Even Me

Tanisha
Stewart

Even Me
Copyright © 2016 Tanisha Stewart

Books may be purchased in quantity and for special sales by contacting the publisher, Tanisha Stewart, by email at tanishastewart.author@gmail.com.

Cover Design: Tyora Moody
www.tywebbincreations.com

Editing and Interior Design: Janet Angelo
www.indiegpublishing.com

First Edition

Published in the United States of America
by Tanisha Stewart

Dedication and Acknowledgments

First and foremost, I dedicate this book to God and my Lord and Savior Jesus Christ. Without Him, I would not be here today.

Secondly, I would like to dedicate this novel to my family and friends. To my mother, Alice Jenkins, my beloved "Alice Jean," who has been the driving force behind most of my life's accomplishments, you have been there through thick and thin, through good and bad, through the struggle, and now through the triumph! Words cannot express how thankful and grateful I am for you. To my little sister, my "favorite girl" Goleana Grant, thank you for always supporting me. I am your biggest fan!

To my brothers James Auston, Thomas Stewart, Arthur Caldwell, and James Stewart, I love you all, and I thank you for supporting me in my endeavors. To my grandmother, Sue Stewart, thank you for your wisdom and your sense of humor, and for always encouraging me. To my father, James Stewart Jr., I love you, and I thank you for your constant encouragement and inspiration. To all of my extended family and my friends, God bless you all. I dedicate this to you!

To my editor, Janet Angelo, thank you for answering my questions and providing constant encouragement, information, and support. Your thoughtful editing really helped bring the story more to life! Also, thank you to my cover designer, Tyora Moody of Tywebbin Creations, for your excellent work.

Next, I would like to dedicate this book to all of my college students past, present, and future. You guys wake me up every morning and keep me on my feet throughout the day. I love you all, and you each inspire me in your own way.

Last, but certainly not least, I dedicate this book to you, the reader. Without you, no one would hear the stories being told. I pray that this book will bless you, and that God will be glorified in and through your life. In Jesus's name, Amen.

Even Me

Chapter 1

Faleesha stared at the empty bottle on the table. She kept it as a reminder of her past life, the life she lived before she became a Christian. During her teen years, she had earned the nickname "the turn-up champion" because she could throw back shots like no one else.

None of her friends knew the reason she drank. On the outside, she was just a sweet, shy girl who liked a little alcohol. But on the inside, she was broken, miserable, and confused because of something painful in her past. She drank to erase her memories and to drown out her fears.

It was always a constant battle with her, trying to do the right thing. Sometimes she wondered if she was really cut out for the life of being a "good Christian." She tried her best to do everything perfectly. Her pastor always said there is no condemnation to those who are in Christ, but Faleesha often found that hard to believe.

She was so consumed by her thoughts that she didn't hear someone banging on her door. Finally, when she heard a girl yell, "Faleesha, answer the door already!" she snapped out of her reverie.

"I'm coming!" she called out as she hurried to the door. "Hey!" she said, greeting her friend Tiara.

"It's about time. Girl, I wore out my knuckles banging on your door."

Tiara breezed past Faleesha and was about to flop on her bed when she saw how neat it looked. Knowing Faleesha's perfectionistic tendencies, she remained standing. "When you supposed to be leaving for college again?"

"Friday," said Faleesha. "Why?"

Tiara put her hands on her hips. "Listen, what I'm about to tell you is not going to be good."

"What's up?"

"Tell me why Shaunte still trying to fight you?"

"For what?"

"Derek."

"I told her I don't want her man!" Faleesha could feel herself getting heated. She glanced at the bottle on the kitchen table, wanting a drink to calm her nerves.

"What you doing with this?" Tiara's eyes followed Faleesha's gaze. She walked over to the table and picked up the bottle. "Guuuurl, don't tell me you done gone back to turning up!"

"No, no." Faleesha shook her head. "I'm done with all of that."

"So why you still got this bottle then?"

Faleesha grabbed it out of her hand and put it on the shelf where she usually kept it. "I just keep it to remind me of where God brought me from, okay?"

Tiara sucked her teeth. "Guuurrrl, ain't nobody got time for that."

CRASH! Their heads whipped around toward Faleesha's kitchen window. It was completely shattered, and a brick was laying on her floor.

"Oh, my gosh!" said Tiara, her hand over her chest. She looked just as startled as Faleesha felt.

They rushed toward the front door and opened it to see what was going on outside. Standing in the middle of the street was Shaunte, a baseball bat in her hand. Two of her friends were standing there with her.

"Bitch! Come outside!" Shaunte snarled at Faleesha.

"Shaunte, what are you doing?" said Faleesha, not believing that she had just thrown a brick through her mother's window.

"Fuck all that, bitch. I said come outside!"

"I'm not coming out there."

"Faleesha, just go!" Tiara urged. "You gotta fight her sooner or later anyway. Just go on and get it over with."

Faleesha looked at Tiara like she was crazy. "Do you see that bat in her hand?" She gestured toward Shaunte and her friends. "Do you really think this is going to be a fair fight? I'm sorry, but I don't feel like getting my brains smashed today!"

"Just go," said Tiara, pulling her cell phone from her back pocket.

Faleesha stared at her. "What are you doing?"

Tiara shot her a strange look. "Nothing, it's just that Reggie and them wanted me to record it."

Suddenly, it dawned on Faleesha how Shaunte had known she was home in the first place. "You set me up?" She glared at Tiara.

"What are you talking about?" Tiara said, trying to inch herself and Faleesha out the door while closing it at the same time.

Faleesha grabbed the door and kept it open. "I'm not going out there. I can't believe you set me up like this."

When a police siren sounded from a couple of blocks over, Shaunte and her friends scrambled toward her car.

"YOU LUCKY, BITCH!" Shaunte screamed through her car window. "Don't leave your house, cuz if you do, we gonna get it fuckin poppin'!" She screeched away in the opposite direction of the sirens.

Faleesha kicked Tiara out of her house. She was gone before the police pulled up in front of the apartment. The officers asked her a bunch of questions, trying to figure out who broke the window and why it happened. Faleesha answered their questions, informing them that Shaunte had come to her house to try to jump her. They asked her if she wanted to file a restraining order, but she declined.

When they were finally finished with their questions, she went to the kitchen to clean up the glass and duct tape some plastic over the window frame. Her mother would be heated when she saw this mess.

Faleesha stared at the bottle on the shelf. She considered whether she should have just one more drink to help her cope with everything that was going on.

"No," she said aloud, shaking her head. She had come too far to give up now. She had stopped drinking two years ago on her three-year anniversary of being saved. If she started again now, all of her progress would be lost.

"I sure hope this new college is as good as it sounds," she said to herself. She was supposed to leave two weeks ago, but because of some other drama, she was forced to wait until this Friday.

She lay down and closed her eyes, rubbing her temples to ease the headache that had just come on. Every cell in her body was longing for a sip of something to help her escape the BS. She contemplated going to the corner store, then she decided that one more drink wouldn't hurt. She would do it to celebrate the new journey she was about to take in her life.

Just as she was stepping into her shoes, a favorite pair of black leather flats that went with all her outfits, her cell phone buzzed with a text message. She picked it up to see what excuse Tiara was coming up with now.

Bitch, I meant what I said. Don't leave your house if you still want to live.

Faleesha didn't have to call the number to know who sent it. Shaunte was serious about wanting to fight her.

"Lord," she prayed, "please just help me get up out of here."

***

Rondell sat on the stone bench across from Terry's headstone. He stared at the name, remembering. He visited this spot every year at the beginning of the fall semester. He could not believe how his life had turned out. He had gone from the streets to college, from foster homes to dorm rooms. He wished his foster brother Terry could be here to say the same, but his life was cut short before he even reached adulthood, another victim of gun violence.

"You would be proud of me, huh?" he said, hoping that Terry was somehow able to hear him.

Suddenly, he heard footsteps coming up behind him. He turned and saw his boy Mike walking over to the gravesite.

"What time you get here?" said Mike, sitting down beside him.

Rondell looked at his watch. "About half an hour ago."

"Well, I'm glad the semester's started up. Things be mad boring when Chris and Tyrone go home." Mike was referring to two guys they had met in their freshman year. Although Chris and Tyrone lived in different states, they, Rondell, and Mike had become fast friends as soon as they met.

"Yeah, I know," said Rondell, scooting over to make room for Mike. "Matter of fact, we supposed to play some two on two later on."

"I don't know why they keep trying to challenge us," said Mike. "We was built for this!" They exchanged dap.

Rondell chucked. "Tell that shit to Tyrone's non-shooting ass."

"Ha! That's fucked up, nigga," said Mike. "I'm-a tell him you said that too."

"Fuck he gonna do about it, 'cept lose?" said Rondell.

They shared another laugh.

"You know what I really wish, though," Mike began. I wish . . . ."

POP! POP! POP!

Mike was cut off by the sound of gunshots. They scrambled to their feet, frantically trying to figure out where the bullets were coming from.

"Shit, man, let's get out of here!" said Rondell.

More gunshots sounded nearby.

Rondell and Mike ducked between the graves as they made their way to Rondell's Escalade. They hopped inside, and Rondell peeled out of the cemetery parking lot, making his way back to the dorms.

"Can't do shit nowadays without hearing fuckin gunshots," he said. He had a flashback of Terry's last day alive.

"I know, man," said Mike, looking out the passenger window. "It's real in these streets."

***

Faleesha made her way through the airport excitedly. She could not wait to get away from her hometown. As much as she loved her mother and some of her old friends, she knew it was time to go.

She considered it a way of escape that God had provided her, as it said in the Bible. She had been so tempted lately to drink as a way to cope, and she knew that going to this new school was the right choice for her life, right now.

She figured that with such a large campus, there would be plenty of opportunities to stay busy, get involved with a great group of Christian friends, and get closer to God, which was where she truly wanted to be.

"Thank you, Lord, for not giving up on me," she said to herself as she glanced at the numbers on her ticket and the numbers on the gates. She was looking for number 413, the same as her favorite scripture in Philippians, one she had come to rely on when she was trying to give up alcohol for good. When she first printed out the tickets, she knew that was a sign that God was not through with her yet, and had good things in store for her.

She was so happy to have this new opportunity in a faraway place where she knew no one. She couldn't wait to meet new friends, join a church and some Christian organizations, and really get cemented in this new life. *I won't let you down, Lord*, she mused as she neared her gate. *Please just see me through this.*

"Oh, I'm sorry!" she said, fumbling to pick up her cell phone that she dropped when she bumped into a young man coming toward her from the opposite direction. She was so focused on getting to her gate that she hadn't even seen him.

"It's cool, man. Wait—Faleesha?" He looked at her like he couldn't believe his eyes.

Faleesha hadn't seen him in twelve years, but she remembered exactly who he was. Her heart pounded, and her only thought was to get away from him as quickly as possible. "Hey," she said, trying to sound casual. Her eyes darted around the waiting area to determine how far she had to walk to board her plane and get away from him.

He looked her up and down and licked his lips. This made her extremely uncomfortable. "Dang, girl. You look even better than before."

"You mean when I was eight?"

He just stared at her, an embarrassed expression on his face.

"I have to go," she said, and she quickly rushed to her gate and was able to get on her plane immediately, as the flight attendant was calling for all rows to board.

She found her seat and sank into it, relieved, her face flushed with nervous tension. She stared out the window, praying that the plane would hurry up and take off, and that he wouldn't be on it.

"Are you okay, Miss?"

Faleesha turned and saw an elderly lady staring at her with concern. She took a slow breath and nodded her head, her cheeks regaining their color.

"Let me know if you need anything," the lady said with a smile.

"Thank you," said Faleesha, forcing herself to smile in return.

Her mind was filled with painful memories as the plane backed out and sped down the runway.

At last, she was in the air, on her way to a new life.

***

"So, what's good for tonight?" said Mike.

"Man, I don't know. There ain't nothin' goin' on in the city. Let's get some shorties or something and go to the movies," said Tyrone.

"I don't know about all that," said Rondell. "We went to the movies last week. Let's do something different."

Tyrone shrugged his shoulders. "A'ight. Let's go bowling then."

"Now *that's* what I'm talkin 'bout!" said Mike as he gave Tyrone some dap.

"Who we bringin'?" Chris looked at Mike to see if he had any ideas.

"I don't know. How about Tara?"

"Nah, she got too much attitude," Rondell interjected.

Tyrone chuckled. "What? You wasn't saying that two weeks ago, when you were . . . ."

Rondell shoved Tyrone before he could finish his sentence.

"Man, shut up! I was drunk!"

"Oh, now you was drunk." They all laughed. "So," Tyrone said, gesturing to the other guys, "does anybody else want Tara to come?"

"I wouldn't mind," said Chris.

"Oh, I think we all know that," said Tyrone.

"Whatever, man," Chris muttered, avoiding their eyes.

Rondell wasn't letting him off that easily. "What? What happened? What'd I miss?"

"Nothing," Tyrone offered. "It's just that your boy Chris here has been crushing on Tara for like six months now."

Rondell's eyes widened.

"Six months?! Yo, brotha. Why you ain't tell me?"

"Not like it would have mattered," Mike muttered.

"I know that's right," said Tyrone.

Rondell had to interject after that comment. "What y'all tryin' a say? I wouldn't have done that to Chris. I ain't like that."

Tyrone crossed his arms and cocked his head to the side. "Oh, really? So what about Sheniqua?"

"What about her?" Tyrone raised his eyebrows at him.

"Man, whatever, yo." Rondell shrugged his shoulders. "You just mad because I got her first."

"A'ight, a'ight," said Chris. "That don't count, but what about Shamara?"

"And Brittany?" said Tyrone.

"And Jasmin?" Mike threw in.

"Tiesha?" said Chris.

"Sara?" said Tyrone. He smirked. "Need we say more?"

Rondell dropped his head in defeat. "Man, y'all whack. A'ight, whatever. You got me. But I don't be meaning to do it."

Tyrone snorted. "R-i-ight."

"Naw, naw, for real, though. I'm just trying to find the right girl."

"By sleeping with everyone you see?" said Tyrone.

"What? Is it a problem when I do it?"

"Cuz you the one talkin' 'bout you trying to change."

"Dee, man, you know you ain't trying to settle down," said Chris.

"Yes, I am."

"Whatever, man," said Tyrone. "Wasn't it you just a month ago who said, and I quote, 'There are too many fish in the sea for me to just have one'?"

"That was then. This is now."

Tyrone chuckled, but he shook his head. He wasn't buying it.

"Yeah, okay," Rondell admitted. "But, really, I'm trying to find the right girl. It's just that none of these chicks at this school is about nothin'. They either got too much attitude, they gold digging, or they manipulative or stupid. And some of them is just flat out ugly."

They all laughed at that last remark.

"I need a woman who I don't gotta worry about all that with. I need a woman who will treat me like a man and give me what I need."

"Preach, boy!" said Mike.

Rondell glanced at him. "Shut up." He continued his speech. "I need a woman who I can call my own, a woman who ain't trying to take my money, stab my back, or sleep with my boy."

"Well, well!" said Tyrone, shaking his head from side to side.

"Y'all some fools," Rondell said with a laugh. "But for real, though, I need a woman who, when I look at her, I can just say—"

Before he could finish his sentence, the door to the residence hall opened. In walked Shelly, a friend of theirs, and a girl they had never seen before. Rondell stared at her in amazement.

"Wow," he said. She was everything he was looking for. She was beautiful. She had long hair that flowed down her back. She was light skinned, what he liked to describe as red-boned. She perfectly filled out a pair of blue skinny jeans and a white T-shirt, and she had completed the casual look with some white flip-flops. She pulled a rolling suitcase behind her.

Rondell watched her, his mouth open in amazement, as she stood for a moment with Shelly. Some other girls got off the elevator and stood talking with them. Rondell was in a state of shock. No sooner had he said what kind of woman he wanted than he looked up, and there she was. He felt butterflies in his stomach, which wasn't like him. Usually nothing threw him off his game.

"Dee!" said Tyrone, interrupting his thoughts.

"Eyo, Dee," said Mike.

"Man, snap out of it!" said Chris, slapping him across the face.

Rondell shook his head. "What?"

"Man, stop staring at that girl like you in a trance or something." said Tyrone. "You seen a woman before!"

"Shut up," he said, taking another sidelong glance at her. She stood with the other girls a moment longer then rolled her suitcase over to the elevator. She must have felt Rondell staring at her because she glanced in his direction as she walked past.

Their eyes met, and she smiled at him and gave a small nod hello. He nodded back and licked his lips as his heart raced again. He watched her as she went to the elevator, pushed the button, and stepped in. She looked straight into his eyes and gave him a brief smile before the doors closed, and she was gone.

"Rondell!" Mike shouted.

"What, man?"

"Man, stop salivating over that girl and help us make a decision."

"About what?"

"Bowling!" said Mike, frustrated.

"Oh, yeah." Rondell didn't sound convinced.

"So who we bringing?" said Chris.

"I don't know. I'm not going." Rondell glanced at the elevator as if he could will it to open and reveal the most perfect woman in the world again.

"Why not?" Mike was exasperated.

"Cuz I got sh- . . . stuff to do, that's why."

"Dee, you ain't never gonna stop swearing, so I don't even know why you trying," said Chris.

"I'm working on it."

"Whatever, dude."

"I'm stopping, okay? We in college now. It's time for a change."

"A'ight, Mr. President," said Mike sarcastically. "But shouldn't you have started that change two years ago?"

"Change is good anytime."

"Yeah, yeah, okay," said Chris. "So, since Dee ain't going, who we bringing?"

Rondell glanced over at the girls, who were dispersing, but Shelly wasn't going with them. She sat on a bench near the elevator and looked at her phone.

Probably waiting for that new girl, he thought.

"I'll be back," he said to the guys, making his way over to Shelly.

"Man, I hope you ain't still thinking about that girl," said Mike, but he got no response.

"So, Shelly!" Rondell smiled as he sat next to her. "How you doing?"

"What do you want, Rondell?" she said in a bored tone, not looking up from her phone.

He held up his hands in surrender.

"What? Why I gotta want something? I can't just be coming over to say hi?"

Shelly looked up and tilted her head, assessing him. "You have that look on your face. You want something."

He and Shelly had been friends with each other since their freshman year of high school.

"Who was that girl?"

"What girl?" Shelly busied herself tapping out a text on her phone.

"You know the one I'm talking about."

Shelly rolled her eyes.

"She's off limits, Rondell. She's a woman of God."

"For real?" he said, surprised.

"Yes. She's deep in the church and everything. I'm supposed to be taking her to visit different places in the area for the next couple of weeks. I'm also going to show her around the campus and a couple places in the city."

"Mmm," he said. "So, she's really a church girl?"

"Yes. She was talking to me about God the whole way here from the airport. She's really nice too."

"Mmm-hmm."

She rolled her eyes again. "Boy, I know what you're thinking! That's why she's off limits for you."

"Off limits? Whatchu mean?" He stood up.

"Yeah, Dee." Shelly stood up as well. "I'm not hooking you up with her."

"Why not?" He crossed his arms over his chest.

She crossed her arms in response and rolled her neck with attitude. "You know why. Your reputation speaks for itself. I don't need to say anything."

"Man, y'all is trippin!" He turned around and jogged toward the stairs.

"EYO, DEE!"

He turned. Tyrone had his arms open. "Where you going, man?"

"I'll check y'all later. I got business to take care of."

"Aw," said Mike, waving him off. "I got *business* to take care of," he mocked.

***

As soon as the elevator door closed, Faleesha let out a sigh. "He was *fine*," she breathed. And she was right.

That guy was hands down the most beautiful man she had ever seen. He was tall, dark, and handsome, and the way he stared at her as she walked past made her feel all shivery inside.

"But that's not what I came here for," she said, interrupting her own thoughts. She had to remember her promise to God. She could not let Him down by getting distracted.

Besides all of the drama she had left behind, this school, with its rigorous psychology program, was just the challenge she needed.

The elevator doors opened, and she walked onto the seventh floor to room 732. She put her key in the lock and opened the door, bringing in the last of her luggage, glad to have that over with. She rummaged through her belongings, looking for something to wear.

It was way too hot outside for jeans, so she finally settled on her favorite pink shorts. She fixed her hair in a side ponytail and put on a visor to shade her eyes from the sun. She didn't have any sunglasses, but she liked the sporty look the visor gave her outfit.

Finally, she slung her purse over her shoulder and walked out of the door, locking it behind her.

She decided to take the stairs down to the lobby, and when she got to the bottom of the final staircase to the first floor, the door opened, and in walked the beautiful man she had seen earlier. Her eyes widened in surprise.

"Hello," she said. He held the door open for her. Their arms brushed against each other as she passed him. She stopped and glanced back. "Excuse me," she said, blushing nervously.

"It's alright." He smiled back. They stood there for a moment.

"Well, thanks for opening the door for me," she said.

"No problem."

She turned and walked away. She felt him staring at her with each step. *Why does he keep staring at me like that? And why is it making me feel like this?*

She gave a brief nod as she passed his friends.

"Hello, how you doin'?" said one of them.

"Good, and you?"

"I'm good. I'm Tyrone, and this is Chris and Mike. The guy you just saw in the stairwell is Rondell, aka Dee."

She looked toward the stairs, but he was gone. Tyrone held out his hand, and she shook it.

"I'm Faleesha," she said.

"Well, it's nice to meet you, Faleesha," he said, licking his lips. Shelly walked over to them.

"Sorry to interrupt you fellas, but me and Faleesha have to go."

"I didn't meant to keep you waiting, Shelly," said Faleesha.

"Oh, no, it's fine," she said. "But I know these guys. They'll have you here talking to them all day long if you let them." They all laughed.

"Well, see you guys later!" said Faleesha.

"Bye, Faleesha," the guys said in unison. Everybody laughed again, and Faleesha and Shelly went out to Shelly's car.

***

"Gesston!" Shelly sang cheerily, coming up behind him.

"What?" He had just taken a big bite of his steak and cheese sub.

"Guess what?"

"What is it?" he said, chewing his food. She put her arm around his shoulders.

"I think I may have found the *perfect* girl for you!" she said, smiling brightly at him.

"And why is that?" he said.

"Because there's a new girl in the psychology department."

"And?"

"And she's a Christian!"

His eyes brightened, and he shifted in his seat.

"A Christian, huh?"

"Yes, a strong Christian, totally in love with Jesus. And she's not married, has no kids, and she's not talking to anyone right now.'"

"How does she look?"

She frowned at him. "Gesston! I thought you weren't supposed to judge someone based on looks."

"I'm not." He chuckled. "Relax, Shelly. I simply asked how she looks."

"Well, for your information, she's beautiful."

"Light or dark?"

"Light."

"Tall or short?"

"About five-five."

"Okay, okay. Fat or thin?"

She slapped his arm. "Gesston!"

He held up his arms in surrender, laughing. "Okay, okay! I was just joking! I don't care what she looks like."

Shelly rolled her eyes. "Yeah, right."

"So, where is this mystery woman of God anyway?" He took another bite.

"She's actually coming over here right now." Shelly gestured to his right. He looked and almost choked. She *was* beautiful. He stared at her as she walked to their table.

"Hi, Shelly!" she said, sitting down.

"Hello, Faleesha, this is Gesston. Gesston, this is Faleesha." They shook hands.

"Nice to meet you, Faleesha," said Gesston.

"Nice to meet you too."

"So, do you like the campus so far?" he asked, trying to sound casual.

"Yeah, I visited a lot of the buildings yesterday. It's really nice."

"How do you like your classes?"

"They're cool, but I have a little bit of catching up to do since I missed the first two weeks."

"Oh, that's tough. May I ask why you came after the semester started?" He took another bite of his sub.

She rolled her eyes and sighed.

"I had some drama with my cousin. She was supposed to drive me up here, but then she changed her mind at the last minute. So I had to catch a flight here instead. I didn't have the money saved, so by the time I had enough, the earliest flight was two weeks into the semester."

"Oh wow, that *is* a lot of drama."

"True, true," said Shelly, nodding her head.

"Well, I'm glad you made it here," said Gesston.

"Thanks."

"So what's your major?" he asked.

"Psychology!" she said excitedly.

"Oh, that's great! We have an excellent psych program, from what I've heard."

"Yeah, it's really rigorous."

"Indeed."

"So what's your major?" Faleesha asked.

"I'm double majoring in Criminal Justice and Political Science," he said.

"Oh, that's cool. So do you want to be a politician or something?"

He smiled and nodded. "Yes. How'd you guess? I'm actually starting an internship at the mayor's office next week."

"That's what's up!" she said.

"I didn't know that," said Shelly. "Congratulations, Gesston!"

"Thank you," he said, smiling. "So, Faleesha, Shelly tells me that you are a woman of God."

She blushed. "Yes."

"So you're saved and sanctified, Holy Ghost filled, and fire baptized—a rare woman indeed!" He shook his head in mock amazement. They all laughed.

"Yes," she said, smiling. "I guess you could say that."

"That's great! God is good."

"All the time."

"Praise the Lord. Have you found a church home out here yet?"

She shook her head. "No, not yet. Shelly took me by two churches so far, and they seemed pretty nice."

"Well I'd love for you to come visit my church. Perhaps we could discuss it over dinner sometime."

"Uh . . . sure. That would be nice."

"Absolutely! How about Saturday at seven?"

"Um, okay."

"Great! I promise you a wonderful evening."

"Thanks." Faleesha was totally surprised at this turn of events. Her shy smile gave away her thoughts.

Gesston stood up. "Well ladies, it was nice talking to you, but I'm afraid I have to go. I'll see you later."

"Bye," they said. Gesston dumped his tray and left.

"He was nice," said Faleesha.

"He's a really good guy," said Shelly.

"He seems like it. But I'm not ready to get into a relationship with anyone."

"Girl, you don't have to marry him! Just have a little fun. You guys could be good friends."

"Yeah, I guess we could."

"Maybe you'll end up together after all."

"You never know," said Faleesha, although she didn't feel any sort of real attraction toward Gesston. Plus, she was trying her hardest to stay focused on God.

***

Gesston made his way to the basketball court with his boys Jamal, Ryan, and Jacob. They met up with Rondell, Chris, Tyrone, and Mike.

"Y'all ready for a whippin'?" said Jamal as he dribbled the ball and shot a layup. After he retrieved the ball, he passed it to Ryan, who shot his own layup.

"Yeah, right," said Tyrone. "When was the last time y'all beat us?"

"The last time we played," said Gesston.

"Whatever, man," said Mike. "Y'all got lucky. Plus it was only by a point."

"A point is a point," said Jacob. "We still won."

"Whatever," said Rondell. "Let's play some four on four."

They played three games. Rondell and his boys won the first game; Gesston and his boys won the second game. In the third game, they all fought hard for the win, but in the end, Rondell and his boys won by two points.

"How you like that?" said Mike.

"Y'all got lucky," Jamal said, panting for breath. "Plus, my ankle still hurts from last time."

"Excuses, excuses!" said Chris.

"I know you're not talking," said Ryan. "How many points did you score? Three?"

"That's three more than you!" Chris shot back.

"Fellas, fellas!" said Gesston, holding his hands up. "It's just a game. No point in arguing. We all win sometimes, and we all lose sometimes."

"Yeah, but we live to fight another day, right?" said Tyrone, quoting the character Pop in the movie *Friday*. They laughed.

"You're nuts," said Gesston. "Listen, I wish I could stay and chat with you all, but I have a date this evening."

"A date? You?" Tyrone smirked. "Since when do church boys have game?"

Rondell and his boys laughed.

"Very funny," Gesston said coolly. "But, you see Tyrone, it's not about how much game you have. A woman, or at least a mature woman, sees the inside of a man."

"Yeah, uh huh," said Tyrone, crossing his arms. "So, who's the ugly—I mean *lucky* lady?" They howled with laughter.

"Actually, she's not ugly at all," said Gesston. "On the contrary, she's quite attractive. You might even say she's beautiful. I think you would be impressed."

"Who is it?" said Chris.

"You may not have met her yet. She's new to the school. Her name is Faleesha McDaniels."

Tyrone's eyes widened. He nudged Mike. "Yo, remember? That's the chick we met last week!"

"Yo, she is bangin!" said Chris.

Tyrone gave Gesston some dap. "Yo, man, I didn't know you had it in you. How'd you bag that?"

"I didn't bag anything. I simply asked her on a date, and she agreed."

"Wow, church boy stepping up in the game!" said Chris, amazed.

Rondell was stunned into silence. How'd Gesston, of all people, make that happen so fast? When the boys looked at him for a response, all he could utter was a half-hearted, "Yeah . . . wow."

Chapter 2

Rondell grabbed his overflowing bag of laundry. It was six o'clock on a Saturday morning, the best time to do laundry. Nobody else was using the machines because they were still asleep from drinking Friday night away.

He made his way down the stairs to the fourth floor. He thought about how he had been a little upset and jealous during the first part of the week after he heard that Gesston had bagged Faleesha.

After a couple days, he got over it, reasoning that she was a church girl, so she was bound to like a church guy like Gesston. He told himself this, but it didn't stop the longing he felt whenever he saw her.

He had never felt this way toward any girl before. He'd been attracted to plenty of girls and they to him, but there was something different about what he felt for Faleesha.

He sighed and opened the laundry room door. He made his way into the room and turned the corner to the row washing machines lined against the wall. His heart jumped. There she was, bending over and taking some clothes out of the washer. She put them in the dryer then saw him.

"Oh!" she said, her hand over her heart. "You scared me!"

"Sorry," he said, smiling as he put his clothes in the washer. He put in the laundry detergent and turned on the machine.

Wow, she thought, *he is too fine*. His strong, masculine body was very evident in the white wifebeater T-shirt and black gym shorts he was wearing. She watched his arm muscles bulge as he lifted himself up to sit on one of the washing machines. She glanced away when he looked at her, not wanting to be caught staring at him.

"So, what you doing up this early?" he said.

She shrugged and met his eyes again. "I just figured nobody would be up at this time."

"You're right. Nobody usually is."

"Except for us today, huh?" She smiled.

"I guess so." He licked his lips.

Don't do that! It's too tempting, she told herself.

"So, what do you have planned for today?"

She hopped up onto one of the dryers. "Nothing, really. Shelly and I were planning to go to the mall, you know, so I could see what kind of stores they have there, but she had to babysit for her cousin's twins. I offered to help, but she said she was alright by herself."

"Oh." He nodded. "So why don't you have Gesston take you?"

"Gesston?"

"Yeah. I heard you guys were dating."

She laughed and shook her head. "Oh, no, I'm not dating Gesston. He took me out to dinner last Saturday to tell me about his church. We're not dating."

"Oh, my bad." Rondell smiled.

Mmm-mmm-mmm! she thought, and then she scolded herself. *Stop that!* She played it cool and said, "It's okay. So what are you doing today?"

"Nothing, really. I was actually thinking about going to the mall myself. I wanted to pick up a couple of things."

"Oh, that's nice."

"Hey, do you want to come with me? I could show you around."

She felt nervous all of a sudden.

"Okay," she said. "That would be cool."

"A'ight, so you wanna go like around two or three?"

"That sounds good. I want to take a nap before I officially wake up and present myself to the world."

He chuckled. "Girl, you just read my mind. I was thinking the same thing."

"So, three it is?" she said.

"Three it is."

***

Faleesha jolted awake at the shrill sound of her alarm clock telling her it was two o'clock and time to get ready to go out. She groaned and rolled over, hitting the snooze alarm, but then she remembered who she was going out with, and she bounded out of bed and into the shower.

She put on her red top and white capris and her red heels. She put her hair in a side ponytail. She had agreed to meet Rondell at his room at three.

His room was directly below hers on the fifth floor, room 532. She tried not to get excited as she made her way down the stairs. She knocked on his door, and he opened it with a smile. Her heart melted. He was wearing red and white as well: a red and white fitted hat, a red shirt, white shorts, and red and white Jordans.

"You been spying on me?" he said, noticing that they matched.

"I was wondering the same thing about you!" She grinned.

They made their way down the stairs to the parking lot where Rondell's vehicle was in a space at the end to protect it from being dinged by everyone else's car doors. Considering that it was a Cadilllac Escalade, he had every reason to protect his baby.

"Oh, this is nice!" she said as he pressed the unlock button on his key remote. The doors unlocked, and he opened the passenger door for her. "Thank you," she said, getting in.

He closed the door and went over to his side. He hopped into the driver's seat and they put on their seat belts. He then turned the key in the ignition. A Jay Z song blasted from the speakers. Faleesha jumped at the sudden sound. He glanced over at her and turned it off.

"Sorry about that. I know you don't listen to that kind of stuff, right?"

"No, I don't. Thanks." She smiled.

"You're a church person, right?"

"Yeah."

"That's cool." He smiled. "So, what's it like?"

"It's a good life. Once you get saved, you see everything so differently."

"Oh, that's cool. So, did you grow up in the church?"

"No, I didn't really start going to church until the ninth grade. My mom had already been saved for like two or three years. But I never went to church with her because I thought it was boring. Then one of my cousins died in a car accident, and I went to the funeral. This lady came up to me afterward and told me that God had a plan for my life. Something about it made me keep going back to the church, and before I knew it, I was saved and filled with the Holy Ghost."

"Wow, that's deep," he said. "How old was you when you got saved and everything?"

"It was the summer before sophomore year, so I was like fifteen."

"Wow, that's what's really good!" he said, smiling. "My mom and dad is saved and all that too. Matter of fact, I think my mom left one of her gospel CDs in here somewhere." He searched through his CDs. "She's always trying to leave them in the car in hopes that I'll listen to them."

"That's cool!" she said. "So, your mom and dad are in the church. Did you grow up in the church?"

He looked at her, then shook his head slowly and turned away.

"Nah, my mom and dad got in the church some years back, but neither of them grew up in it." He continued searching through his CDs. "They had some pretty rough lives. I did too." He finally found the one he wanted. "Here it is. Shirley Caesar. Do you listen to her?"

"Yeah, that's mad old school! She can definitely sing though."

"That's what my mom said." Rondell smiled at her.

Faleesha smiled back. "My mom has all of her CDs."

His eyes widened. "Really?"

"Yeah. She had a really rough life too, and she said that listening to Shirley Caesar helped her get through those times."

He stared at her. "Well, I'm glad that both our moms are doing good now."

"Me too."

They chatted until they arrived at the mall. When they walked inside, they saw a camera crew set up around a photo booth.

"I wonder what this is about?" said Rondell as they passed by. One of the women seemed to be directing the cameramen. They were taking pictures of a little girl with a dog. The woman turned and saw Rondell and Faleesha, and her eyes widened.

"Hey, guys!" she exclaimed. She ran over to them. They stared at each other in confusion, then at her. "Could you guys do me a favor?" she pleaded. "Please? I'll pay you."

"Uh . . . what is it?" said Rondell.

"Well," she gushed, "we're taking pictures for a new design on the photo booth, and we need a picture of a couple. You guys look so cute together in your red and white! So, could you take some pictures for me, please? It won't take long. I promise."

Rondell looked at Faleesha. "You wanna do it?"

She shrugged. "Sure . . . I guess . . . if you want to."

"YES! I love you guys!" The woman hugged them both with a bit more exuberance than necessary and led them to a table where they filled out and signed a bunch of forms to give their approval to be in the photos. Afterward, they posed, and the pictures were taken. When they were done, they were both given some copies to keep.

"Those pictures came out pretty good," said Faleesha.

"I know, right? We look good together." Rondell smiled at her. She blushed. They made their way around most of the stores then they decided they were having too much fun to leave, so they went to the movies then out to eat. At the end of the evening, it was like they had known each other forever.

"Today was so much fun," Rondell said when they stood in the lobby of their residence hall waiting for the elevator. "You are so cool!"

"So are you. We gotta do this again sometime," said Faleesha.

"Definitely." The elevator doors opened, and they both got in. "Hey, could I get your number so we can keep in touch?" Rondell asked.

"Sure!"

They exchanged numbers, and Rondell got off at the fifth floor. Faleesha smiled all the way up to her room. Rondell seemed like a really good guy.

***

"NO, Mommy, NO!"

Rondell fought off the man who was trying to take him away, and rushed over to his mother. He wrapped his arms around her knees, tears streaming down his cheeks. She stared down at his upturned face, her eyes afraid and confused.

"Ma'am," the Man said. "We need to go now."

"Delly," she whispered, her voice quivering. "Delly."

"Mommy, no," he said. "I don't want to go with him."

"Baby, I know. But Mommy is sick. The nice man is going to take you to his friends so Mommy can get better."

"What about Daddy? When's he coming back from his trip? Why can't I go with him?"

She stared at the man for a moment with a pained expression, then back at Rondell.

"Baby, Daddy is going to be gone for a while on his trip. You just have to go with the nice man until Mommy gets better. Then Daddy will come back from his trip, and we will all be together again."

"But, Mommy!" Tears of hurt streamed down his face.

"Come on, baby. Everything will be okay." She hugged him then gently pushed him toward the man. Rondell got in the car. The man *kept trying to talk to him, asking him questions, but all he could think about was his mother. He remained silent the whole way to his new home.*

Rondell popped up in his bed. He wiped the tears from his face and sighed deeply. It was the dream again, the one that haunted him frequently.

Memories of his childhood were as painful today as they were when he was living them. He shook his head and tried to clear his mind, but he couldn't, so he got out of bed. He did fifty pushups. That didn't work, so he did the same amount of situps. That didn't work either.

Finally, he slipped on some sweatpants and a T-shirt, grabbed his iPod, and rushed down the stairs. When he got outside, he stretched for a couple minutes then started jogging.

He plugged in his earphones, and the voices of Mobb Deep filled his consciousness, drowning out his thoughts. He jogged and jogged until the sun came up. He turned around to head back to campus but stopped to rest a minute, panting for breath. He closed his eyes, and his heart burned once again with the memories of his past.

He fought back the tears before they could escape his eyes, then he ran as fast as he could to the dorm. By the time he got back, he was exhausted. He dragged himself to the shower and then to his room. He fell face first onto his bed and remained there for the next six and a half hours.

***

Gesston stared as Faleesha made her way over to the table where he and Shelly were eating lunch.

"Hey guys!" she said. She smiled as she sat down. "How's everybody's day going?"

"Mine is good so far," said Gesston. "Better now, though." He took a bite of his apple.

Shelly giggled.

"Okay, so how about you, Shelly?" said Faleesha.

"My day is going pretty good. How's yours going?"

"Good. I have like seven chapters to read by the end of the week, though." She rolled her eyes.

"Oh, that sucks," said Shelly.

"How about you hang out with me tonight?" said Gesston. "I bet I could help you take your mind off of those chapters."

"No, thanks. I don't want to get behind again."

"Aw, come on," he said, gently nudging her shoulder. "You won't get behind. You can start reading tomorrow." He stared at her.

She stared back.

"Come on," he persisted.

"Okay," she said.

"Thank you!" Gesston smiled as if he'd chalked up a huge win for himself.

***

"You're really not feeling Gesston, are you?" said Shelly as she closed the door to her room. She and Faleesha had just come back from lunch. Faleesha plopped down in an armchair.

"Nope."

"Why not? He's nice. He's cool too. And, he's cute."

"I don't know. I'm just not interested. I don't think he's my type."

"So what is your type?" asked Shelly.

An image of Rondell popped into Faleesha's mind, but all she said was, "I'm not looking for a relationship right now."

"Girl, you are too much. How old are you?"

"I'm twenty. Why?"

"What do you mean, why? You're young and single. You've got to want a man, especially at twenty."

"I'm not saying I don't ever want a man. I'm just saying that I don't want one right now. My purpose in life right now is to build my relationship with the Lord."

"So that means you can't have fun?"

"No, it just means I'm not getting distracted."

"How would you be distracted? Gesston is in the church too."

"I know, and that's a good thing. But I don't think God sent me here to get a man. It was to focus on school and to get to know Him better." Shelly stared at her for a moment then shook her head.

"Okay, fine. You win." They stared at each other for a few seconds then they both started laughing.

"Girl, you a trip," said Faleesha.

Chapter 3

It was a beautiful sunny Saturday, a hot day for early October. Nobody was staying indoors on this day—no one, that is, except Faleesha, which annoyed Shelly to no end. When Faleesha didn't stop by her dorm room to say hi and see what was up for the day, Shelly went to her room to tell her everyone's plans.

"Faleesha, you have to come!" Shelly pleaded for the third time.

"No, I don't really like swimming."

"Girl, ain't nobody really gonna be swimming. We're just gonna chill. It'll just be a bunch of us having a good time."

Faleesha stared at her suspiciously. "And what exactly constitutes a good time?"

Shelly rolled her eyes and sighed.

"You know, just a bunch of us girls chillin' and relaxing at the pool. Come on! You'll get to meet some of the other girls."

Faleesha thought about it for a few moments.

"Okay, I'll go."

"Finally!" Shelly exclaimed. "I swear, getting you to do anything fun is like pulling teeth."

Faleesha looked at her with an expression of mock hurt. "Hey! That's not true!"

Shelly rolled her eyes again. "Yeah, okay, mmm-hmm." She got up to leave. "Well, I'm going to my room to get my bathing suit and stuff. I'll meet you in like an hour, okay?" Shelly headed toward the door, but Faleesha grabbed her arm.

"Gesston's not going to be there, is he?" He had seriously been irritating her lately. He kept showing up everywhere she went, and she was running out of excuses not to give him her number. Shelly chuckled.

"No, Faleesha, Gesston won't be there."

Faleesha sighed with relief. "Good."

***

Rondell, Mike, Tyrone, and Chris made their way to Rashonda's apartment complex. She was having a pool party, and they couldn't wait to check out all the girls.

"Fellas, thank you for coming!" said Rashonda, greeting them at the door. "All the girls are already in the pool waiting for you guys to show up and make things fun."

"Oh, yeah!" said Mike. They took off their shirts and shoes and followed Rashonda to the pool. When they got there, they saw Shelly, Shalonda, Maria, and Faleesha. Rondell's heart dropped. He tried not to stare at her as he entered the pool.

"Hey, ladies!" said Mike.

"Hi," they all said.

Faleesha immediately felt nervous when the guys walked in. She hadn't expected any of them to be there, or she wouldn't have worn her bikini without a T-shirt or something over it. When she saw Rondell, however, a part of her was glad that he would have a chance to see her assets. As soon as this thought crossed her mind, she felt ashamed, and her smile vanished.

Rondell stared at her as he entered the pool. She tried not to stare back. His abs were beautiful. *Mmm-mmm-mmm,* she thought, but quickly pushed it from her mind before it could go any further. She nodded hello at him. He nodded and smiled back. *Don't smile at me with that gorgeous smile of yours! It makes it so difficult to resist you.* She forced herself to look away from him.

"So," said Rashonda as she emerged from her back door carrying a volleyball. "Who's up for a game?"

They played three games, boys against girls. The girls won the first game, but the boys won the other two by shutouts.

"GOT EM!" shouted Tyrone as he gave Mike and Chris dap.

"What-ever!" said Rashonda. "Anyways, can you fellas come inside and help me carry this couch outside?"

"We gotchu," said Mike. He, Tyrone, and Chris hopped up out of the pool and followed Rashonda into her apartment. Rondell stayed at the pool.

Seizing her opportunity, Shalonda swam over to him. "Ooh, you been working out or something?" She felt his arm.

He glanced at Faleesha then backed away from Shalonda.

Yeah, that's right, thought Faleesha, but then she quickly shook the thought from her mind. *Forgive me, Lord.*

"What's wrong, Dee?" Shalonda whined. "I can't touch you?"

"Nope."

"Why not?"

"Don't you got a man?" he said.

She sucked her teeth. "Who? Curtis? He ain't 'bout nothin'. We been broke up. I need a *real* man." She batted her eyes at him and moved closer to him. He moved away again. "Stop playing!" she whined.

"Eyo, Dee!" Chris yelled from the back door. "Come help carry this couch!"

"A'ight!" he yelled back. He looked relieved as he jumped out of the pool and jogged into the apartment.

"What? She moving or something?" said Shalonda, rolling her eyes.

"I don't think so," said Shelly.

"She *need* to stop calling my man to do everything for her."

Shelly snorted. "Shalonda, please. Rondell is not your man!"

"Well, he *would be* if he wasn't all up in *her* face!" Shalonda sucked her teeth and rolled her neck as she gestured rudely toward Faleesha.

Faleesha's head snapped back like *excuse me?*

"Yeah, that's right," said Shalonda with attitude.

"What's right?" said Mike as he, Chris, and Rondell stepped out the back door carrying the couch. Tyrone came out behind them carrying a drink. Shalonda cut her eyes at Faleesha and turned away.

"Nothin'," she said.

"Shalonda!" Rashonda called.

"What?" she yelled back.

"Your dacquiri is ready!"

"Ooh, goody! Let's get this party started, boys!" She jumped out of the pool, and half of her butt was showing because she got a wedgie as she climbed out. "Oops!" she said in mock embarrassment, fixing her bikini bottom and switching her behind the whole way into the apartment.

"That girl is so nasty!" said Maria.

"Did you see what she just did?" said Shelly.

"She only did it because she wanted Rondell to see her nasty booty," said Shelly.

"Mmm-hmm, girl, you know you right!" said Maria.

Shelly and Maria continued their conversation, mostly about Shalonda, but Faleesha was distracted by the sight of Rondell standing at the deep end of the pool, his muscular body poised and ready to dive in.

"Hey, Faleesha, come on in! I'll meet you halfway." He dove in and burst from the surface, a big smile on his face. He beckoned her to come over to him. She stepped into the pool and went toward him, and he swam toward her. They met at the edge of the pool.

"Amazing dive," she said.

"Thanks, it was nothing." He smiled again. "Hey, I haven't talked to you for a couple of days, so I wanted to see how you're doing."

"I'm doing good. How are you?" She kept her chest under the water, not wanting him to see her cleavage, though a part of her wouldn't mind if he did and admired what he saw.

"I'm alright. I went out to the mall the other day. You know they already put our pictures up?"

"For real?" she said. "That was quick!"

"I know, right? They look pretty good too."

"Really?"

"Yup."

In that moment, Faleesha felt her bikini top loosen. She gasped and caught it before it slipped off. Rondell looked angry at whoever was behind her.

"Yo, what is wrong with you, girl!" he said.

Faleesha turned and saw Shalonda staring at her with a smug expression on her face.

"Oops," she said, and she swam to the ladder and climbed out of the pool. She sauntered to a lounge chair and situated herself with much bending over, making sure Rondell got an eyeful of her ample cleavage and behind.

Faleesha could feel the anger rising inside her. She fought to maintain her composure.

Rashonda had watched it all happen. "Shalonda!" she said. "You know that wasn't right." She jumped into the pool and tied Faleesha's straps back in place.

"Thank you," said Faleesha. Rashonda nodded then got out of the pool and marched over to Shalonda, her hands on her hips. "Well?" she said.

"What?" said Shalonda with an attitude, adjusting herself in her chair, one leg stretched out, the other bent at the knee, swaying back and forth in languid nonchalance.

"That was very childish," said Rashonda.

"So?" said Shalonda. "What she gonna do about it?"

"Excuse me?" said Faleesha, but she stopped herself from saying anything more.

"Don't worry about her," Rondell said. "She's like that to everybody."

Faleesha nodded and took a couple of deep breaths, making sure she didn't even glance in Shalonda's direction. *Be ye angry, but sin not*, she thought. She repeated the scripture in her mind as she got out of the pool. She walked toward Rashonda's back door.

"Faleesha! You don't have to leave!" Rashonda called after her. Faleesha just shook her head and kept walking. Shelly and Rashonda followed her.

"Girl, I am so sorry about that!" said Rashonda.

"It's not your fault," said Faleesha.

"I know, but I feel really bad. You seemed like you were having fun."

"I was. Don't worry about it," said Faleesha. She dried off with her towel then pulled on her shorts and shirt.

"I'll leave with you," said Shelly.

"Aw, now my day is really ruined!" said Rashonda. She crossed her arms and pouted. "Are you sure you're okay?" she said to Faleesha.

"Yeah, I'm good. I just think it's best that I get away from Shalonda right now."

"I feel you on that. But listen, I really enjoyed your company today. Me, you, and Shelly should hang out sometime."

"Oh, definitely!" said Faleesha.

"Okay," said Rashonda. She started to go back to the pool but turned toward Faleesha again. "Oh yeah, and I'll tell your man that you'll call him later."

Faleesha blushed. "What do you mean?"

"Mmm-hmm," said Rashonda, and winked mischievously. She headed back out to the pool.

"I don't know what she's talking about," said Faleesha, grabbing the rest of her things.

"Yeah, right!" said Shelly.

***

"I don't know what's wrong with that girl," said Gesston.

"What do you mean?" said Jacob.

"She's sending me mixed signals. It's like, she'll go places with me, but then she'll refuse to give me her number. I don't understand it."

"Well, maybe you should stop stalking her," snickered Jamal.

"What do you mean stop stalking her? I don't stalk her!"

Jamal jumped up from his seat.

"Ri-i-ight. So you just coincidentally be on her floor, outside of her classes, and around her best friend all the time?"

"Okay, okay." Gesston held up his hands in surrender. "I get it. I'll stop."

"You got to make that woman want you, man!" said Jamal.

"Yeah, grow some backbone!" said Ryan.

"So how do I do that?"

"I don't know . . . make her jealous or something." said Jamal.

"Jealous how?" said Gesston.

"Start talking to Shelly or something," said Ryan.

"Wait, wait. I don't like that idea," said Jacob.

"No, I think it sounds pretty good," said Gesston. "But what if that doesn't work?"

"Then maybe she doesn't want you," said Jamal sarcastically.

"Okay, so I'll hook up with Shelly," Gesston said, rubbing his hands together. He thought about it some more. "I think we got something here."

***

"I know you don't think that lil nigga's coming to MY room!" Terry said defiantly. He threw a fierce look at Rondell.

"Terry, watch your mouth. Rondell is going to stay with us for a while, and he is the closest to your age, so yes, you will be sharing a room with him."

"Man, whatever!" said Terry, glaring at his foster mother. He thundered up the stairs.

She turned to face Rondell. "Now, let me show you the rest of the house." They went into the kitchen where two other boys were playing Connect Four.

"Sherman, Daniel, this is Rondell." They turned to look at him then back to their game. She showed him the bathroom before they headed upstairs. "This is your room." She opened the door. There was a bunk bed, a window, and a rug on the floor, but not much more. She put his suitcase on the top bunk.

"You can have this bunk. I think Terry sleeps on the bottom."

"Okay."

"Well, I'm about to go to the store. If you need anything, just ask Daniel or Sherman."

"Okay."

"Well, I'll be back." She walked out of the room and closed the door behind her. He heard her go down the stairs and out of the house. He walked over to the window and watched her get into the car, start it up, and drive off.

"Yeah, and she told him he could stay in MY room!" said Terry. He banged the door open and walked into the room with two older boys.

"How old are you?" one of them asked.

"Six," said Rondell.

"Little nigga," sneered Terry.

"How old are you?" Rondell shot at him.

"I'm eight!" he said proudly.

"Big difference," said Rondell sarcastically.

"Whatchu say?" said Terry. He moved closer to Rondell.

Rondell squared off in response.

"Chill, Terry," said one of the older boys. "It's his first day."

"Whatever." Terry walked over to the bunk bed. "This is MY shit!" He flung Rondell's suitcase to the floor. Rondell jumped toward him. One of the older boys held him back.

"No fighting up here."

"Why not?" said Terry. "He wanna be a man, let him be a man!" Terry stepped up to Rondell. "Step, punk!" he said.

Rondell just stared at him.

"I said STEP!" Terry growled. He shoved Rondell, causing him to trip over his suitcase. Rondell got up quickly and punched Terry in the jaw.

"Sucka!" he said, and charged at him. Rondell was ready this time. He dodged Terry, but then he felt a foot sweep him and hands push him to the ground. He looked up and saw all three of them staring down at him. He tried to get up but was kicked back down by Terry. The boys pounded him with a barrage of blows, punching and kicking and stomping him. Just when he felt that he was about to lose consciousness, the door banged open.

"WHAT IS GOING ON HERE?" his foster mother screamed. They jumped back from him and pushed past her, running down the stairs.

***

"He gave me joy like a river
Joy like a river
Joy like a river in my SOUL!
He gave me joy, joy, joy like a river
Joy like a river in my SOUL!"

Everyone jumped up out of their seats, shouting, "HALLELUJAH! THANK YOU, JESUS! PRAISE THE LORD!"

The singer handed the microphone to the praise leader.

"How many people got joy like a river today?"

The people shouted in response.

"I said, how many people got JOY like a RIVER today!"

They shouted louder.

"HALLELUJAH! Bless the Lord, everybody! I thank the Lord today because He gave me joy like a river in my soul. And you know where that joy comes from? Do you know how I got it?"

"JESUS!" somebody shouted.

"That's right! The Lord saved me, sanctified me, and filled me with the Holy Ghost one day. And I'm GLAD about it!"

"GLORY!" someone shouted.

"I said I'm GLAD ABOUT IT! I'm glad about this joy that I got deep down in my soul." She was so filled with joy that she broke out into song. The church knew the lyrics and echoed each line as she sang:

"I don't know what you come to do!
(I don't know what you come to do)
And you and you and you and you!
(You and you and you and you)
But I come to clap my hands!

(My hands)
I come to stomp my feet!
(My feet)
I come to leap for joy!
(For joy)
I come to praise the Lord!"

The entire church erupted in praise. Everybody was up out of their seats praising the Lord and giving glory to God for who He is. The Holy Spirit's presence was evident in the church. People were shouting, singing, dancing, and clapping. Everybody praised the Lord. This went on for a while because the Spirit was so strong. Everyone could feel the power of the Holy Ghost in their midst.

After the praise break, everyone went back to their seats feeling blessed and happy. The pastor went up to the pulpit.

"Now, ain't God good?" he said.

"Yes!" someone shouted.

"Yes, He is," said the pastor. "How many people got a testimony about how good God has been to them?"

A lot of people raised their hands.

"Do we have any visitors in the house?" His eyes swept the room. "Sister Faleesha!" he said, spotting her. "I'm so glad to see you back!"

"I'm glad to be here!" she said.

"Praise the Lord," he said. Then he called out again for any visitors. A few people stood up, and he greeted them.

Faleesha felt very comfortable at this church. So many of the people were so warm and inviting, and she really felt at home.

When the service was over, she walked out with Shelly and Gesston to Gesston's car.

"So, Shelly, did you enjoy the service?" said Gesston.

"Yes! It was nice."

"Well, I hope to see you here a lot more," he said, staring at her. Shelly glanced at Faleesha then blushed.

"Um, okay," Faleesha said, feeling awkward under his intense gaze. "I'll come back."

"Make sure you do," he said.

"I will."

"Good," he said with a smile. "Good," he repeated, to himself more than to her.

When they got back to campus, Faleesha and Shelly opened their doors at the same time.

"Thanks for bringing us to church," said Faleesha.

"Mmm-hmm," said Gesston.

"Yes, thank you Gesston," said Shelly. "We really appreciate it."

"Oh, anytime," he said to Shelly. They moved to get out, but Gesston grabbed Shelly's arm. "Hey, Shelly, wait one second. Can I talk to you in private? Just for a minute."

Shelly looked at Faleesha.

"I'll see you in a little bit," said Faleesha. She walked into the dorm as Shelly got back into the car.

Faleesha walked across the lobby to the elevator. *I got to hurry up and get these heels off!* They were hurting her feet. She was used to wearing cute, comfortable flats most of the time. She waited a few moments, and finally the doors opened. Rondell walked out.

"Hi!" she said with a smile.

"Hey, girl," he said. He gave her a hug. "Whoowee! You smelling good, girl. And look at you!" He held her arm up as she twirled around. "That's a nice dress. Where you coming from? Church?"

"Yeah," she said.

"Oh, that's what's up. How was it?"

"It was good. I really enjoyed it."

"Especially 'cause you was with your man though, huh?" he smirked.

"My man? And who would that be?" said Faleesha, a teasing glint in her eye.

"Gesston."

"Oh, please." She tried to slap his arm, but he dodged her.

"Ooh, you better stop that, girl. That is NOT Christian-like!"

"Shut up!" she said, giggling. "And stop saying that. Gesston is NOT my man."

"Could have fooled me," he said, his eyes twinkling mischievously. "All them dates y'all been going on. I was finna ask if I was invited to the wedding."

"Oh, no you didn't!" said Faleesha.

"Oh, yes I did," he said. They both laughed.

"Where are you about to go?" said Faleesha.

"Work," he said.

"Oh. What are you doing later?"

"I'll probably do some homework when I get back, then get some sleep. I been tired lately."

"Aw, poor baby!" said Faleesha. "Not getting enough sleep?"

"Nope. Can't hardly sleep." he said, and his smile faded.

"Why? What's wrong?"

He opened his mouth to answer then closed it. "Nothing. Just can't sleep," he said finally.

"Come on, you can talk to me." Her voice was sincere, and he felt like he probably could tell her anything, but just then, the door to the stairwell burst open. Tyrone rushed past them then stopped and turned around.

"Fool, you ain't gone yet? We gonna be late!"

"I was about to leave," said Rondell.

"Man, stop flirting. Let's go!"

"Shut up," said Rondell. He turned back to Faleesha. "I'll see you later, okay?"

"Okay," she said, and as she watched them run out the door, she wondered what was weighing so heavily on his mind. *Show me how I can help him, Lord*, she prayed.

***

"So what were you and Gesston talking about?" Faleesha said as she collapsed onto Shelly's couch.

"Nothing," she said, sitting next to Faleesha. "He just invited me to this art exhibit thing."

"Oh, that's cool."

Shelly's cell phone rang.

"Hello? Yeah . . . why?"

"Who's that?" Faleesha said.

"Rashonda," said Shelly. "Yeah, girl. We'll be right there."
She hung up.

"What happened?" asked Faleesha.

"Rashonda's baby daddy got arrested," said Shelly. "She's
all shook up about it. You know how dramatic she is. We best
get over there."

Chapter 4

They pulled up to Rashonda's apartment and got out of the car.

"I didn't know Rashonda had kids," said Faleesha.

"She has a daughter," said Shelly. "She's four."

"Oh, okay."

They knocked on the door.

"Who is it?" called a muffled voice from inside.

"It's me," said Shelly. The door opened. Rashonda stood there, tears running down her cheeks. She wiped her face and allowed them to walk in.

"Hi, Faleesha," she said, followed by a loud sniffle.

"Hello." Faleesha gave her a hug. Shelly hugged her too.

"So what happened, girl?" said Shelly.

"I don't know. It happened so fast. I was at Snickers, and he just . . . ."

"Girl, I thought you quit!" Shelly interrupted.

"I know, but . . . ."

"What's Snickers?" said Faleesha.

Rashonda looked down, ashamed. "It's a strip club," she said.

"Oh," said Faleesha. Then she looked at Rashonda, and realization dawned. "Oh!" she said again.

"But it's not like you think," Rashonda said quickly. "I only work there to support my daughter. It's so hard to find a job with the right hours for me to stay in school, and I was going to quit."

Faleesha held up her hand before any more words could come out of Rashonda's mouth. "Rashonda, I am not here to judge you. I want to help you."

"So, you don't think bad of me?"

"Honey, I have no right to look down on you. If it weren't for the grace of God, I could be in the same place. Besides, anybody can change."

Rashonda let out a deep breath.

"Thank you so much. I'm sorry, I just figured because you're a Christian and all that, you wouldn't like me because I sin." She began crying again.

"It's definitely not like that, Rashonda. I wasn't always in the church. I may not have done the same things as you, but sin is sin. We're all sinners saved by the grace of God. I don't have a right to look down on anyone. I'm here to help lift you up."

"Thank you," said Rashonda, and they hugged.

"So tell us what happened," said Shelly.

"I was at Snickers working, and there was this guy who kept trying to touch me and you know, that's against the rules. So I told him to stop, but he wouldn't, and Tyrone was there, but I didn't know he was, and . . . ." She started crying again. Her shoulders heaved uncontrollably.

"Shhh," Shelly said soothingly, rubbing her back. She looked at Faleesha.

"Rashonda, try to calm down, honey, okay?" said Faleesha. She handed her a tissue from her purse. Rashonda sniffled and wiped her tears.

"Tyrone was there, but he was drunk and not thinking straight and he pulled a gun on the guy, and the guy smacked the gun out of his hand, and they started fighting. Tyrone hit the guy in the head with a bottle and knocked him out. Then I guess somebody called the police because they came in and arrested him. He called me from jail and said they found drugs on him."

"Wait, are you talking about Tyrone that was here at the pool party?" said Faleesha. Tyrone didn't seem like the fighting type to her. He was more of a jokester than anything.

"No," said Rashonda. "Not the Tyrone that hangs with Rondell and them. My baby's father is a different Tyrone. You haven't met him yet."

"Oh, okay."

Shelly glanced around the living room. "Where is Lisa?"

"She's in her room. She fell asleep right before you guys came." They sat there silently for a few moments. Rashonda stared into space. Finally, she sat back in her chair and sighed.

"I don't know what I'm going to do. I mean, I have to pay bills, but I can't get another job because it's already enough of a struggle working at that place, and I don't want to work more hours because I was planning on quitting. And now I'm-a have to pay for some kind of babysitter for Lisa since Tyrone won't be here at night . . . ." The tears rushed back to her eyes. She stared at Shelly and Faleesha. "My back is against the wall. What am I supposed to do?"

***

"I don't think this is working, man," said Gesston.

"What do you mean?" said Jamal.

"She's still ignoring me. I completely diss her in front of Shelly, and I keep taking Shelly places, but Faleesha doesn't seem to notice."

"Maybe she doesn't *want* you," said Jacob. "Ever consider that possibility?"

"But why not?" he whined.

"Man, stop acting like a little boy!" said Ryan. "Get with Shelly. She's cute, and she definitely wants you."

"But I don't really like her like that," said Gesston. "I want Faleesha."

"But Faleesha doesn't want *you*," said Jacob. "Let it go."

"Man, whatever," said Gesston. "I'm just going to have to turn up the heat or something."

"Turn up the heat how?" said Jacob.

Jamal and Ryan stared at Gesston, waiting for his response.

"Don't worry. I got this." Gesston rubbed his hands together, thinking.

"Don't do anything stupid," said Jacob.

"Mmm-hmm," he said, very unconvincingly.

***

Rondell watched as Terry opened yet another box of brand new Jordans.

"Yo, those is fresh, son!" said Jessie.

"I know, huh?" said Terry. "I'm 'bout to get ALL the chickenheads with these."

"Yeah, right," said Quincy.

"Why do you say that?" said Terry.

"Cuz you STILL ugly, nigga!" They all burst out laughing at Quincy's joke. Terry pushed Quincy roughly.

"Shut up, man. I GETS girls."

"Ri-i-ight," said Rondell.

Terry turned to him. "I KNOW you ain't talkin'," he said. "I get more than YOU."

"Ohhh!" Quincy and Jessie chorused.

"Whatever, man," said Rondell.

"Nah, nah," said Terry. "You a prime example. You a pretty boy, and I still gets more girls than you. And why is that?" He stared at Rondell, his eyes full of malice. He pulled out a wad of cash from his pocket. "It's cuz I GETS money!" He smacked Rondell in the face with the bills.

Rondell charged at him, knocking him backward onto the floor. They wrestled for a few moments, but when they got too serious, Jessie and Quincy broke them up.

"You need to stop hatin'!" Terry panted.

"You need to quit talking junk!" said Rondell.

"Ain't my fault you broke!" said Terry. Rondell swung at him, but Jessie and Quincy broke them up again. Rondell banged open the door furiously and walked out, stomping down the stairs.

"Bum nigga!" Terry snickered.

A few hours later, when Terry and Rondell were alone in the kitchen, Terry's beeper went off.

"Who's that? One of your 'clients'?" said Rondell.

Terry chuckled. "Nah, it's one of my biddies." Terry smirked, and Rondell got his meaning, but he just shook his head.

Terry looked at him as if he was debating something in his mind. "You know, Dee," he said, "if you want to get money, I could put you on."

"What are you talking about?" said Rondell.

"You could work for me."

Rondell chuckled sarcastically. "Negro, please, I don't need to work for you."

"Come on, man!" said Terry. "Don't you plan on going to college one day?"

"What are you, my father now?"

"Nah, I ain't trying to be nobody's daddy. But you're a schoolboy. I seen all them As on your report card."

"How did you get my report card?" said Rondell, surprised.

"Never mind all that. What I'm saying is, you need money. And you gotta save up for college, so you need to be thinking of the future."

"Man, you crazy," said Rondell. "I'm only thirteen years old, and you talking about college."

Terry threw his hands up. "See, that's what's wrong with you young bloods nowadays. I'm trying to get you to stack chips now so you won't have to worry about college later, and you crying about you only thirteen."

"I don't need your drug money," said Rondell, sitting back in his chair.

"Man, it ain't like you going to be doing it forever! I'm stacking my chips now so I can retire when I'm thirty."

"Man, you're full of it." Rondell got up from the table to carry his plate to the sink when Terry grabbed his arm.

"I'm just trying to help you, man."

They stared at each other for a few moments. Rondell searched Terry's eyes. They were full of sincerity. He sat down.

"So, how long I got to do this for?"

A smile broke out on Terry's face.

"See, now you talkin'!"

***

"Jesus is my doctor
He writes down all of my Scriptures
He gives me all of my medicine
In my room

"Oh, Jesus, won't you
Come on, in the room
Come on, in the room

"Jesus is my doctor
He writes down all of my Scriptures
He gives me all of my medicine
In my room"

"Hallelujah!"

"Thank you Jesus!"

"Praise God!"

The praise group continued to magnify the name of the Lord, and then they all sat down while the speaker remained standing.

"How many people know that the Bible says that men should always pray and not faint?" Everyone nodded their head, and a few said amen.

"Praise God, hallelujah. This world needs prayer," said the speaker.

"Yes!"

"Praise God! I said the world needs prayer, whether it be in church, in the home, or in prayer meetings like the one we are having right now."

"Amen!"

"Now, I'm going to give you a short sweet word today. The Lord gave it to me while I was driving to work this morning, and I was rejoicing in my Spirit because it is so good.

The word for today is 'Pray in obedience, and you will reap great rewards'."

"Hallelujah!"

"That's right. Praise God, for the Lord is good. Now, we're going to turn to the book of Daniel chapter 6. When you have it, say Amen."

The rustling of pages filled the room. Faleesha was excited because Daniel was one of her favorite books in the Bible. It helped her to remember to always remain steadfast in her faith.

"Now, I'm pretty sure you all have heard the story of Daniel in the lion's den. But today, I'm going to look at the situation from a slightly different perspective."

He went on to explain that Daniel stayed obedient to the Lord by continually crying out to Him in prayer. Because of his obedience, Daniel was not only saved from the mouths of the lions, but the king who put him in the den began to glorify God himself.

Whenever Faleesha heard or read this story, she wondered what she would do if she were in a situation like Daniel's. She prayed that God would keep her strong so that she would remain obedient to His Word regardless of the circumstances she might encounter.

***

"I told you that chick was a THOT, brutha!" said Tyrone, giving Chris dap. He, Rondell, Mike, and Chris were all in Tyrone's room playing *Call of Duty* and talking about girls.

"Yeah, true, but I ain't know it was like *that* though, feel me?" said Chris.

"I'm telling you—I heard about her," said Tyrone.

"What did you hear?"

"I heard that all you gotta do is tell her she's pretty, and you're in there!"

"You right about that," said Chris.

"That's definitely how you catch AIDS or an STD," said Mike. "I hope y'all used protection."

Chris leaned over in his seat and pushed Mike's head. "Man, *shut* up!"

"What?" said Rondell. "He's speaking the truth."

"Dee, man, I know you ain't talking, with all the hoes you done ran through," said Chris.

"And I used protection every time, homie." Rondell shook his head and looked away.

"Protection don't always work," said Tyrone.

"True, but it's better than not using anything at all," said Rondell.

"Yeah, whatever." Chris blew out his breath in exasperation. "Alright, I used protection. Y'all happy now?"

"Good," said Mike.

"So, anyway, back to my story," Chris said, "before I was rudely interrupted, Shorty was a straight up THOT, just like you said, Ty."

"What she do?" said Tyrone.

Chris's eyes widened. "Bruh, everything."

"*Everything?*" said Tyrone.

"YESSSS, brutha."

"Wow," said Mike. "That's really sad."

"Yo, bruh, don't kill my vibe, man!" Chris was annoyed all over again. "Why you so sensitive all the time?"

"I'm not sensitive," said Mike. "I just don't like to see girls who give it up so easily like that. It's usually because of something in their past."

"Psssht!" Chris sucked his teeth. "Yeah, okay," he said. "So you telling me that you believe every single 'Daddy made me a THOT' story?"

"It's not a joke, Chris," said Mike. "Stuff like that really happens."

"True," said Rondell, not taking his eyes off the game.

"Whatever. She tried to come at me sideways with some wack ass excuse like the one you just gave," said Chris. "Talking about she a hoe because she was molested as a child. The way I see it is, you wasn't that scared of it if you ready to hop on any nigga that come through!" He laughed sarcastically at his last remark.

"That's not funny, Chris," said Mike.

"Why not?" said Chris.

Mike just looked at Rondell, but he just stared at the screen, focused on the game.

"Why you looking at him?" said Chris.

"It's just not funny," said Mike.

"Yeah, but what Dee got to do with this?" said Chris.

"Don't tell me you hit it too," said Tyrone.

"No," said Rondell, refusing to make eye contact with him.

"Okay, so what's good then?" said Chris.

"Nothing," said Rondell. "Just drop it."

Chris got up out of his seat and turned off the TV.

"Yo, what you doing, man?" Tyrone exclaimed. "You just killed our mission!"

"Shut up, man. You suck anyway," said Chris. He stood in front of Rondell and stared down at him. "Dee, what's good?"

"None of your business, nigga."

"What you mean, it's none of my business? I want to know what the big deal is."

"Like I said, it's none of your business." Rondell looked at Mike, then at Tyrone. "Yo, I'm 'bout to be out." To Chris he said, "Move out the way," and he got up and headed to the door.

"So you 'bout to just leave?" said Chris. "All cuz I talked about some girl?"

Rondell didn't respond. He just walked out the door and closed it behind him.

"What's wrong with him?" said Chris to Mike.

"It's not my place to talk about it," said Mike. "Let's just get back to the game now that you messed us up."

***

Rondell made it back to his room, his entire body trembling with rage as he walked. He closed the door behind him and sank down onto his bed as the memories washed over him.

***

He sat at the kitchen table staring blankly into space. His report card stared back at him. It was all As as usual. His foster mother had just "rewarded" him for his grades, but her reward was nothing like what he expected.

He felt confused. He knew that what she did to him was wrong, but he didn't understand why she did it. He never asked her for anything, and especially not that.

He didn't know what to do. She said that she would make sure he never saw his mother again if he told, so he felt like he had to keep it inside. He didn't know who to tell anyway. Who would listen to him?

He considered trying to get in touch with his caseworker, but as far as he knew, he already had a new one by now. He had been assigned so many caseworkers since he had entered the foster care system that he had lost count. None of them lasted very long, and only a few of them seemed to actually care about him.

But it didn't matter, because even the ones who cared eventually were replaced.

"What you doing in here all silent?" said Terry, who had just come into the kitchen from the back door.

"Nothing," Rondell said dully.

Terry walked over to his report card and picked it up. He looked it over then chuckled. "Aw, come on man! One A-minus is nothing to cry about!"

"I'm NOT crying!" said Rondell defensively.

"Hey, man, why you getting all angry?" Terry looked concerned.

"It's nothing!" said Rondell. "Just leave me alone."

After a few moments, Terry said, "Where's Charlene?" He was referring to their foster mother.

Rondell sat there staring into space. A lump formed in his throat, but he pushed it back. "I don't know."

"She finally got to you, didn't she?"

Rondell looked at Terry, his tension rising. "What are you talking about, man?"

"You know what I'm talking about. She got to you, didn't she?"

"I don't know what you're talking about," said Rondell. "So I think it's best if you shut the fuck up." He stood up to face Terry, ready to square off if need be.

"Hey, man, chill," said Terry. "I understand how you feel. But she got to all of us, one by one. She does it to everybody."

"She ain't do nothing to me!" Rondell said in denial.

"Dee, man, you can chill. I know."

"Did she get to Mike?" said Rondell, concerned for his younger foster brother.

Terry shook his head. "Nah, I don't think so. Not yet, at least."

"We gotta protect him." Rondell's mind raced, searching for a plan.

"I know," said Terry. "He might be the only one left."

***

"So, Faleesha, how do you like your classes so far? Is it really cramped in this office sharing it with the other student workers? Do you have enough air in here, or does it get too hot? You know these windows can open, right?"

Dr. Spandinelli, Faleesha's advisor, walked over to the window and opened it. Faleesha opened her mouth to answer, but she didn't know which question to address first. Dr. Spandinelli continued to talk. "There," she breathed. "That's so much better, right?"

"Yes, thank you," said Faleesha. She had just finished organizing her desk the way she liked it. She was a student worker in a research lab, and Dr. Spandinelli was not only her advisor but her boss. Things had been pretty hectic over the past few weeks. She had been doing a lot of running around, getting her classes settled and attending church meetings. It had been a whirlwind of events, but everything was turning out pretty good.

"So, how do you like it out here so far? I know you're quite a ways from home. I probably could not do that. I was born here, raised here, got my degrees here, and now I work here! Ha ha, isn't that funny? So, how are your classes so far?"

This lady has way too much energy, thought Faleesha. She watched as Dr. Spandinelli bounced around the office straightening things here and there and talking the whole time. At certain points in the "conversation", Faleesha wondered whether she was talking to herself.

"So, what do you think of that?" She stopped in front of Faleesha.

"I'm not sure what you're . . . ."

"No, that's way too soon. I'm always jumping ahead of myself. My husband tells me three times a day, 'Kathy, just slow down. Slow down!' But I can't do it! I guess I have one of those bubbly personalities, you know. I think I was born with it. Sometimes I just have so much to say that I try to say everything all at once." She flailed her hands in the air. "And all of these words start tumbling out, and people get confused, and then I get confused, and I can't remember what I was going to say!" She took a breath. Faleesha stared at her in amazement. She was exhausted just listening to the woman.

"Am I scaring you?" said Dr. Spandinelli.

"No," said Faleesha, forcing herself not to laugh.

"Well, I just want you to know that I am always here for you, and if you have any questions, you can talk to me at any time."

"Thank y-. . . ."

"Oh! I'm late for my meeting!" She looked at her wristwatch. "I have to go now, Faleesha. But I will see you later, and we will talk more then, okay?"

"Okay," said Faleesha.

"Okay, well, you enjoy the rest of your day, and get out there and enjoy some of this sun! There's enough for all of us!" She let out a peel of laughter then rapidly switched to a regular facial expression. "I'll see you later. Do you want this door closed?"

"No, that's . . . ."

"Okay, buh-bye!" she sang out.

Faleesha chuckled and shook her head. "This is going to be an interesting experience," she murmured to herself.

***

"So, which building are you working in again?" said Faleesha. She and Shelly made their way to their usual table in the cafeteria.

"It's the one across from the library. Oh, that reminds me! I have to get a book for my criminal justice class. I totally forgot!"

"What, do you have to write a paper or something?" They sat down.

"Yes, and it's due Monday!"

"That's not too bad."

"It is for me. I'm a very slow reader."

"Oh," said Faleesha, biting into her apple.

"Hey, ladies!" Gesston strolled up to them with a tray of food in his hands. He bent over and kissed Shelly on the cheek before he plopped down in his seat. She blushed and glanced at Faleesha.

"So, how are you doing today, Shelly?" he said.

"I'm doing good," she said with a smile.

"Hi, Faleesha," he said in a monotone then quickly returned his attention back to Shelly. "So, what are you doing later tonight?"

"I was going to start reading for my criminal justice class."

"Oh. Well, why don't you come out with me for a little while?"

Shelly shot a nervous glance at Faleesha. "Um, where are we going?" she said to Gesston.

"Just out to dinner," he said nonchalantly.

"Dinner?"

"Yeah, I want to take you somewhere nice."

Her face turned red, and she looked back and forth between Gesston and Faleesha.

"Okay," she said. "I guess."

***

Faleesha's message alert sounded on her cell phone. She fought to suppress a smile when she saw who had sent it.

"Who's that?" asked Shelly.

"Nobody."

"Girl, I know it's somebody with you smiling like that."

"I'm not smiling," said Faleesha.

"Faleesha! Who is it?" said Shelly.

Before Faleesha could get the words out of her mouth, Shelly's door banged open. They both jumped. Rashonda stalked in, her face livid.

"What's wrong?" said Shelly.

"Do you know I just lost my job?" Rashonda shouted.

"You *did*?" said Shelly.

Rashonda threw her hands up. "Yes, I did. Roger gonna call me up talking about he needed to see me. I didn't think it was nothing because we had meetings and stuff before. So I went up in there, and he goin' try and sugarcoat the situation, talking about how I'm such a good worker, and blah blah blah, so I just told him to get to the point. Then he said that he can't have employees whose guests are a potential danger to the other patrons, so he was going to have to ask me to step down from my position, like I'm some got-dang . . . ." She stopped short and looked at Faleesha then tried to calm herself. She took a few deep breaths.

"I don't know what I'm going to do. I mean, I got a little money saved, and I still got my work study position, but that ain't going to cover everything." She was pacing back and forth. "I gotta find another job quick, but I ain't going to any more strip clubs. I'm done with that." She plopped down onto Shelly's couch.

"Well, the good thing is that you got to leave that place," said Shelly.

"I know," said Rashonda, "but now I need another job, and I don't even know where to look!"

"How about Lenore's?" said Faleesha, referring to a department store at the mall. "I heard they were hiring."

Rashonda just stared at her, her arms crossed over her chest.

"What?" said Faleesha.

"I can't work at Lenore's," said Rashonda. "That place would never hire me."

"I don't know why you say that," said Faleesha, but Rashonda glared at her in a way that said *I don't feel like talking about it with you.*

They thought for a few moments, but no one came up with anything else.

"Well . . . ." said Faleesha.

Rashonda and Shelly looked at her expectantly.

"We could pray about it," Faleesha said in a quiet voice.

Rashonda snorted at those words. "Girl, God won't hear my prayers. He don't like me! You forget I was a stripper."

"So? God hears the prayers of a sincere heart. And besides, you're not a stripper anymore."

"I know, but the whole God thing doesn't work for me anyway," said Rashonda.

"What do you mean?"

"I'm a sinner, Faleesha. I'm not about to get all hypocritical and turn around asking God for help just because I suddenly need it." Rashonda sucked her teeth and shook her head.

"Okay." Faleesha sighed and sat back in her seat.

***

Faleesha was walking across the parking lot toward the cafeteria when she saw Shalonda about to cross her path with two other girls. She wanted to go in another direction to avoid the drama that would most likely ensue, but it was too late. Before she could change directions, Shalonda spotted her.

Just play nice, Faleesha said to herself.

Shalonda eyed her nastily as she walked past. "Hmph!" she sneered, and twirled her head around, her weave swirling with her.

"I like your hair," said Faleesha, trying to be nice.

Shalonda and her friends stopped and turned around. Shalonda crossed her arms and rolled her neck as she spoke.

"Look, don't be trying to get all friendly with me, trick. I know what you trying to do."

"What are you talking about?" said Faleesha, puzzled.

"You *trying* to get with my man Rondell."

"I'm not trying to get with anybody," said Faleesha. "We're just friends."

"Pssht . . . yeah, right!" said Shalonda, sucking her teeth. "I'm on to your little game. But don't play yourself, Boo Boo," she said, pointing her finger in Faleesha's face. "Rondell is *mine!*" She twirled around again and walked off with her friends.

Faleesha stared after them for a moment then shook her head.

"That girl is ridiculous," she said to herself.

Chapter 5

Jacob, Jamal, Gesston, and Ryan sat at their usual spot in the cafeteria. After several minutes of conversation, mostly dominated by Gesston, Jacob looked at him and said, "Man, what's gotten into you lately?"

"What do you mean?"

"You seem so obsessed with this Faleesha-Shelly triangle."

"Oh, that." He bit into his steak and cheese. "Yeah, I'm still working on it."

"I think you should just let Faleesha go, man. She obviously wants nothing to do with you."

"You don't know *what* Faleesha wants." Gesston stared him down from across the table.

"You're going way too far with this thing," Jacob said. "Plus, you're not considering everyone's feelings."

"What do you mean?"

"I mean Shelly, man! What is she, just a pawn to you? You can't use people like that!"

"I'm not using anybody," said Gesston. "I take her out places, and we hang out and have fun. What's the harm in that?"

"The harm is that females catch feelings, dude! Sooner or later, she's probably going to think you two are in a relationship, and if she finds out that you are just using her to make her best friend jealous, think about—"

"Think about what, man?" Gesston said, cutting Jacob off. "Stop being so sensitive. We're all adults here. Nobody's putting a gun to Shelly's head making her do anything with me. Once I'm done with her, she'll find someone else."

"Once you're *done* with her? Really? Do you even hear what comes out of your mouth?" Jacob stared at him incredulously, but Gesston just made a dismissive sound and took a long swig of his Coke.

"You're the definition of a *pig*, man!" said Jacob. He got up from the table and started to walk off.

"And you're the definition of why nice guys finish last," said Gesston.

***

Rondell stood against the building, waiting for Terry. The street light above him flickered then dimmed. He had been waiting for over an hour.

Terry was supposed to be bringing the rest of the product. One of their customers had ordered extra that day. He checked his pager for the fifth time to see if he had any missed messages. Nothing. He sucked his teeth and shifted his position. Suddenly, he saw three dark figures closing in on him.

"Aw, sh*t!" he swore. It was too late for him to run. When they got up to him, he saw who they were: Mancho, Lenny, and D-Rock from a couple blocks over.

"Wassup?" sneered D-Rock.

"Yo, don't start nothing with me," said Rondell.

"Looks like it's too late for that," said Mancho. Lenny stepped in closer. Rondell was surrounded. The only way out was to fight.

"So what you got on my stack, lil homie?" D-Rock glared at him, waiting for an answer.

"I ain't got nothing for none of y'all!" said Rondell. "Now back up off me before you regret it."

Lenny flipped out a blade. It glistened in the dim light.

"Regret what?" he growled.

Before Rondell realized what was happening, three gunshots sounded in the air. D-Rock, Lenny, and Mancho whipped their heads around to see who was shooting.

Rondell took this opportunity and charged through them, and ran up the street as fast as he could. More gunshots sounded, and Rondell could hear the other guys' sneakers hitting the pavement as they ran. He jumped over a few fences, fell and ripped his shirt, and lost his pager, but he kept running. Finally, he made it home. He slammed the door behind him and tumbled up the stairs.

"DON'T BE SLAMMING MY GOT DAMN DOOR!" *his foster mother screamed from her room.* "AND STOP RUNNING THROUGH MY HOUSE LIKE YOU CRAZY!"

Rondell stood in his room trying to catch his breath and figure out what just happened. Two minutes later, he heard the front door slam then footsteps on the stairs. Terry rushed into the room, closing the door behind him. A big smile was on his face. Rondell surged with anger.

"Where was you just at! Do you know I almost got killed? Huh? D-Rock and them—"

Terry held up his hand to stop him.

"I know! I was there. Who you think just saved your life?"

Rondell was quiet for a moment.

"That was YOU?"

Terry nodded his head, smirking.

"Where the hell did you get a gun?"

"Your momma," *said Terry.*

"Don't play like that," *said Rondell.* "Seriously, where did you get a gun?"

Terry held up his hands. "Don't worry about all that. It protected you, right?"

Rondell didn't answer.

"That's all that matters," *Terry said.*

***

Faleesha lay in her bed, tossing and turning. Try as she might, she just could not sleep. Her mind kept drifting from Rashonda to Shelly and Gesston to Rondell and back to Rashonda.

She was really worried about that situation. She felt so heavy in her spirit. When she could no longer take the tossing and turning, she rolled over and looked at her alarm clock. It was exactly 3:00 a.m.

She suddenly felt an urge to pray. She got out of her bed and onto her knees. She clasped her hands on her mattress and bowed her head.

"Lord," she prayed, "I want to come to You on behalf of Rashonda. Lord, You know her situation. I am praying that You will work it out in her favor. Though she does not yet know You, I pray that You will use this situation to draw her to You. Lord, I also pray for Rondell. The other day, he said that he could not sleep. Lord, I pray that whatever is troubling him, You will fix it. Use this situation to help him turn his life over to You. I also pray that You will keep me from temptation and help me to be a light to the people around me. I want You to use me for Your glory. Help me to help other people come to You. Let Your light shine through me so that others can see You in me. Lord, I have no idea what to do, but You know. Show me what to say, what to think, and what to do. I pray all these things in the name of Jesus. Thank You, Lord, for all things. Amen."

After she was finished praying, she got back into bed. Immediately, her eyes became heavy. Before she knew it, she was fast asleep.

***

"I got a job!" Rashonda exclaimed. She had just walked up to Shelly and Faleesha who were sitting on some benches outside.

"What!" Shelly beamed. "That's wassup, girl!" She and Rashonda hugged.

"Praise God!" said Faleesha. "Where you work at?"

"Actually, Lenore's," said Rashonda, "just like you suggested, Faleesha. They have a late-night position doing some stocking and inventory, and I happened to catch the hiring manager just as she was leaving. She had me fill out an application, interviewed me, and hired me right on the spot."

"That is so good! I am so happy for you," said Faleesha.

"Yeah, me too. And that's not all. My cousin switched to first shift at her job so she said she can watch Lisa for me."

"Ooh, girl, see, I knew God was going to work it out for you!" said Faleesha.

"Well, I don't know about all that, but I'm definitely feeling blessed right about now," said Rashonda.

"So, when do you start?" asked Shelly.

"Next week. Just in time to not get too far behind in my bills."

"That's great!" said Shelly. "I am so happy for you, girl."

"Thank you, girl. I'm happy too. I didn't know what I was going to do."

***

Faleesha had just flipped on her TV after a long day of writing papers when she heard a knock on her door. She pressed the mute button on the remote and walked to the door.

"Who is it?" she said.

"The police!" said Rondell. She fought back a smile and opened the door.

"Boy, you know you need to stop," she said. He smirked as he walked in. She closed the door behind him.

"What you up to?" he said, plopping down on her couch.

"Nothing." She took a seat in an armchair. "Just got finished writing three twenty-page papers."

"Word?" Rondell grinned. "Sounds like a fun day."

"Yeah, the time of my life." Faleesha smiled.

"So, you want to take a walk or something to unwind?"

Her heart fluttered slightly. "Um, sure," she said casually, trying to play off her excitement. "That would be nice."

"Cool. Let's roll!" he shouted, springing up from the couch.

Faleesha laughed. "You are too much."

***

"So, Shelly, the night is young. Want to go out to MJ's for some ice cream?" Gesston and Shelly had just finished a date to the movies.

Shelly blushed. "Sure," she said. "That would be great."

"Excellent!"

Gesston seemed more excited than the occasion called for, but Shelly pushed that thought from her mind. They got into his car, and he drove them to MJ's. When they got inside, the waitress seated them at a small table for two where they could sit across from each other.

"I love MJ's," said Shelly. She smiled and glanced around the ice cream shop. "It's such a cozy atmosphere here."

"It is nice," Gesston said absentmindedly as he looked through the menu.

"Ooh!" said Shelly.

Gesston looked up. "What is it?"

She pointed toward the door. "There goes Faleesha and Rondell! Hey, they can sit with us. Double date!"

"Shelly, I don't think—"

"Faleesha! Dee!" They heard her and turned in her direction. She gestured for them to come over. They pulled another small table close to where Shelly and Gesston sat.

"How you been doing, Shelly?" said Rondell, giving her a hug and a kiss before he sat down next to Gesston. Faleesha sat down next to Shelly.

"Good, and you?"

"Everything's good." Rondell turned his attention to Gesston. "What's up, church boy?"

Gesston grunted in reply, not looking up from his menu.

"So, where are you guys coming from?" said Shelly.

"Nowhere, really," said Faleesha. "We were just taking a walk."

"Ooh, romantic!" said Shelly.

Faleesha shot her a look.

Rondell started cheesing.

"What?" said Shelly, a mischievous glint in her eye.

"Let's talk about you," said Rondell. "Where are you lovebirds coming from?"

Shelly blushed. "We just came from the movies."

"Oh, what did you see?"

"The Five-Year Engagement."

"Ooh, romantic!" said Rondell, sarcastically. Shelly slapped his arm playfully.

"Are you all ready to order yet?" said Gesston. He was glaring back and forth between Rondell and Shelly. Neither of them appeared to notice his frustration. The waitress came over to the table.

"Hello-o-o!" she said in a singsong voice. "Can I start you guys off with something to drink?"

Shelly opened her mouth to speak, but Gesston cut her off.

"Actually, we just came for ice cream."

"Sounds great. What would you like?" She poised her pen over her notepad and looked at him expectantly.

"I'll have one scoop of vanilla, nothing more."

"Gesston, sweetie, you don't want any fudge or anything?" said Shelly.

"Nope," he said curtly, handing the waitress his menu. "I'm all set."

"Ma'am, what would you like?" the waitress said, turning to Shelly. She glanced at Gesston, concerned, but gave her order, and Rondell and Faleesha ordered theirs.

The awkward atmosphere continued the entire time they were there. Shelly tried repeatedly to bring everyone together, Faleesha avoided any references to dating, and Rondell attempted to lighten the mood by making jokes.

This, however, was constantly curbed by Gesston's sour attitude. He ignored everyone and only looked up from his ice cream now and then to glare at Rondell or Shelly before putting his head back down.

When it was time to leave, he threw his money onto the table, scraped back his chair noisily, stood to his feet, and strode to the door, leaving everyone behind.

"Gesston, wait!" said Shelly. He turned around. She gestured toward Rondell and Faleesha. "Didn't you guys walk here?" she asked.

Gesston snapped his head back like, *Oh, no you ain't!*

Rondell held up his hand. "We good."

"You sure?" said Shelly.

"Yeah, campus is not that far."

"Okay . . . well, it was nice seeing you guys tonight," said Shelly, and she did a little wave goodbye. As soon as she was in Gesston's car, he turned his key in the ignition and screeched out of the parking lot, narrowly missing a group of teens.

"What was up with that dude?" said Rondell.

"No idea," Faleesha murmured. They walked back to the campus, mostly silent. When they were about two hundred yards from campus, Rondell stopped short. Faleesha looked at him. "What?" she said.

"I bet I could beat you back to the dorms," he said, grinning mischievously.

"Yeah, right!" she said, smiling. "I may be small, but I'm fast."

"Alright. 1, 2, 3, GO!" he shouted, and he took off without warning.

"Hey!" Faleesha shouted after him. "Cheater!" She chased after him but could barely catch up. He, of course, made it to the dorm before her.

"Dusted on you!" he shouted. "WHOO!" he whooped, his fists in the air.

"You had an unfair advantage," she said breathlessly.

"How so?"

"Well, first of all, you didn't even count right, so you definitely cheated. And second of all, your legs are longer."

"How I didn't count right?" he said. "I said one, two, three, go. You should have been ready to move like your boy Gesston." She stared at him, not comprehending his meaning for a moment, and then they both burst out laughing. She slapped his arm playfully.

"Shut up, jerk," she said. They got on the elevator and went up to her floor. When they stepped out of the elevator, Rondell challenged her to another race. She was ready this time, and took off before he could count, but he quickly caught up with her and pushed her aside as he ran past, beating her to the door.

"Oh, my gosh, you are such a cheater!" she said, slapping him on the arm. He chuckled.

"Hey, you got something to drink in there? All this exercise made me thirsty."

"I guess so," she said, and opened the door. She went over to the fridge.

"What you want?"

"What you got?"

"Some orange juice, soda, bottled water . . . ."

"OJ is cool," he replied. She took one out and threw it to him.

"Thanks," he said, and gulped it down.

She stared at him in amazement.

"What?" he said.

"You wasn't joking about being thirsty."

He grinned.

"You want another one?"

He shook his head and shot his empty bottle into the recycling bin.

"Nah, I'm good." At that moment, her phone rang. She answered it.

"Hello?"

"Faleesha?" It was Shelly, her voice shaky.

"What's up girl? You okay?" she said, glancing at Rondell.

"Who's that?" he mouthed.

"Shelly," she mouthed back.

He gestured to say he was about to leave.

She nodded to say okay.

He got up, went over to her refrigerator, and took two bottles of orange juice before he left. She shot him a teasing glare, and he grinned at her mischievously as he closed the door. She rolled her eyes and turned her attention back to her conversation with Shelly.

"I don't know what I did wrong!" said Shelly. "I mean, it seemed like everything was cool, then he just got mad at me." She sounded really hurt.

"Oh, Shelly, I'm sure everything is fine," she said soothingly. "He was probably just in a bad mood."

"I know, but did you see the way he looked at me?" She sniffled. "And then the way he was talking . . . he ignored us the whole night."

"Well, did you guys talk on the way home?"

"No, I tried to start a conversation, but he was driving so crazy that I didn't want to distract him and cause an accident."

"True."

"I don't know, it's just . . . I know we're not like, official or anything, but I really thought we were moving toward a relationship. We basically been talking since the beginning of the school year, and now, all of a sudden, he hates me."

"Oh, Shelly, he doesn't hate you! Maybe he just wanted to be alone or something." Faleesha shrugged as she spoke. "I mean, we did kind of interrupt you guys."

Shelly was silent for a bit. "Yeah, I guess that could explain it. His mood did seem to change the minute you guys showed up."

"Oh, then yeah, that's probably it," Faleesha said, more convinced now. "If he wasn't acting like that before we got there, then maybe he just wanted to be alone with you."

"Yeah, I guess so," Shelly said, her tone considerably lighter.

"You going to prayer meeting tomorrow?" Faleesha asked, changing the topic. Shelly had attended church faithfully up to that point and had recently begun to attend prayer meeting as well.

"Yeah, I should be able to make it. I'm excited to hear part two of last week's message."

"Ooh girl, me too," said Faleesha. For the rest of their conversation, they chatted about church, the prayer meetings, and songs they wished the choir would sing.

After they hung up, Faleesha marvelled at Shelly. "Lord," she said, "You are truly working in Shelly's life. She's reading her Bible, going to church, and going to prayer meetings . . . next thing you know, she'll be saved! Thank you, Jesus!"

***

"So, tell me again exactly what happened."

Rondell removed the ice pack from his eye and stared up at Terry.

"I told you already. I got jumped. I got robbed. The money and everything's gone."

Terry stood silent then picked up his empty Heinekin bottle and hurled it against the fence, shattering it.

"FUCK! SHIT! This is BULLSHIT!" He paced back and forth then collected himself. "Okay, so fifteen hundred dollars . . . I got that in my stash. If I pay that back to Ace, then you can pay me back."

Rondell held his hand up in protest. "No, I got it," he said.

"What you mean?" Terry stared at him.

"I'll take it out of my stash."

"But you only got like two Gs saved, don't you?"

"I don't care. I'm out."

"Boy, is you crazy? What about your school?"

"What about my school?" Rondell countered. "I ain't been keeping up with the work anyway. I might as well drop out. I ain't never gonna be nothing no way. Don't no nigga from the hood ever make it nowhere."

"Yo, don't talk like that. You ain't going out like that," Terry growled with conviction.

Rondell stared up at him. He had never heard Terry speak so passionately.

"Don't ever let nothing like that come out of your mouth again," Terry added. "You gonna make it out this hood. You hear me?"

"Yeah," Rondell said softly.

"What?" he said.

"Yeah, nigga!" said Rondell.

"A'ight. Say it like you mean it." They began walking toward the park.

"So, like I said," Terry began, "I pay Ace, you pay me—"

Rondell held up his hand again. "No, I meant what I said. I'm out."

Terry looked at him like he was crazy. "Don't tell me that sucka D-Rock and them got you shook."

"No, it's not that. I'm just not into it anymore."

"Why not?"

Before Rondell could answer, they heard a voice shouting from behind them. "THERE HE GO! THERE HE GO!" They both turned just in time to see a car screeching toward them, D-Rock in the passenger seat, gun pointed at Terry.

"Oh, SHIT!" they shouted in unison. Rondell began to run, but Terry pulled his gun out of the back of his jeans. Rondell turned back.

"Terry, what you doing?"

POP! POP! POP!

Terry's first bullet knocked the gun out of D-Rock's hand, and the other two struck the side of the vehicle.

"DIE, NIGGA, DIE!" he shouted. The car screeched around the corner and out of sight. Rondell stared at Terry in shock, his mouth open.

"What?" said Terry with a smirk.

"You crazy? You gonna get us killed!"

"Man, chill. Them punk bustas ain't gonna do nothing."

They heard police sirens in the area as they walked home. They were a few blocks from the house when they heard the car screeching around the corner again. This time, D-Rock's gun was pointed directly at Terry. He shot the bullet just as a police car turned around the other corner, coming from the opposite direction. Terry fell down, the car and the police car collided, and Rondell screamed all at the same time.

"TERRY! NO-O-O!" He fell to his knees. One of the officers got out of the car and pointed his gun at D-Rock and his crew. The other officer walked toward Rondell and Terry, gun in one hand and walkie-talkie in the other.

"Yes, this is Officer Smith reporting. I've got a gunshot victim on the corner of . . . ." The rest of his words were a blur as Rondell's world came crashing down around him.

Chapter 6

Shelly, Faleesha, Jacob, Jamal, and Ryan sat in the cafeteria eating lunch and joking around.

"Alright, alright, I got another one!" said Ryan, catching his breath from laughing. "So there was this zebra, right? And he went through his whole life unsure of himself because he didn't know whether he was black with white stripes or white with black stripes."

Shelly rolled her eyes. "Ryan, you are too much!"

"Wait! Wait!" He held up his hand. "This is good, I promise." He chuckled. "Alright, so the zebra goes through his life confused, then he dies and goes to heaven."

"I thought all *dogs* go to heaven, not zebras," said Jamal.

"Shut up, man, you're messing up the plot."

"Alright, whatever. Continue."

"So, anyway, he dies and goes to heaven, right? So at the gates of heaven, Peter lets him in. Soon afterward, Peter notices that the zebra walks around with his head down as if he's sad about something. So one day, Peter decides to see what's up.

"He says, 'Young zebra, why are you so upset?'

"And the zebra replies, 'Well Peter, all my life I've been confused.'

"'About what?' says Peter.

"'Well,' said the zebra, 'I've always wondered whether I was black with white stripes or white with black stripes.'

"'Oh,' said Peter, nodding his head. 'That's a good question. Why don't you ask God?'

"So the zebra goes to the Lord and says, 'Lord, can I ask you something?'

"'Yes, young zebra. What is it?'

"'Well, I've always gone through life with this question, and I really want to know the answer. Am I black with white stripes or white with black stripes?'

"The Lord looked at the zebra lovingly and said, 'Well, young zebra, you are what you are.'

"So the zebra left the Lord and went back to Peter.

"'What did the Lord say?' asked Peter.

"'He didn't really give me an answer. He just said, 'You are what you are.'

"'Oh, that's easy," said Peter. "I know what you are now. You're white with black stripes.'

"'How can you be so sure?' said the zebra.

"'That's easy too,' said Peter. 'If you were black with white stripes, He would have said, 'You is what you is'!'"

Ryan sat back triumphantly. Everyone stared at each other then erupted in laughter.

"Man, you're a corn-ball!" said Jamal.

"Hey, hey, I told you it was good!" said Ryan.

"Man, you're a fool!" said Jacob, shaking his head with a chuckle. He looked up in the direction of the door, and his smile dropped. He rolled his eyes and shook his head. "Oh, Lord, here we go."

"What?" said Shelly, and they all turned to see what he was looking at. Gesston stood in the cafeteria line dressed in baggy jeans rolled up at one knee, a wifebeater T-shirt, a fitted cap turned to the side, some "stunna" shades, and a basketball under one arm. When he saw them, he smiled and attempted (unsuccessfully) to "limp" toward them, trying his best to look hard.

"Oh, God," said Ryan. "This fool has lost his mind."

"Yep, that explains it," said Jamal.

"Wazzap!" said Gesston, giving Jamal dap. "Wassup, Shawtay?" he said to Shelly, kissing her on the cheek.

"Hi," she said. She looked nervous.

"Zup, Faleesha."

"Hi," she said, trying not to laugh.

"So, what's up with you, Gesston? You got a class project or something?" said Jacob, gesturing toward Gesston's outfit.

"Whatchu mean, homie? This all me!" Gesston spun around to show off his outfit, trying to mimic an iconic Michael Jackson move.

"Are those grills?" said Jacob, unable to hide the disgust in his voice.

"Fo sho! You know I got to rock my bling err now and then, feel me?"

Shelly and Faleesha stood up at those words.

"We have to go," said Faleesha.

"Why you leavin' so soon, Shawtay?" said Gesston.

"I think her name is Shelly," said Faleesha, "and we've got somewhere else to go right now."

Shelly shot her a look of relief, and they left the cafeteria before Gesston could say another word.

"Man, these hood rats is trippin!" said Gesston as he sat down. "Faleesha want me though. Y'all see that??"

Jacob was furious at this fool's behavior. "Gesston! What are you doing?"

"Whatchu mean, Woaday?"

Jamal and Ryan burst out laughing.

Jacob said, "What I mean is, why are you waltzing in here like you're some gangster from the 1990s?"

"Whoa, whoa, wait pardna." Gesston raised his hands. "Why so serious?"

"STOP!" Jacob banged his fist on the table. Some girls at the table next to them jumped at the sound. "Sorry," he said, calming himself.

Jacob leaned in close to Gesston so that no one at the surrounding tables could hear them. "You have gone too far with this thing," he said, staring straight at Gesston. "This charade has got to stop—*now*. You are supposed to be a man of God, but you're acting like you lost your mind!"

"What are you, *rebuking* me?"

"That's exactly what I'm doing," said Jacob. "This whole act you're putting on has to stop."

Gesston sucked his teeth. "Man, you're not my father."

Jacob stood up. "Yeah, you're right. I'm not your father. But I am your friend. And I'm not going to let you continue with this behavior."

"Who do you think you are?" said Gesston, rising from his seat as well. Jacob saw that the situation was not going to end well. He shook his head and looked at Gesston.

"I'm going to say this, and I hope you listen to me. You are bringing a reproach to the kingdom of God. You need to check yourself before it's too late."

Gesston brushed off his words with a cocky shrug. "Man, whatever. You just—"

Jacob cut him off. "I've got nothing else to say to you until you act like you've got some sense." He turned and walked away, not bothering to look back.

***

"So, when are you coming to church with me?" said Faleesha. She and Rondell were walking back to their dorm after a campus event.

"Um . . . ." He trailed off, looking in another direction.

"Um, what?"

"I'm not really a holy dude. I drink, I party, and I do other things that aren't too godly."

"Well, you don't have to be perfect to go to church," she said.

"Yeah, I know, but I don't think I'm really ready for all that right now."

"Why not?"

"I don't know." He shrugged. "Maybe one day."

"Oh, okay," she said, slightly disappointed.

"You mad at me?"

"No," she said. "It's just . . . ."

"Just what?"

"Well, I don't know if this is the right thing to say, but it seems like nobody really cares about God. Nobody wants to go to church. Nobody wants to be saved . . . ." She trailed off. He stared at her for a moment like he was thinking about something. "What?" she said.

"You're really into Jesus, huh?"

"Yeah."

"Why?"

"Because He changed my life."

When she said those words, something touched Rondell's heart. He'd heard people talk about God before, but something about the simplicity of her response really struck him. "That's deep," he said.

"Yeah. God has done so much for me and my family. I feel like I just have to share it with somebody."

They were silent for a few moments, and then, before he knew it, the words were tumbling out of his mouth. "You know what? I'll go with you to church this Sunday."

"Really?" she said, her eyes widening.

"Yup." He nodded. "I'm gonna see what it's all about."

"Yes!" she said, raising her fists in excitement.

He laughed. "Girl, you crazy."

"Why?"

"Cuz all I said was that I was going to church. You act like I said you just won a marathon or something."

***

Rondell was lying on his bed, listening to music when he heard a soft knock on his door. He ignored it, hoping they would go away. Instead, they knocked louder. He sat up and pressed pause on his remote. "Who is it?" he said, irritated.

"It's me and your father. Can we come in?"

Rondell sucked his teeth. "Yeah." He sat on the edge of his bed and waited for the inevitable—another discussion.

His mother and father walked into the room with huge smiles on their faces. He knew what they were smiling about. It had to be his report card. He was happy to see them happy, but he wanted to wipe the stupid smiles off their faces.

"Did you hear me, Delly?" said his mother. "We got your report card. You have all As!" She clapped her hands in excitement.

"We are so proud of you, son," said his father. "God has truly answered our prayers."

"Hmph." Rondell was not impressed.

"This is so exciting!" said his mother. "I can't wait to tell all the mothers in the church."

Rondell sucked his teeth. "Why you telling them? It ain't none of their damn business."

"Rondell," said his father, his voice stern.

"What?"

"Watch your mouth."

His mother persisted. "Rondell, honey, aren't you excited? All of your hard work has paid off! We have to go somewhere to celebrate!" She put her hand on his father's shoulder. "Let's go somewhere nice."

"Why y'all wanna take me somewhere?" said Rondell. "Ain't like I did it for y'all."

His mother's smile wavered slightly. "I know," she said. "But we just want you to know how proud of you we are."

"Why?" he said. "This don't mean shit."

"Rondell, you got one more time to cuss at your mother."

"Or what?" said Rondell, stepping up in his father's face.

"Or you got me to answer to." His father stared him down. "You think you so tough, boy? Huh? Where you think you got that from?"

"Not you!" said Rondell. "Nigga, I don't even know you!" At those words, his father backed down a little. Rondell could tell he had hurt him, but he didn't care.

"Rondell, honey," said his mother, tears in her eyes. "We just trying to love you. That's all. We just trying to love you."

Rondell stared at her with hard eyes. "Well, y'all should have thought about that a long time ago."

A tear rolled down his mother's cheek. She wiped it away and turned to his father. "Let's just leave him alone," she said.

Rondell slammed the door behind them and plopped back onto his bed. He felt bad for hurting them, but at the same time, he was glad they left before they could see him shed tears of his own.

***

Rondell, Mike, Tyrone, and Chris all hopped into Rondell's Escalade. It was Saturday and the weather was perfect, so they decided to take a spur of the moment trip to the beach. Rondell figured it would help take his mind off of going to church the next day. Ever since his conversation with Faleesha, he had been nervous about going. He turned his key in the ignition and began to drive. They all rode in silence for a few moments, then Mike spoke up.

"Man, it's way too quiet in this truck!"

Rondell glanced at him out of the corner of his eye, not taking his focus from the road. "Put on some music or something, then."

"A'ight," said Mike, and he grabbed Rondell's CD collection. "Let's see what we got here. Drake? Nah, not in the mood for all that. What's this? Busta? Are you serious?" He chuckled. "You definitely need an upgrade, my dude." He shuffled through some more. "Whoa, whoa, wait, hold up!"

"What is it?" said Tyrone from the back seat.

"Shirley Caesar? Is this Gospel music?"

Rondell glanced at the CD. "Man, put that back," he said, the truck swerving slightly.

"Eyes on the road," said Mike. "I don't know. I kinda wanna hear some Shirley Caesar right now."

Tyrone snorted. Chris sucked his teeth. Rondell glanced over again.

"Mike, man, stop playing and put on some music."

"Naw, naw, for real though," said Mike. "What's wrong with getting in tune with some Negro spirituals every now and then?" He took the CD out of the case.

"Mike, do not put that on," said Chris. "It's Saturday, man. We're going to the beach. Got to get in the mood."

"I'm trying to cleanse my spirit before looking at all the girls in bikinis."

Tyrone burst out laughing. "Mike, you're an idiot, man."

"Please. Do not put that on," Chris said again.

"Why?" said Mike.

"Because I find it offensive, that's why."

"What? You a preacher now?"

"No, far from it. I don't believe in all that God nonsense."

"Word?" said Mike, his eyes wide. "You don't believe in God?"

"Hell no!" said Chris.

"Why not?" said Mike.

"Because that's bullsh*t, that's why. God doesn't even exist. Humans and animals evolved. We weren't created by some old man up in the sky."

Mike's eyes got even wider.

"Yo, Chris, you crazy, man."

"No, I'm in my right mind," said Chris. "Do your research. This world was created by cosmos and consciousness, and we evolved."

"Cosmos and *what*?" said Tyrone, confused.

"Yo, Chris, man, you going to Hell," Mike said, shaking his head.

Tyrone burst out laughing again.

"I'm not going anywhere," said Chris.

Mike brushed him off and turned to Tyrone. "So anyway, Ty, what do you believe in?"

Tyrone shrugged his shoulders. "I mean, I believe in God and everything, but right now, I'm just trying to get some money and some honeys. Maybe I'll start going to church when I'm forty or something."

"A'ight, a'ight, I respect that," said Mike. He turned to Rondell. "So what about you, Dee?"

"What about me?" said Rondell.

"Do you believe in God?"

Rondell sighed, his shoulders slumping slightly. "Man, I don't know what I believe."

"So, what's up with the Shirley Caesar then?" Mike asked, holding up the CD.

"That church girl got him whipped," said Tyrone.

Mike grinned. "Oh, so *Faleesha* gave this to you."

Rondell snatched the CD from Mike and put it in his door pocket. "Naw, man, my mom put that in here."

"Oh, I see." Mike let the subject drop.

"Can you hurry up and put on some music?" said Chris.

"Alright, man, stop naggin'!" said Mike. He found an old Ruff Ryders CD and put it on. Rondell turned up the music so that it blasted from the speakers.

***

"Wazzup, Ma?" said Gesston, coming up from behind Shelly. She turned, and he kissed her on the cheek.

"Nothing," she said, blushing at his attention. "What you been up to?"

"Nat'n. Just chillin'."

She giggled.

"What?" he said.

Shelly looked at him as if she was deciding what to say. "Can I ask you something?" she finally said.

"What is it, baby girl?"

"Why are you acting all different now?"

"Whatchu mean, Shawtay?"

"Like, the way you're dressing and talking. It's all different."

"Oh, that," he said, picking at his wifebeater. "This is just me."

"It wasn't you before."

"Well, it is now. Why, you like it?"

She shrugged her shoulders. "I mean, I guess it's okay."

"Good," he said. "So, what you got planned for the night?"

"Just some studying."

"Oh."

"Why do you ask?"

"Oh, nothing," he said slyly. "I just wanted to see if you wanted to go somewhere with me."

Her eyes widened. "Where?"

"This girl Cheyenne invited me to her beach party tonight."

Shelly's expression changed to shock. "You're going to a party?"

Gesston shrugged nonchalantly. "Yeah, why not?"

"I didn't know you . . . did stuff like that."

"What? Girl, a little dancing never hurt nobody!"

She giggled.

"Right?" he said.

"I guess not."

"So, you game or not?"

She smiled and looked into his eyes. "Sure."

"That's wassup!"

***

Rondell and his boys played some volleyball against some girls they met at the beach. After a couple of games, they all collapsed in the sand.

"I'm so thirsty," one of the girls said.

"Me too," said Tyrone.

"You boys want something to drink?" said another girl.

"Heck yeah!" said Chris.

"Okay! Be right back!" she said, running in the opposite direction of the drink stand. Rondell stared after her, puzzled.

"Where she going? The drink stand is *that* way." He pointed.

"Oh, we brought our own supply," said one of the girls, smirking mischievously.

"Thass what I'm talking about!" said Tyrone.

"Ummm . . . ." said Rondell, then he looked away, his voice trailing off.

"What?" said Tyrone.

"I don't drink no more," he said.

Chris sucked his teeth. "Come on, man. You ain't drank with us in months! It ain't like you was a alcoholic or nothin'."

"I know, but . . . ."

"But what?" said Tyrone. "Come on, man. Have some fun."

"Yeah, have some fun!" said the girls. The other girl returned.

"Who's ready for some Ciroc?" She sat down and pulled a bottle out of her bag. Everyone else looked at Rondell.

"What?" he said.

"You down, or what?" said Chris. Rondell sat silently for a few moments then sighed, giving in.

"A'ight, man. Whatever."

"Yes! That's my boy!" said Tyrone. The girl who brought the drinks filled their cups and passed them around.

***

Gesston and Shelly pulled up to the beach house. He turned off the ignition then took a deep breath.

"What's wrong?" said Shelly.

"Nothing. I'm just a little tired, that's all."

"Well, it was a long drive," she said. "But that will wear off once we get inside."

"True, true," he said, smiling. "Okay, let's go!" They got out of the car and walked to the house. A couple of people from their school were standing around outside, drinking. Gesston nodded at them as he and Shelly entered the house. It was already full of partiers, and the music was blaring.

"Ooh, this is my song!" said Shelly. "Want to dance?"

Gesston stared at her uneasily. "Um . . . ."

"What's wrong?"

"Nothing," he said, shaking his head.

"Come on, let's go!" she said, pulling him to the dance floor.

***

"Yo, this party is rockin'!" said Tyrone. He, Rondell, Mike, and Chris were posted up on the wall sipping some drinks. He looked out at the crowd, nodding his head to the music and moving his body to the beat.

Suddenly, he spit his drink out and burst out laughing as something caught his eye. He poked Chris. "Yo, man, look at Shelly freakin' some dude on the dance floor. That nigga got NO rhythm!"

Chris looked then burst out laughing as well.

"You right!" he said, taking another sip. "No rhythm at all."

Rondell and Mike heard them laughing and looked at Shelly.

Mike scrunched his eyes up, not believing what he was seeing. He tapped Rondell.

"Yo, Dee. Is that *Church Boy*?"

Rondell looked in the direction Mike nodded toward. "What the—that's Gesston!"

"Ohh!" said Tyrone in a loud whisper. "Hypocrisy!" He and Chris burst out laughing again.

"That's cra-a-azy!" said Mike.

"I know," said Rondell.

Just then, a group of girls walked up to them.

"You fellas want to dance?" one of them said, eyeing Rondell.

"Yo, Dee! I think she likes you!" Tyrone sang.

"Ty, you is DRUNK!" Chris slurred. They both burst out laughing again.

"Come on, fellas," said Tryone, downing the last of his drink. He put his arm around one of the girls. "Let's show Church Boy how we gets it in."

Chapter 7

"Rise and shine!" said Mike, opening the shades. Sunlight streamed into the room. Rondell squinted open his eyes. He sat up, and immediately, his head started pounding.

"Oh, man," he said, holding his head in his hands. Mike leaned against the windowsill.

"Where are we?" said Rondell, looking around the room.

Tyrone and Chris sat on the floor, playing chess.

"We at Kimberly's beach house," said Mike.

Rondell scrunched his eyes. "Whos's Kimberly?"

"Cheyenne's sister."

"Oh." He lay back down then sat up quickly again. "Yo, where's my phone?" He patted his pockets frantically. He found it and checked the time. "Oh, man." It was two o'clock in the afternoon.

"What's up?" said Mike, concerned.

"I was supposed to go to church at ten."

Chris looked up from his game. "Church?" he said disgustedly.

"Yeah, I was supposed to go with Faleesha." He checked his phone. He had three text messages from her and four from another number not saved in his phone.

"Who's this?" he said, confused.

"Who's who?" said Mike.

He checked the messages from Faleesha first. She had sent him one at 9:00. *Wake up!* Then another at 9:45 that said, *Got here early. I'll wait for you outside.* Then another at 10:05 that said, *You must be running late. I'll sit in the back and save a seat for you.*

"Aw, man, she's gonna be heated."

"So?" said Chris.

Rondell shot him a glance then looked at his phone again. "But who's this other number?"

He looked through his messages and read them out loud to himself. "Hey, baby, I really enjoyed you tonight." He wrinkled his nose. "Your lips are so perfect."

He looked up at Mike. "Man, what did I do?"

"Oh, I know who that is," said Tyrone.

"Who?" said Rondell.

"That's Shalonda."

"Shalonda?" It was Rondell's turn to be disgusted. "Oh my gosh. How did that girl get my number?"

"She asked to use your phone at the party."

"What party?" he said, his head swimming again.

"The party we went to last night. You don't remember?" Tyrone poked Chris. "Yo, brotha. I told you he was wasted!" He burst out laughing.

"This ain't funny, Ty, man. You know I can't stand that girl."

"Why not? She got a big booty."

"And what she talking about my lips for? I ain't do nothing with her, did I?" Rondell was suddenly scared. "Man, what did I do?"

"Chill, relax," said Tyrone, putting his hands on Rondell's shoulders. "Y'all was dancing, and then out of nowhere, she grabbed you and started kissing you. Me and Mike pulled y'all apart cuz we know you don't like her. Then, the whole night after that, she kept trying to get you to go to one of the bedrooms with her."

"Oh, my gosh." Rondell shuddered in disgust. "That girl is nasty—and I *kissed* her? What was I drinking?"

"Man, I don't even know," said Tyrone. "I think you had more to drink than all of us. We all went back out to the beach to play some volleyball, but before we could start the game, you threw up and passed out. We had to carry you back here."

"For real?"

"Yeah. It was wild."

"Dang. I don't remember nothing."

***

"So, Shelly, how are things with you and Gesston?"

Faleesha and Shelly had just left the cafeteria line and found a place to sit. Shelly sat down across from her.

"We're good!" Shelly said, her eyes dreamy.

"What are you looking so happy for?" said Faleesha. Shelly shrugged nonchalantly.

"Oh, nothing," she said with a smirk.

"Ooh, tell me!" Faleesha said excitedly. "Are y'all official?"

Shelly stared at her for a moment then gave in and nodded her head yes.

"Ooh, get it, girl!" said Faleesha. She raised her hand to give Shelly a high five.

They slapped hands just as Rashonda and Maria came and sat with them.

"Get what, Miss Thang?" said Rashonda, eyeing Shelly.

"Hi, Rashonda!" said Faleesha.

"Hey, girl!" said Rashonda. Faleesha turned to Maria.

"Maria, right?" she said, remembering her from the pool party.

"Yup!" she said, biting into her apple.

"How are you doing?" said Faleesha.

"Pretty good," she said. "Classes are kicking my butt though."

"I know what you mean, girl," said Rashonda. "So anyways," she said, turning back to Shelly. "What conversation did we just interrupt?"

Shelly blushed and looked at Faleesha. "Oh, nothing," she said.

"Nothing my ass!" said Rashonda, then she looked at Faleesha. "Sorry."

"It's okay," said Faleesha.

"So I can't know?" said Rashonda to Shelly.

"Know what?" said Shelly.

"Know why you all giddy and stuff."

"Well, me and Gesston are together now."

Rashonda and Maria gasped. "For real?" said Rashonda.

"Yup!"

"Ooh, girl, I should have seen this coming!" said Rashonda.

"What do you mean?" said Shelly.

"Don't act like you don't know. I seen how you was freakin' him at Cheyenne's sister's party." She swiveled her head with an attitude.

Faleesha's head snapped back like *what?* She pinned her eyes on Shelly and said, "Party? You and Gesston were at a *party?*"

Shelly nodded guiltily. "Yes," she said, ashamed.

"What's wrong with that?" said Rashonda. "Jesus went to the club."

"What?" said Faleesha. "No, He didn't!"

"Yes, He did." Rashonda glanced around, hoping everybody was on her side. "When He turned water into wine."

"Rashonda," said Faleesha, "Jesus did not go to clubs. That was at a wedding."

"Whatever," she said, rolling her eyes. "There's nothing wrong with going to parties. All you do is dance, hang with friends, and chill. What's wrong with that?" She waved her hand dismissively.

Faleesha sighed. "Rashonda—"

"What? Am I going to hell now because I party?"

"Rashonda!" said Shelly. "Chill!"

"Yeah, girl. Calm down," said Maria.

"I don't need to calm down," said Rashonda. "Christians need to stop being so judgmental."

"Rashonda, I'm not judging anybody," said Faleesha, finally able to get a word in.

"Whatever," she said, sitting back in her seat.

"So anyways," said Shelly, "how did everybody do on their midterms?"

The conversation continued, but the tension remained. Faleesha could not understand why Rashonda went off on her like that. She tried to search her mind for a time when she had treated her unfairly or judged her. She couldn't think of anything. She decided to remain silent for most of the rest of the conversation.

***

Faleesha was walking back to her dorm after her night class when she saw Rondell. He was walking out of the dorm toward the parking lot. He noticed her and smiled.

"Wassup, girl?" he said as he approached her, a tinge of nervousness in his voice. "Can I get a hug?"

She hugged him briefly then pulled back.

"What's wrong?" he said. "You mad at me?"

"No, I'm not mad at you," she said, her voice distant.

"What's wrong then?"

"Nothing," she said, crossing her arms in front of her chest.

"Hey, I'm sorry about Sunday."

"It's okay," she said, looking down.

"Faleesha," he said, touching her arm gently. She looked up at him. He stared into her eyes. "For real. I'm sorry." She felt her neck and ears heat up from his touch. She smiled slightly, but then her expression changed to worry.

"Rondell?"

"What's up?" he said.

"Do you think I'm judgmental?"

"Huh?"

"I'm asking because—"

"There you are!" Shalonda exclaimed, brushing up on Rondell. He stepped back.

"Shalonda, what are you doing?" he said, his nose wrinkled in disgust.

"Hey, boo!" she said sweetly. "Why haven't you been answering my text messages?"

"Because I never gave you my phone number," he said flatly.

"Boy, stop playing," she said. "You gave me your number at Kimberly's party. Remember? Then we kissed?"

Faleesha's heart dropped at those words.

"You kissed her?" she said, before she could stop the words from coming out of her mouth.

"Faleesha, it's . . . ."

"Excuse me?" said Shalonda, turning to face Faleesha as if she just realized she was there. "Why are you all up in my man's face?"

"Shalonda—" Rondell started.

"No, baby, I got this." Shalonda turned to Faleesha again. "Get out of my man's face, trick!"

"Shalonda!" said Rondell.

"I don't have time for this," said Faleesha, her head swimming. She turned and headed toward the dorm.

"Faleesha, wait!" said Rondell. She kept walking.

"Baby, forget her," said Shalonda, grabbing his arms. "Let's go to your room."

"Get off of me!" he said, pushing her away.

"What's wrong?"

"Shalonda, I don't want you."

"Yes, you do."

"No, I don't."

"Then what happened at the party? What was that all about?"

"Nothing happened at the party. I was drunk!"

"Oh, now you was drunk!" She crossed her arms. "You weren't saying you were drunk when you were kissing me."

"Look, Shalonda." Rondell took a breath, trying to remain calm. "I'm sorry about the party. I really was drunk that night. I don't have feelings for you. We can be friends, but that's it."

She scrunched her face as if she was working up some tears. "Why?" she said with a pout, a tear rolling down her cheek. She wiped it away.

"I'm sorry. I just don't see you that way."

Her expression suddenly changed to an attitude. She sucked her teeth.

"Fine. Whatever." She stalked away.

"Dang!" Rondell said to himself. "What just happened?" He stood there for a moment then headed to his original destination.

He was going to meet Mike, Chris, and Tyrone at the gym for some two on two. When he crossed the parking lot to the entrance, his phone buzzed, alerting him of a text.

It was Mike. *Where u @, brotha???*

Rondell sucked his teeth as he typed his response. *Hold your horses. I'm outside.*

He entered the gym a few seconds later, just as Tyrone shot a three-pointer. The ball swished perfectly through the hoop.

"BOOYAH!" he yelled. "KOBE!"

"Too bad you can't do that in an *actual* game," said Chris.

"Aw, whatever, man!" said Tyrone.

"What I'm wondering is what took *this* dude so long?" Chris gestured toward Rondell. They all looked at him.

Rondell shrugged his shoulders. "What y'all trippin for? It's full court! There's nobody even here!"

Mike dribbled the ball a little then put it on the ground and sat on it. "We just wondering why you was so late."

They all stared at Rondell expectantly. He finally gave in.

"A'ight, this is what happened. I was on my way over here, and I bumped into Faleesha." Chris sucked his teeth. Rondell looked at him. "Wassup?" he said, wondering where all the hostility was coming from.

"What did she do, rebuke you? Preach a sermon? That's why you were so late?"

Rondell eyed him before continuing. "Not at all. So anyway, me and Faleesha was talking, and I was apologizing to her about missing church the other day. Then, out of nowhere, Shalonda busts up in the conversation, blockin'."

"That girl be tripping," said Mike.

"So then she tells Faleesha that I kissed her at the party."

"Word?" said Tryone, his eyes lighting up with excitement. "Aw, shoot! Drama!"

"Shut up, Ty," said Rondell. "So anyway, before I get to explain, Shalonda goes off on Faleesha, Faleesha walks away, then I set Shalonda straight, and she walks away, and now I don't know what to tell Faleesha, man."

"Is that it?" said Chris, his arms crossed cockily.

"What you mean?" said Rondell. He was getting irritated with Chris's constant attitude.

"Just what I said. Is that it?"

"What's really good with you, man?" said Rondell, shaking his head. "So anyway," he said, turning to Tyrone and Mike, "what do y'all think I should do?"

Tyrone chuckled. "You really asking *me*, man?"

"Well, I think you should—" Mike started, but Chris cut him off.

"Just drop the Jesus freak and get with Shalonda," he said rudely.

"Chris," said Rondell, starting to get frustrated. "I don't want Shalonda."

"Why not? I don't see what the problem is. Ain't like Jesus Freak is giving it up anyway."

"That's more to life than that," said Rondell.

Chris burst out laughing in Rondell's face. "You serious, brotha? Did I really just hear you say that? The hell it ain't! You been hanging around that church girl for too long. She's starting to turn you out!"

"What the fuck is that supposed to mean?" said Rondell, stepping closer to Chris.

"Just what I said." Chris stared him down. "You soft. You weak. You whipped. That girl is turning you out. She got you going to church and everything. Next thing you know you'll be leading Bible studies and teaching Sunday school."

"What's wrong with church?" said Mike. Rondell and Chris ignored him, staring each other down.

"Forget you, Chris," said Rondell.

Chris's head snapped back. "Forget me?" he said. "Is that what's really good? You really 'bout to drop your boy for some

Jesus freak?" He pushed Rondell, almost causing him to trip over Mike's basketball, but Rondell was ready for him. He quickly regained his balance and swung at Chris, but Tyrone stepped between them, blocking the blow.

"Chill, brotha!" said Tyrone. "We boys!"

"That's right," said Mike.

"Y'all need to squash this," said Tyrone.

"Squash what? I ain't got no problem," said Chris.

"A'ight," said Tryone. "Chris said he ain't got no problem. Dee, you cool?"

Everyone waited.

Rondell stood still for a moment, his body surging with anger.

"Whatever, man," he said, and the tension among them relaxed.

"A'ight then," said Tyrone. "Let's play some ball!"

***

Faleesha stared at the TV screen, only half-watching it, her mind consumed with thoughts of Rondell, Shalonda, Shelly, Gesston, and Rashonda.

"I can't believe he kissed her!" she said to herself.

She tried her best to shake the thought from her mind, but she couldn't. She had allowed herself to develop strong feelings for Rondell, and now that he was potentially with someone else, she didn't know what to do. It was getting harder and harder for her to remain focused.

Then, her mind wandered to the whole incident with Rashonda. She could not figure out why that girl had said those things to her earlier. She was trying her best to be nice to everyone, but it seemed like everyone was taking her words the wrong way. "I need to pray," she blurted out. She pressed mute on her remote control, sat back, and began to pour her heart out to the Lord.

"Lord," she prayed, "I don't understand what's happening. I don't know what I did to Rashonda. Lord, if I was being judgmental or critical in any way, I pray that You please forgive me and help me to do better. I also pray for Gesston. Lord, he is slipping. I pray that You help him to come to repentance and to turn his heart back to You. I also pray for Shelly, that You not let her be led astray. And last but not least, I pray for myself and Rondell. Save him, Lord. And please keep me from temptation, because I really like him. In Jesus's name, Amen."

At some point during her prayer, she had closed her eyes. As soon as she opened them, she heard a knock on her door.

"Who is it?" she called out.

"It's me," said Rondell.

Her heart leapt with excitement. She tried her best to keep from smiling too eagerly as she opened the door.

"What are you doing here?" she said, stepping aside to let him in. "I was just . . . thinking about you." She closed the door behind him.

"I wanted to apologize for what happened earlier with Shalonda," he said, sitting on the arm of her couch.

"It's okay," she said. "If you guys are together, then—"

"Oh, we're not together," he said quickly. "Shalonda is *not* my girlfriend."

"Oh, okay." She paused. "Why not?" As soon as she asked, she knew she should not have, but he didn't seem to mind.

"I have other interests." He stared into her eyes and licked his lips. She looked away, unable to hold eye contact because she felt so nervous.

"Oh, for real?" she said, taking a step back.

He noticed her nervousness and changed the subject.

"What you watching?" he said, stretching across her couch to reach the remote. "Why you got your TV on mute?" He sat back up with the remote in his hand.

"I was praying."

"For real?" he said. "What about?"

"Just . . . things."

"Did you tell Jesus on me?" he said with a smirk.

"Boy, shut up!" she said, pushing his shoulder. He flipped backward onto the couch, exaggerating the effect.

"Oh, oh," he moaned, rolling back and forth, clutching his shoulder. One of the couch pillows became loose underneath him, and he tumbled to the floor. Faleesha burst out laughing and helped him up.

"Are you okay?" she said.

"Yeah, I'm alright," he said, a big smile on his face. "I guess the Lord didn't think my joke was funny, huh?"

She sucked her teeth. "Boy, you need to stop. You fell because you were acting silly, not because God struck you down." She pushed the couch pillow firmly back into place then plopped down next to him.

"Hey, you got something to drink?" asked Rondell.

"Yeah, I got some orange juice," she said, getting back up. Rondell held out his hand for her to sit back down. She did.

"I got it," he said, walking to the fridge. "You want one?"

"Sure," she said. "And you only take one, greedy. I remember last time." He grabbed two orange juices and handed one to Faleesha as he sat down next to her.

"Man, I love me some OJ," he said after he gulped his down.

"I see," she said. She had only finished a quarter of her bottle.

"Yeah, that was one of the only things I liked about my first foster mother. She never forgot my orange juice." He shot his empty bottle into the recycle bin and said, "Score!"

Faleesha stared at him. "You were in foster care?"

He nodded.

"What was it like?"

His expression changed slightly as he thought about his past. Painful memories immediately rushed to his mind. Before he could answer, his phone rang. It was Mike calling. "Hold on," he said, and looked at Faleesha to see if it was okay to talk. She nodded.

"Wassup?" he said.

"Yo, Dee, I need you to bring me to the store right quick."

Rondell sucked his teeth. "For what?"

"I gotta pick up some groceries for my mom, man."

Rondell sighed "Man, I don't feel like going to no store right now."

"Let me borrow your car then."

"Man, hell n—" He stopped himself, glancing at Faleesha. "I'm-a be right there. Meet me in the parking lot." He hung up the phone and turned to Faleesha. "I gotta go," he said.

"I heard," she said. "It's okay."

Rondell stood up. "I'm-a talk to you later, okay?" He licked his lips. Her heart melted.

"Okay," she said. She walked with him to the door.

"See you later," he said, walking out.

"Bye." She started to close the door behind him, but he turned back and stopped her.

"Wait," he said.

"What?"

"I'm going to church this Sunday."

She smiled excitedly. "Really?"

"Yeah, for real."

"Great!"

"A'ight. See you."

"See you," she said, and closed the door.

Chapter 8

Rondell sat at the kitchen table with his arms crossed, a blank expression on his face. It was the day after Terry's funeral. The only people who showed up were his foster mother, the other guys who stayed at the house, and the funeral director.

Terry had never attended school that much, so he didn't have that many friends. Throughout the entire day of the funeral, Rondell felt numb. Every significant person in his life had been taken from him. His parents were gone, he had no brothers or sisters that he knew of, and now Terry, the only really stable person in his life, was dead. Miraculously, they had been through three foster homes together. Their foster parents never understood their constant fighting, but that was their way of expressing their love for each other.

Rondell hated his life. He hated being a foster kid, the one no one seemed to want. People didn't really want to adopt him because he was too old. He'd not only been shipped from house to house but from school to school as well. No one from his mother or father's family wanted him. His parents were both considered the "black sheep" of their families, and it was assumed that he, their offspring, could only amount to no good. He waited for his parents his first couple of years in foster care, but they never came to get him. After a while, he gave up hope, figuring they didn't want him either.

He sat there, lost in his thoughts. He was so out of it that he didn't realize his foster mother was speaking to him.

"Rondell!" she exclaimed. She waved her hand in front of his face. He snapped out of it.

"What?" He looked up at her.

"I said do you want something to eat?"

"No."

"Well, you got to eat something. Ain't nobody 'bout to accuse me of neglect."

"Ain't like you cared before."

"What did you just say to me?"

He stood up.

"I said, ain't like you cared before!"

"Boy, don't be jumping up in my face!" she yelled back.

"Whatchu gonna do?" he said evenly. "Kick me out? Nah, you wouldn't do that, cuz then that's TWO paychecks gone."

"You better watch your mouth!"

"Make me."

"Boy, you got one more time to get smart with me." Her voice was serious.

"Or what?"

"Or I'm calling CPS to get you out of here."

"So what? You ain't my mother anyway."

"That's right, and your real mother ain't want you. That's why you here."

Rondell flipped over the table and lunged toward his foster mother.

She ran, and he was blocked by two of the other guys staying there, Mike and Quincy.

"Chill, Dee," said Mike. "Focus on your future."

"I ain't got no future, man," said Rondell, calming down. "I'm a lost cause."

"Don't talk like that, bro," said Mike. "Just focus on school so you can get up out of here and go to college."

Rondell shook his head and started toward the stairs. He turned back.

"It's too late. I already failed. I ain't going back." He went up the stairs to his room and slammed the door.

***

Rondell and Mike walked through the grocery store, picking up items for Mike's mom.

"Why your mom always want so much stuff?" said Rondell. The cart they had was almost full, and they still had quite a few items left. Mike was checking through the list.

"Man, I don't know. Food runs out mad quick at the crib." Mike had seven younger brothers and sisters. They moved toward the dairy aisle. "Let's see," said Mike, reading the list and pushing the cart at the same time. "Milk, eggs, OJ . . . ."

"OJ," said Rondell. "I might need some of that myself." He patted his pockets to make sure he had his wallet. Mike grabbed two orange juice cartons and put them in the cart.

"That's right," he said. "You did always love orange juice." He smiled, but when he saw Rondell's distant look, his expression changed to concern.

"What's up, man?"

Rondell shook his head, "Nothing. I was just thinking about back in the day."

Mike nodded with understanding. "Terry and all them?"

Rondell nodded. "Yeah. I can't believe it's been seven years."

"It has been that long, huh?" said Mike.

"Yeah. And then right after Terry passed, remember your mom came back for you?"

Mike nodded. "That was the best day of my life, man."

"Yeah, I remember," said Rondell.

"How's everything with your parents?" said Mike.

Rondell's parents had come for him a few weeks after Mike's mom came and got him.

"Same old stuff. My mom's still trying to get me to come to church, and my dad's always preaching."

"Why don't you go?" said Mike.

"What? To church?"

"Yeah."

"Brutha, we just went to a party a few nights ago!"

"Yeah, I know, but what harm could it do?" said Mike.

"Man, why you so worried about *me* going to church?"

Mike shrugged. "It seems like a good thing to me."

"So why don't *you* go?" Rondell stopped in the middle of the canned food aisle and stared him down.

"I don't know," Mike said. "Nobody ever asked me."

Rondell looked at Mike.

"What?"

"You serious?" said Rondell. "You been waiting for somebody to ask you to go to church?"

Mike nodded shyly. "Yeah. I be watching the preachers on TV and stuff, and I get this feeling when I watch them like I can feel God speaking through them. But I don't know where to go because nobody ever asked me, and nobody in my family is into church. But I always wondered about it, know what I mean?"

Rondell stared at Mike in shock.

"What?" said Mike finally. "Why you staring at me like that?"

"Wow," said Rondell. "So this whole time you been a undercover Christian."

They burst out laughing.

"Nah, I ain't no Christian, man," said Mike. "I never got saved. The preachers on TV say you just have to say this prayer to do it, but I always wanted to do it in church, know what I mean?"

"Wow, Mike. You a deep dude, man. I never would have expected all of this out of you. What, you be reading the Bible and stuff?"

Mike nodded his head "Yeah, every now and then. But I don't really understand it."

"I need to set you up with Faleesha, man!" said Rondell. "She'll have you preaching by the time she's done with you."

Mike laughed. "Man, you crazy."

"But for real though," said Rondell. "If I go to church this Sunday, you'll go?"

"Yeah, I'll check it out," said Mike.

"A'ight," said Rondell. "I just told Faleesha that I would go to church this Sunday, so if I go, then you gotta go with me."

"A'ight, man!" said Mike. "What time does the service start?"

"I think like ten," said Rondell.

"A'ight, I gotchu," said Mike.

***

It had been a few weeks since Jacob had stopped talking to Gesston. Since then, Gesston hadn't changed. He'd been to the club a few times, hung out with Shelly, and even missed a few church services.

But regardless of all that he had done, he had made no progress on his goal of getting with Faleesha. He strolled through the cafeteria fronting like he was cool. He spotted Jamal and Ryan sitting at a table and walked over to them.

"Wassup, y'all?" he said, and took a seat. They stopped their conversation and looked at him.

"What's up, Gesston?" said Ryan. Jamal just stared at him.

Gesston bit into his apple. "Nuthin much. Just coolin'."

"Coolin'?" said Jamal.

"Yeah, man. Coolin', chillin', it's all the same," he said nonchalantly.

"Gesston, man." said Ryan, looking concerned. "We've been worried about you."

"For what?" he said, taking another bite.

"Because, man, you been walking around with this ghetto fabulous act for almost a month now. You been missing church and Bible Study, and I even heard somebody say you were at the club."

Gesston chuckled. "Yeah, man, I been around."

"Gesston, that's not cool, man. Seriously."

"I'm just waiting for Faleesha to stop frontin'."

Jamal stared at Gesston like he'd lost his mind.

"Are you serious, brutha? You're doing all this for Faleesha?"

"Yeah."

"Gesston, man." Ryan paused, shaking his head. "You have got to let that girl go. You've been trying to approach her for months. She doesn't want you. It's almost Thanksgiving. When are you going to give it up?"

"Plus," Jamal interjected before Gesston could speak, "you seem to be forgetting that Faleesha is a woman of God. Even if she did want you, you're going about it all the wrong way."

"She likes that chump Rondell!" Gesston glared at them defiantly. "That's why I had to step up my game. But she's still not budging. Might have to take it up another notch with Shelly."

"What do you mean, take it up another notch?" said Ryan. "You're not sleeping with this girl, are you?"

"Not yet," said Gesston.

Ryan was incredulous. "Not yet? What do you mean, not yet?"

"Fornication is a major sin, Gesston," Jamal added.

"You've got to stop playing this game," said Ryan.

"Or what?" Gesston sat back with his arms folded in a defiant pose.

"Or we ain't cool no more," said Jamal.

"Oh, so now you guys are going to drop me like Jacob did?"

Ryan leaned his arms on the table and looked straight at him. "Gesston, we are trying to hang in there with you, bro, but you're taking this thing too far."

"I think y'all are taking *yourselves* too seriously."

Ryan and Jamal sat there for a moment, unsure of what to say. Ryan sighed and rose from the table. Jamal followed suit.

"Alright, man," said Ryan. His voice had a note of finality. Jamal nodded.

"Whatever." Gesston shrugged irritably and jumped up from the table as well. "Y'all some squares!"

He stalked off.

***

"Ooh girl, this would look cute on you!" Shelly gushed, holding out a cute top for Faleesha to try on. She, Faleesha,

Rashonda, and Maria were at the mall hanging out and shopping. Faleesha scrunched up her face.

"I don't think so. Green is not really my color."

Shelly sucked her teeth. "Girl, you got to try something new. Just try it on. Please?" She pouted. Faleesha rolled her eyes.

"Fine." She went into the dressing room. After a few minutes of scrutinizing herself in the mirror, she came out and showed the girls.

"Ooh," they chorused.

"Somebody's sexy!" said Maria.

Faleesha grinned. "Girl, stop acting up."

"I agree," said a male voice behind her. She turned around, and there was Rondell. He, Chris, Mike, and Tyrone were all standing there looking at her admiringly.

"What are you doing here?" she said, blushing.

"Yeah, why are y'all in a women's clothing store?" said Rashonda.

"I'm trying to pick out something cute for my date tonight!" said Tyrone in a girly voice. They all laughed.

"Shut up, Ty," said Rondell. He looked at Faleesha. "Chris is picking out a birthday present for his girl."

"Aw, how sweet!" said Maria.

"Who you go out with, Chris?" said Rashonda.

"Shonda!" said Shelly, scolding her.

"What?" she said, swiveling her head.

"Um, *business*?"

"What? I can't know who Chris's girl is? Is that classified information?"

"You don't know her," said Chris.

"How you know who I know?"

"She don't go to our school."

"So? I know people outside of our school."

"A'ight. Her name is Brittany."

"Brittany what?"

"Spears," said Mike, chuckling.

Chris punched his arm. "Shut up, man!"

"Why you calling his girlfriend Britney Spears?" said Rashonda.

"Rashonda!" said Shelly. "You're so nosy!"

"Her last name is Carmichael, okay?" said Chris, getting annoyed.

"Brittany Carmichael?" said Rashonda. "That name sounds familiar. Ain't she a cheerleader at that high school over on Front Street?"

"Yup! That's the one," said Tyrone.

"Eww Chris!" said Rashonda, wrinkling her nose. "That is a little girl!"

"Well, she's all grown up now!" said Tyrone, laughing. He gave Chris some dap. "Besides, she's eighteen."

"Ty, you so wild!" said Maria.

"Why don't you tame me?" he said, eyeing her. She eyed him back.

"Okay, okay, enough flirting," said Shelly. "What are y'all doing once y'all are done in here?"

"Probably the movies or something," said Rondell. "Why?"

"Because we might want to join you. Is that cool?"

Rondell looked at Faleesha. "Yeah, that's cool." He licked his lips. Faleesha blushed.

"Okay," said Shelly. "So, Chris, pick out your gift, Faleesha, change back into your shirt—but you need to buy that cute top!—and we'll all walk to the movies together."

"Pssht!" said Tyrone, snapping his head back.

"What?" said Shelly.

"Who died and made you the boss?"

"Boy, shut up!"

***

Faleesha watched as her advisor, Dr. Spandinelli, who was also the professor of her physiological psychology class, bounced around the room, gesturing wildly while explaining things and moving very close to the students one moment then very far away the next.

Where in the world does this lady get her energy? Faleesha mused. The mere thought of all that gesturing wore her out.

"So, as you can tell, Darwin's Theory of Natural Selection had a major impact on the field of psychology as well as those of the natural sciences, which brings me to another point about something I discussed with my husband three weeks ago as we were shopping for new bifocals. Hey, did you know where bifocals actually came from? Oh, wait, I'm getting ahead of myself. Let's go back to the Theory of Natural Selection. So anyway . . . ."

Faleesha looked around the room as Dr. Spandinelli rattled on. Some people were texting with their cell phones underneath the desk. Some had their heads down, asleep. One girl in the back even had the nerve to have her headphones on, nodding her head to the music.

That is terrible, Faleesha thought as she tried to stifle a giggle. She looked around the room to see who was paying attention. A few people in the front and middle rows seemed to be listening to what the professor was saying, and some were even writing notes. She glanced into the back corner of the room and caught Chris, Rondell's friend, staring at her. She nodded at him and smiled. He rolled his eyes and turned his head.

What's his problem?

"So, does anyone have any questions before we move on?" said Dr. Spandinelli.

Chris raised his hand.

"Yes, Christopher?"

"So, going back to the whole Theory of Natural Selection, how does the Bible's description of the creation of the human race fit in?"

Faleesha's ears became hot. *What is he doing? That boy is just stirring up trouble.*

"Well, that's a good question," said Dr. Spandinelli. "Actually, there is sufficient evidence to support the Theory of Natural Selection over biblical theories of our ancestry. In my opinion, I would rather rely on scientific facts and evidence than a bunch of man-made philosophies from people who are opposed to logic and reason anyway."

Faleesha swallowed. She was hurt by Dr. Spandinelli's comment. She considered herself a very logical and reasonable young woman.

She turned her hurt into prayer. *Father, forgive her. She doesn't know You.*

Another student raised his hand.

"Yes, Stephen?"

"Wasn't the Bible, like, mistranslated a bunch of times anyway?"

"Yeah," said a girl in the back. "Noone even knows what it's really saying anymore. The language is so outdated with all the thees and thous."

That's just the King James Version, Faleesha wanted to add, but she remained quiet.

"Exactly," said Dr. Spandinelli. "That is precisely why we, as educated people, should focus on gaining the truth rather than relying fairy tales, which most of the Bible is. By the way, did anyone know that the actual root word for science is *scientia*, the Latin word for knowledge?"

The lecture continued, but Faleesha could hardly pay attention. She felt horrible. Why did Chris do that? He knew she was a Christian. Why did he purposely start a discussion like that?

She wracked her brain trying to think of what she had said or done wrong to him to make him want to annoy her purposely. She couldn't think of anything. She resolved to talk to him after class and apologize for whatever she had done.

"Chris!" she said, catching up to him in the hallway. He turned around and looked at her with a smug expression on his face.

"Yeah?" he said, his arms crossed.

"I just want to know if I did or said anything to offend you lately. I'm only asking because you gave me a weird look before you made that comment in class about the Bible."

"Your *presence* offends me, Faleesha."

She was taken aback. "What do you mean? I don't remember doing anything to you, so I don't know what you mean by that comment."

"Hi, Chris!" said one of the girls from the class. She hugged him and gave him a kiss on the cheek.

"Wassup?" he said.

"Hi, Faleesha," the girl said, a little less enthusiastically.

"Hey," said Faleesha.

"So what are you going to do, Church Girl? Huh? You gonna sic Jesus on me?"

"You're a Christian?" The girl looked shocked.

"Yes, why?" Faleesha waited, her face open and expectant.

"Oh . . . it's just . . . I thought you were smarter than that, I guess."

Faleesha's jaw dropped. She could not believe what she had just heard.

"Oh, I didn't mean anything by that!" said the girl, trying to be reassuring.

"Ashley!" Another girl called from down the hall. "We have to go now!"

"Okay!" she yelled back. She turned to them. "I've got to go. See you guys later!" she said cheerily, and she ran away.

Chris turned to walk away as well, but Faleesha grabbed his arm. "Chris, wait. I think we should—"

He jerked his arm away from her, causing her to lose her balance.

"Look, I don't really care what you think," he snarled. "I'm done with this conversation. Go read your Bible or pray or something, Jesus Freak."

He gave her his back and walked away. Faleesha felt like she had just been spat on. She put her head down and swiftly walked in the direction of her dorm. She blinked to hold back her tears until she got to her room, and then she broke down sobbing. She felt more alone than she had in a long time.

Chapter 9

"Hey baby," said Shelly. She kissed Gesston on the lips.

"What's up, girl?" he said, smiling.

"Nothing!" She sat down and cuddled close to him. She had a dreamy, faraway look on her face.

"What's going on?" said Gesston.

"Well," she said, turning her body toward him. "There is something."

Gesston felt nervous. "What is it?"

"Well, I was thinking, Thanksgiving break is next weekend, and we've been dating for like three months."

Gesston stared at her expectantly. She didn't say anything.

"So . . . ?" he said.

"So, I was thinking we should celebrate. I think we should take our relationship to the next level."

Gesston suddenly felt like someone had poured a bucket of ice down his back. Sure, he talked a bunch of trash to Ryan and Jacob about sleeping with Shelly, but he never really intended to go through with it. Even he knew that was wrong.

Okay, this just got real, he said to himself.

"Um, Shelly . . . ." He chuckled nervously. "Um, don't you think it's kind of soon?"

"What do you mean, kind of soon? We've been together for three months!"

"Well, it hasn't *really* been three months . . . ."

"I know, but almost," she said. "I want to express my love for you."

Gesston felt like he had been punched in the gut. He took a deep breath while frantically searching his mind for what to say.

"Um, you know what?" he said finally. "Maybe after the break." He figured that by that time, she would forget about it.

"Which one?" she said.

"What do you mean?"

"Which break? Thanksgiving or Christmas?"

"Um, I'm thinking Christmas," he said. "That should give us more time to um, grow our relationship."

"Okay!" she said happily. "I can't wait. It's going to be *so* romantic!"

Gesston smiled uneasily. *Oh, Lord, what have I gotten myself into?*

***

Rondell's cell phone alarm went off, jolting him out of a deep sleep. It was "judgment day," aka Sunday, aka he was supposed to meet Faleesha at the church at ten, and this time, he knew he better be there, and on time, too. He sat up in his bed, yawned, and wiped his eyes. Then he dialed Mike's number.

"Hello?" said Mike, sounding like he had been asleep.

"Man, you always up early. What you doing still 'sleep?"

"Aw, man I was up all night, throwing up."

"What happened? You sick, or you was drinking?"

"I think I'm sick," he groaned. "It must be something I ate from that place up on the corner."

"Man, I told you not to order from there no more! I don't think they legit."

"Well, I learned my lesson now," he said. "You still going to church, right?"

Rondell was silent. He wasn't sure if he still wanted to go without Mike.

"I don't know," he said uneasily.

"You should go, man. You already promised Faleesha, right?"

"Yeah, I did."

"So go then. Put in a good word for me with the Lord."

They both burst out laughing at that statement.

"Man, shut up and go back to sleep," said Rondell.

"A'ight. Let me know how the service goes."

"A'ight." He ended the call and lay back against his pillows. He told himself that he better get up and get moving, but he felt an overwhelming urge to crawl back under the covers and sleep some more. He looked at his phone. It was eight o'clock. He decided to set his alarm for 8:30. That would give him plenty of time to get ready.

Rondell jolted awake. His alarm should have gone off by now. He checked his phone. It was 9:15. "What happened to my alarm?" he exclaimed.

He checked his alarm settings and sucked his teeth. He had accidentally set the alarm for 8:30 p.m.

He got out of bed and went to the closet to get his outfit he had picked out the night before. Much to his dismay, his shirt had fallen to the floor, and it was completely wrinkled. He remembered pulling it out from the other clothes and thinking he should button the first two buttons so it wouldn't slip off the hanger. To make matters worse, his iron had broken three days ago.

"This is bullsh . . . ." He stopped himself when an idea came to mind. He could put his shirt in the dryer! That would definitely get the wrinkles out. He quickly ran down to the laundry room and put his shirt in the dryer for about ten minutes.

He took it out and it was perfect—all the wrinkles were gone. "Good as new!" He smirked, pleased with himself. He checked the time on his phone. It was 9:30. He went back to his room and stopped short when he got to the door.

He had forgotten his keys, and the door automatically locked behind him when he left. "SHIT!" he swore. Then he looked up at the ceiling. "Oh, sorry," he said, apologizing to

God. He spent the next ten minutes searching for one of the Residence Life staff to open his door for him.

Once he got in his room, he grabbed his clothes and quickly showered. At 9:55, he was racing across the parking lot toward his Escalade. He was definitely going to be late, but he figured he had gone too far to stop now. He got on the highway and sped toward his destination.

Suddenly, he heard a loud pop, and his truck began to shake. He pulled over and got out. His right rear tire was flat. He didn't have a spare. Knowing he was taking a risk, he decided to keep going.

"I can still make it," he said to himself. He put on his hazard lights and drove very slowly. He heard another loud pop, and his truck began to shake more violently. He pulled over again and got out. Now both of his rear tires were flat.

He called roadside assistance, and the operator told him that it would take them about an hour to get to his location for a tow.

"I don't believe this," he said miserably. His phone beeped with a text message from Faleesha.

Where are you?

Hey, he typed. *I won't be able to make it today. Long story. SMH.*

Okay, she replied. He could feel her disappointment in that one word.

"This is unbelievable," he said, and sat back to wait for the tow truck.

***

"So, what's everybody doing for break?" said Shelly. She and Faleesha had just sat down across from Ryan and Jamal in the cafeteria.

"I'll be getting some chitterlings and collard greens!" said Ryan, enunciating every syllable. Everybody laughed.

"Ryan, you are so corny," said Shelly.

"Why do I have to be all of that?" he said.

"Because you don't have to enunciate every syllable like that."

"Why not? I *am* an English major, after all. Besides, I think using slang is pretty ignorant." He bit into his apple as Jamal's jaw dropped.

Ryan glanced over at him. "What?"

"I use slang," said Jamal. "Whatchu tryina say?"

"Exhibit A," said Ryan, gesturing toward Jamal.

Faleesha and Shelly giggled.

Jamal pushed Ryan's shoulder. "Aw, shut up, man!" he said, but he was laughing too. "For real, though. What's wrong with using a little slang every once in a while?"

"Slang won't get you jobs."

"Proper English won't get you friends."

"Who said I'm looking for friends? Straight and narrow all the way, baby!"

"Oh, so now you bringing the Word into this?" Shelly rolled her eyes. "You are too much."

"Why not?"

"Who's talking about the Word?" said Jacob. He had just walked up to their table and sat down.

"Ryan and Jamal are debating," said Shelly. She and Faleesha were enjoying the conversation.

"Who's debating?" said Rashonda as she and Maria came and sat down as well.

"Ryan and Jamal," said Jacob. "Hey ladies," he added, greeting them.

"Hey," they said in unison.

"What are y'all debating about?" said Rashonda.

"That's what I'm trying to figure out," said Jacob. "I hope it's not some foolishness."

"Oh, it is," said Faleesha. "They're debating whether we should talk slang or use proper English. It's very enlightening." She grinned as Rashonda rolled her eyes and said, "Lord ha' mercy," and sucked her teeth.

"Well, the debate is over anyway because I won," said Ryan.

"No, it's not, and no, you didn't," said Jamal.

"How so?" said Ryan. "The Word of God trumps opinion any day."

"Well, I got some scriptures for you, too," said Jamal.

"Oh, really?" said Ryan coolly. "Bring it."

"I gotchu. Paul said, 'I became all things to all people that I might save some.'"

"Okay, but what does that have to do with what we're talking about? That's completely out of context! Also, I still win because the scripture I used came from the mouth of Jesus, while yours came from Paul. And we all know that Jesus trumps Paul."

"You guys are nuts," said Jacob, shaking his head.

Shelly chimed in. "And to think this all started because I asked Ryan what he was doing for break, and he said eating chitterlings instead of chitlins!"

"For real?" said Rashonda. "So, let me see if I got this straight. It sounds like Ryan won the debate."

"Oh no, he didn't," said Jamal.

"How so?" said Ryan.

"Because first of all, my brother, what I said was completely in context with our conversation because I was talking about interacting with other people. The souls that we win for Christ not only become our friends, but our brothers and sisters for eternity."

"Okay, I understand what you mean by that, though your explanation is shoddy at best," said Ryan. "However, you still did not address the fact that the words of Jesus outweigh the words of Paul."

Everybody looked at Jamal.

"Okay, but I wasn't finished." Jamal leaned forward on the table. "The Lord always has a ram in the bush."

Everybody burst out laughing.

"Really, Jamal?" said Faleesha. "You are so crazy."

"What does a ram in the bush have to do with eatin' chitlins?" Rashonda asked, and Shelly said, "That's what I'm talking 'bout!"

Everyone laughed again, and when they settled down, Jamal said, "Can I finish?"

"Go ahead," said Ryan. "I definitely want to hear this one."

"Well, my brother," said Jamal, shaking his head from side to side. He cleared his throat in an exaggerated fashion and launched into his "preacher" voice. "You previously stated that Jesus's words trump Paul's words any day. This is true. But, you fail to realize that the words of Paul are not only the words of Paul, because the words of Paul are truly the words of Jesus."

He pulled a mini copy of the Bible from his back pocket. "Everybody, if you will open your Bibles and travel with me to the book of 2nd Timothy, we will read from the 3rd chapter and the 16th verse."

He flipped the pages. "Please bear with me," he said, heaving a dramatic sigh. "I can feel my 'help' coming on."

"Jamal, you are too much!" said Maria, overcome with laughter.

"Where is he going with this?" said Jacob.

"Who knows with Jamal," said Faleesha, her tone droll.

Jamal found the scripture and cleared his throat again before speaking. "If you look at the first part of the scripture, you will see that it states that all scripture is God-breathed. Other translations state that it is God-inspired."

"Okay," said Ryan, staring at Jamal expectantly.

"So, my brother," said Jamal, not missing a beat, "so what my Bible tells me is that since all scripture is God-breathed, and all scripture is God-inspired, then the words of Paul were, in fact, not the words of Paul himself, but the words of Jesus. And since the words of Paul were actually the words of Jesus, Jesus cannot trump Himself. I'm going to say that again because some of y'all didn't get it."

Faleesha burst out laughing. "Jamal, you are too much!" she said, trying to catch her breath.

"I can't do this anymore!" said Shelly, laughing as well.

"I don't get it," said Rashonda.

They all looked at her, and then the whole table erupted in laughter.

"What?" she said.

"I'm going to help you out, my sister," said Jamal. "I understand where you're coming from, because at one point in my life, I didn't get it either."

"You need to stop," said Jacob, but Jamal was on a roll.

"When I said that Jesus cannot trump Himself, what I meant was that since Jesus is the one who inspired the scriptures, it was actually Jesus who spoke through Paul when he made that statement. If you need further clarification, let me take you to the book of Matthew, the 9th chapter, and the 9th through the 13th verses."

Jamal went on to explain how Jesus called Matthew, a sinner, to be one of His disciples, and how He was eating dinner with all of the sinners from around the town at Matthew's house. He explained how Jesus became all things to all people, not only in a natural sense of having compassion for people in need, feeding the hungry, and calming storms, but in a spiritual sense by sending the Holy Spirit to be our healer, our provider, our protector, and our savior.

Rashonda—and everyone else for that matter—was completely engrossed in Jamal's words. At some point during the conversation, he had stopped playing and started preaching and expounding on the gospel. By the time he was done, both Rashonda and Maria had tears in their eyes.

"Are you alright, Maria?" said Jacob. Everyone looked at her.

"I just wanted to know, could you pray for me and my family, because . . . because . . . ."

She burst into tears and put her head down, covering her face. Everyone crowded around her, hugging her and assuring her that everything would be okay.

When she calmed down, she explained that she'd had a rough life, and her family was struggling financially, and her mother was starting to give up hope, and she was the only one in her family who had made it to college.

All of her younger brothers and sisters were looking up to her, and her mother as well, but she didn't feel that she had what it took to succeed in school because she was already on academic probation for her low GPA.

"I just don't think I'm smart enough!" she cried. "But I don't want my mom to give up hope because she's been through so much,"

"Honey, Jesus can fix all of your problems," said Faleesha.

Maria looked up at her. "He can?"

"Yeah, girl! There's a scripture that says to cast all of your cares on Him because He cares for you. So, all of your problems and worries, we can put them in Jesus's hands, and He will fix them."

"Really?" said Maria. She smiled and held out her hands. "Can we pray now?" Everyone gathered around her and held hands.

Jacob led the prayer, and at the end, everyone said amen. Once the prayer was over, they all settled in their seats again. Maria looked at Faleesha like she wanted to say something, but then she looked away.

"What's up?" said Faleesha.

Maria shook her head. "Nothing. It's probably too much."

"What is it?"

"It's kind of embarrassing," Maria said nervously.

"Go ahead, girl. Don't be ashamed."

"Well," Maria started, and she took a deep breath. "In case you haven't noticed, I've been hanging around you guys a lot lately. The reason is that I want to change my life. I want God. I see how all of you are so strong in Christianity, especially you, Faleesha. I've been watching you, but I mean that in a good way. I want to know what I have to do to be saved."

"Glory to God!" said Faleesha and Jacob in unison.

"That's good, girl!" said Shelly.

"Praise the Lord!" said Ryan. They prayed the prayer of salvation with Maria right there, and she was smiling with joy by the time they finished.

"Wow," said Ryan. "Who knew our silliness would lead to all of this?" He was amazed.

"See, the Lord told me that was going to happen," said Jamal.

Ryan looked at him sideways and shoved his shoulder.

"Boy, shut yo mouf!"

They all laughed at Ryan's slang, the perfect way to end a silly debate that led to a new life in Christ.

***

Faleesha felt so happy as she packed her bags to go home for Thanksgiving break. She had just had the most beautiful day. Maria got saved! She'd had no idea that God was working in Maria's heart, or that Maria had seen her as an example to look up to, especially since she didn't feel like such a good example.

That had touched her heart so much that she had almost started crying right there at the lunch table. She truly had been trying her best to live by the Word and treat people the way Jesus would treat them.

She was so grateful that despite the moments of discouragement she had faced, God had shown up and shone out in somebody's life, glory to His name.

***

"GOT 'EM! WOOO!" Tyrone shouted and jumped up from his seat. He, Mike, Chris, and Rondell were in Rondell's room playing video games before they left for Thanksgiving break.

"Stop exaggerating, brotha!" said Mike. "You only won by two points."

"Ahh, you a sore loser," said Tyrone. "A win is a win." Rondell's cell phone rang.

"Who dat, the pizza?" said Tyrone.

Rondell looked at the number on his phone. "Yep, that's them. Let me answer this." He pressed the talk button. "Hello? You outside? Okay, I'm coming." He hung up and went to get the pizza and soda.

When he came back, Tyrone and Mike were arguing about who had won the most games.

"A'ight, a'ight, so you got this semester, but what about the summer when we played against each other online?" said Tyrone.

"Oh my gosh, Ty!" Mike exclaimed. "I whipped you all summer too!"

Tyrone jumped up from his seat again. "You lyin', brotha! Remember *Call of Duty*? You sayin' you whipped me in *Call of Duty*?"

"Hey, y'all stop bickering and get some pizza," said Rondell.

"'Ey, you got some napkins?" said Chris, his hand oily.

"Naw, man, get some tissue or something." said Rondell, taking a bite of his pizza.

"Tissue?" said Chris, disgusted. "That's nasty, man!" He looked at Mike.

"What?" said Mike, chewing his pizza.

"Baptized!" said Chris, smearing his oily hand on Mike's forehead.

Mike pushed Chris against the wall in response.

"That's disgusting, man!" he shouted. He wiped his forehead with the bottom of his T-shirt.

"No, *that's* disgusting," said Chris, leaning against the table.

Mike stood there for a moment, his fists clenched in anger. He took his shirt off and sat down on the couch.

"Oh, come on, man!" Chris goaded him. "Stop pouting in the corner like a little girl." Mike ignored him. "Besides, I don't see what the big problem is. You said you want to go to church. That's what they do there. Get used to it."

"You play too much, Chris," Mike said in a quiet voice.

"Well, speaking of church," said Tyrone, turning to Chris. "That was messed up how you went in on Faleesha the other day after class."

Rondell snapped to attention. He stared between Chris and Tyrone. "Whatchu talkin about, Ty? Chris went in on Faleesha how?"

"Relax, man," said Chris, putting his hands in the air in mock surrender. "It wasn't nothing."

"It didn't seem like nothing to me," said Tyrone. "Mad heads said she was crying when she walked away."

"Crying? You made her cry?" Rondell stepped closer to Chris.

"Ty, you always starting trouble, man."

"I ain't start nothing," said Tyrone. "You started it. Besides, it's *his* girl." He pointed to Rondell. "He has a right to know."

Chris backed up slightly and gestured in defense. "Wait, wait—first of all, she's *not* his girl. And second of all, what I say to Jesus Freak is nobody's business but mine."

"Stop calling her that," Rondell in a level tone, his eyes narrowed at Chris.

Chris looked at Rondell. "What, you got a problem with that?"

"Yeah, I got a problem with it."

"Well, that's what she is, so whatchu wanna do?"

"Oh, so it's like *that*, brotha?" Rondell stepped closer. "You just gonna straight disrespect me like that?"

"It is what it is," said Chris.

Rondell lunged toward Chris, but Mike jumped from his seat and blocked him.

"Chill, Dee! Chill!"

Tyrone was holding Chris back. "Yeah, both of y'all need to chill. We boys. Let's squash this."

"Like I said before, I don't got no problems," said Chris.

"What about you, Dee?" said Tyrone.

They all stared at him. Rondell stared back at them.

This was the second time Chris had come at him and then backed off as if nothing had happened. Rondell could feel his anger surging, so he decided to leave until he cooled down. He snatched his coat from the back of a chair.

"Whatever, man," he said, walking toward the door.

"Where you going, Dee?" said Mike.

"I'll be back." He slammed the door behind him.

Chapter 10

Faleesha was standing outside next to the dorm parking lot, waiting for a cab to take her to the bus station. She was going home that night for break. She shivered and tapped her feet, trying to shake off the cold.

A sudden movement caught her eye, and somebody burst out of the front door of the building, making a lot of noise in the process. She was startled by the sound, but even moreso when she saw that it was Rondell. He was so angry that he stormed right past her without seeing her.

"Hey!" she called out after him. He stopped short and turned around.

"Faleesha? What you doing out here, girl?" His angry expression softened as he walked toward her.

Her heart melted when he smiled.

"I'm just waiting for my cab."

"Where you going?" he said, looking at her luggage. "Home?"

"Yeah." She nodded.

"You want a ride instead?"

She felt her neck heat up with nervousness. "Oh, thanks, but the cab should be here any minute."

"You sure?"

"Yeah, I'm good."

"A'ight. I'll wait here with you until they come."

She blushed.

He grinned. "What?" he said.

"What do you mean?" she said.

"Why you always so shy? Do I make you nervous?" He stepped closer to her.

She stepped back.

"Where you going?" he said, then stepped forward again.

She stepped back again and felt the wall behind her.

"Boy, stop!" she said, giggling. She gently pushed him back. His chest felt so firm, she wanted to touch it again.

He stared at her.

"What?" she said.

"You are so pretty," he said softly.

She felt her neck and ears heating up again.

"Thanks." Thinking it best to change the conversation, she said, "Where are you coming from? You looked really upset when you came out the door."

"Upstairs in my room," he said, and she could hear the irritability in his voice.

"What's wrong?"

"Nothing. Just get sick of people sometimes."

At that moment, headlights beamed in their direction as the cab pulled into the parking lot.

"That's my ride," she said.

"So you're leaving me?" he said, faking like he was hurt.

"I'll be back, silly."

"Let me carry your bags." He grabbed her suitcase and her backpack and started toward the cab.

"Oh, you don't have to," she said, walking after him.

"I gotchu," he said over his shoulder. He put her bags in the back seat then held the door open for her.

"Thank you," she said, and as she started to get in the cab, he gently grabbed her arm.

"Wait."

She looked at him.

"Can I get a hug?"

She smiled and put her arms around his neck. He put his arms around her waist and pulled her close. He hugged her firmly then slowly pulled back, his cheek against her cheek. He kissed her on the cheek before he let her go. "Have a safe trip," he said, smiling.

Her entire body felt like it was on fire.

"You too," she said, and she got in the cab.

He closed the door, and as the cab drove off, she turned and waved at him through the back window. He waved, and when the cab turned a corner and was out of sight, he walked back into the dorm.

She was in a happy daze the whole way to the bus station. She couldn't believe he kissed her! But she wished it had been on the lips . . . .

***

Faleesha rushed through the bus station, trying to find her gate. She looked back and forth between the numbers on her ticket and the numbers at the station until she found her bus.

When she got to the crowd of people waiting, she accidentally tripped over something on the ground and bumped into the person in front of her. The woman turned around with an attitude. It was Shalonda.

Oh, Lord, Faleesha thought. *Here we go.*

"Why don't you watch where you're going?" said Shalonda, pushing Faleesha backward.

"Hey! It was an accident!" Faleesha said angrily.

"Who you think you getting smart with?" said Shalonda, stepping toward Faleesha.

"Ladies, ladies!" said a security guard. He stepped between them. "Do I need to ask you to leave?"

"No," said Faleesha.

Shalonda sucked her teeth. "Punk," she said to Faleesha.

"Hey, no need for name calling," said the security guard. "Do you need to leave?" he asked Shalonda.

"I'm good," she said with an attitude. She picked up her suitcase and walked toward the other side of the crowd.

"Thank you, Lord," said Faleesha. She definitely didn't need any drama. It was bad enough that her happy mood was ruined.

***

Shelly heard a knock on her room door. "Coming!" she said with a smile, thinking it was Gesston. She opened the door and saw Rashonda standing there.

"Girl, what are you doing here?" said Shelly.

"Girl, I am so glad you're on campus!" said Rashonda, walking into the room.

"What's up?" said Shelly, closing the door.

"I need you to do me a huge favor."

"What is it?" said Shelly.

"Well, you know how I wanted to see Tyrone before Thanksgiving, right?"

"Yeah, I suppose so," Shelly said, hedging. She was fairly certain she knew what was coming next.

"So, tell me why my cousin Craig gonna cancel on me at the last minute, and now I have no ride!"

"That's messed up," said Shelly.

"I know!" said Rashonda, and her expression softened. "Can you take me?"

Shelly's head snapped back. "Girl! Are you crazy? That's like an hour and a half drive!"

"I know!" said Rashonda. "But I *need* to see him!" she wailed. "Please, Shelly? *Please?*"

Shelly stared at her for a moment, her hands on her hips. She sucked her teeth and rolled her eyes. "Let's go," she said. "You lucky you my girl. You know that, right?"

"YES!" Rashonda jumped up and down ecstatically. "Thank you *so* much!"

"Yeah, mmm-hmm. You owe me for gas too."

When they got to the facility, they had to go through the security process, removing everything from their pockets, going through metal detectors, the whole bit. Finally, they were allowed in to see Tyrone. He was seated near a corner, away from the other inmates and their families. When he saw Rashonda, his face broke into a huge smile.

"Hey, girl!" he said, giving her a hug.

"Hey, baby!" she said excitedly, kissing him on the lips.

"What's up, Shell?" He hugged her too, and they all sat down.

"Nothing much," said Shelly, "except Rashonda here owes me a big favor now."

"Bae, how you been?" said Rashonda, ignoring Shelly's remark.

"Girl, we just talked yesterday," said Tyrone. "I'm good."

"I know, but I don't like you in here," she said, touching his arm.

"I know, I know—so how's our daughter?"

"She's good. She got all As on her report card, but she misses her daddy."

Tears welled in his eyes when he heard those words. "Tell her I miss her too, and I'll be home soon."

"When you getting out?" said Shelly.

"I don't know. It's still up in the air. We trying to get the date moved up, so hopefully in about three or four months."

"I'll be so happy when you get out of here!" said Rashonda.

"Girl, me too!" he said. "When I get out, things will be different. I'm making some changes right now."

"What kind of changes?"

"I'm done with the street life," he said, his voice taking on a serious tone. "No more drinking and drugging. I'm getting a real job, and me, you, and Lisa is moving to a better neighborhood."

"Ooh, I can't wait!" said Rashonda.

"Me either," he said. "I also been getting into some other stuff I'll tell you about later."

"What stuff?"

"I'll tell you later."

"Why can't I know now?" she pouted.

"Because you'll know later," he said, not budging. She stared him down. He stared right back. Finally, she sucked her teeth and rolled her eyes.

"Whatever," she said. "You never want to tell nobody nothing."

"Girl, you are a trip!" said Shelly, laughing. "You guys are so cute. You have definitely found your match."

***

Gesston sat in a corner in the cafeteria, deep in thought. They had all just come back from Thanksgiving break and were talking excitedly about their upcoming finals.

Thoughts were swirling in Gesston's mind. He was thinking about all of the things that had happened up to that point in the semester. He was also thinking about what to say to Shelly.

"Hey, boo!" a female voice called out, interrupting his thoughts.

He looked up. It was Shelly. She leaned over and kissed him on the lips before sitting down across from him.

"What's up?" he said, trying to sound casual.

"Nothing. Why didn't you answer your phone last night?"

Gesston searched his mind for what to say, but decided that it wasn't time to tell her the truth.

Instead, he merely said, "Oh, my bad. I was busy."

"Oh, okay," she said, biting into her sandwich. When she swallowed, she looked at him and smiled.

"What?" he said.

"I was just wondering—have you given any more thought to our special night?"

"What special night?" he said, playing stupid.

"You know . . . our first time together."

"Oh, that. Yeah, I've been thinking about it."

"I was thinking we should get a hotel room."

"What?" He was starting to feel closed in.

"It would be so romantic!" she said, a dreamy look in her eyes. "We could go away for the weekend to somewhere nice and get one of those suites with a spa and Jacuzzi."

"Wow. You really have this all figured out, huh?"

"Of course, silly!" she said. "I want our first time to be perfect!"

***

"So, Maria, when you coming to church?" said Faleesha.

She, Rashonda, Shelly, and Maria were hanging out at Rashonda's apartment.

"Oh, I already started going!" she said. "I really love Pastor Bryant. He really breaks everything down."

"When did you go?" said Faleesha, surprised.

"Oh, I didn't tell you? Jacob took me last Sunday."

"Jacob? Ooh, get it, girl!" said Rashonda. Maria laughed.

"Not like that," she said. "Jamal, Ryan, and my sister were there too. She came up to visit me so I wouldn't have to spend Thanksgiving alone."

"Oh, that's nice," said Rashonda.

"Oh, and guess what?" said Maria.

"What?" said Shelly.

"I got tutors for all of my classes! I went to the student center this morning, and they looked at all of my grades and said that if I work hard, I should be able to pull at least a C- in all my classes. If I get all Cs, that's enough to get me off of probation!" She let out a little squeal of excitement.

"That's good, girl!" said Faleesha. She slapped high five with Maria.

"But I think I have another problem," Maria added.

"What's up?"

"Well, there's this guy I like, but . . . he's not really like, a Christian."

"Who is it?" said Rashonda.

"Shonda!" said Shelly, shooting her a look.

"What?" said Rashonda.

"You are *too* nosy."

"Whateva," said Rashonda, flipping her weave. "Don't act like you don't want to know too." She turned back to Maria. "So anyways, who is he?"

"It's Tyrone," said Maria. "The one that hangs with Dee, and Mike, and Chris." She looked at Faleesha. "Is that bad?"

Faleesha felt uneasy all of a sudden. She didn't know how to respond without potentially offending anyone, especially Rashonda. She remembered the last few times she had spoken about things and how Rashonda had gotten an attitude with her.

"Well," she said, trying to tread lightly, "it's not necessarily a bad thing, but I think you should wait before you get into any relationships."

"Why should she wait?" Rashonda interrupted, not letting Maria answer.

"Yeah, why?" said Shelly.

Oh, God, thought Faleesha. *Here we go.* Looking only at Maria, she said, "Well, since you just got saved, having a boyfriend could be a distraction."

"A distraction how?" said Rashonda, interrupting again. "I mean, as long as she goes to church every Sunday, what's the problem?"

"Yeah, and Tyrone's not a bad person," said Shelly.

"True," said Rashonda.

Maria just sat there, waiting to hear more.

Help me, Lord, Faleesha prayed in her mind. "I'm not saying that Tyrone is a bad guy. I'm just saying that when we get into relationships, we sometimes get so caught up in them that it can lead us away from God."

"Okay, but wait," said Shelly, clearly offended. "How would you know anything about relationships if you've never been in one? I don't see you with a man."

Faleesha flinched. She couldn't believe what Shelly had just said. She had shared that information with her in confidence, and Shelly knew that it was something that she was kind of embarrassed about.

"Whaaat?" said Rashonda. "So you mean to tell me you in college, and you've never had a *boyfriend*?"

Tears formed in Faleesha's eyes, but she blinked them back, refusing to let anyone see her pain.

"Yeah, that's why she acts all giddy and nervous around Rondell," said Shelly.

"Shelly," said Faleesha, keeping her voice level as she maintained composure. "Just because I have never had a boyfriend doesn't mean that I don't know what I am talking about. There are plenty of things about me that none of you knows anything about. Besides, this is not about me. This is about Maria's question. Can we get back to that please?"

Looking at Maria, Faleesha said, "To answer your question, the Bible says not to be unequally yoked."

Maria frowned. "What does that mean?"

"It means that a saved person should not get into a serious relationship with a person who is not saved."

"What?" said Rashonda. "Are you *serious*? See, that's why I can't get down with church. That's why I can't be no Christian. Too many rules and regulations for me."

"Well, it's not about rules and regulations," said Faleesha. "It's about—"

"So wait, wait," said Rashonda, cutting her off. "You're telling me that if I got all saved and sanctified, I would have to break up with Tyrone?"

Faleesha sighed. "Rashonda, that's—"

This time, Shelly cut her off. "And what about me and Gesston? And you and Rondell?"

"Me and Rondell?" said Faleesha, her voice rising.

"Faleesha, don't play dumb," said Rashonda. "Everybody knows you like him."

"But I'm not dating him," said Faleesha defensively.

"Okay, but you still like him," said Rashonda. "Ain't that a sin too?"

Before Faleesha could answer, Rashonda fired another question at her.

"So you're telling me that God doesn't want y'all to be together, even if you like each other, just because he's not saved?"

"Yeah, and what does that even mean, anyway?" said Shelly. "Saved from what? What are you saving me from?"

"Shelly," Faleesha began, but she was cut off again.

"And that's not true!" said Shelly. "Because me and Gesston been together for three months!"

"Shelly," Faleesha started again, but Rashonda cut her off.

"No, wait. I want her to answer *my* question."

Faleesha was getting frustrated. "WILL Y'ALL LET ME FINISH?" she yelled.

"Hold up," said Rashonda, putting her hand up. "No need to get an attitude with *me* in *my* house."

"Oh, so you can get an attitude with me, but I can't get one with you?" said Faleesha.

"Not in my house," said Rashonda.

"Okay," said Faleesha, grabbing her things. "I'll see y'all later." She walked out the door.

Chapter 11

Faleesha walked up to Rashonda's front door. The new semester had just started. Her Christmas break was horrible. She could not wait to get back to school. She had struggled with urges to drink from the moment she got home to the moment she left. The only thing that kept her from slipping was her constant attendance at church and Bible study.

Was it supposed to be this hard? She often worried whether she had failed God in some kind of way, because in her opinion, it shouldn't be this much of a struggle, considering that she had given up drinking a couple of years ago! The pastor's words, "There is no condemnation to those in Christ," taken from Scripture, kept coming back to her, but she still could not bring herself to believe it. She must be doing something wrong to struggle this much.

In addition to her battles with trying to stay free from drinking, she constantly worried about the situation with Rashonda and the other girls. She felt bad that they had left on such a bad note. She hadn't really spoken to Rashonda or Shelly over break due to their last conversation, except when Rashonda called her out of the blue to invite her to her house when she got back. She had no idea why.

She wasn't holding anything against them, but she was getting tired of always having to defend her faith. She knew that it was all a part of the Christian life, facing backlash because of her beliefs, but that didn't make her like it any more.

She stared at the door. *Do I really want to go in here?* Before she had a chance to talk herself out of it, Rashonda opened the door.

"Faleesha!" she said, smiling. "Come on in!" Faleesha stared at her quizzically as she walked in. Shelly and Maria were both there, sitting at the kitchen table.

"What's this about?" said Faleesha.

"Do you want something to eat?" said Rashonda. "I made fried chicken. There's some mashed potatoes, macaroni and cheese, and collard greens too."

"Yes, thank you," said Faleesha. "But what's this about?"

"Oh, we'll talk later," said Rashonda, brushing it off. "Right now, let's eat some food."

"Ooh, girl, you can *cook!*" said Maria, biting into her fried chicken. Faleesha and Shelly nodded in agreement. "Can I have some more?" said Maria. Rashonda looked at her like she was crazy.

"Girl, finish that plate first, then we'll talk about another one." They all laughed.

"Where's your daughter?" said Shelly.

"Oh, my cousin is watching her for a couple of hours," said Rashonda.

"Oh, okay," said Shelly.

They continued to talk and laugh, but there was a certain level of tension in the room. Finally, Faleesha could not take it anymore.

"Rashonda, what's this about?" They all stared at her.

Rashonda knew that it was time to spill the beans. She stood up, looked too nervous to speak, and sat back down.

"Well," she said, clearing her throat. "The reason I invited you all here is because I have something to say." She paused.

"Okay," said Faleesha, wondering what it was.

"Well," said Rashonda, "I just wanted to talk to you guys about something."

"Which is . . . ?" said Shelly.

"Well," she said, taking a deep breath, then she stopped again.

"Come on, girl. Spit it out!" said Maria.

Rashonda looked at her and nodded. "Well," she started, but Shelly cut her off.

"Rashonda Shanay! If you say 'well' one more time, I'm done!"

"Okay, okay," said Rashonda. "I have a confession to make. But first, I have an apology." She turned to Faleesha.

"Faleesha, I'm sorry for always starting trouble with you. The reason I did that was because I'm jealous of your walk with God. You're so strong in the faith, and I should be where you are."

Faleesha's jaw dropped. This was totally unexpected.

"Rashonda!" she said. "You can have the same thing!"

Rashonda dropped her head. "I know," she mumbled. "I did. I'm a backslider."

"A backslider?" said Maria. "What is that?"

Rashonda looked at her. "A backslider is somebody who walks away from God. I left the church to be with Tyrone. At first, we were just dating. I was a church girl, and he was a boy from the streets. My mom and everyone at the church kept telling me not to be with him, but girl, I'm-a keep it real with you. I was horny."

Shelly's mouth dropped open. "Rashonda! I cannot believe you just said that!"

"Well, it's true. So anyways, me and Tyrone kept getting closer and closer, and then one day, we ended up having sex. After that, somebody's cousin from the church found out, and that person told everyone, and then my mother found out."

"Did she kick you out?" said Maria.

"No, no," said Rashonda. "She would never do that. I left my mother's house to move in with Tyrone because I figured the damage was already done." Her voice started to crack as she continued. "I couldn't take all those people talking about me and staring at me and shunning me in the church, so I left."

She wiped a tear from her eye. "And the whole time, I could hear God calling me back, but I didn't come." She broke down.

"Rashonda," said Faleesha, rubbing her back. "It's okay."

"No, it's not okay," said Rashonda, rocking back and forth. "I'm not saved no more. I ruined it. I got pregnant, had Lisa, then I started stripping to make ends meet. I stayed in school to try to prove something to myself, but I know I ain't fooling nobody." She cried even harder at those words.

"Rashonda," said Faleesha, "we all make mistakes."

"What mistakes have you made? You always seem so perfect."

Everyone's eyes were on Faleesha now. She considered telling them about her drinking problem and the other things she had been through, and she knew it would probably help them to know what God had saved her from, but she couldn't bring herself to do it. "Trust me, I'm not perfect," she finally said. "We all make mistakes—even me."

"Not like mine, and now Tyrone is locked up. I feel like that's God's way of showing how much he hates me."

"That is *not* true," said Faleesha. "Now, you listen to me."

Rashonda looked at her.

"God does *not* hate you. You made mistakes, and you fell, but we all do from time to time. You are *still* saved, and you are *still* a child of God. And God loves you with an everlasting love. He said in His Word that He would NEVER leave us or forget about us. You are still on God's mind. And just like the Prodigal Son, God is your Father, waiting for you to come back with open arms."

Rashonda sat there silently, taking in those words. She looked at Maria and said, "Please don't get with Tyrone."

Maria looked confused. "Why not?"

"Don't get with him. Don't do what I did. You are saved now. Stay in the church, and keep getting to know God. Faleesha's right. It's not the right time to get into a relationship. Don't do what I did."

The sincerity in Rashonda's voice touched Maria's heart, and she knew her friend was right. "Okay," she said.

"But what about you?" Faleesha said, looking at Rashonda. "Are you going to come back?"

Rashonda sat there for a few moments. "Soon," she said finally. "Not right now, but soon."

***

Gesston sat in the back of the cafeteria, confused. All through winter break, he had struggled with an identity crisis. Should he stay in church, or should he totally rock his newly acquired gangsta persona? He could see the benefits of both.

In church, he was an assistant youth leader. A lot of the younger kids looked up to him. Church was really all he knew. He was born and raised in it.

But on the other hand, with this new direction he was going, he had more friends. People thought he was cool. Other guys envied him because of his grills and his chain, and a lot of girls tried to talk to him now as well, something that never used to happen. He even had a girlfriend, though she wasn't really the woman he wanted . . . .

A pained smile crossed his face as he thought of Faleesha. He really liked her, but she didn't seem to have any interest in him. She wanted Rondell. He couldn't stand it when that happened—girls in the church always seemed to go for guys in the world.

"What's wrong with you?" A voice interrupted his thoughts. He looked up. It was Shelly.

"I was about to leave," he said, as soon as she took a seat across from him. He really did not want to hear any more about their special night, as Shelly called it.

Her face fell.

"What's wrong?"

"Nothing," she said, tears in her eyes.

"You sure?"

"Yeah. It's just . . . you barely even talked to me over break. And then, whenever we did talk, it was only for like five minutes because you were always so busy."

"Shelly," he began. He was going to finally tell her the truth, but she cut him off.

"But you know what? I've been doing some thinking."

Gesston's heart leapt with excitement. Was she breaking up with him? He hoped so. "About what?" he said, trying to contain his smile.

"I was thinking we should postpone our first time together until Valentine's Day. That way, it will be really special and memorable, and it will help spice up our relationship." She smiled with that dreamy look in her eyes that he had come to dread so much.

Gesston slumped in defeat.

"What's wrong?" said Shelly. "Did you want to do it sooner? I mean, we can move the date up."

"No." Gesston sighed. "Valentine's Day is fine."

"You don't sound too thrilled about it."

"I was just thinking about all the work I have to do this weekend."

"Oh, that's right," she said. "You're starting your internship next week, right?"

"Yeah."

"Well, I won't keep you waiting." She smiled and took a sip of her hot chocolate. "Go do your work, and I'll call you sometime tonight."

"Okay," he said, and got up from his seat. He started to walk away.

"Wait!" she said.

He turned back. "What's up?"

"Aren't you forgetting something?"

"What?" He glanced at the table and felt his pockets for his phone, wallet, and keys.

"Not that, silly! Aren't you going to kiss me goodbye?"

"Oh, yeah, sure, just so much on my mind, is all." He leaned over and kissed Shelly on the lips.

"Much better," she purred.

"Yeah."

On his way out the door, he heard someone say, "Yeah, that Gesston dude is definitely paying her to date him."

Gesston turned around. It was two guys who lived on his floor, Rashad and Terrell, standing there smirking at him.

"Nick Cannon, brotha?"

"AHH!" They burst out laughing and gave each other dap.

"Y'all talking 'bout me?" said Gesston, switching to his street lingo.

"Yeah," said Rashad. "We talking 'bout how there's no way you could really bag a girl as fine as Shelly."

"Oh, really?" said Gesston, crossing his arms. "And why is that?"

"Cuz you ain't got no game," said Terrell. He and Rashad laughed in his face.

"Yo, why y'all hating on my boy Gee?" said Chris. He had just walked by and caught a part of the conversation.

"Cuz ain't no way he really bagged Shelly," said Rashad.

Chris gave him a look. "Why is that so hard for you to believe? Cuz *you* couldn't get no play with her?"

Rashad's smirk changed into a frown. "I gets girls," he said defensively.

"A'ight, a'ight," said Chris, holding his hands up. "No need to get all upset. I'm just saying, don't hate on Gee cuz he's with Shelly."

Rashad nodded.

"That chain real?" said Terrell, pointing at Gesston's chest.

"You know it," said Gesston proudly.

"How much that cost? Like a stack?"

Gesston nodded.

"Where you get it from?" said Rashad.

Gesston folded his arms across his chest in a cocky pose. "Don't worry about all that. I just do what I do."

"A'ight, a'ight," said Rashad, giving him dap. "I ain't mad atcha."

"I'm-a see y'all later," said Chris.

"A'ight, man," said Terrell. They all parted ways.

***

"So what side do you usually like to sit on?" said Maria. She and Faleesha were walking into church together.

"Oh, it really doesn't matter," said Faleesha. They walked around until they found two empty seats.

"Hey!" Maria called out, waving at someone. It was Jacob, Jamal, and Ryan. They looked over in the girls' direction and waved back as they walked to their seats. Faleesha smiled, but her smile faded when she realized that Gesston was not with them. She was worried about him. Gesston had missed a lot of church last semester, and his pattern seemed like it would continue this semester.

Moreover, Shelly also skipped church whenever Gesston was not there. Faleesha sensed that Shelly was losing interest in God, and that saddened her. She breathed a silent prayer for them both as the service started.

"Praise the Lord, everybody!" said the praise team leader. "Today is Youth Sunday, and you know we are about to have a good time. Y'all like that?" People began to clap. "I said, do y'all like that?"

People stood up and started clapping.

"Glory to God!" said the praise team leader. "Now, I want everybody to give it up for the youth department. They have worked hard the entire year to raise funds for the homeless shelter on Orchard Street. This year, the youth raised five thousand dollars!" The whole church erupted in praise.

"Praise God!" the leader shouted. "We are very proud of our youth department. Jesus said, 'Whatever you have done for the least of these, you have done for me.' Let's give them another hand."

Everyone shouted and clapped their appreciation. Faleesha looked over at the teens sitting in the youth section of the congregation. It warmed her heart to see them smiling with true happiness.

"Thank you, Jesus," she said softly.

"Now, everybody, we have some special guests in the house. I would like everyone to welcome the praise dance team from Holy Trinity Church on Brown Street. Let's give them a hand as they come forth."

Faleesha clapped and shouted excitedly with everyone else. She loved praise dancers. She thought it was so beautiful how they could really express the words of a song through movement. She smiled as the group made their way to the front of the church.

"Ooh, this is my song!" she said to Maria. It was Micah Stampley's "Take My Life." Faleesha sang along with the lyrics.

"Holiness, holiness is what I long for,
Holiness is what I need
Holiness, holiness is what you want for me
Holiness, holi—"

"What the heck?" Faleesha said out loud, shocked when she saw that Shalonda was one of the praise dancers.

Faleesha could not believe her eyes. Shalonda was right there in the front of the church, dancing as innocently and beautifully as the rest of the team.

Faleesha just stood there in shock. When the song was over, the church erupted in praise, and they called for another performance, so the group began to dance to Mary Mary's "God in Me."

"I can't do this." Faleesha excused herself and went to the bathroom until the song was over. "Lord," she prayed, "please forgive me. I know I should not have walked out like that, but this is crazy."

She stayed in the bathroom another five minutes before she went back to the service.

Chapter 12

Faleesha sat at her desk organizing her work into separate folders. This semester was going to be no joke. Somehow, she had to find an internship on top of taking all advanced courses. *This is what I get for transferring*, she thought, flipping through her syllabi.

After carefully looking at all of the due dates for various assignments, she realized she had three ten-page papers due by Friday. Today was Monday.

"Oh, Lord," she said. "How am I going to do all of this and find an internship?" Just then, the door opened, and one of her officemates walked in. "Hey Keisha," she said, smiling.

"Hey girl," said Keisha, putting her bags on her desk. "I have *so* much work to do this week, it's not even funny."

"I know what you mean, girl," said Faleesha. "I got three papers due Friday, and I haven't even bought any of my books yet. Plus, I have until Friday to find an internship."

"Oh, girl! That is brutal."

"I'm saying though," said Faleesha. Just then, the door opened again, and two more girls walked in, Beth and Mary Jane.

"Hi, ladies!" said Beth as she and Mary Jane went to their desks.

"Hey," said Faleesha and Keisha. Then, the door opened again and their last officemate, Rebecca, walked in.

"Okay," said Rebecca as she gestured in the air. "Is it me, or are all of these professors going crazy this semester?" They all laughed at her antics.

"I know what you mean," said Keisha. "Faleesha and I were just talking about all of the work we have to do."

"Well, at least we're all in the same boat," said Beth. "We will get through this together!" She walked around the office, slapping high five with everyone.

They heard a knock on the door.

"Come in!" Beth called. "We're decent." The other girls chuckled as Dr. Spandinelli walked into the office.

Beth's face reddened in embarrassment, and she covered her mouth in shame. "Dr. Spandinelli!" she gasped. "I'm so sorry! I didn't mean . . . ."

Dr. Spandinelli held up her hand. "I'm fine. It's okay. I've been doing this a long time, and I've heard much worse." She smiled, and her eyes sought out Faleesha. "I'm glad you're here," she said. "Could you come over to my office for a sec? We need to have a conversation."

Faleesha felt her face heat up. What did they need to have a conversation about?

"Okay," she said, and walked across the hall with Dr. Spandinelli. She tried to contain it, but she felt very nervous inside.

"So, how are your classes going so far?" said Dr. Spandinelli. "Are your professors piling the work on yet?"

"Absolutely," said Faleesha, smiling.

"Especially that Dr. Michaels, huh? I've had so many students come into my office on the brink of a nervous breakdown because of his classes that I can't even count them. Very encouraging, isn't it?"

"Sure!" said Faleesha, a bit too brightly. She felt even more worried now.

"Well, anyway, what I wanted to talk to you about is very important."

Faleesha straightened up. She hoped she wasn't in trouble.

"I know you've been searching frantically for an internship in the area, and I think I might have one for you.

I'm ready to start the data collection phase of my latest research project, and based on your level of work, I want to recruit you as part of the team to conduct a portion of our interviews. I know that this is a major responsibility, especially with all of your classes this semester, but I really would like for you to work on this."

Faleesha was floored. This was totally unexpected.

"What do you think?" said Dr. Spandinelli.

"Wow," said Faleesha. "Thank you so much for this opportunity!"

"Oh, no problem! And I already cleared it with the Dean, so it's definitely doable as an internship. So what do you say?" She looked at Faleesha expectantly.

"Yes!" said Faleesha.

"Great! We'll get started next week."

***

Rondell washed and dried his bedsheets then returned to his room. He was putting his sheets on his bed when he heard a knock on the door. "Come in!" he called, thinking it must be Mike and the boys.

"Hey," said a female voice. Rondell quickly whipped his head around.

"Shalonda!" he said, surprised. She smiled at him and sat down at his desk facing him. She crossed her legs seductively. Her skirt was so short that it barely covered her thighs, and her tight v-neck top was so low-cut that it showed her ample cleavage to full advantage.

He wrinkled his nose in disgust.

"What?" she said, smirking at him.

"Ain't you cold?" he said. "Girl, it's like thirty degrees outside."

She smiled at him and adjusted herself in his chair. "It is a little chilly. Why don't you come warm me up?"

"I don't have time for this today."

She pouted. "Why not?" she said in a whiny voice. "Don't you want me?" She opened her legs so that her thong panties showed underneath her skirt.

"We already went through this," said Rondell. "I told you I don't have feelings for you like that."

"Come on, Rondell. Stop playing! You slept with both my girls Tamara and Rhianna. Why can't I get none?" She crossed her arms in front of her.

"I'm not that kind of dude no more."

"Okay, but you're still a man! I know you have needs." She got up and sauntered over to him. "I just want to fill those needs." She began to pull up her top.

"Shalonda, chill!" said Rondell, his irritation building with each minute.

She pulled off her top and tossed it on the floor, then she reached behind her to unzip her skit, wriggling her butt to step out of it. She moved closer to him.

"Didn't you hear me?" Rondell said, stepping back as she slinked closer to him. She pressed her body up against him.

"Come on, Rondell. Just one time—I promise I won't disappoint you."

Rondell felt himself getting aroused. It had been several months since he'd been with a girl. He was determined to change his life in all respects, including this one. He had ignored his desires for sexual intimacy, promising himself that he was waiting for the right girl, but he felt his resolve weaken.

"A'ight," he said, his voice husky with tension. "Just one time."

"Yes!" said Shalonda, excitedly. She threw herself onto his bed and gestured toward him. "Come on, baby," she said seductively. "I want you to finish undressing me."

He slipped off his shoes and got on the bed, lowering himself on top of Shalonda. Then he froze. He didn't really want to do this. He didn't even like Shalonda as a person. Her actions and attitude were disgusting to him. He didn't even know why or how he had allowed himself to go this far with her.

"What are you doing?" she said, interrupting his thoughts. "Aren't you going to kiss me?"

He recoiled at those words, snapping out of his funk. He shook his head and rolled off her. He sat on the edge of his bed, putting his shoes back on.

"What are you doing?" she repeated, sitting up as well.

"I don't want to do this."

"What do you mean you don't want to do this?" She was angry now. "So you just gonna stop?"

He stood up and looked down at her. "Yeah. You gotta go."

"I can't believe you!" she yelled. "How you gonna get me all hot then just stop?"

"Look, I ain't call you over here. You came yourself." He pointed to the door.

"So what? You can't just say you gonna do something then renege."

"Shalonda," he said in an even tone, "I don't want you like that."

"What's this about?" she said, standing up to face him. "Huh? Is this about Faleesha? Don't tell me that wack ass church girl got you turned out."

"What are you talking about?" said Rondell, his irritation returning.

"Nothing!" Shalonda snatched her top from the floor and put it back on, adjusting her boobs in her push-up leopard print bra with more drama than necessary. "You done let that church girl turn you into a punk. She got you whipped, and she probably ain't even giving it up. How you gonna pass up a real woman like me for that lame?"

Rondell had had enough. "Shalonda, get out of my room."

"Whatchu gonna do if I don't?" she said defiantly. "Why I gotta leave? You mad cuz I'm calling it like it is? You a punk now, Rondell. That girl—"

"SHALONDA, GET THE FUCK OUT MY ROOM!" Rondell hollered. He was rapidly passing his boiling point. His fists shook with rage. He was really about to punch this girl in the face if she didn't leave—now.

She didn't move, so he grabbed her by the arm and steered her toward the door. He flung it open and forced her outside.

"GET YOUR HANDS OFF OF ME!" she shouted.

"SHUT UP!" he shouted back.

"What's going on here?"

Tyrone, Chris, and Mike had just rounded the corner.

"Nothing," said Shalonda. "Your boy is wack, that's all. Church girl done turned him out."

Rondell had had more than enough of Shalonda and her attitude. "Shalonda, shut the fuck—YOU KNOW WHAT? You know why I don't want you? Huh?" He stepped close to her face and glared into her eyes. "It's cuz you a mothafuckin THOT. That's why. You fuck every nigga you see, and my boy Jerell said you gave him crabs."

Shalonda's jaw dropped at those words.

Chris burst out laughing.

Tyrone was full of excitement. "Aw, shit! Aw, shit!" he kept repeating.

SLAP! Shalonda smacked Rondell across the face.

Mike quickly intervened before Rondell could strangle her. "That's enough! That's enough!" he said, pulling her toward the stairwell. "He don't want you. Leave him alone. Don't come back over here."

"Whatever," she said, still with an attitude. "I don't want his wack ass no way." She wrenched herself from Mike's grasp and thundered down the stairs, tripping on her five-inch heels.

Mike walked over to Rondell. "Dee," he began, but Rondell held his hand up.

"I don't even want to talk right now, man."

He felt . . . he didn't even know how he felt. He was angry that Shalonda had just slapped him. He was disappointed that he had almost slept with her. But most of all, he was full of remorse because he swore. And that confused him.

He didn't understand why something that he used to do without even thinking about it caused him so much grief now. What was wrong with him? Was he really turning into a lame?

He shook his head. "I don't even understand this whole situation, man."

"Understand what?" said Mike, looking concerned. "What's going on, man?"

"It's like . . . I'm trying to change my life around, but everything just keeps getting worse." Rondell shrugged his shoulders. "I don't get it."

Chris sucked his teeth. "What you trying to change for anyway?" he sneered. "There was nothing wrong with you before."

Rondell stared at Chris.

"I'll tell you what you *need* to do," Chris continued. "What you *need* to do is get rid of that Jesus freak. She's the one who got you all messed up in the head, bringing you to church to get brainwashed with that outdated Bible. Just live your life, man. Do what you want to do. You ain't hurting nobody. You a grown ass man. You don't need no pimping ass preacher trying to get your money and control your life, cuz that's all that church shit is about."

"Chris, man, why you always so hostile about Dee going to church?" said Mike.

"Because it's a waste of time!" Chris exclaimed, exasperated. "Why can't nobody see that?"

"It's not a waste of time," said Mike. "People's lives get changed by turning to God."

"Bullshit! People's lives don't change from going to church! Some of them is worse than the ones you see out here in the streets. It's all an illusion, man. Open your eyes. Ain't nobody got time for that shit."

"Just because some people ain't really 'bout that life don't mean everybody does the same thing," said Mike.

"How the fuck would you know?" said Chris. "Wait, don't tell me that Jesus freak done got to you too!"

"This ain't got nothing to do with me," said Mike.

"Word to moms," Tyrone chimed in. "My grandmother go to church faithfully, and she is the realest person I know."

"Man, whatever." Chris looked as if he wanted to spit on the floor. "That don't mean nothing. Rondell's a man. Let him speak for himself. He ain't saying nothing because he knows I'm telling the truth." He turned back to Rondell. "Ain't that right, Rondell?"

Rondell stared at him then shook his head. "I'm not having this conversation right now."

"Why not?" said Chris.

"Because I don't want to get into all that."

"Why not, though?"

"Because I said so. Fall back."

Chris stared at Rondell a moment longer then sucked his teeth. "Whatever, man. Just don't try to talk that church shit around me."

***

Faleesha could not wait to see Rondell. She had thought about him all throughout the break, especially how he had kissed her on the cheek. She replayed it over and over again in her mind, but she pushed away the thought because she knew she could not be with him.

They had talked on the phone a few times over break, and they always had such good conversations. She sighed. "I wish he was saved," she said to herself. "Lord, please save Rondell so I can have him." She laughed at her words, and then she felt a little guilty. "I'm sorry, Lord. That was selfish."

Suddenly, she heard a knock on her door. She crossed the room and opened it. It was Shelly and Rashonda. "What's up?" said Faleesha.

"Let's go to the cafeteria. We's hungry!" said Rashonda.

Faleesha laughed. "Girl, you crazy." She grabbed her coat.

They went down the stairs and exited the building. As soon as they got outside, Faleesha spotted Shalonda and her friends.

"Oh, God," she said. She usually tried to avoid Shalonda at all costs. Whenever she saw her, there was always some drama.

"What's wrong?" said Rashonda.

"Nothing," Faleesha muttered, but her hunch was right. As they passed by Shalonda and her friends, they heard Shalonda mention Faleesha's name in her conversation.

"I don't even know what he sees in her," she said, her arms crossed over her chest. "All she do is go to church and read the Bible. I mean, come on, that's wack. What are they even going to do together? Pray?" She sucked her teeth. "Ain't nobody got time for that." Shalonda and her friends laughed.

Faleesha's face grew hot. Rashonda turned and looked at her expectantly.

"What?" said Faleesha.

"Ain't you going to say something to her?" she said, gesturing toward Shalonda.

"No."

"That's right," said Shalonda, overhearing them, daring Faleesha to respond.

Rashonda shot her a look and said, "Nobody was talking to you, Shalonda."

Shalonda looked at her. "This is between me and Faleesha. Me and you is cool."

"What do you have against her?" said Rashonda. "She ain't never did nothing to you."

"She always all up in my man's face."

"Rondell is not your man," said Faleesha.

Shalonda's head snapped back. She stepped closer to Faleesha. "Who you think you talking to like that?"

"She talking to *you*," said Rashonda. Shalonda looked at Rashonda and stepped back a little bit.

"Look, I said me and you was cool, but if you want to take it there, you can get it too."

"Get what?" said Rashonda, stepping in Shalonda's face.

"Rashonda . . . ." Faleesha tried to step between them.

"Bitch, don't touch me!" yelled Shalonda, and she mushed the side of Faleesha's head. Rashonda swung at Shalonda in response. Shalonda looked dumbfounded as she stumbled back holding her jaw.

"Really, Rashonda?" she said, clearly shocked. "That's how you really feel?" She kicked off her shoes and wrapped up her weave. "Let's scrap then, hoe."

"Londa," said one of her friends. "Chill."

"No, she wanna act all tough, let's get it!" she said, squaring off.

Rashonda stared her down. "You don't want it with me, girl. I was born and raised in Philly. Ask about me."

"Yeah, well I'm from Brooklyn, bitch. We out here, too."

"Let's just squash this," said Shelly. "It's not worth it."

"She shoulda thought about that before she put her hands on me," said Shalonda. "If this bitch too scared to fight," she said, gesturing toward Faleesha, "then this one will." She jabbed a finger in Rashonda's face.

"What did you just call me?" said Rashonda.

"You heard me," said Shalonda. "I said you a bitch—"

Rashonda's fist connected with Shalonda's jaw before she could finish her sentence, and everything was a blur of arms flailing, fists punching, and weaves flying. Shelly, Faleesha, and Shalonda's two friends all had to pile in to separate them.

"THIS AIN'T OVER, BITCH!" screamed Shalonda as her friends pulled her away, her nose bloody and her lip busted.

"I can see that I still have to teach you how to watch your mouth!" said Rashonda as Faleesha and Shelly held her back.

"I see 'Jesus' still ain't got nothing to say though, right?" said Shalonda, spitting in Faleeesha's direction.

Faleesha just shook her head in disappointment.

"Yeah, that's right! She don't want it!" Shalonda said, and she stumbled into the building with her friends holding on to her, helping her walk.

"You alright?" Faleesha said to Rashonda.

"Yeah, girl, my face is clean and clear. Shalonda took all the punishment. But what I'm wondering is, what's wrong with you?"

"What do you mean?"

"Why you keep letting Shalonda punk you?"

"She's not punking me."

"Yes, she is!" said Rashonda. "She be talking mad crazy, and she put her hands on you. Are you scared of her or something?"

"No, I'm not."

"Then why do you let her treat you like that?"

"FALEESHA!" a male voice shouted. They turned and saw three dark figures running toward them. It was Rondell, Mike, and Tyrone.

"Hey," said Faleesha.

"You a'ight?" said Rondell, looking concerned.

"Yeah, why?"

"I heard you and Shalonda was fighting."

"Who won?" said Tyrone. "I got my money on Faleesha!"

"Shut up, Ty," said Rondell. "You a'ight?" he asked her again.

"Yeah, I'm okay," she said. "I didn't fight her. Rashonda did."

"Oh," he said. "Well, what happened?"

"She got up in my face running her mouth, so I closed it," said Rashonda.

"Word?" said Tyrone excitedly. "That's what I'm talking about!"

"Shut up, Ty," said Rondell.

"Why you always telling me to shut up?"

"So anyways," said Rashonda, "can we take this conversation to the cafeteria? I was hungry before, but I'm really hungry now. I worked up an appetite!"

***

Faleesha, Rashonda, Shelly, and the boys entered the cafeteria. When they walked in, they spotted Maria sitting with Jacob, Ryan, and Jamal. They looked like they were having a deep conversation.

"Let's go sit with them," said Rashonda. They all got their food and made their way over to the table with Maria and the boys.

"What's up, Church Boys?" said Rondell as he, Tyrone, and Mike sat down.

"Nothing, just talking with Maria here," said Jacob. They all exchanged dap.

"What y'all talking about?" said Rashonda.

"I just had some questions about church," said Maria.

"Oh, for real? You in the church now, Ma?" said Tyrone. She smiled.

"Yeah," she said. "I just got saved a couple of weeks before Thanksgiving break, and now I'm joining the church."

Tyrone nodded. "That's what's up. So y'all be having Bible study and stuff?"

"Yeah, it's really cool!" she said. "The pastor really breaks it down."

"Oh, well, that's cool," he said. "Congratulations."

Jacob said, "You know, Tyrone, you're welcome to come out to church some time too if you'd like."

Tyrone almost choked on his sandwich. "Oh, um, I—"

"It's okay, man." Jacob held his hand up. "Everybody has their own time. I'm just saying that whenever you're ready, you can definitely come on over to our church."

"Thanks, man. I appreciate that."

"No problem," said Jacob. Then he turned to Rondell. "What about you, man?"

"Huh?" said Rondell.

"You want to come to church some time?"

"Dang!" said Tyrone. "Jacob going in!" Everybody laughed. "You trying to be a pastor or something, man?"

"No, man, not at all. I just wanted to invite you guys out to church. We chill together sometimes, and we play basketball, so it's only right to invite you to church. Know what I mean?"

"Yeah, I feel you, man," said Tyrone. "I respect that. I think I'll get into church and all that when I'm older."

"Why wait?" said Jacob.

"I don't know, man. I'm young. I feel like there's more to do in life before I settle down into church and all that. I'm just trying to make money right now."

"I understand," said Jacob. "What about you, Rondell?" he asked again.

"Well, me and Rondell was supposed to go to church before break," Mike interjected. "But a few things came up."

"Oh really?" said Jacob. "Why don't you guys come this Sunday?"

"Yeah, I'll go," said Mike. "You coming, Dee?"

Everyone looked at Rondell. He felt uncomfortable with all their eyes on him.

"Yeah. I guess so."

"That's great, man!" said Jacob. "I'm glad you fellas are coming out to join us."

"Is there like a dress code or something?" said Mike. He looked eager at the prospect of going to church.

"No, not at all. Just come as you are."

***

Rondell, Mike, Tyrone, Shelly, Rashonda, and Faleesha exited the cafeteria together.

"So, fellas," said Shelly, "do you guys want to come chill with us in my room?"

"That's cool with me," Rondell said, looking at Faleesha as he spoke. He licked his lips.

Faleesha blushed.

"Yo, Dee," said Tyrone, looking at his cell phone.

"What?"

"Could you bring me to the pharmacy right quick? I need to pick up a prescription."

"You sick?" said Rashonda.

"Nah, it's for my cousin."

"Oh. Which one?"

"Shonda!" said Shelly, in a mock scolding tone.

"What?" she said.

"You are *so* nosy."

"Aw, hush," said Rashonda. Then she turned back to Tyrone. "So are you guys going to come chill when you get back?"

"Sure," said Tyrone. "Ain't like we doing nothing else."

"Okay, cool."

Rashonda and the girls parted ways. Rondell, Tyrone, and Mike hopped in the car.

"Yo, Dee, what time Chris get off work?" said Tyrone.

Rondell shrugged his shoulders. "I don't know, man. I think he said midnight." He sounded irritated.

"What's wrong with you?" said Tyrone.

"Nothing. Which pharmacy you trying to go to?"

"The one up on Center Street."

"A'ight." Rondell turned his key in the ignition, and Jay Z blared from the speakers. Tyrone turned down the volume.

"Why you always got your music so loud, man?"

"Cuz that's how I like it," Rondell said sarcastically. "Is that a problem?"

"Naw, man, I'm just saying, you messing up your ears."

"Whatever, Grandpa."

"Yo, Dee, what's wrong with you, man? Why you acting all agitated?"

"Maybe I don't want to hear nothing from you about it. Maybe I want to drown everything out sometimes. Is something wrong with that?"

"I mean, that's cool and everything, but don't take it out on me."

Rondell turned up his music. He glanced at Tyrone a few moments later then shook his head. He didn't know why he spoke so harshly to him. Tyrone didn't done anything wrong.

They pulled into the parking lot of the pharmacy. It was empty except for one car in the back of the parking lot near a streetlight. The trunk of the car was open, and the driver's back was to them. He was talking on a cell phone. He turned so that his face was in profile, and the gold chain draped against his chest glistened in the light.

"Yo, Dee, is that Church Boy?" said Tyrone.

Rondell squinted. "Yeah, I think that is him." He drove over and parked next to him. "What's up, man?" he said, getting out of his Escalade.

Tyrone and Mike hopped out as well.

Gesston gave each of them dap. "I just need a jump. The insurance company said they're going to send somebody out, but it's going to take an hour."

"Oh, I got cables in the whip," said Rondell.

"Thanks, man." Gesston looked dejected.

"You a'ight, Church Boy?" said Tyrone.

Gesston sucked his teeth. "Yeah man. I'm good." He didn't sound convincing.

"A'ight. Well, I'm 'bout to go in the store." Tyrone pointed behind him. "I'll be back."

Rondell jumped Gesston's car, and it started right away. "Good as new," he said with a smirk.

Gesston sucked his teeth again. "Whatever, man."

Rondell unhooked the cables and put them back in his trunk as Gesston walked over to the driver's side door.

"Yo, Gesston, what's up with you, man?"

"Whatchu mean, what's up with me?"

"Why you acting all uppity?"

"I ain't acting like nothing."

"I noticed you ain't hanging with Jacob and them no more."

"Yeah, so?"

"And I also heard you got into some beef with Drake and them."

"Yeah, so?" he repeated. "What, you keeping tabs on me now?"

"No, what I'm saying is, you don't want it with Drake and them, man. Them dudes is straight punks. They're out of your league. They got guns, and they'll use them, cuz none of them can fight for shit."

"I don't give a fuck," said Gesston. "I could get guns too."

"Gesston, I'm not trying to get in your business, but you really need to stop messing with these dudes."

"Man, fuck them niggas."

"This is not a game. You not in some churched-out fantasyland. These is real niggas with real guns. Stay in your lane."

"Man, fuck you!" said Gesston.

"Nigga, what you just say?" said Rondell. He stepped to Gesston.

"You heard me. You trying to make me out to be some type of punk. I ain't scared of nobody."

"Look," said Rondell. "Ain't nobody call you nothing. What I'm saying is if you a church boy, then be a church boy. Don't mess with these street niggas."

"Whatever, nigga." Gesston got in his car and backed it out. He rolled down the window. "Thanks for the jump," he said, and he screeched out of the parking lot.

Rondell shook his head. "Whatever, man." He got back in his truck.

Mike got in the passenger seat. "You can't be three people at once," Rondell said.

"Whatchu talking about?" Mike felt like he'd missed something while he was in the store.

Rondell turned to Mike. "I'm talking about Gesston—don't that nigga work as an intern in the mayor's office? How you gonna be a gangster, a church boy, and a politician?"

"Why are you so worried about him?" said Mike.

"Cuz that nigga is mad fake! He ain't tough, but he always trying to act all hard."

"That's not your problem, Dee, so why do you care what that fool does? What's really wrong with you?"

"And why you tell Jacob we was going to church?" Rondell said irritably.

"I thought you wanted to go."

"Well, I don't."

"Well, you don't gotta go if you don't want to."

Just then, Rondell's back passenger door opened, and Tyrone hopped in.

"Why you take my seat, man?" he said to Mike. Then he looked out the window. "Gesston left already?"

"Obviously," Rondell said sarcastically.

Tyrone looked at Mike. "This dude *still* got an attitude?" He turned to Rondell. "What? You feeling bloated or something, homie? You want me to go back in there and get you some tampons or some Midol or something?"

Rondell looked at Mike and Tyrone, and all three of them burst out laughing.

"Shut up, Ty!" said Rondell, and he pulled out of the parking lot.

When they got back to the dorm after dropping off the prescription at his cousin's house, Tyrone said, "Y'all still want to go chill with Shelly and them?"

"Yeah, that's cool with me," said Mike. They both looked at Rondell.

"What about you, Dee?" said Mike.

Rondell tried to suppress a smile. "Yeah, that's cool."

Tyrone burst out laughing. "AH!" he said. "Church Girl got your boy whipped!"

Rondell pushed his shoulder. "Shut up, Ty," he said with a grin.

"Look at him all smiles now," said Mike. "All we had to do was mention Faleesha."

"Whatever, man."

"You really like her, huh?" said Tyrone.

"I mean, she a'ight." Rondell tried to look cool and collected, but his heart was pounding.

"Yeah, whatever man." Tyrone chuckled. They turned toward the dorm. When they got inside, Tyrone glanced at the stairwell.

"What?" said Mike.

"Twenty dollars says I can dust both of y'all to Shelly's floor."

"Yeah, right!" said Mike.

"You down?" said Tyrone, looking at Rondell.

"Yeah, I'm down."

"A'ight. On the count of three: One . . . two . . . three . . . Go!" He charged toward the stairs with Rondell and Mike close behind. When they got to the last landing, Tyrone tripped and fell up a few stairs. Mike and Rondell burst out laughing. They fought to contain their laughter and catch their breath as they helped Tyrone up.

"You a'ight, man?" said Rondell, still laughing and panting.

"Yeah, I'm good." He leaned on Mike and Rondell as they got up the last few stairs, groaning in pain. When they were in the hallway, he wrenched his arms from their grasp and raced to Shelly's door.

"WOOOO!" he screamed, pumping his fists in the air. "I won! Where my money at?"

"You cheated!" said Mike.

"I know," said Rondell. "How you gonna fake an injury?"

"Y'all just hating. We ain't establish no rules before the race, so all's fair. Where's my money?"

"Whatever, man," said Mike, and he and Rondell both shelled out $20 to Tyrone.

"Thank you, and thank you!" said Tyrone, snatching the money.

Shelly opened her door. "What is all this commotion?"

"We was just racing up the stairs, and Ty cheated," Mike said.

They made their way into Shelly's room. Tyrone plopped down next to Rashonda on the couch.

"Hey, man, a win is a win." He turned to Shelly. "We saw your man up at the pharmacy."

She looked excited. "Oh, really?"

"Yeah, he needed a jump."

"Oh, for real? His car *has* been acting up lately."

Tyrone yawned then Faleesha yawned right after him.

"I'm tired," said Tyrone. "I gotta go to work in the morning."

"I'm tired too," said Faleesha, rubbing her eyes. "I think I'll go to my room."

"Want me to walk you?" said Rondell.

"How y'all just going to leave?" said Rashonda. "Everybody just got here."

"Well, *we* been here for a while," said Faleesha.

"I'm-a see y'all later," said Tyrone, hopping up.

"Me too!" said Mike.

"Y'all is wack!" said Rashonda.

"Don't you gotta go home to your daughter anyway?" said Mike.

Rashonda checked her cell phone. "That's right! I gotta pick her up in half an hour. Then I have to return this car to my cousin Craig. Thanks for reminding me!" She jumped up and grabbed her purse. "Bye, Shelly! Bye, everybody!" She put on her coat and dashed out the door.

"Well, I'm 'bout to leave too," said Faleesha.

"Okay," said Shelly. "I gotta call Gesston anyway and see if everything's okay."

"Alright then," said Faleesha. She, Rondell, Tyrone, and Mike all exited Shelly's room together.

"Yo, Ty, I want a rematch for my money back," said Mike. "Race you to our room."

"A'ight, I gotchu," said Tyrone. Both of them took off running down the hall. They banged open the door to the stairway and thundered down the stairs.

Faleesha just shook her head. "Your friends are crazy."

Rondell smiled. "Yes, they are," he said. He smiled. They made their way to the elevator.

"So, are you ready for church on Sunday?"

His smile faded slightly. "Yeah, I guess so." He pressed the call button, and the doors opened. "Express service," he said, and grinned as if he never had to wait for an elevator.

"Yeah, that was pretty quick," she said. When they got to her floor, they made their way down the hall to her room. "Well, here's my stop!" she said. She turned to put her key in the lock.

"Wait," said Rondell. She looked at him. He was staring at her intently.

"What?" she said.

"Can I get a hug?"

She blushed. "Okay." He put his arms around her and pulled her close. She put her arms around his neck.

"Mmm," he murmured. "You fit so perfectly." She pulled back slightly, a nervous expression on her face.

"What's wrong?" he said, staring into her eyes.

"Nothing," she said, smiling.

He licked his lips.

She blushed again. "Well, I'll see you later." She pulled away from his embrace.

His hand caught her hand, and he intertwined his fingers with hers. She looked up at him. He smiled, and then he leaned in and kissed her on the cheek. She felt the fire rush from her face to the rest of her body.

"Good night," he said, his face still close to hers.

"Good night," she whispered.

Chapter 13

Rondell was on his way back from the mall when he spotted someone who looked familiar walking down the street. He pulled over and beeped his horn. The person flinched at the sound and whipped his head around. Rondell rolled down his window.

"Yo, Quincy!"

Quincy jogged toward him with a smile. He reached his hand through Rondell's car window to give him dap.

"Wassup, baby?" said Quincy.

"Where you headed to?"

"My girl's crib." Quincy pointed behind him. "She live right around the corner."

"You want me to drop you?"

Quincy hopped in the car in response. "Thanks, man." He rubbed his hands together and blew on them to warm them. "Yo, it's mad cold out there, brotha."

"I think I got an extra pair of gloves in the back." Rondell reached into his back seat and gave Quincy his hat and gloves. Quincy looked at him in surprise.

"Thanks, man!"

"So, whatchu been up to?" said Rondell. "You still in school?"

"Nah, man, I dropped out when I turned sixteen."

"Did you get your GED?"

Quincy shook his head no. "I signed up for this program, but the director tried to slay me, so I dropped out of that too."

"So what you doing to support yourself?" said Rondell.

"I got kicked out of my foster home, so I just stay with my girl at her mom's crib. She pregnant—my girl, that is."

Rondell's eyes lit up with surprise. "Word? That's a lot, man. Congratulations on the baby."

"Yeah, I know. Thanks." He chuckled. Rondell glanced at his friend's eyes. Quincy was only eighteen, but he looked so tired.

"It's real out here in these streets, man," said Rondell, turning his eyes back to the road.

Quincy nodded. "Yeah, I know. I be out here."

"Quincy . . . ." Rondell began, a stern tone in his voice, but Quincy cut him off.

"I know, man, but I gotta provide for my family. I didn't have the luxury of my parents coming to get me like you and Mike had. I gotta do what I gotta do."

"But you ain't got no record, nigga!" said Rondell. "You could get a job!"

"Easy for you to say!" Quincy shot back. "I ain't some rich college boy like you. You blessed, man. Look at this shit. You got a car, you got clothes, you in college, you got everything. I ain't got nothing."

"And what about your baby on the way?" said Rondell. "You gotta think about the future."

"Man, you sound like Terry. He was all about the future, and look where that got him."

Rondell pulled over. "Get out my car, man."

"What?"

"You disrespecting Terry's name. Get out my car."

"My bad, man." Quincy held his hands up. "I ain't mean it like that. I'm just saying, everybody don't got it as easy as you."

"Oh, so you think my life has been easy?" said Rondell. "I been jumped, shot at, stabbed, moved from house to house, school to school, abused, neglected, and forgotten. Plus, you forget I was right there when Terry died. He died right in front of me. I sold drugs just like you did. I was out in these streets just like you was."

They pulled in front of Quincy's girlfriend's house.

"I understand all that," said Quincy. "But you had a happy ending. I didn't."

"Can you sign up for that program to get your GED?"

"Yeah, I guess."

"Then do it."

"Man, I don't be understanding all that stuff . . . ."

"Stop making excuses, and get your life, man!" said Rondell. "If you need help, I'll tutor you. You got my number."

Quincy nodded but said nothing, and got out of the car. He was halfway to the front door of the house when he turned back. "Hey, is you a preacher or something, Dee?"

Rondell looked taken aback. "No. Why?"

"Cuz you got me feeling all inspired and shit."

Rondell burst out laughing. "Shut up, man."

Quincy chuckled. "A'ight, man, I'll see you." He waved.

"I'll see you," said Rondell, and he drove off.

***

Rondell and Mike walked up to the front doors of the church. Rondell reached out to open the door then paused nervously. Mike looked at him.

"You a'ight, man?" he asked. Rondell licked his lips and nodded.

"Yeah, man, I'm good." As soon as he opened the door, two older women smiled and gave them a warm welcome. Rondell instantly felt at ease.

"Well, don't you two young men look nice?" said one of them. She reached out and hugged Rondell, then Mike.

"Um . . . thanks," said Rondell, awkwardly.

"Well, don't be shy. Come on in!" She gestured for them to walk toward the doors to the inner sanctuary. "I'm Sister Shirley, and this is Sister Joann."

"Hi," said Rondell and Mike in unison. Sister Shirley held the doors open so that Rondell and Mike could walk through.

"Now, honey, this is Brother Roger," Sister Shirley said, gesturing toward an older man wearing a black suit. "He is one of our ushers, and he will seat you. If you need anything, tell him to come and find me, okay?"

"Okay." They turned to Brother Roger as the two women walked away.

"Good morning, fellas!" said Brother Roger.

"Good morning," said Mike. He smiled.

"What's up?" said Rondell.

"Now, where do you guys usually like to sit?" Brother Roger asked.

Rondell quickly spoke up. "Well, this is our first time coming, so we would like to sit in the back." Mike shot him a glance, but he ignored it.

"Okay," said Brother Roger. He led them to the second to last row of pews, empty except for a family of four sitting at the other end.

"This good?" he asked.

"Huh?" said Rondell, taking in the scenery.

"This row good?" he repeated.

"Oh, yeah. Thanks."

Mike slid into the pew first, and Rondell sat next to him in the aisle seat.

"Well, if you need anything, I'll be walking around," said Brother Roger.

"Okay, thanks," said Rondell. He and Mike looked around the church. Everything was neat and clean. The stained glass windows had pictures of angels etched into them. The pews filled quickly as people filed in and took their favorite seats.

"Hey, Dee, there go Faleesha and them toward the front. Let's go sit with them," said Mike. He started to get up, but Rondell stopped him.

"Nah, we good."

"Why not?" said Mike.

"We good back here."

Mike sighed. "Whatever, man."

Rondell looked around the church and felt like everyone knew he didn't belong there, and it made him nervous. He had never stepped foot inside a church in his life. He tried to remain calm, but the tension became too much for him. He stood up.

"I gotta go," he said to Mike.

Mike stared at him with concern. "Wassup, man? What's good with you?"

"I don't belong here, man." Rondell shifted from one foot to the other as he glanced around. His nervousness was apparent.

Just then, Sister Shirley appeared at his side.

"You alright, honey?"

"I'm sorry, but I don't feel like I should be here," Rondell said. He felt a lump forming in his throat. He tried to swallow it.

Sister Shirley gave him a nurturing look. "This is your first time coming to church, huh?"

He nodded. She put her arm around his shoulder and held him gently. She was so warm and inviting, like a mother. A tear almost escaped, but Rondell blinked it back.

"It's going to be alright," Shirley said, rubbing his back reassuringly. "How about you give it a try, just this one time, and we'll see where it goes from there?"

She looked up at him. All of a sudden, he felt peace. He exhaled and nodded.

"Praise God," she said with a warm smile. "Well, I'll be walking around. Just let me know if you need anything."

"Okay," he said, and he sat down again. Sister Shirley smiled again and gave Mike a little wave before she walked away.

"Whew!" said Mike. "I thought you was fitnin' ta bounce on me!"

When music began to play softly, people stopped their conversations and straightened in their seats. A man walked up to the mic in the center front of the platform.

"Bless the Lord, everybody," he said.

"Bless the Lord," said some of the people in the congregation.

"Well, as most of us know, today is Testimony Sunday where we have sort of an open mic portion of the service so that people can come and share things that the Lord has done for them. Is that alright?"

Some people clapped in response.

"I said is that alright?" he repeated with emphasis.

"YES!" a few people shouted, and more people clapped.

"Alright, alright," he replied with a warm smile. "Now that's more like it! But before we get into the testimony service, we will have an opening prayer led by Sister Brown, then after that, we will have praise and worship. We ask that everyone please stand to receive Sister Brown. Thank you."

People clapped lightly as he walked away from the mic, and Sister Brown approached it. "Good morning, everyone!" she said, her voice sweet and clear.

"Good morning!" some people responded.

"We will now begin our opening prayer. Please bow your head."

Rondell looked around as everyone bowed their head. He and Mike did the same.

"Father God, in the name of Jesus . . ." she began to pray, and as the prayer continued, Rondell felt himself becoming more and more relaxed.

When she was finished, everyone said amen and sat back down.

After the prayer was over, the choir sang a variety of praise songs, some fast and joyful, others slow and introspective, inviting an attitude of worship. At first, Rondell tried to look disinterested, but after a while, he found himself nodding his head and tapping his feet to the music. Every time he looked at Mike, he seemed to be all in it, standing up, trying to sing along, clapping his hands, and stomping his feet. Rondell was so fascinated to see his friend carrying on like this that he couldn't help but chuckle, but at other times, he found himself wanting to get up and clap too.

When the singing was over, the testimonial portion of the service began. At first, it seemed like no one was going to approach the mic, but then a young kid, maybe about nine or ten years old, got up and thanked God for helping him with school. After that, more people approached the mic. Some sang songs, some recited poems, and some just talked. One guy even rapped! Rondell found himself relating to some of the stories people told of their struggles and how God brought them through, and at some points, he even found himself getting choked up, but he fought back his emotions.

When the testimony portion was over, they took an offering and passed the collection plate. From what he had heard about church from Chris, Rondell expected this part of the service to bring out the true colors of the pastor, meaning, he expected the man to be all about the money, but he actually seemed pretty cool about it. Pastor Bryant stressed the importance of giving to the church, but he also said that he wasn't expecting people to give too much if they didn't have it. He said just to give what was on your heart to give.

Rondell and Mike weren't sure how much to give, so they each dropped a $20 bill in the plate and kept it moving. When the offering was over, it was finally time for Pastor Bryant to speak. He cleared his throat.

"Good afternoon, everyone."

"Hey, Pastor!" someone from the audience said.

"It's a blessing to see you all today. I thank God for all that He has done in the service thus far. We thank God for every song, every prayer, every praise, and every worship. And we certainly thank God for every testimony. Speaking of testimonies, I feel pressed in my spirit today to share a portion of my own testimony. As some of you may know, my story may be a little different, but God gets the glory anyhow. Can I get an amen?"

"Amen, Pastor!" a few people shouted.

"Amen." He smiled. "So, to start off, I did not grow up in the church. I was raised in the foster care system, so I was moved from home to home and school to school, and I never really had the opportunity to be part of a church family."

Rondell's jaw dropped in shock. He and Mike looked at each other. From just looking at the pastor, they expected his life to be completely different from what he just said. Rondell's ears pricked up, and he sat up in his seat and became totally engrossed in the pastor's story.

"So anyway," he continued, "because I was shifted from environment to environment, I never really had a stable foundation. I never really had anything to hold on to, as most other children do. I was angry, and I lashed out at everyone. I didn't care about school. I didn't care about anything. The only thing I cared about was my set of homeboys. We found a way to stick together despite our constant movement. Many times, we said, 'We all we got.' We said this because for us it was true. None of us really had a strong family background. So, as you can imagine, since we didn't really have anyone to teach us, we taught ourselves. We got involved in criminal activity, and most of us were in some type of juvenile facility by the age of thirteen."

He chuckled. "And for the ones that didn't end up in juvy, it was only because they didn't get caught." He paused and straightened his tie.

"We robbed people. We shot at people. We sold drugs— you name it. Everything we were big enough and bad enough to do, we did it. It was all fun and games at first, but then, after a few years, things started getting real. So, first, one of my homeboys caught a body.

"For those of you who are not up on street vernacular, that means he killed someone. He was sentenced to life in prison. He is still there to this day. Then, after that, some of us started to turn on each other. Before you know it, one homeboy turned on another homeboy and snitched or told on him for something he did, and then he was in jail. So things got tense, and it just wasn't the same anymore. But we kept on getting deeper and deeper into the street life.

"It wasn't until I lost two of my closest friends in the same night that my life began to change. I was so devastated and disoriented from losing them that I got caught running through a red light and was pulled over by the cops. They found a large portion of drugs in my car. I was sentenced to fifteen years in prison."

Some people in the congregation gasped.

"Fifteen years, y'all," he repeated. "So, during my early years in prison, I continued much of the same behavior. I picked fights, I didn't follow the rules, and I walked around with a chip on my shoulder because of my anger. To make a long story short, there was this guy there, this 'jailhouse preacher' as everyone called him, who was always trying to tell everybody about Jesus. He pestered everybody about reading the Bible and praying, and most people really weren't trying to hear what he had to say. So one day, I decided to check him out and see what this whole God thing was all about. I went and had a conversation with him, and while we were talking, he shared some things with me, and I shared some things with him, and not long after that, God began to manifest Himself in my life. The two of us founded the Jail to Jesus program, and now, even though both of us are out of prison, we go back on a weekly basis to minister to the prisoners."

Everyone stood up clapping and praising God in a jubilant response. Rondell and Mike got up and clapped too.

"Praise the Lord," the pastor said as everyone sat back down. "So anyway, let's get to the message for today. The topic I would like to share with you is titled Getting Past Your Past. Now, this topic is near and dear to me, because all of us have a past. Some people's histories are long and extensive, while others are much shorter. But we all have a past. I already shared with you some of the things that happened in my past. Because of those things, as I said, I was very angry. Even after I came to Christ, I struggled with anger for a while because of my past. But God is a healer. If we want to move forward with Him, we have to be willing to get past our past."

"PREACH, Pastor!" someone shouted.

"Amen," he continued. "For a scripture reference, I would first like to turn to the book of John, chapter 5." He described the story of the man who had been in the same condition for thirty-eight years, and Jesus came to heal him, but all the man had was excuses. He blamed other people for the fact that he had been in his predicament for so long. But Jesus cut to the chase and healed him.

Then the pastor went to the book of Romans and explained that when we come to Christ, He transforms us day by day through the Word of God.

Rondell expected to be bored with all the preaching, but instead, he found himself relating to what the pastor said. The pastor raised many points that so closely resembled his life that it scared him.

Then it was time for the altar call. The pastor first explained what it meant to be saved, and then he invited anyone who wanted salvation to walk to the front of the church.

Rondell looked at Mike, who gestured eagerly for Rondell to go with him down to the front, but Rondell shook his head no, the fear evident in his eyes. Finally, Mike sank back in his seat, clearly disappointed. Rondell turned away from him, pretending to be annoyed. He felt horrible that he had blocked Mike from going forward, but he just couldn't go up there.

After the service, Mike was silent the whole way back to school. This drove Rondell deeper into guilt. He hoped that he hadn't ruined Mike's chances with God.

***

Rondell felt horrible. Mike barely spoke to him all day Sunday after church. Today was Monday, and he still seemed upset. They made their way to the cafeteria for lunch. They got their food then looked for open tables.

They saw a couple of seats at a table with Jacob, Ryan, Jamal, Faleesha, Rashonda, and Maria. Rondell wanted to make an excuse not to sit with them, but before he could open his mouth, Mike was already making his way over there. Rondell gave in and followed, hoping they wouldn't ask about the service.

"Hey, fellas!" said Jacob as they sat down.

"What's up?" said Mike, giving the guys dap as he sat down.

"Hey," said Rondell, also giving dap before sitting down.

"It was good to see you at service yesterday," said Jacob. The girls' heads all shot in their direction at once.

"Y'all came?" said Faleesha.

Rondell nodded.

"Oh, I didn't even see you guys."

"Yeah . . . we sat in the back," said Rondell, a guilty look on his face.

"Oh," Faleesha said. Her shoulders slumped. She was disappointed she hadn't been able to talk to them at church.

Rondell glanced at Mike.

"So what did you think?" said Jacob.

"I enjoyed it," said Mike.

"What about you, Rondell?" said Jacob.

"Oh, it was a'ight," he said nonchalantly.

"Good, good," said Jacob. "So, did either of you have any questions about anything?"

"No!" said Rondell quickly, hoping to change the subject.

"Well, I had some questions," said Mike, looking at Rondell as he spoke.

"What about?" said Jacob.

"When the pastor had the altar call . . . ." Mike shifted in his seat. He was unsure how to say this.

Rondell felt himself getting hot.

Mike continued. "When he gave the altar call, he mentioned something called the Holy Grail—or something like that."

"Huh?" said Jacob, and then he realized what Mike meant. "Oh, you mean the Holy Ghost."

"Yeah, that was it," said Mike. "What is that?"

"Well," said Jacob, "to make a long explanation short, the Holy Spirit, or the Holy Ghost, as the pastor called it, is God's Spirit."

"Wait, wait," said Maria. "I don't mean to cut you off, but this Holy Ghost—how does it apply to like, God and Jesus? I know God is the Father, and Jesus is the Son, so what is the Holy Ghost? Why do they need another one? Is that like the cousin or something?" She gave a nervous little laugh at her analogy, and the others joined in, chuckling with her.

"No, no," Jacob said, his eyes kind. "You are right. God is the Father, and Jesus is the Son, but the Holy Ghost is the third person on the team. They all work together, and they are all God, and they are all one, but they each have separate levels of authority, even though they all can do the same things. The Father is first in command, the Son is second, and the Holy Ghost is third."

Mike looked confused. "So how can they be one if they are three separate beings?"

"It's a very difficult subject, and I don't think anyone fully understands it, honestly," said Jacob. "I've asked multiple people throughout the years, and I've read and studied the Bible myself and prayed about it, and I believe God showed it to me in a way I can understand it best.

"Think of ice, snow, and frost. All of them are water, meaning they are all H2O, but in different forms. It's the same with the Father, Son, and the Holy Spirit. They are all God, but they each play different roles. The Father assumes the head role, that of the Ultimate Judge. Jesus assumes the secondary role, Savior now and Judge later. The Holy Spirit assumes the tertiary role, because when we get saved, He begins to live inside us and transform us so that we can be what God wants us to be. And He also serves as a sort of inner judge because He tells us right and wrong and helps us to change for the better."

"Oh, okay." Mike nodded, understanding. "That makes sense." He chuckled. "I might need some of that Holy Ghost inside of me. I don't know what I'm doing sometimes."

Jacob laughed as well. "Me too, man. We all do. And the great thing about God is that He freely gives us the Holy Ghost as soon as we get saved."

Mike sat back silently for a moment, but then he leaned toward Jacob. "Hey, Jay."

"Yeah," said Jacob, chewing on his sandwich.

"So . . . I had one more question." Mike straightened his shirt nervously.

"Shoot."

"So when like, when you feel like God is calling you or speaking to you, do you lose your chance if you don't go?"

"What do you mean?"

"Like if there is an altar call, and you feel like God is telling you to go up there, and you don't go, do you lose your chance with God?"

Jacob stared at Mike for a moment. "Well, what I would tell someone is that life is a very delicate thing because it is so short. If you are at a point where you feel like God is calling you, you should most definitely answer that call. That's not to say that He won't call you again, but at the same time, tomorrow is not promised to any of us, whether we're saved or not."

Mike nodded. "True, true." He sat back in his chair deep in thought with a faraway look in his eyes. Jacob knew this was the right time to remain silent to let his words touch Mike's spirit.

***

Faleesha sat on her couch, daydreaming about Rondell. She often found herself thinking about him, and sometimes, she changed her thoughts to a different topic, but most times, she found herself lost in fantasy.

She was so caught up in her thoughts that she barely noticed someone knocking at her door. She shook her shoulders, snapping out of her dream.

"Who is it?" she said through the door.

"The police," said Rondell from the other side.

She blushed as she opened the door. "Boy, you know you need to stop." She smiled as he walked into her room. She closed the door and sat next to him on the couch.

"Why you always got your TV on mute?" said Rondell, grabbing her remote.

"I was just . . . thinking."

He looked at her with a curious expression, his eyebrows raised. "About . . . ?"

She found herself blushing again. She was so attracted to him it wasn't even funny. "Nothing," she said quickly, lowering her head slightly.

Rondell smirked. "You was thinking about me, wasn't you?"

She felt her face heat up. "No," she said, shifting in her seat.

"Mmm-hmm," he said, still smirking.

"So how come you didn't sit with us during service?" she said, changing the subject.

This time, it was Rondell's turn to feel nervous. "Well, we just . . . um . . . ." He fidgeted, and then he let it all out in one big rush. "We just preferred to sit in the back since it was our first time and all."

She stared at him for a moment.

"Okay," she said finally.

"You mad at me?" he said, looking into her eyes.

Her heart fluttered. "No," she said. "It's cool."

Rondell was relieved.

"So . . . ." she began slowly. "What did you think of the sermon?"

He shrugged. "It was cool. I actually kind of related to the pastor's testimony."

"Really?"

He nodded, playing with his collar. "Yeah."

"Oh yeah," she said. "That's right. You did say that you were in foster care, right?"

Rondell's expression changed slightly. "Mmm-hmm." He nodded.

"So . . . what was it like for you?" she said quietly.

"It was . . . um . . . it was basically like what the pastor said."

"Were you moved around a lot?"

"Yeah." He looked away. "Yeah, I been through a lot."

Faleesha was silent for a moment. "So . . . what kinds of things have you been through?"

"Pretty much everything." He stared at her uneasily. "I don't really like talking about it."

"Oh, I understand," she said, nodding.

Rondell opened his mouth to change the subject, but then he felt the urge to tell his story. Before he knew it, the words were flying out of his mouth. He told her everything, about his parents, about Terry, about everything. He had never shared his story with anyone, ever. By the end of it, he felt so relieved, as if a huge weight had been lifted from his shoulders.

"Wow," she said when he was finished. "That was a lot."

"Yeah."

"I'm really glad you're here," she said, resting her hand on his.

Her eyes were so full of warmth and sincerity that it touched his heart, but it also kind of turned him on.

"Faleesha," Rondell said softly.

"Hmm?"

"Can I kiss you?"

Just like that, she was nervous again. She had fantasized about kissing Rondell so many times, but now that the moment was here, she didn't know what to do.

"Um . . . ." she said.

"It's okay if you don't want to," he said.

"Well, um," she said, looking away, then back at him. "I've never done that before."

"Never kissed anybody?" he said, shocked.

She shook her head no.

He inched closer to her. "Well," he said softly. "Don't you want to know what it feels like?"

Her entire body felt like it was on fire. She nodded. He moved in closer to her, and she instinctively closed her eyes.

His lips touched hers softly, and she felt like she was in a dream. He moved closer to her as the kiss deepened. She felt herself leaning backward on the couch, and then, somehow, she ended up on her back with Rondell on top of her, his legs between her legs. Her mind was telling her to stop, but her body wanted to keep going. Rondell's hands ran up and down her legs and thighs. His hand went briefly up her inner thigh, and then he let it travel to one of her breasts. He cupped it gently, and Faleesha's eyes popped open. She stopped the kiss.

Rondell opened his eyes. "What's wrong?"

Faleesha didn't know what to say.

He sensed her discomfort, so he got off her and sat on the end of the sofa while she straightened to a sitting position.

"Sorry," he said. "We must have gotten carried away."

"Yeah," she nodded. They sat there for a few moments.

"Um, I think I should leave," he said.

"Sorry," she said.

"It's cool." He got up and walked to her door. She followed behind him. "Well, I'll see you later," he said after opening the door.

"Okay. See you."

Faleesha closed the door behind him and burst into tears.

Chapter 14

Rondell, Mike, Chris, and Tyrone were at the basketball court, waiting their turn to play four on four. They were paired up against four other guys from their dorm: Jermaine, Rick, Rob, and Tito.

"Ready to get that ass busted?" said Jermaine.

Ty chuckled. "We'll see, young boy."

"Young boy?" said Jermaine. "A'ight, we got you." Jermaine and his crew left to go to the water fountain outside the gym.

"Them some follow-the-leader ass niggas," sneered Chris.

He and his boys shared a laugh.

"Oh yeah!" said Ty, remembering something. "Eyo, Dee. What's this I hear about you and Mike meeting in the pastor's chambers?"

Rondell stared at Tyrone quizzically.

"What are you talking about, Ty?" said Chris.

"Yeah, what are you talking about?" said Rondell.

"I heard y'all went to church on Sunday," said Tyrone.

Chris sucked his teeth.

Rondell felt himself getting hot. "Where you hear that?"

"I overheard Jacob talking about it to one of his friends."

Rondell sucked his teeth. "I'm-a have to talk with that nigga."

"Why? What's good?" said Ty.

"Cuz I don't want him spreading my business out like that."

"Ain't like nobody was going to find out anyway," said Chris.

"Well, I prefer to tell people myself!" Rondell shot back.

"So, what happened?" said Chris. "Did y'all go down to the altar and let 'Passa' pray for you? Did he tell you Jesus was gonna fix it?"

Mike looked irritated at that comment. "No, it wasn't even like that."

"Right," said Chris. "All them churches are the same, especially the Black ones. All they do is sell people dreams while they pimping their pockets."

"Why are you so against the church?" said Mike.

"What are you, a preacher now?" said Chris. "Should I start calling you Reverend Mike?"

"Leave him alone," said Rondell. He still felt guilty about Sunday.

"Or what?" Chris said evenly.

Rondell could feel his blood beginning to boil. "Chris, I'm getting sick of you coming at me."

"I'm not coming at you. I'm trying to save you from being brainwashed." He spat.

"I think I can handle myself. Besides, you don't know nothing about me," said Rondell.

"Nigga, I know enough."

"Is that so?"

"Yeah, I know you been letting this church shit get to your head ever since you met that Jesus freak."

"I told you not to call her that."

"And I told you that I'll call her what I want."

"See, that's what I mean. You keep testing me."

"I ain't testing nobody. If you wanna get it poppin', what's good?" Chris stepped to Rondell.

Rondell looked taken aback, and then he stepped up.

"Word? That's how you feel?"

"Yeah," said Chris. "It's clear to me that you let this chick get you all in your feelings, so now you want to choose some bitch over your boys. So let's get it poppin'."

"Chill," said Mike.

"No, fuck this nigga," said Chris.

"Fuck me?" said Rondell.

"You heard right."

Rondell's fist connected with Chris' jaw faster than he could think. Chris spit blood on the floor. He gripped his jaw and glared at Rondell.

"Nigga, you knocked my fuckin tooth out!" He charged at Rondell, but he was no match for him. Rondell easily slammed him to the floor before Mike and Tyrone broke them up.

"Chill, man! We boys!" said Mike.

"Nah, fuck that shit!" said Rondell. "Jealous ass nogga." He snatched his coat up off the ground. "And why you always starting shit!" he said to Tyrone as he stormed off.

"I'll check y'all later," said Mike, and he followed Rondell out the door.

***

Gesston exited the pawnshop, slipping his new chain over his head. He took a deep breath and sighed. He was getting tired of trying to impress people. He had been under a lot of stress lately because of the situation with Shelly and his new "friendships" with the guys at his dorm.

Shelly kept pressuring him to have sex with her, which he knew in his heart he could never do. And the guys at the dorm kept downing him for being a church boy, as they called it, so he always found himself fighting to earn their respect.

But sometimes he wondered whether it was worth it. Maybe he should just go back to being regular old Gesston, the church boy with no girls and no street credibility. He was furious with Jacob because of how he turned his back on him, but after a while, his anger turned to guilt.

He knew he was headed down a destructive path, and the fact that he had all but abandoned his position as the assistant youth leader at his church didn't help either, but he was so far gone at this point that he didn't know if it was possible for him to return.

Gesston was so lost in his thoughts that he had completely passed his car and wandered into the middle of a side street.

Someone blasted a car horn, swerving to keep from hitting him.

"GET THE FUCK OUT THE STREET, NIGGA!" the driver screamed through the window.

This pissed Gesston off. He pounded the hood of the car angrily with his fist. "Why don't you watch where the FUCK you going?"

The driver jumped out of the car. Immediately, Gesston recognized him as Drake, a guy from the neighborhood that he'd had run-ins with before.

"Whatchu say, nigga?" said Drake, shooting Gesston a fierce look.

"You heard me."

Suddenly, a police siren let out a short shrill note, just enough to get their attention.

Gesston and Drake turned their heads at the sound. They saw a cop parked across the street, staring at them intently.

"A'ight, nigga," said Drake, backing up and returning to his car. "I'll see your bitch ass later."

"Whatever, mufucker," said Gesston.

***

Gesston got into his car and slammed the door shut. The entire encounter with Drake had pissed him off. He was tired of that guy trying to son him.

His cell phone rang. He answered it without looking.

"What?" he barked.

"Is this a bad time?" It was Shelly. She sounded nervous.

"Yes."

"What's wrong, baby?" she said sweetly.

He rolled his eyes. "Nothing you can help me with."

She was silent for a moment. "Well, I'm sorry you're having a bad day." She sounded hurt.

He immediately felt guilty. "Sorry for being rude."

"It's okay," she said softly.

"Why were you calling?"

"Well . . . ." she said, her voice perking up. "It might actually be something that will cheer you up."

He felt uneasy. "What's going on?"

"I found this GREAT discount for us at the Red Hill Hotel," she gushed. "They have a Valentine's Special, and I was able to book us this awesome suite. I checked it out today and paid the fee. It is going to be so romantic and so special for our first time."

"Shelly," he began, but she continued talking.

"I also picked out some sexy lingerie," she said, and in a seductive voice, she added, "for your eyes only."

"Shelly."

"What?"

He was silent for a moment. He was trying to find a nice way to break things off with her, but he couldn't think of anything to say. He was silent for so long that she finally spoke.

"Hello? Are you still there?"

"Yeah, I'm still here," he said, hoping she noticed his sarcasm and got the hint.

"You were going to say something?" she said expectantly, clearly not getting it.

"You ordered the room already?"

"Yes! I wanted to get the one with the most perfect view."

"Okay . . . ."

"What's wrong?"

"Nothing."

"You aren't saying anything."

"I don't know what to say."

"Aren't you excited?"

"Yeah, sure," he lied, not too convincingly, but Shelly was in her own little world.

"Me too!" she said. "I can't wait."

"Yeah, me either."

"Are you sure you're alright?"

"Yeah." He exhaled loudly. "Listen, I gotta go. I had to meet up with someone, and I'm running late." He hoped she couldn't tell he was lying again.

"Oh, okay. I won't hold you."

"Thanks."

"Drive safely."

"Mmm-hmm." He hung up the phone before she could say anything else. He sat there trying to think of how to get out of this situation, but it seemed like the only way out was to come clean.

"SHIT!" he exclaimed, slamming his hands on the steering wheel.

***

"Yo, Dee! DEE!"

Rondell stopped walking and turned around.

"Why you walking so fast, man?" panted Mike as he caught up to him.

"Adrenaline," he said sarcastically.

Mike didn't say anything. They began walking again, heading to the dorm.

A few people greeted them as they passed. Mike responded, but Rondell just ignored them.

They took the elevator up to Rondell's floor. When they got to his room, Rondell slammed the door shut and plopped down in his armchair. He flipped on his TV and turned on his gaming system. He began to play *Call of Duty: Black Ops*, but he couldn't concentrate. Mike just sat on his bed, watching him, not saying a word. After Rondell had failed his third mission, he turned to Mike.

"'Ey, what the fuck are you looking at, man?"

"Nothing. Do you want to talk about it?"

"About *what*, man?" said Rondell, throwing his hands in the air, the game controller sailing to the floor. He swore and kicked it even farther.

"About what happened with you and Chris."

Rondell sucked his teeth. "Man, fuck that nigga. And fuck Ty too. Always starting shit like some got-damn female."

"Chill, bruh," said Mike. "We boys."

"Them niggas ain't my fuckin boys," Rondell spat. "Chris ass been hating since day one, and Ty ass always starting shit."

"He was just joking around."

"Fuck that shit. Don't defend that nigga. He knew what he was doing from jump."

"True, but that's—"

"Nigga, I don't give a fuck what you got to say about it. Fuck them niggas and fuck you too if you want to take their side."

"Yo Dee, what are you really mad at, brutha?" said Mike, feeling his own anger rising.

"Fake, grimy ass niggas, that's what. I should have never done this college shit. Nothing but a bunch of pussy ass niggas that might as well be bitches."

"You talking crazy now," said Mike, standing up.

"No, I'm talking real." Rondell stood up too. "I'm from the fuckin gutter. I can't relate to these lame ass niggas."

Mike crossed his arms. "So what you gonna do then, man? You gonna quit school? Throw your life away?"

"Man, fuck this life." Rondell picked up his game controller and sat back down. "I told Terry's ass I wasn't built for this shit. I should have never listened to y'all. I should have dropped the fuck out like I planned."

"Dee, man, calm down." Mike sat next to Rondell on the sofa and put his hand on his shoulder.

Rondell swatted his hand away. "Don't fuckin touch me."

Mike stood up again. "So what, you want to fight me now?"

"Get the fuck out of my room."

"Why?"

"I said get the fuck out!"

Mike could see that Rondell's anger was building more and more by the second. "A'ight, I'll check you later." He walked to Rondell's door and opened it. He stepped out then poked his head back in. "Or, you could check me when you calm down."

Rondell didn't answer. He just stared at the screen, focued on his game. Mike closed the door and walked away.

***

Faleesha could not stop thinking about what had happened between her and Rondell. One side of her felt extremely guilty. She had prayed and cried about it several times, but she could not shake the guilt. The other side of her wanted it to happen again—and wanted to do more.

She went to the cafeteria for lunch and sat at a table with Jacob, Jamal, Ryan, Shelly, Rashonda, and Maria. They were all talking and laughing, but she felt too guilty to participate.

"Hey, girl!" said Maria, smiling.

"Hi," said Faleesha half-heartedly.

"You a'ight?" said Rashonda.

Faleesha took a bite of her apple.

"Mmm-hmm."

"You sure?" said Jacob.

Faleesha looked at him. He stared into her eyes intently. She felt extremely nervous. *Can he tell? Does he know?*

"Yeah, I'm fine," she said.

"So anyway," said Rashonda, "guess what, guys?"

"What?" said Maria.

"My baby should be coming home soon!" She looked extremely excited.

"Ooh, get it girl!" said Shelly.

"When is he supposed to be getting out?" said Maria.

"Well, right now, they are looking at June."

"That's great!" said Shelly. "So you only got like, four months to wait."

"Yup!" said Rashonda, clapping her hands. "Trust and believe, I am counting down the days."

"Amen!" said Shelly.

"But tell me why Tyrone keeps trying to get me to go to y'all church?" said Rashonda, gesturing at Jacob and the guys.

"Oh really?" said Jacob. "What's wrong with that?"

She shrugged her shoulders. "I mean, nothing, but like, why would he do that?"

"Why not?" said Maria. "You used to go to church, right?"

"Yes, I did," said Rashonda, looking at Jacob and the guys uneasily. "But y'all already know my story."

Jacob looked at her. "Well, Rashonda, I don't mean to get in your business, but—"

"She be in everybody else's business!" said Shelly.

"Shut up, girl!" said Rashonda, laughing.

"It's the truth," said Shelly.

"I don't mean to get in your business," Jacob began again. "But I do hope that you know that regardless of what you may have done, you can come back to God."

"Yeah, I know, but . . . ." Rashonda paused, looking at Jacob as if she wasn't sure whether she should continue.

"But what?"

"Look, I love the Lord and everything, but I can't go back to church, because if I do, then I know that I can't do the things I want to do."

"Such as . . . ." Jacob prompted.

"Jacob!" Rashonda exclaimed.

"Ooh, girl, he's getting under your skin!" said Maria.

"No, I really want to know," said Jacob.

"Look, honey, I'm talking about sex," said Rashonda.

"Shonda!" Shelly looked like she was embarrassed for Jacob.

"What?" said Rashonda. "He asked."

"You're right. I did." Jacob nodded.

"Yes, you did," said Rashonda. "And that's just the reality of the situation. I mean, we have a child together, and we love each other, so that's just what we're going to do."

"Preach!" said Shelly, giving Rashonda a high five.

"Well, if I may, Rashonda . . . ." said Jacob.

She looked at him expectantly. "Go ahead."

"Well, actually . . . ." He turned to Faleesha. "You can probably handle this better from a female perspective."

Everyone looked at Faleesha. She felt heat rising up to her cheeks and ears. A lump formed in her throat. She looked at

Rashonda, then at Jacob. "Um . . . ." she said, full of shame, but trying not to show it on the outside. "I think we already had this conversation."

Jacob stared at her as if discerning something.

He turned back to Rashonda. "Okay," he said. "Well, I was going to say that you and Tyrone should consider marriage."

Nothing had prepared her for that one. "Marriage?" she said, her expression skeptical.

"Yes, marriage. You said you have a child together, right?"

"Yes."

"You said you're in love with each other, right?"

"Yes."

"How long have y'all been together?"

"Six years."

"So why not get married? Why not just go ahead and do it the right way? What's stopping you?"

Rashonda looked at Jacob like she had never thought of that before. She looked as if she was really considering it. She opened her mouth to speak, but before she could say anything, Shelly interjected.

"What do you mean, the *right* way?" Clearly, she was offended by Jacob's words.

"What I mean is God's way," said Jacob, his voice quiet and careful.

"And what is God's way?" said Shelly.

"God's way is that we not enter into fornication, which of course is sex before marriage, but that instead we put Him first by getting married before having sex."

"Pssht!" said Shelly, snapping her head back. "And what's the point of that?"

"The point is to put Him first," said Jacob. "It's about trusting God's wisdom over our own desires."

"But what about our *needs*?" said Shelly, her face blushing crimson. "I mean, it's biologically proven that we need sex to survive as a species. So why does God have such a problem with it?"

"It's not that God has a problem with sex. It's just that He wants us to do it in the context of marriage because in marriage, two become one spiritually, which is the right framework for becoming one physically."

"Wait," said Shelly, shifting in her seat. "So you mean to tell me that you're a virgin, and you're waiting to get married before having sex?"

Jacob opened his mouth to answer, but Shelly cut him off.

"See, I didn't think so."

"Actually, Shelly," said Jacob, "I was going to say that yes, I *am* a virgin, and I fully intend to wait until I'm married to have sex."

Shelly's jaw dropped for a second time that day. "Bullshit!" she exclaimed.

"Shelly!" said Rashonda.

"What?"

"It's the truth," said Jacob.

"So you mean to tell me that you've never, ever had sex?" said Shelly.

"Yes, that's what I'm saying."

"Don't you want to have sex sometimes? Don't you want to know what it feels like?"

"Of course I do!" said Jacob. "I'm a man. And I'm not saying that I don't struggle with it, but—"

"So what if you wait for marriage, and then you and your spouse are not sexually compatible?"

"To tell you the truth, that's something I used to worry about. But now I'm at a point in my life where I just trust God, and if it does come to that, I know that He will help us work it out."

"Wow," said Shelly. "See, that's one of the reasons I can't get into church like that. You all put way too much emphasis on trusting God, like He is really going to help you with your sex life."

"Who's to say that He can't, or that He won't?"

"Whatever," she said. She turned to Jamal and Ryan. "So you mean to tell me that you guys are virgins too?"

"Yes," they said in unison.

"That is impossible!" She practically spat the words. "As much sex that is going on at this school, especially in y'all dorm, and not one of y'all has had sex?"

"I don't know what to tell you," said Jacob. "Other than it's the truth."

"Well, I don't believe it." With that, Shelly got up from her seat, but she didn't move to leave.

"We made up our minds before we got here to do it God's way or no way at all," said Jacob.

She waved at him dismissively. "Yeah, whatever." She turned and stalked off with more drama than necessary.

***

Faleesha made it to her room and closed the door. She put her back against the wall and sighed, slipping down to the floor as the tears streamed down her face. She felt horrible that she could not be of help when Jacob was talking to Shelly. It's like, she knew what to say, but she didn't feel like she had a right to say it because she had almost done it. She had almost had sex with Rondell. She felt like scum because that was her first time ever kissing someone, and she had allowed herself to get that far.

"I'm sorry, Lord." She sniffed. "I'm sorry."

Just then, she heard a knock on her door. She flinched at the sound then scrambled to get up in a hurry, wiping her face. She cleared her throat.

"Who is it?" she said.

"It's me," said a familiar voice. She opened the door. It was Rondell's friend Mike.

"Hey," she said, wondering why he was there.

"What's up?" he said. "You okay?"

"Yeah," she said, sniffling.

"You sure?"

"Yeah."

"Why are you crying?"

"It's nothing. I'm good."

He looked like he wanted to say something else, but he stopped himself. "Okay," he said, finally. "Well, the reason I came to talk to you is because of Rondell."

"What's going on?"

"Well, him and Chris got into a fight the other day, and he hasn't spoken to any of us since."

"A *fight*?" she said. "Is he okay?"

"Yeah," said Mike. "But he hasn't been answering anybody's calls, and when we go to his room, he won't even answer the door. He just tells us to leave."

"Wow," she said.

"So, I was wondering if you could try to talk to him."

"Me?"

"Yeah, maybe he will see a pretty face and calm down." He smiled at her, waiting.

She blushed. "I don't know," she said, nervous at the thought of seeing Rondell again so soon.

"Please? I don't want him to just shut down. Midterms are coming up, and I don't think he's been going to class."

"Oh, wow." She took a deep breath and exhaled slowly. "Okay, I'll try to talk to him."

"Thanks," said Mike.

"Sure. It's okay."

Mike fidgeted with his jacket zipper, not sure what to say next. Finally, he said, "Well, I hope you feel better. See you around."

"See you," she said, and she closed the door and sank back down to the floor, wondering what she should say to Rondell.

Chapter 15

Faleesha stood in front of Rondell's dorm room door, too afraid to knock. They hadn't seen each other since the kiss. She was always nervous around him anyway, and now that they'd gotten physical, she wasn't sure she could trust her feelings.

Tears of shame and guilt rushed to her eyes once more, but she fought them back. She had to make sure Rondell was okay. She took a deep breath and knocked lightly on his door.

"I *told* y'all niggas to leave me alone!" said Rondell.

"Um . . . it's me," said Faleesha.

He was silent for a moment, and then she heard him walking to the door. Her heart pounded uncontrollably as he twisted the knob.

"Hey," he said softly when he saw her face.

"Hey," she said. "Can I come in?"

"Sure." He opened the door so she could walk in. "What's up with you?" he said, walking back to his bed and sitting down after closing the door behind her.

"Nothing," she said, trying to sound casual as she took a seat in the chair across from him, looking everywhere but at him.

"What's wrong?"

"Nothing," she lied. "Is everything okay with you?"

"Why you ask that?" The muscles in his jaw tensed.

"Well, Mike said—"

"Mike?" He exhaled loudly. "Mike said *what*?"

"He said you've been upset lately."

"Well, Mike needs to stay out my damn business."

She flinched when he swore.

"Sorry," he said.

"It's okay," she said, keeping her voice pleasant and light. "So, have you been keeping up with your classes?"

"Yeah, I've been submitting my assignments online."

"So, do you want to talk about what happened with Chris?"

"No."

"Okay. Are you going to be alright?"

"I'm fine." He gave her a defiant look. "He's the one with all the drama."

"Well, I know that sometimes—"

"But I do want to talk to *you* about something."

She fidgeted nervously. "What about?"

"About me and you."

"What about us?"

"What happened the other day."

"Oh," she said, her face reddening. "I'm sorry."

"No need to be sorry. I thought it was great. I want to kiss you again."

Her heart raced at those words.

He stood up, and she stood up too, thinking it best to depart.

"I guess I better go," she said. "I don't think we should do this . . . ."

He wrapped his arms around her and pulled her close.

"Rondell . . . ."

He gently cupped her chin with his hand and turned her face up to his. He gazed into her eyes. She lost focus. He was staring at her with such intensity that it set her insides on fire.

No one had ever looked at her like that before—ever.

His lips covered hers, and he kissed her again, slowly at first, and then more passionately. His hands gently caressed her back, and then they traveled down to her bottom.

He cupped her butt gently, then squeezed. "Mmm . . . ." he moaned.

Her eyes popped open. She pushed him away.

"What's wrong?" he said, still lost in a daze from the kiss.

"I can't do this."

"Do what?"

"If we keep going . . . ."

"What?"

"I don't want to have sex."

"Why not?"

"Because it's against God's word."

"Huh?" He looked confused.

Her nerves were getting the best of her. She didn't know what to do with her hands so she stuffed them in her jeans pockets. Finally, she said, "It would be a sin."

"What do you mean a sin? Isn't that a little old-fashioned?" Rondell smirked.

"Sex before marriage is a sin."

"So, you're telling me that I can kiss you, but I can't have sex with you."

"I can't kiss you anymore either," she blurted, and braced herself for his response.

He was taken aback. "Why not?"

"It brings too much temptation."

"So you just going to play with me like that?" He felt his anger rising.

"I didn't mean to play with you," she said, full of shame and embarrassment. "Please understand."

"No, I don't understand."

"I'm sorry, Rondell. I have to go." She turned toward the door.

"You going back to your room so you can pray for me and my sinful ways?"

Her face fell at his tone. The sarcasm was unmistakable.

He sucked his teeth. "I can't believe this shit. All y'all Christians always running to God with all your problems. What has God ever really done for anybody? Huh?"

Faleesha did not know how to respond. She had never seen Rondell angry before.

"What has that nigga ever done for *me*? Huh? You got an answer for that? Did He tell you that in your prayers?"

"Rondell . . . ."

"Matter of fact, where was that nigga when my mom was on crack and my dad was in jail? Huh? Where was He when I was moved from foster home to foster home for seven muthafuckin years? Where was He the day I lost my best fuckin friend? When I was getting shot at and stabbed and staying out all night selling drugs cuz nobody gave a FUCK about me? Huh? Where was He then? Where was He when those old ass forty-year-old ass women was fuckin touching on me when I was fuckin six years old? Where the fuck was He at? Huh? Where was He?"

He stepped closer to her.

She stepped back.

"You don't know the answer, do you?" he challenged. "I didn't think so."

Silent tears streamed down her face.

He sucked his teeth. "Just go on and get the fuck out of my room."

***

Shelly and Gesston opened the door to their room at the Red Hill Hotel.

"It is *so* beautiful!" Shelly exclaimed. She walked throughout the room, touching the furniture and admiring all of the details. "What do you think?" she said, looking at Gesston with a bright smile on her face.

"It's . . . nice," he said. A lump of guilt formed in his throat. He swallowed it. It took everything in him not to bolt from the room.

"Well, I wanted to start off with us getting nice and relaxed. I ordered us a bottle of wine and some cheese."

"*Cheese*?" said Gesston, wrinkling his nose.

"Yeah, cheese. It's really romantic. Plus I don't want us to get too full before we consummate our relationship."

"Consummate?" Gesston couldn't believe this. Where did she come up with this stuff?

"Yes! I want it to be nice and slow." She pulled a chair out from a table for two. "Come on. Let's sit down." She gestured for Gesston to sit.

Gesston sat down across from her at the table. He ate the cheese and drank the wine, forcing himself to nod and smile in all the right places while Shelly talked, but he was barely paying attention to her words. He thought he heard her mention some juicy gossip. At least that would be interesting.

"Who's a virgin?" he asked taking a sip of wine.

"I said, are *you* a virgin?"

"Yes!" he said wholeheartedly. Maybe the Lord was making a way of escape for him! Maybe Shelly would drop him for another guy now that he had admitted it.

She looked a little disappointed.

Yes! he thought. *Now maybe I can get out of here.*

"Oh, I figured that," she said, "especially after the conversation I had with Jacob and them."

He sat up in his seat. "Jacob and who? About what?"

She waved dismissively. "Oh, nothing. They were just talking a bunch of nonsense. I'm so glad you're not like them."

His heart burned at her last words. At that moment, he felt the heaviest guilt that he had ever experienced in his life. What was he doing here with her? How far was he really going to go with this thing? He had to come clean.

"Shelly . . . ." he began, his voice hesitant.

"Don't you worry," she said, smiling. She was already tipsy. "I've got something to help you come out of your shell."

"What do you mean?" he said, desperate for a way out.

"Just watch," she said. "Sit back and relax." She got up from the table and went over to a boom box that was sitting on another table. She took a CD out of her purse and put it in the player. "Turn your chair around," she ordered, trying to sound like a sexy dominatrix.

He turned the chair around to face her, all the while wondering why he was going along with this.

She dimmed the lights and turned on the CD. TLC's "Red Light Special" began to play.

"What are you doing?" said Gesston.

"Shhh," she said. "Just watch." She began to dance seductively to the music. She slowly took off her coat and let it fall to the floor. Then she began to dance more provocatively, moving her hips to the beat while removing more and more of her clothing.

Gesston just sat there, frozen in place. By the end of the song, she was sitting in his lap, completely naked. He was turned on by her body, but in his mind, he wanted nothing more than to escape.

"Gesston," she moaned. "I want you to do whatever you want to do to me." She leaned down and kissed him deeply.

He felt sick to his stomach. Sure, he would love to have sex with Shelly, but he knew that if he did, he would not be able to live with himself. He had to do something—now.

He stopped the kiss.

"What's wrong?" she said, breathlessly.

"I can't do it."

"What do you mean?"

"I can't have sex with you."

She froze. "What do you mean?" she repeated, her voice rising.

"We have to stop," he said, trying to get up.

She got off his lap so he could stand.

"What's going on?" she asked, suddenly feeling ridiculous standing there naked.

"Shelly . . . I can't do this."

"Okay, you said that, but why not?" She grabbed her coat and wrapped it around her.

"It's not right."

"But we love each other!"

"No, we don't."

"What?" Her voice was shaky.

"This is not right," he repeated.

She sucked her teeth. "I hope you are not talking that same bullshit as Jacob and them."

"What are you talking about?"

"This no-sex-before-marriage thing. Is that what you're talking about?"

"No."

Her features softened.

He hesitated. "Wait . . . I mean yes."

She folded her arms across her chest and put one foot out, full of attitude.

"They're right," Gesston continued. "I can't do it for that reason. But that's not the only reason." He looked away from her and stared at the floor.

"Well, what's the other reason?"

He didn't answer.

"Is it my body? Am I too fat?"

"No, no . . . Shelly, it's not that."

"Then what is it?" She sounded desperate.

"I . . . don't have feelings for you like that." There. He had said it.

She stood there for a moment as if she hadn't heard what he said, and when it hit home, her expression changed to one of pain mixed with anger and confusion.

"What do you mean you don't have feelings for me? You're my man! We've been together for over four months!"

"I . . . I never felt that way about you." He swallowed, bracing for the onslaught.

"Fuck you mean?"

"This is bad. I was wrong."

"So why the fuck were you with me this whole time then?"

"I don't want to say it."

"No, you going to tell me, muthafucka. You telling me everything. Spit it out."

"Faleesha."

"Faleesha?" she shrieked. "The fuck Faleesha got to do with this?"

"I got with you to make her jealous. It didn't work."

"What the fuck . . . you got with me to make her *jealous*? What are you, twelve? Where they do that at? Huh? You mean to tell me that I wasted four months of my life with you just for you to try to use me to get at some *other* bitch? Naw, nigga, you got me FUCKED up!"

At those words, she took off her earrings and began to roll up her hair.

"What are you doing?" said Gesston, bewildered.

"You got me fucked up," she repeated, fastening her hair with a bobby pin. Once she was finished, she charged at him without warning. She struck him with a barrage of blows, kicking, slapping, and punching him everywhere. He was caught off guard, so she got him on the ground, but when he finally came to himself, he grabbed her arms and pulled her down to the floor with him, restraining her.

"GET THE FUCK OFF OF ME!" she screamed, wrestling against him. He refused to let her go until she ran out of energy. When she finally calmed down, she began sobbing uncontrollably.

"Shelly. Shelly. I'm so sorry." Gesston swallowed another lump in his throat.

"Fuck you. Get out!"

"I'm so sorry."

"GET THE FUCK OUT!" she screamed again.

"Okay," he said. He let her go and got up off the floor. "Okay," he repeated. "I'll give you the money for the room."

"GET THE FUCK OUT!" She leapt to her feet and snatched her clothes off the floor.

"Okay," he said again. He walked to the door and jumped back just in time as the empty wine bottle whizzed past his head and shattered against the wall.

"YOU LUCKY, MUTHAFUCKA!" Shelly screamed. "I didn't mean to miss your ugly head!"

"I'm sorry," he repeated. Before he exited the room, he happened to glance at his reflection in the mirror next to the door. He was now sporting a black eye and a busted lip.

***

Rondell hopped in his truck at around three o'clock in the morning. He planned to go to the twenty-four-hour gas station up the street from the dorm to cop two more forty-ounce bottles of Heineken. He had been drinking all week, and he knew he shouldn't, but he didn't care.

His life was so confusing. He felt like he was literally going crazy on the inside. He had fought with Chris, snapped at Mike, cussed out Faleesha, and stopped going to classes.

He didn't understand why he was acting this way. All he could think about was his foster brother Terry, his parents, Faleesha, and God. He didn't know why he felt so burdened, but it just seemed like every time he tried to make a step forward in life, something pushed him back.

He pulled into the gas station and almost hopped out of his truck before he realized the station was closed. He squinted his eyes to read the sign on the door.

"What?! Closed for renovations? Nigga, I was just here yesterday!" He sucked his teeth and turned the key in the ignition. He sighed, leaning back in his seat. The next twenty-four-hour gas station was about a fifteen-minute drive from here. He knew he shouldn't be driving since he was more than a little intoxicated, but he felt like he really needed something to help him block out his thoughts.

He drove to the gas station, but it took all his concentration to stay in his lane. He ended up buying four bottles instead of two. He put them in the passenger seat and turned the key in the ignition once again.

He glanced at the bottles and immediately felt guilty. He had said at the beginning of the school year that he wasn't going to drink anymore, yet here he was with four bottles and six others in his room that he had emptied just this week. He considered returning them to the store, but decided against it.

"Fuck it. Too late now."

He drove back to the dorm, his hands gripping the steering wheel, his body hunched forward so he could focus on the road. He was sure he would be pulled over at any minute, and that made him feel even guiltier. He didn't know why he felt so guilty over everything lately. He had been drinking for most of his life up to this point.

He decided to turn on some music to drown out his thoughts. He quickly glanced through his CD collection, grabbed a CD out of an old Ruff Ryders case, and put it in. He turned it to his favorite track and let it play.

The music blasted from his speakers, but it wasn't Ruff Ryders. It was some gospel song.

He pulled over and put on his hazard lights. He flipped through his CDs and found the Shirley Caesar case. Just as he thought, the Ruff Ryder CD was in it.

"Mike!" he exclaimed, remembering he had switched them that day they all went to the beach. He took the Ruff Ryders CD out of the case and went to switch it in his CD player, but then he froze when the lyrics of the Shirley Caesar song caught his attention.

I realize
That surely and eventually

We gotta leave
This world behind

That's why I'm making
Ohh, making preparations,
To meet the Lord
To meet the Lord.

A woman came to me one day . . . .

Rondell sat back and listened, intrigued by what he heard.

She came and said Shirley,
I've got something to tell you now

I'm not ready
I'm not ready
I'm not ready to give up my wicked ways

Then she told me this:
"Every time,
Every time I make a step toward the Kingdom

Mean old Satan,
Gives me hard times."

I told that woman, yes I did
Said I told that woman, "How can you hold out any longer?
Oh, when you see that Jesus
Jesus, He loves you so . . . ."

She said, "I'm getting ready
Yeah! I'm getting ready
To meet the Lord
To meet the Lord."

Rondell sat there, lost in the lyrics of the song. He had never listened to any of the CDs his mother left in his car because he hadn't been interested. But now, for some reason—he didn't know whether it was the alcohol or what—but it seemed like this lady was really singing his life right now. Her voice was so soulful, and the lyrics rang true for him.

After the song was over, he turned off the music. He reflected on his life and all of the things that he had done and that had happened to him.

Tears tried to escape, but he fought them back as he pulled out onto the road.

When he got to the dorm parking lot, he stared at the bottles. There had to be a better way to live than this. There had to be a better way to handle his problems.

He realized that he no longer knew who he was. More than that, he didn't know who he was supposed to be.

***

Gesston, Chris, Jermaine, and Terrell were all posted up outside their dorm talking about money, girls, and basketball.

"Like I said," said Chris, "Lebron James is the greatest of all time."

"*All* time?" said Jermaine. "Nigga, definitely not. Just cuz he's one of the best right now doesn't make him better than all of the greats that came before him."

"Okay, okay. Like who?" said Chris.

"Michael *Jordan?*" said Jermaine. "Kareem Abdul-Jabbar, Larry Bird—bruh, the list goes on and on."

"People give those old heads way more credit than they deserve, just cuz they paved the way," said Chris.

"Nigga, *what?!?*" Jermaine exclaimed. "That's straight *blasphemy*, my dude."

Gesston flinched at that last remark.

Chris noticed. "What?" he said, challenging Gesston. "What's up with you, Gee?"

Just then, Jacob walked up to them.

"Aww, look at Church Boy, all collared up and corduroyed out," said Chris, mocking him.

"What's up, Chris?" said Jacob, unfazed by his remark. He gave them all dap. When he got to Gesston, he paused.

"Hey, man. I need to speak to you."

"About what?" said Gesston, his heart pounding. It had been a couple of months since he had last spoken to Jacob, Jamal, and Ryan. He missed them deeply, but he couldn't bring himself to apologize for his behavior.

"Uh oh, judgment is coming!" said Chris. He, Jermaine, and Terrell chuckled.

"It's kind of private," said Jacob.

"You can say it in front of them," said Gesston, but he felt uneasy.

"No, I think it's best if I tell you privately," said Jacob. Now he looked a little uneasy. That scared Gesston, because Jacob was the kind of guy who always seemed calm, cool, and collected.

"No, I would rather hear it right now, right here," said Gesston. "Bring it."

They stared at each other. When Jacob saw that Gesston wasn't going to budge, he sighed.

"Okay, man." His shoulders slumped. "I'll tell you."

"Go ahead," said Gesston, trying his best to look nonchalant.

"God spoke to me about you this morning. I would have called you, but I felt it was better to tell you face to face."

"Aw, shit!" said Chris. "This is getting good!" He rubbed his hands together excitedly.

Jacob looked at him warily. "Please, man." He held his hands up.

"Look, man. Just say what you got to say," said Gesston, fidgeting. He was starting to feel edgy. His heart was already racing. He wished he had agreed to speak with Jacob in private, but it was too late now.

"Okay," said Jacob, turning his attention to Gesston. "Look, man, God said that you're treading on dangerous ground. He said that if you don't repent now, something worse is going to come."

"What do you mean something worse?" said Gesston. "And besides, since when does God speak directly to you about me?"

Jacob saw right through his defense and ignored that last remark. "What happened to your eye?" he said, cutting to the chase.

"None of your business," said Gesston.

"Look, Gesston—" Jacob started, but Gesston cut him off.

"Was that all you had to say?"

"Gesston—look, man, you don't have to stay on this road. It will only get worse from here. If God spoke to *me* about you, we both already know that means he has been telling you the same thing. This is not who you are. Just come back, man. Please."

There was so much fire and concern in Jacob's eyes that Gesston wanted to burst into tears. Every word that Jacob had spoken was true: God *had* been speaking to him, but Gesston had been ignoring Him. He knew he wasn't really about this gangsta life like he'd been pretending to be, but he felt that he had gone too far to get back to God now.

"What do you mean, that's not who he is?" said Chris, interrupting them. He had a look of disgust on his face.

"I'm talking to Gesston," said Jacob, giving Chris a look. "He knows what I'm talking about."

Chris wasn't done yet. "How you just gonna tell this man who he is? Just cuz he's not living up to your holy expectations doesn't mean that you have any right to judge him."

"Chris, I'm not judging anyone. Gesston knows exactly what I'm talking about, and like I said before, this has nothing to do with you."

Jacob was starting to look a little agitated. Chris was getting under his skin. He tried to shake it off and turn back to Gesston. He held his hands out. "Come on, man. Let's pray."

"Pssht!" Chris sucked his teeth. "I'm done." To Gesston, he said, "Gee, you really gonna listen to this nigga?"

"Look Chris," said Jacob, "I understand that you don't believe in God. But you don't have to be so disrespectful. I said it before, and I'll say it again. I wasn't talking to you. I was talking to Gesston."

"Okay, now it sounds like you disrespecting me," said Chris.

"Look, Gesston is my best friend. I've known him all my life. This has nothing to do with you."

Gesston remained silent and decided to see how this would play out. He could tell that Jacob was really getting heated.

"So what you gonna do about it, Church Boy?" Chris sneered. "You a little far from your prayer closet." He stepped between Jacob and Gesston.

"Chris, back away from me," said Jacob.

"Or what?"

"Or I'll give you a whole lot more than a missing tooth."

Both Terrell and Jermaine burst out laughing at Jacob's last remark.

"Oh, shit!" Jermaine howled. "GOT 'IM!"

Chris looked heated. "Oh, really? You wanna bang, Church Boy? Square up then."

Jacob held up his hands in apology. "Look, man, I'm sorry. I was out of line. The only thing I wanted to do was talk to Gesston. I didn't come here to start a fight."

Chris sneered again. "Yeah, that's right. I knew you was a punk."

"I'm not afraid of anyone. I fear no man." Jacob turned to go. "Gesston, I'll be praying for you, man." He walked away, clearly discouraged, his head hanging low.

***

Shelly lay in her bed, staring at the ceiling. It had been a rough night. She could barely sleep because of what had happened with Gesston.

Every time she closed her eyes, she relived the moments of him breaking her heart, and her standing there naked in front of him feeling like a fool.

A tear slipped down her face. She wiped it away and sighed.

Just then, someone knocked on her door. She wondered who it could be this early in the morning. She looked at her clock. It was 7:30 a.m.

"Who is it?" she called out, irritably.

"It's Rashonda. Get out the bed and let me in, girl!"

Shelly's heart raced. She couldn't let Rashonda see her crying like this. She would ask questions and want all the details, and Shelly was in no mood to tell her anything. She shot up out of bed.

"Hold on, girl!" she said, dashing to her bathroom to splash some water on her face. She patted her face dry with a towel then hurried to open the door for Rashonda.

"I didn't think you would be in your room this early!" said Rashonda.

"So why did you *come* this early?" said Shelly.

"I need a favor."

"What kind of favor?"

"Listen, my cousin Craig backed out on me once again, and I *have* to see Tyrone. Shelly, please! It's Valentine's weekend!"

"Rashonda, no, I am not going all the way out there again, especially not this early in the morning."

"Shelly, please! I don't have anybody else who can give me a ride, and I need to see him. I know you and Gesston probably got plans for the day, but I need to see my man too. Come on, girl, you know how it is."

Shelly stared at Rashonda, but she knew it was no use resisting. Rashonda would never stop begging until Shelly caved in. She sighed.

"You got gas?" she said, throwing her hand up in aggravation and rolling her eyes.

"Yes, girl!" Rashonda said, digging into her purse. She took out forty dollars. "I even got extra, honey."

Shelly took the money. "Okay. Come on in. Let me throw on some clothes."

Rashonda sat down on Shelly's couch. "Thank you *so* much, girl."

"Mmm-hmm," said Shelly with a tinge of sarcasm in her tone. She rummaged through her closet, found some jeans and a sweater, and hopped in the shower. Then she did her hair and came out. "You ready?" she asked Rashonda.

"Yup!" she said, hopping up off the couch.

They rode the elevator in silence then they made their way through the parking lot to Shelly's car. She popped the locks with her key fob, and they both got in.

"Why you so quiet, girl?" said Rashonda. "And why you look so depressed? It's Valentine's Day!"

"No, Valentine's Day was yesterday!" Shelly snapped.

"You know what I mean," said Rashonda as Shelly backed out of her parking space. "Why do you look so unhappy? Was he wack or something?"

"What are you talking about?"

"Gesston, silly! Did he put it on you last night or what? Why are you back at the dorm so early? I need details, girl!"

"Rashonda, I really don't feel like talking about anything right now, especially not Gesston." Her chin quivered.

"What's wrong? Is everything okay? What happened? I'll beat that boy if he hurt you!"

"I don't want to talk about it."

"I mean . . . y'all are still together, right?"

Shelly shook her head as a tear slipped down her cheek. "Nope." She sounded as depressed as she felt.

"Shelly, you *have* to tell me what happened. What did he do? Do I need to call Shaquan and them?" Shaquan was one of Rashonda's male cousins.

"No. I'll be okay."

"So what happened?"

"I can't talk right now. It's a long story, and I'm hung over. Plus, it's still too fresh. I'll tell you when we get back."

"Okay."

Shelly put on some music, and they drove without talking the rest of the way.

When their names were finally called to visit Tyrone, Rashonda jumped up excitedly and raced to the door. Shelly barely could keep up with her. When Rashonda got to Tyrone, he opened his arms to receive her. They embraced and lost themselves in a long, deep kiss. After a few moments, a guard came up and tapped Tyrone on the shoulder.

"Hey," he said. They stopped kissing for a moment.

"Come on, man," said Tyrone. "It's Valentine's Day."

The guard shrugged. "Whatever," he said. "Just make it quick."

They kissed for a few more moments then forced themselves to pull apart, holding hands.

"Bae, I love you so much," said Rashonda.

"I love you too, girl." Tyrone smiled into her eyes.

"You look so *different*!"

"What you talking about, woman?"

Rashonda turned to Shelly. "Doesn't Ty look different?"

"Oh, hey Shelly," said Tyrone, just noticing that she was there. "Sorry for being rude."

"It's cool," said Shelly. "You *do* look a little different."

"Is it the haircut?" he said, rubbing his head.

"No, it's something else," said Rashonda, staring at him closely. "I can't describe it."

"Well . . . it might have to do with some things I been working on." Tyrone gave Rashonda a big smile. "But I'll tell you about that later."

"What things? Tell me now!" said Rashonda.

Tyrone chuckled and looked at Shelly. "You see what I have to deal with?"

"Mmm-hmm," said Shelly.

Rashonda swatted his arm. "Shut up, boy. I didn't do nothing. But why won't you tell me, though?"

"Baby . . . ." he said, shaking his head. "I ain't even fooling with you, girl." He turned back to Shelly.

"So, Shell, how's things been going?"

Shelly swallowed a lump in her throat. "I been okay!" she said brightly, trying to sound convincing.

"You tired?"

"Why you say that?"

"You look a little down."

"I'll be okay."

"You sure?"

"Now who's nosy?" said Rashonda, cutting in.

Tyrone chuckled. "Stop it. I get it from you."

They talked and laughed together for a few more moments, and then Shelly sat off to the side so that Rashonda and Tyrone could talk privately. When it was time to go, Rashonda and Tyrone said a final "I love you" then kissed again. After that, Shelly and Rashonda left.

When they got in the car, Rashonda said, "I love that man *so* much," her eyes dreamy. "Thank you for bringing me."

"Mmm-hmm," said Shelly, turning her music on and trying to hold back the vomit that was rising in her throat.

***

When Shelly and Rashonda got back to her room, Rashonda plopped down on Shelly's couch.

"So, tell me what happened with you and Gesston."

"Shonda," said Shelly, holding up her hand in protest. Just then, there was a knock on Shelly's door.

"Who is it?" said Rashonda before Shelly could speak.

"It's us." Rashonda opened the door. Faleesha and Maria walked into the room. She closed the door after them.

"Hey, girl," said Maria. She and Faleesha sat down next to Rashonda.

"Hey," said Shelly.

"What's wrong?" said Faleesha, looking at Shelly.

"Nothing." Shelly directed a piercing look at Rashonda to silence her, but it didn't work.

"Come on, Shelly," said Rashonda. "You have to talk about it some time."

"Talk about what?" said Maria. "What happened?"

Shelly sucked her teeth at Rashonda. "Why do you always have to open your big mouth?" Her voice trembled as she spoke.

"Shelly," said Faleesha. "What's going on?"

All of them were staring at her, concerned. Shelly felt as if the room was closing in on her. She sat on her bed and hugged her knees.

"I really don't want to talk about it."

"Come on, girl," said Faleesha. "We're your friends."

At those words, a few tears slid down Shelly's face. She wiped them away. "I was willing to give him everything!" she said, bursting into tears. She buried her face in her arms.

"Aw, Shelly," said Rashonda, and all three of them rushed to her, Faleesha and Maria on either side of her rubbing her back, and Rashonda kneeling in front of her. "Shelly, honey," she said again, grabbing some Kleenex from her purse. "What happened?"

"Everything I did, and I wasn't good enough." Shelly wept. "I'm never good enough."

"Honey, that's not true," said Rashonda. "Tell us what happened."

Shelly broke down and told them everything that had happened the previous night between her and Gesston.

"That trifling ass nigga!" said Rashonda. She glanced up. "Sorry, Faleesha."

"It's okay," said Faleesha. "Shelly, I'm so sorry. I had no idea."

"It's not your fault," Shelly said, staring blankly.

"Yeah," said Maria. "He's definitely not worth it, girl."

"You're right about that," said Shelly.

"You'll find somebody better," said Rashonda.

"Mmm-hmm," said Shelly, but she wasn't convinced.

"Why don't we watch a movie or something?" said Faleesha. "Help take your mind off things."

Shelly sat there staring into space. "I got a better idea." She looked at Rashonda, then Maria. "Let's hit the club tonight."

"The club?" said Rashonda. "You sure you want to go clubbing with what just happened last night?"

"Yeah, girl. I got to get all these feelings out." She looked at Faleesha. "I know you probably can't come, or at least, you *won't* come, but we'll be alright."

"What's that supposed to mean?" said Faleesha.

"Yeah, why you say it like that?" said Rashonda.

"Nothing," said Shelly. "I didn't mean nothing by it. I just know that since Faleesha's in the church, she probably thinks it's sinful to go clubbing."

"Why don't we just watch some movies?" said Maria.

"Uh-uh," said Shelly. "I'm not trying to be stuck up in my room. That's too depressing. I need to go out, get some air, have some *drinks* (she glanced at Faleesha), and find me a *real* man."

"Shelly, do you have a problem with me?" said Faleesha.

"No, of course not."

"Are you sure?"

"Yeah, girl, we good. I just know you won't be able to participate tonight. But we'll be good. Maria, you coming?"

"I'm not really into that scene anymore, but I'll come for support."

"Cool! It's going to be so much fun!" said Shelly, and she glanced in Faleesha's direction again.

Chapter 16

Rondell finished yet another bottle of Heineken and put it on his desk along with his other bottles. For some reason he didn't yet understand, he felt compelled to save the empties, as if he needed a stark reminder of what he was doing.

Since he had locked himself in his room, he had experienced every negative emotion possible: anger, sadness, depression, loneliness, regret, and remorse. He grieved his life; he grieved the loss of Terry; he grieved his actions of the past few weeks. His self-imposed exile helped somehow, as if he needed to come face to face with the hard realities of his life with no one else's help.

The only times he left his room were to get more liquor and to grab some food. He had sent emails to all of his professors saying he was sick, and requested that they let him submit all of his assignments online. To his surprise, they all agreed, stating that they were giving their permission because he was such a good student.

As a result, his daily routine was to get up, eat, drink, do his work, drink, play video games, watch TV, drink, eat, listen to music, drink, and finally, to crash into sleep. If he ran low on food or alcohol, he crept out during the early morning hours when most people were asleep, and went to twenty-four-hour stores and fast food spots.

He ignored all phone calls and texts, even from his parents and Mike. He knew he was wrong, but he felt that he was too far gone to turn back now. He got up to turn off the lights when his phone buzzed with yet another text message.

He sucked his teeth in irritation. To his surprise, it was Shalonda.

Hey, I just wanted to say sorry for hitting you. I hope you forgive me. He went to delete her message, but decided to write back. He figured that if he couldn't have the woman he wanted, he would have to settle for the woman who wanted him. He decided to reply.

We good.

Within seconds, she replied. *Really? ☺ Why don't you let me come and make it up to you? ;)*

He rolled his eyes. Shalonda was such a fuckin THOT. He took a breath before he responded, contemplating whether he should really go through with this. Then he sighed and texted back.

Cool. Come on up.

Again, within seconds, she texted, *Okay, baby. See you soon! ☺*

He put his phone on his desk, brushed his teeth and washed his face, brushed his hair, then sat on his bed, waiting for Shalonda to get there.

She arrived about ten minutes later.

"Hey!" she said when he opened the door.

"What's up?"

"Nothing!" she said cheerily. "Just been thinking about you lately." She looked around his room, and her eyes fell on all of his bottles. "Dang, boy! You finished all of these yourself?"

"Yup."

"Did you save some for me?" she said with a wink.

"There's one in the fridge," he said, gesturing for her to get it herself.

"Yes!" she said. She opened it and drank a few swigs straight from the bottle. She burped. "Ooh, sorry!" she said. "I was drinking a little bit earlier."

"You good," he said, trying to mask his disgust.

"So, you ready?" she said, gesturing toward his bed.

"Yup."

"Alright, Daddy, let's get this party started."

**

Shelly sat on her bed, staring at the bottle of pills. She had been contemplating what she was about to do for two months.

She had gone back and forth about it, over and over again, and she kept coming to the same conclusion: She just wasn't meant to be happy.

See, Gesston wasn't the first man who rejected her. She had grown up without her father, so she had never known what it was like to have a man love her, hold her, or tell her that she was beautiful.

She had searched for love in other men, but she was never able to find it. Instead, she saw herself surrounded every day by people who were in loving relationships, people like Rashonda and Tyrone, but nobody ever wanted *her*.

It was always someone else who was happy, never her. She'd had multiple boyfriends in the past, but those relationships usually ended after a couple of months. The guys always ended up cheating on her and leaving her for someone else.

She was sick of it! She opened the bottle and popped one of the pills in her mouth. She grimaced at the taste. It was so bitter that she almost spit it out.

"No," she said, shaking her head. She was going to do it this time. She went to the fridge and grabbed a bottle of water. She carried it back to her bed and opened it. She took a few sips to help get the pill down.

Then she took another, and another, drinking about half the water bottle.

"I've got to pace myself better," she said. Then she took three pills at the same time and almost choked getting them down.

When she had taken about three-quarters of the bottle of pills and gone through two bottles of water, she was tired. She decided she was done. After all, it was a pretty large bottle of pills, and she had taken almost all of them. She lay down and waited to float out of this place . . . .

She was lying there for about ten minutes when she heard a knock on her door. "Who is it?" she slurred, her voice angry.

Even in death, somebody always had to ruin it for her.

"It's us!" said Rashonda.

She contemplated not opening the door, but she knew that if she didn't, they would just keep knocking. She got up and staggered to the door.

"What do y'all want?" she said as Faleesha, Maria, and Rashonda came in.

Rashonda gave her a look like she knew something was up. "Um, Faleesha said we should check up on you. She said she had a funny feeling."

Shelly felt uneasy at those words. "Oh really?" She didn't realize how glazed her eyes looked already, and that she was swaying the slightest bit as she tried to keep her balance.

"Yeah," said Faleesha. "Are you okay?" She looked concerned.

"Yeah, juss waiting for these pills to kick in . . . ."

"What, you *still* got a headache?" said Rashonda, going over to the bottle of pills. "Girl, I told you you was drinking way too much."

"Wait!" said Shelly as Rashonda picked up the bottle of pills, but it was too late.

Rashonda made a strange face as she shook the bottle. "Shelly, honey . . . ."

Her eyes were full of fear as she looked at Maria and Faleesha.

"What did you do?" she said to Shelly.

"What do you mean?" Shelly felt dizzy and lightheaded. "Leave me alone. I juss wanna sleep . . . ."

"Please tell me this is *not* the bottle of pills you bought last night on the way back from the club."

"Yes," Shelly said in a small voice.

"Shelly?" said Rashonda, tears rushing to her eyes. "This bottle is almost empty!"

"I'm sick of this life," said Shelly. "I'll be better off outta here."

A tear slid down Rashonda's face. "Shelly, we love you. We can help you."

"It's too late," said Shelly. She took a couple of steps toward her bed and collapsed onto the floor.

"SHELLY!" Rashonda screamed.

The last thing she saw before she lost consciousness was Faleesha calling 911 and Maria looking shocked and frightened.

***

Rondell lay in his bed, disgusted with himself. He could not believe that he had just had sex with Shalonda. She left early in the morning to get ready for class, and she had been blowing up his phone ever since, texting him repeatedly. He didn't even read her messages. He deleted them as they came in.

He looked at his clock—3:00 p.m. He contemplated going outside to get some fresh air, but he decided against it. He didn't want to run into anybody that he didn't want to talk to. He lay in the bed dozing when he heard someone knock at his door. He ignored it, thinking it was Shalonda coming back for more. The person kept on knocking. He contemplated getting up, but decided not to. She would get the picture after a while. He stayed in the bed.

"EYO DEE!" It was Mike. "You in there, man?"

Rondell sucked his teeth. That was another person who kept blowing up his phone. Why couldn't these n*ggas just realize that he didn't want to be bothered?

Mike kept on knocking. That really pissed Rondell off. Just as he was about to get up and give him a piece of his mind, he heard another voice.

"RA coming in! Safety and wellness check!" His door unlocked, and he jumped out of bed. When the door opened, there stood Mike, Tyrone, and Nick, the Resident Assistant. They all looked concerned.

"Hey, you alright in here, man?" said Nick, looking around the room. His eyes fell on Rondell's bottles.

"Yeah, I'm good, man," said Rondell, clearly annoyed.

"You sure? Mike and Tyrone said you haven't been to class in over a week."

"I'm sick." He didn't care if he lied. "I've been doing my work online." He glared at Mike and Tyrone.

"Alright, man." Nick held his hands up. "We were just concerned about you. Did you drink all of these bottles?"

"I am twenty-four years old, man," said Rondell, crossing his arms over his chest. "Do you need to see my ID?"

"Look, man, I'm not here to start trouble. I just want to make sure you're okay."

"I'm good. Like I said, I been submitting all my work online. You can email my professors if you want proof."

"No need for all of that." Nick stepped toward the door. "Just wanted to make sure you were okay."

"I'm good."

"Okay," said Nick, turning to leave. "Knock on my door if you need anything."

He exited the room and went down the hall. Mike and Tyrone just stood there.

"Y'all niggas really called Nick on me?" said Rondell, heated. "I told y'all I didn't want to be bothered."

Mike was the first to speak. "Look, Rondell, we your boys. That's not going to change. We was just worried about you because you usually don't cut us off for this long. Plus, something happened with Shelly this morning, and we wanted to make sure the same thing didn't happen to you."

Rondell's heart dropped. "What do you mean, something happened to Shelly?" He and Mike had known Shelly since high school. They had always hung tight with each other.

"She . . . she tried to kill herself, man."

"What?" Rondell was frantic. "Why? Where she at? Where they take her?" He started rummaging through his drawer for some clothes to put on.

Mike held out his hand to stop him. "Chill, man. They not letting nobody see her. She's in isolation. Parents only. We already called."

"Oh," said Rondell. He went back to his bed and sat down. "Shit, man, what happened? Why she try to kill herself?" He felt dizzy all of a sudden. His head was spinning.

"It was over Gesston," said Tyrone.

"What that nigga do? I'll fuck that nigga up, yo! Straight up!" Rondell's anger was building.

"Maria said—"

"Maria? Since when you talk to Maria like that?" said Rondell.

Tyrone licked his lips and his eyes darted back and forth. "We been hanging out lately. But anyway, Maria said that Shelly rented a room for her and Gesston to get it in on Valentine's Day cuz I guess Gesston been holding out since day one." He chuckled for a moment. "Corny nigga." He went back to his story.

"So when they got to the room, she stripped for him, then he dissed her and told her he was only with her to try and make Faleesha jealous."

"Nigga, *what*? How *old* is that nigga? Fuckin lame ass, square ass, wanna be down ass nigga!"

"That's messed up," said Mike.

"I know," said Tyrone.

"Yo, Dee. What you been doing in here, man?" said Mike, gesturing toward all the bottles.

"Nothing. I just wanted to be alone."

Tyrone glanced at Mike and then at Rondell. "Shalonda came up to us asking about you right before we went to get Nick."

"Yeah," said Mike. "She said something about you not answering her messages after last night."

Rondell couldn't meet their eyes.

"Dee, you didn't," said Mike.

Rondell shrugged.

"What is really good with you, Dee?" said Tyrone, surprised. "You know that bitch be burning!"

"I know," said Rondell, his head still down.

"So why did you do it?" said Mike.

Rondell tried to fight back the tears, but one escaped. He wiped it away. "I don't know, man. I'm fucked up."

"What's been going on with you, man?" said Mike, sitting next to him.

"I ain't shit," said Rondell. He told them how he had cussed at Faleesha and made her cry.

"Man, that was my fault," said Mike. "I asked her to come talk to you when you stopped going to class."

Rondell just looked at him.

Tyrone pulled the desk chair across the room and sat facing Rondell. "I understand you feeling bad and everything, but you can't just throw your life away, man. Look at how far you've come. You grew up in the system, and now you about to graduate next year from college as one of the top GPAs of your class. That's good shit, bruh. Most people wouldn't make it like that. You can't just let all that go."

"Word, man," said Mike. "Terry would be proud."

Rondell thought about this. "So y'all *really* think I'm actually doing something with my life?"

"Yes!" they said in unison.

"Mad dudes be hating on the low."

"Fuck out of here," said Rondell.

"For real!" said Mike. "I always looked up to you."

"Bullshit, man!" said Rondell.

"For real!" said Mike. "You and Terry was both like a father to me."

"I never knew that, man," said Rondell, his voice quiet.

"It's true. Y'all always tried to look out for me before my mom came and got me."

"Yeah, even Chris has respect for you, despite everything that went down," said Tyrone.

"Man, fuck Chris," said Rondell.

Mike gave him a friendly nudge. "Come on, Dee. Y'all gotta squash it sooner or later."

"Naw, that nigga tested me way too many times."

"Yo, you know that nigga Jacob almost got it in with Chris?" said Tyrone.

"*What?*" said Rondell.

Tyrone burst out laughing and clapped his hands. "Yes, nigga!"

"Fuck outta here, Ty. That's bullshit."

"I'm not lying, nigga!"

"*Church* boy Jacob almost got it in with Chris?"

"Yes, nigga!" Ty repeated, gasping for breath.

"Why?" said Rondell, chuckling despite himself.

"Jermaine and them said that Jacob came up to them trying to talk to Gesston, but Chris kept butting into the conversation with that atheist shit. So Jacob finally got sick of his ass, and him and Chris was 'bout to square up. This is what you missed being holed up in here, brutha!"

Rondell burst out laughing as he imagined Jacob about to fight Chris.

"Yo, did anybody record that shit, nigga?" said Rondell.

"Naw, but Jermaine and them was crying when they told the story, they was laughing so hard," said Tyrone.

"They said Jacob was mad heated," said Mike.

"Wit' his Poindexter ass!" said Tyrone.

All three of them howled with laughter at that last remark.

"That's fucked up, Ty," said Rondell, wiping his eyes.

"I know, but Chris need to stop with that disrespectful shit," said Mike. "Jacob's really 'bout that church life, and he don't never mess with nobody."

"True, true," said Tyrone. "Maria said he be holding Bible studies in his room and everything."

"Word?" said Rondell.

"Yeah."

"Sound like that's the nigga everybody need to be looking up to then," said Rondell.

"I know," said Mike. "Jacob's a good dude."

"Yeah," said Rondell.

"Wit' his square ass!" said Tyrone. All three of them burst out laughing again.

***

Faleesha sat at her desk, trying to concentrate. There were so many things on her mind it wasn't even funny.

It seemed like everywhere she went, bad things happened. She had almost fornicated with Rondell, and he cursed her out when she told him she couldn't go through with it. She was having extreme difficulty balancing her work schedule with her internship and schoolwork. And then, Gesston used Shelly to try to make her jealous, and Shelly blamed Faleesha for it and tried to commit suicide. It was all just so messed up.

She was lost in her thoughts to the point that she didn't even notice her advisor standing right in front of her until she looked up.

"Oh!" she said, jumping back in her seat. "You scared me. I didn't even hear you come in."

Dr. Spandinelli had a serious expression on her face. "Faleesha, we need to have a conversation. Please come to my office."

Faleesha's heart dropped at her words. This did not sound good. "Is everything okay?" she asked, getting up and following her to her office.

"We'll talk," said Dr. Spandinelli, her expression grim. She turned and walked into her office and Faleesha followed her.

Dr. Spandinelli closed the door behind them and gestured for Faleesha to take a seat.

They stared at each other for a few moments. Finally, after what seemed like forever, Dr. Spandinelli spoke. "Do you have any idea why you're here?" she said softly.

"N-no." said Faleesha. "I—"

"It seems that I may have overestimated you in terms of your competency and capabilities for this level of work."

Faleesha's heart dropped. "What do you mean?" She was trembling.

"I had Denise, my graduate student, spot-check your work, and she found a significant number of errors in the way you coded the data over the past two weeks. The weeks before that were fine, but these past two weeks were not good at all."

"I'm sorry," said Faleesha. "I've just been going through a lot, and—"

Dr. Spandinelli held up her hand to stop her. "Please, no excuses. Everybody has hard times, and believe me, I understand, but there were a *lot* of errors in your work. Denise is going to have to work extra hours to get everything situated again."

"I can fix the errors." Faleesha felt desperate. Everything was falling apart, and now her work was too.

"No, no. I understand that you want to rectify the situation, but I can't afford to take that risk. I'm unfortunately going to have to permanently dismiss you from the project."

"I'm fired?" said Faleesha, tears filling her eyes.

"Yes, unfortunately. It's no hard feelings, but this is a huge grant, and I really can't afford to jeopardize our future funding."

Faleesha was speechless.

"I'm sorry, Faleesha, but I've got an appointment in about fifteen minutes." Dr. Spandinelli looked at her watch to emphasize her point. She got up from her desk. "I will see you in class on Thursday."

Faleesha nodded her head and stood to her feet. They awkwardly shook hands before leaving the office.

Faleesha's head was spinning. She could barely believe what was happening.

Dr. Spandinelli began to walk briskly in the opposite direction, but she stopped short. "Oh!" she said, turning around. "I don't know if this is any conciliation, but you did complete all of your required hours for the internship, so you should be all set regarding that. Also, I've decided to keep this between us. No one else knows except Denise, but she's not necessarily a social butterfly, so . . . I hope that helps."

Faleesha swallowed. "Thank you," she said in a very small voice.

"Sure thing!" said Dr. Spandinelli. Faleesha had the passing thought that this woman managed to sound effervescent even while delivering bad news. She wasn't sure if that was a good thing or a bad thing.

"Just take it as a learning experience, and I'm sure you will have another opportunity in the future."

"Thank you," Faleesha repeated.

Dr. Spandinelli nodded, then turned and walked away.

***

Rondell, Mike, and Tyrone were walking back to their dorm after playing basketball in the gym. They had just been beaten by Jermaine, Terrell, and a guy named Manny from a different dorm.

"I can't *believe* you missed that last shot, man!" said Tyrone, looking at Rondell.

"Hey, I told you my stomach been messed up from all that drinking."

"Well, you need to get your alcoholic ass back in gear, man! We can't be losing to Jermaine and them. Those niggas suck, and now we suck even harder!"

"We'll get them next time," said Mike. "Right, Dee?"

"Of course," said Rondell.

"RONDELL!" They all turned to see Shalonda bearing down on them like a freight train on stilettos.

"Shit!" said Rondell, realizing that she had finally caught up with him.

"Uh oh!" said Tyrone. "You in trouble now!"

"Fuck you, Ty," said Rondell.

"Ron-dell!" Shalonda said in a singsong voice when she got close to them.

"What's up?" he said awkwardly.

"Can I talk to you?"

He did not want to talk to her, but he knew that if he didn't, she would cause a scene, so he walked out of earshot to speak with her.

"What's going on?" he said.

"Have you been getting my text messages?"

He briefly considered lying, but decided against it. "Yeah."

"Well?" she said, crossing her arms and looking at him expectantly.

"Well what?"

"What do you think?"

"Think about what?"

"The question I asked you!" She struck a pose and waited.

"What question?"

"Rondell, did you even *read* my messages?"

"No."

"Why not?" She pouted.

"I was busy."

"Well, I was asking you where you think we should go from here."

"Where I think we should *go* from here?"

She stepped closer to him, her features softening. "Yeah," she said, touching his arm. "I want to be your girl."

He recoiled at the thought. "Shalonda!" he said, trying to mask his disgust.

"What?"

"Look, I was drunk when we—you know."

"Why you always say that?"

"I *was*. You saw the bottles."

"Well, it didn't *seem* like you was drunk with the way you was putting it on me. You are definitely the best I ever had, hands down." She smiled and purred, "I want you again tonight, baby."

"I can't do that."

"Why not?"

"I made a mistake with you."

"What do you *mean* you made a mistake?"

"I was drunk, so I wasn't thinking straight."

She sucked her teeth and rolled her eyes. "You *always* talking about you drunk when we get together."

"I *was*. And it was only one time."

"No, it was *three* times, all in the same night, so don't try to play me. And what about the party?"

"We didn't do nothing at the party. And I was drunk then too."

"So what are you saying?"

"The same thing I *been* saying. I made a mistake, and I apologize for that, but I'm not feeling you like that. I don't want to be with you."

"How can you say that with everything that happened between us the other night?"

"Look, Shalonda, I don't know what I said or did to you, but I was drunk, and I don't want to be with you. You're going to have to find another man." He started to walk back over to where Mike and Tyrone were.

"So you think you can just keep playing me like that?"

He turned back around. "I'm not trying to play you. I made a mistake, and I was wrong, but it's *you* who keeps coming for me, not the other way around."

"Nigga, whatever!" She brushed off his comment. "Alright, I got something for you."

"Something like what?"

"Don't worry about it. Just know I got something."

"Whatever," he said, waving her off as he returned to where Mike and Tyrone waited.

***

Faleesha knocked on the door to the pastor's office. She had made an appointment to seek counseling from his wife Deborah. She felt overwhelmed from all the drama she was facing lately and needed someone to talk to.

"Come on in!" said Deborah.

Faleesha walked in and almost immediately felt at peace. Deborah was very warm and welcoming.

"Hi, Faleesha," she said with a smile, standing up to hug her. When they hugged, Faleesha burst into tears. Deborah just rubbed her back and told her it was going to be alright.

They stood there hugging for a while, and she allowed Faleesha's tears to flow. Deborah handed her a Kleenex to wipe her eyes and blow her nose.

"I'm sorry for crying all over you," said Faleesha, taking a seat.

"It's no problem, honey. We all need to cry sometimes."

"Thank you," said Faleesha, wiping her tears.

"Mmm-hmm. So, what's been going on with you lately?"

Faleesha almost started crying again. "I've been going through a lot."

"Go ahead. You can let it out," said Deborah.

Faleesha felt free to talk, so she told her everything. Without mentioning any names, she told Deborah about Rondell, Shelly, Gesston, her classes, losing her internship, everything. When she was finally done, she felt relieved.

"Whew! That *was* a lot, honey."

"I know. Thank you for listening."

"Of course—any time."

"So . . . what do you think I should do?"

"Well, before I give any advice, I want to pray with you that God will grant us wisdom to handle these situations."

"Okay," said Faleesha. She held out her hands, and Deborah took them and prayed with her. When they finished, she sat back.

"Okay, now what do you want to tackle first?"

"Well, the thing that's bothering me the most is what happened with Rondell." She swallowed. "I'm very ashamed that I almost . . . did those things with him."

"Well, the first thing I want to let you know is that it is natural for you to want to have sex. Some people are blessed with the gift of celibacy, but most of us are not." Deborah chuckled. "Those desires are common for most adults, young and old. Once you get a certain age, you start getting attracted to people, and those feelings become stronger and stronger. But please remember that you are not alone.

"First, God is always with you. You have the Holy Spirit living inside of you, and He understands everything we go through. Also, you are not alone in a sense of being the only person to have those feelings. I struggled with the very same thing when I was your age, and believe me, I know it is tough!

"But keep in mind that you have already repented. Now you have to forgive yourself, stay in prayer, and try not to put yourself or allow yourself to be put into situations where sex could happen."

"So I shouldn't talk to him anymore?"

"I'm not saying that. I'm just saying that when you do talk, make sure it's in an open area with other people around. If you two are attracted to each other, sparks will fly, especially if you are in his or your bedroom with the door closed. Does that make sense?"

"Yes."

"So that would be my advice for that situation. I know it's hard, but with God, all things are possible. And also, I am here, day or night, if you ever need prayer or spiritual support."

Faleesha smiled. "Thank you so much!"

"Now, as far as your friend, honey, that is not your fault. I know it is a very difficult thing to witness somebody trying to end their life, but what that young man did to her was not your fault.

"For that situation, I would advise you to give her space, and to keep them both in prayer. Also, if you need to talk, I'm always here for you.

"I know from this meeting, you might be thinking, *well, all she is telling me to do is pray*, but honey, let me tell you from personal experience, prayer changes things. Also, talking it out with someone you trust is extremely helpful. I know it is for me."

"It's great to know that you're here for me," Faleesha said.

"You can always count on me," Deborah said. "I can't tell you how many times I have felt like the world was closing in on me, but after I poured my situation out to God and talked to a close friend, I received the healing I needed. Some things take much more time than others, but it definitely works."

"I believe you!" said Faleesha. "I feel like a weight has been lifted just by talking to you."

"Oh, don't I know it!"

"Can we meet a couple of times a month just to stay in touch?"

"Of course! We can even go out to lunch if you'd like. As a matter of fact, I have a group of young ladies your age that I meet with as a group and one on one. We have a great time together, and I would love for you to join us. I am here to support you, and remember, you are not alone. We are all in this together."

"Wow," said Faleesha, feeling empowered. "Thank you so much."

Chapter

A fter his discussion with Mike and Vicente, Ronnie
decided to go back to class. He dreaded but at
lunch his and threw their away to help him get back in
to game. He had no idea how to the house, and the
reactions were too to took his mage with something or
him alcohol.

He had been telling how much time he spent
working lately, on his magazine had class on time and
he only had had good. He shook his head trying and he
was so keep happen again life and so much his eyes
were days.

At the factory, as he enters the when class picked up
to even few minutes there the small and and that at keep seeing
so older guy who forced very in him. At that he that he did
might have seen one of a foster mothers' both hands and the
in looked at home natural for this.

He thought he must have left of his in his many
class ever in remembered the father in line about of
The day he sees the man at it him to and and his day.
He was of the of the everything com me so a role. He
shrugged at surprise and looked at his way.

Ronnie was getting and a space of back the man
soon to him it his voice was familiar in a the football
left at home. He was the part of from the period that had
so invited him.

Chapter 17

After his discussion with Mike and Tyrone, Rondell decided to go back to class. He cleared out all his bottles and threw them away to help him get back in the game. He needed to make a run to the grocery store. He figured it was time to stock his fridge with something other than alcohol.

He had been running low on cash since he hadn't been working lately, but his manager had a crush on him, so when he told her he'd been sick, she just wrote him up and told him not to let it happen again. He was set to start back work the next day.

At the grocery store, he cruised down the aisles, picking up a few things here and there, and he noticed that he kept seeing an older guy who looked very familiar. At first, he thought he might have been one of his foster mothers' boyfriends, but the man looked too professional for that.

Then he thought he must have been one of his many caseworkers, but he seemed to have too good of an attitude.

Lastly, he figured the man must have been one of his dad's friends who visited the dealership from time to time. He shrugged his shoulders and kept moving.

When he was getting some orange juice, he heard the man speak to a clerk. His voice was familiar, and then Rondell remembered. He was the pastor from that church Faleesha invited him to!

Once it clicked in his mind who the man was, he realized that he had to get out of that store as quickly as possible.

He grabbed the orange juice and darted down another aisle before the pastor could see him. He didn't know why he was so nervous. The man probably had not even seen him the day he visited the church. But just in case he had, Rondell wanted to get out of the store as quickly as possible.

He made it through the checkout line without being spotted or seeing the pastor. He pushed his cart out of the store and made his way to his Escalade. When he was a couple of yards away, he couldn't believe what he saw. The pastor was at his own car parked right next to Rondell's.

There was no way to play it off now. He popped his trunk and started loading it, staying focused on the task in the hope that the pastor would not notice him or recognize him.

How the hell did this nigga get out the store before me? As soon as he had the thought, he realized that he had called the pastor a nigga. Even though he hadn't said it out loud, he was pretty sure it still counted, and God wasn't too pleased. Feeling guilty, he looked up at the sky. *Sorry, God.*

"Hey, young man!" said the pastor.

Shit! Rondell turned around. No use pretending not to hear. "Hey," he said, feeling awkward but trying to look casual.

"Don't I remember you from somewhere?" said the pastor, shaking Rondell's hand.

Rondell considered lying and saying no, but for fear of being sent straight to hell, he told the truth. "Um . . . yeah. I visited your church a while back."

The pastor snapped his fingers. "Yes! That's it. I knew you looked familiar. It was you and another young man, right?"

"Yeah, my boy Mike," said Rondell, staring at him and wondering how he remembered all that.

"Well, I was glad to see you that day, and I hope you come back soon. It's real in these streets, and we all need God in our lives."

When the pastor spoke, it was like Rondell could feel every word. He knew the pastor had been there, because he had told his story during the service that day. But Rondell wasn't at the point where he felt like the church life was the direction he wanted to take. He couldn't see himself being like Jacob and them, all suited up and walking around with Bibles in their hands. He just wasn't that type of dude. He was from the streets.

"That's true," Rondell finally said. "But I don't think it's for me."

"Why you say that?" said the pastor.

"I'm not sure I even believe in God like that." He figured that would turn the pastor away, if he presented himself as a lost cause.

"Oh, no, you believe, alright," said the pastor, nodding his head with confidence as he looked Rondell right in the eyes. "That's why you've been questioning."

Rondell's heart dropped. Why did it seem like this guy who he had only seen twice in his life, including today, seemed to know everything about him?

"What do you mean?" said Rondell, feeling nervous.

"You know what I mean. I can tell by your eyes that you have seen some of the same things I have seen. I'm telling you, God is the answer."

"That's what y'all all say, but how do you even know you got the right one? And who's to say that if there is a God, that He will even answer *my* questions? Who am I to God?"

"God has been speaking to you your whole life, young man. You just didn't know it." He paused. "And as for your question of who the right God is, for me, the right God is the one who has been there for me all along, the one who kept me strong when I had nothing and no one, the one who watched out for me while I was out in these streets selling drugs and doing whatever else my hands could do—the one who, no matter how far I went, knew just how to come and get me and bring me where I needed to be. That's the right God for me. And you will find Him too. Just keep on searching."

"Well, we'll see," said Rondell, feeling like this conversation was getting just a little too deep for him. "I'll keep searching like you said, but I don't think I'll be coming back to church. It's not for me."

The pastor put his hand on Rondell's shoulder. "Believe me, I have been exactly where you are right now, and I can tell you, you'll be back. Just come when you're ready."

Rondell shook his head.

The pastor chuckled. "I'll see you around. Stay safe out here."

"You too," said Rondell.

The pastor got in his car, started it up, backed out of his spot, and waved as he drove off.

Rondell just stood there, taking in everything he had said.

***

Faleesha was walking back from her last class of the day. She could not wait to get to her room. She had cramps and a headache, and all she wanted was sleep.

She passed a few small groups of students standing around talking and hanging out. She said hi to a few people that she knew from her classes.

She passed by the student center building, then she heard a loud female voice coming from the front steps.

"LONDA! There she go! There she go!"

Faleesha turned around, trying to see who they were looking for. She saw a few people coming toward her with their cell phones pointed at her. She looked in another direction, confused, and saw Shalonda and three of her friends coming straight toward her.

Faleesha felt heat rushing all through her body as Shalonda and her friends stopped right in front of her, and a crowd formed around them.

"AH, SHIT! WORLD STAR!" some guy from the crowd shouted.

"What's going on?" said Faleesha to Shalonda, trying to remain calm.

"Didn't I tell you to stay away from my man, bitch?"

"Shalonda, what are you talking about?" said Faleesha, her head swimming. She was starting to feel the need to throw up.

"I *told* you," Shalonda said, stepping closer to her. "Stay away from Dee. But you can't seem to follow directions. But just so you know, Boo Boo, I had him the other night, and it was *all* good!" She nastily ran her hands down her body.

"What are you talking about?" Faleesha repeated.

"Bitch, don't you get it? Me and Rondell went at it three times in one night, and he was the best I ever had. I rocked his world in ways you could only dream of. So once again, I'm telling you to stay the fuck away from *my* man!"

Faleesha's heart dropped. She could not believe what she had just heard. Tears welled in her eyes, but she blinked them back. "You slept with him?" she said.

"Yeah, that's right," said Shalonda, rolling her neck with an attitude. "And honey, let me tell you, it was *good*."

Faleesha stood there for a moment then stepped back. "Well, I'm glad y'all are happy." She turned to walk away.

"Bitch, who you think you getting sarcastic with?" said Shalonda, but Faleesha kept walking.

"Londa, you going to let her do you like that?" said one of her friends.

"Hit her!" said the other one.

Shalonda spoke again, this time her voice full of aggression. "You not going to just walk away from me!"

Before Faleesha could turn around, she felt herself being dragged backward onto the ground by her hair and then punched in the face.

"NO-O-O-O!" She heard an angry male voice, and she felt herself being lifted off the ground. It was Tyrone, Rondell's friend. Mike was also there, and he was the one who yelled at Shalonda.

Two other guys were holding Shalonda and her friends back, but they were fighting to get loose.

"THIS IS NOT 'BOUT TO GO DOWN LIKE THAT!" Mike thundered. "Y'ALL RATCHET ASS THOTS IS NOT 'BOUT TO JUMP ON HER!"

With that, Mike and Tyrone pushed through the crowd, their arms supporting Faleesha, protecting her from harm.

"YOU LUCKY, BITCH!" said Shalonda. "I'll see your ass next time."

"No you won't!" said Mike. "I'll hit a bitch, and it'll be you. Try me."

At those words, Shalonda shut up.

When they were out of earshot, Mike turned to Faleesha. "You okay?"

She nodded and sniffled, tears streaming down her face. "Thank you, guys."

"Aw, anytime, sweetheart," said Tyrone.

"Yeah, anytime," said Mike.

When they were a safe distance away, Tyrone stopped and chuckled. "Yo, Mike," he said, "I didn't know you had that much *bass* in your voice. You sounded like Mufasa, my nigga! NO-O-O-O-O!" he said, laughing and mimicking Mike's defense of Faleesha.

They all burst out laughing.

"Shut up, Ty!" said Mike, pushing on his shoulder.

"For real!" said Tyrone. "I'm 'bout to hire you to be *my* bodyguard."

"Y'all are so silly!" said Faleesha, still laughing.

"There you go," said Tyrone, sweetly. "No more crying."

"Thanks for making me laugh," said Faleesha. "I've never been in a fight in my life."

"Oh, it's no problem," said Tyrone. "And just so you know, they didn't mark you up or anything. Your face is still as beautiful as ever."

Faleesha blushed at those words.

"But what I *really* wanna know is," he said, turning to Mike, "was you really 'bout to hit Shalonda?"

Mike sucked his teeth. "No!" he said. "I would never put my hands on no female, but she ain't have to know that."

"*My* nigga," said Tyrone, imitating Denzel Washington from the movie *Training Day*.

"Tyrone, you are so silly!" said Faleesha, feeling so much better now.

***

It turned out that the people who recorded the incident between Faleesha and Shalonda had put it on social media.

There were countless videos set to different kinds of music and themes, all of which showed her being dragged down by her hair and punched in the face. They all conveniently stopped at that part. No one showed the part where Mike and the others stepped in to help her.

Along with the videos, she was constantly tagged by people who posted memes of her on the ground. All of them had captions saying she got the ultimate beat-down.

To make matters worse, some freshman made a rap song and a music video called "I'll Go *Shalonda* on that Hoe" featuring snippets of the incident along with a new dance he created mimicking Faleesha being dragged back and punched in the face.

As soon as the music video was on the internet, whenever she walked down the hallway, groups of guys broke out dancing, saying, "I'll go *Shalonda* on that hoe!" bursting into laughter afterward.

Faleesha was considering dropping all of her classes and going back home.

She had come to this school to be in a better environment, to lead people to Christ, and to get closer to God. Although she had gotten closer to God, no one around her seemed interested in Jesus, and she was now the laughingstock of the entire school.

She made her way to her psychology class and sat all the way in the last row, far from her usual seat in the front of the room. More students filed in. Finally, Chris came in and sat in the last row as well, a few seats over from her.

Faleesha felt herself heating up. She had forgotten that Chris usually sat in the back row! She silently prayed that he wouldn't say anything to her because she didn't think she could take any more drama.

They sat in the class waiting for Dr. Spandinelli to arrive. A few students across the classroom turned around in their seats, talking to each other. Others sat with their heads down, waiting for the class to get on and over with so that they could go back to their rooms and sleep.

So far, Faleesha hadn't heard anyone mentioning the fiasco that had occurred with her and Shalonda—yet. She hoped it stayed that way, because she was sick of it.

At that moment, the person in front of her turned around to face her. It was Jake, a guy who usually sat in the front, like she did.

"Hey, Faleesha, right?" he said, leaning toward her.

"Yes?" she said, feeling tense.

"I'm Jake, and I'm a reporter for the school's underground newspaper. We cover trending stories that occur around the campus."

He held out his hand for her to shake it. She shook it with hesitation.

"I just wanted to thank you because your incident with Shalonda has really put us on the map. Almost all of the videos and memes we've created have gone viral, and I'm sure you've heard the Shalonda song everyone's been singing lately."

Faleesha's ears felt like they were on fire.

"*You* put all of those pictures and videos out?" she asked, keeping her voice steady.

"Most of them, yes." He looked proud of himself.

"Why would you do something like that?"

"Because drama sells, honey. But anyway, that's not what I wanted to talk to you about." He shifted in his seat to face her more directly. "What I *really* wanted to say was, we interviewed Shalonda the other day, and she had a lot to say about you. What I wanted to know was would you be willing to share your side of the story? I'm sure everyone would love to hear from the victim herself."

Faleesha could not believe what she was hearing. "No!" she exclaimed, louder than she meant to.

"No?" He looked confused.

"I can't even believe you guys would do something like that to someone. Do you realize how much you could hurt people?"

"Oh, it'll blow over," he said, totally disregarding her feelings. "But since it's hot now, we need you to share your side."

"No. I'm not doing that."

"Maybe you don't understand what I'm saying—"

Jake was cut off by Chris of all people.

"She heard you just fine. She doesn't want to do it, so leave her alone wit' your fake reporter ass."

"*Excuse* me?" said Jake.

"You heard what I said."

"Weren't you just out blasting her in the hallway a couple of months ago?"

"And your point is?"

"Well, this is an A and B conversation—"

"And I'm about to C your ass out," said Chris. "Matter of fact," he said, standing up, "how about I whoop your ass right now on camera and post that shit to your website? How 'bout we see how much *that* sells, huh?"

Jake's face reddened, and he turned around, picked up his things, got up, and raced out the door of the classroom. He almost knocked over Dr. Spandinelli as she entered the classroom.

"Whoa, what got into *him*?" she said, looking out the door as he scurried down the hall.

"Bitch ass nigga," said Chris under his breath.

***

Ironically, Jake became the butt of many jokes after Chris shut him down. Someone recorded the incident in the classroom, thinking that Jake and Chris were going to fight. They posted the part of the video where Jake was running out of the classroom, and titled it "Fake Ass Reporter Gets Sonned."

Soon after that, the incident with Faleesha and Shalonda took a turn for the better. New videos were posted that showed the part where Mike came on the scene and shouted, "N-O-O-O-O!" Someone had edited it by adding some scenes from the *Lion King* and *Planet of the Apes*.

Remixes of the "Shalonda" song called "I'll Go Mufasa on that Bitch" and "King Konging on These Hoes" started circulating. The dance to both songs was an imitation of Mike yelling at Shalonda and her friends, and someone added in a part where you beat your fists against your chest like an ape. The remixes took over the popularity of the original song, and now everyone joked about Mike being Faleesha's bodyguard.

Mike didn't really sweat it. He and Tyrone seemed to get a kick out of all the attention. Everyone on campus had always known that Mike was a sweetheart, but now, whenever he walked down the halls, a girl would yell out, "Mike! *Save* me!" in an exaggeratedly helpless voice, and a guy would jump to her rescue, shouting, "N-O-O-O-O!" in a deep voice while beating his chest with his fists.

Faleesha chuckled and shook her head. People were so silly. She was just glad that she wasn't in the spotlight anymore. It had been almost two weeks since the incident with Shalonda, and things were finally starting to die down.

She sat in her room by herself having a quiet afternoon, startled when she heard a knock on her door. She got up to answer it. "Who is it?" she said.

"Us!" said Rashonda.

Faleesha opened her door, and Rashonda and Maria came in giggling.

"What are you guys laughing about?"

"Girl, did you see the latest Mufasa video?" said Rashonda. "They are really blowing Mike all out of proportion."

"Which one?"

"I'll show you!" She pulled up the video on her phone. This video portrayed Mike as part of the Bobby Shmurda video for the song "Hot Nigga," and someone had photoshopped the actor Terry Crews shirtless onto Mike with gorilla arms beating his chest as he shouted, "N-O-O-O-O!"

They were rolling with laughter by the time the video finished.

"They really need to stop!" said Faleesha, fighting to catch her breath.

"Girl, I know!" said Rashonda, wiping her eyes. "But Mike is mad sexy, though, with his chocolate self."

"I know, girl," said Maria. "I always thought he was gorgeous."

"Don't you have a man?" said Faleesha to Rashonda.

"So? That don't mean I can't look."

"True," said Maria.

"But anyways, we need to hook him up with somebody. He is too fine and too sweet not to have a girlfriend."

"Rashonda!" said Faleesha.

"What?"

Maria added, "Girl, you always up in somebody's business. What if he's not looking for anyone right now?"

"Trust me, honey," said Rashonda. "Men are *always* looking. We just gotta find out his type."

"You are too much," said Faleesha.

"He did used to talk to this girl named Kiki back in high school, but she was wack," said Rashonda.

"What happened?" said Maria.

"Now who's nosy?" Rashonda said.

"We need details!" said Maria

"Okay, well, from what Shelly told me, Kiki dumped Mike for some other dude because she thought Mike was too nice. The other dude turned her out, and now she's a number one THOT."

"Dang, that's deep," said Maria. "So he hasn't been with anyone since?"

"Not that anyone knows of. But he's a good man, so we gotta find somebody for him."

"Yes, we do," said Maria, already pondering the options.

"So anyway," said Rashonda, turning back to Faleesha, "I am so glad that the video of you and Shalonda is done circulating. I can't tell you how many people I almost smacked for doing that stupid dance. Talking about some 'I'll go Shalonda on that Hoe.' B*tch, *where*? Wit' her non-fighting ass."

She shook her head in disgust then snapped back to attention. "Oh, I am so sorry, Faleesha. I shouldn't be doing all this cussing in front of you."

"It's okay," said Faleesha.

"But seriously, though. We need to get you some lessons or something."

"Lessons for what?"

"I hated to see her on that video pulling your hair and hitting you like that. She is so lucky I wasn't there."

"I'm not a fighter," said Faleesha.

"Well, I am," said Rashonda. "You sure you don't want me to get her?"

"No, I'm okay."

"You sure, now? Cuz all you need to do is say the word, and I will do her dirty, drag her ass down the steps and pull all them tracks out."

"Rashonda, you are so mean!" said Faleesha, but she couldn't help laughing.

"Talkin 'bout she from Brooklyn," said Rashonda, enjoying the attention. "According to Tyrone, who lives down the street from her, she ain't even from New York! She's from some no-name town in Connecticut."

"Really?" said Faleesha.

"Yeah, girl, I got *all* the goods."

"I'm sure you do!"

Changing the subject, Rashonda said, "Hey, Maria, what's up with you and Tyrone lately anyway?"

Maria's eyelids fluttered slightly. "What do you mean?"

"He asked about you the other day when I was talking to him and Mike. He was practically drooling when he mentioned your name, so what's up?"

"Nothing. We're just friends."

"Mmm-hmm. Don't tell me you let him in the cookie jar."

"What?" Maria said, looking bewildered.

"You know what I'm talking about. You giving him the goods?"

Maria's face reddened and her mouth dropped open.

"Rashonda, leave that girl alone," said Faleesha, a quiet warning in her voice. "You really are too much."

"Why everybody always on my back?" said Rashonda. "I just want to know—"

She stopped talking when her phone rang. Her eyes widened when she looked at the caller ID.

"It's Shelly!" she gasped.

"Answer it!" said Faleesha.

"Yes, go!" said Maria, gesturing for her to hurry up.

None of them had had the chance to speak to Shelly since she tried to end her life. Only her parents were allowed in her hospital room, and even now that she was at home, her parents weren't letting anyone near her.

"Hel-lo!" Rashonda sang into the phone, trying too hard to sound cheerful. "Honey, how are you?"

"What's she saying?" said Maria.

Rashonda held her finger up. She chuckled. "Girl, that's Maria. Me, her, and Faleesha all here talking. We miss you, girl."

She paused for a moment. "Okay." She turned to the others and said, "She misses us too!"

"Aw, teardrop!" said Faleesha.

"Tell her we can't wait to see her," said Maria.

"Maria said we can't wait to see you," said Rashonda to Shelly, then she paused again. "Of course, girl! We will be right over!" She hung up the phone excitedly and jumped to her feet.

"She said she wants us to come over!"

"YAY!" Faleesha and Maria said, clapping their hands in unison.

"Wait. How are we going to get there?" said Maria. None of them had a car. Rashonda reached into her purse and pulled out some keys.

Dangling them from her fingers, she said in a singsong voice, "My cousin Craig let me borrow his car!"

They excitedly made their way to the car and hopped in when Faleesha got an idea.

"Wait!" she said.

"What?" said Rashonda, checking her rearview mirror.

"We should get her a gift."

"Yes!" said Maria.

They made their way to a gift shop and purchased some beautiful flowers and a teddy bear.

When they got to Shelly's house, they got out of the car and hurried to the front door.

"I can't wait to see her!" said Maria.

"Me either," said Faleesha. They rang the doorbell.

A woman who had to be Shelly's mother answered the door. "Hello, ladies," she said.

"Hello," they said in unison.

"I'm Rashonda, and this is Maria and Faleesha," said Rashonda, introducing everyone to Shelly's mother.

"Oh, so you're Faleesha." Shelly's mother looked concerned.

"What's going on?" said Faleesha.

"Well, I don't . . . I don't know how to tell you this, but just before you got here, Shelly said she didn't want you to come. I tried to get her to call you guys and tell you, but she wouldn't. She said she only wants to talk to Rashonda and Maria."

Faleesha felt like she had been stabbed in the heart. Maria and Rashonda looked shocked to hear this.

"I'm so sorry," said Shelly's mother. "She's been in and out of moods since she came home. I would invite you in, but I don't want to set her off."

"It's okay," Faleesha said in a small voice. "I can wait in the car."

"Are you sure?" said Shelly's mother.

"Yes, I'll be fine." She nodded her head for emphasis, convincing herself. "You guys can go on in."

Rashonda handed her the keys. "Here," she said. "You can turn the heat on as long as you want. It's very cold out here."

"Thanks," said Faleesha, taking the keys.

"We won't stay too long," said Maria.

"Yeah," said Rashonda.

"Okay," said Faleesha.

She walked back to the car, cranked the engine, blasted the heat, then put her head in her hands and sobbed.

***

Rondell, Mike, and Tyrone were walking to the corner store a few blocks from their dorm.

"Bruh, I have no idea why I let you convince us to walk to this store," said Tyrone, rubbing his hands together to keep them warm.

Rondell sucked his teeth. "Man, shut up. It's not even that cold out here."

"Speak for yourself," said Mike, hunching his shoulders against the cold wind.

"Man, do y'all want to go back to the dorm or something?" Rondell pointed his thumb toward the dorm.

"Nah, we made it this far. Might as well get to the store and get Rondell's errand over with," said Tyrone, giving his friend a good-natured shove.

"Stop complaining then," said Rondell.

Just then, two girls walked past them from the other direction. After they passed, they turned around to get another look at the guys, and one of them spoke.

"Hey!" she said.

They turned to face the girls.

"Hey, is your name Mike—from the Mufasa videos?"

"Yeah, that's me," Mike said with a reluctant grin, shoving his hands in his jeans pockets and hunching his shoulders in embarrassment.

"Damn, you're even sexier in person!" she said.

Mike blushed. "Thanks."

"Oh, my gosh! I can't believe it's really you!" said the other girl.

Mike looked even more embarrassed.

"Well, anyway," the first girl said, taking out a pen and some paper. "Take my number. I need a real man in my life."

She handed Mike the paper, then she and her friend walked away. Mike crumpled the paper and threw it in a nearby trashcan.

"What are you doing, man?" said Tyrone.

"That's the third one this week!" said Mike.

"So what?"

"I'm not interested."

"Why not?"

"Cuz none of them actually want *me*. They just caught up in the hype over that video."

"Bruh, you better *cherish* this, man! You ain't got to marry nobody, but there's nothing wrong with hanging out with a couple of beautiful women."

"I'm not looking for anyone right now."

"Why not? I never really see you trying to get at nobody."

"I'm looking for something real, and I haven't found it yet."

"But if you ain't trying to holla at nobody, then how you gonna know for sure?"

"I guess I just don't trust too easily due to some things that happened in my past." He looked at Rondell.

Rondell nodded, understanding where he was coming from.

Tyrone looked back and forth between them.

"What happened?" he said.

"Nothing," said Mike.

"Man, every guy gets his heart broken by a female at least once. But that don't mean to just completely shut down."

"I understand that, and that has happened too. But this is something a little different."

He looked at Rondell again.

"I feel you," said Rondell.

"What are y'all talking about?" said Tyrone. "What's the big secret?"

"Just something in the past. Don't worry about it."

"But for a minute there, Mike, I was worried you was trying to take *my* girl," said Rondell, changing the subject.

Mike looked at Rondell for a second then pushed his shoulder. "Man, shut up. You know I would never do that."

"I don't know," Tyrone said, getting in on the joke. "You played that bodyguard role real well."

"Forget y'all," said Mike.

"Nah, I'm just messing with you," said Rondell. "But I do appreciate you stepping in for Faleesha—both of y'all."

"No doubt," said Tyrone.

"You know it," said Mike.

Tyrone chuckled. "Shoot, even Chris stood up for her!"

"I know!" said Rondell. "I appreciate that too."

"Yo, Dee, you know you gotta squash that, right?"

"I'll see him when I see him."

"Aw, come on," said Tyrone.

"Eyo, my man," said a young Hispanic man who walked up to them. He was speaking to Rondell.

"Hey, what's up?" said Rondell, trying to figure out if he knew the guy from somewhere.

"My man, can I talk to you for a second?"

"Uh . . . sure," said Rondell, confused.

He handed Mike, Tyrone, and Rondell each a gospel tract.

"The Hood Meets Jesus," said Rondell, reading the title.

"It's my testimony," said the man. "I tell about how I got locked up and did a nine-year bid for hustling. Then I finally found out through the Bible that when you live by the sword, you die by the sword, feel me?"

"Uh-huh," said Rondell, wondering where he was going with this.

"So, once God saved me, I started going to church, and He cleaned me up from the inside out. I put the church name and address on the back of the pamphlet."

"Oh, okay," said Rondell, looking at the back.

"Hey, Rondell, this is Faleesha's church!" said Mike, recognizing the address. "Pastor Bryant, right?" he said to the man.

"Yes, he's an awesome pastor, man. He really mentored me when I was locked up, and he helped me get a job when I got out. He's a good dude, my man. You guys should come on down. We need more men on the street team, cuz the ladies is out here killing it."

He gestured toward a group of young women talking to someone across the street.

"True," said Rondell.

"So, what do you think? You want to come down and visit sometime?"

"We'll see," said Rondell.

"Alright," said the man, looking relieved. "I hope to see you soon. And you can come as you are. Don't worry about a dress code or anything."

"Cool," said Rondell.

"What's your name, man?" said Mike.

"Julio. I'm sorry, I forgot." He looked a bit nervous like he was new at this. He shook their hands. "Well, it was nice meeting you fellas, and I hope to see you at the church."

"A'ight, man," said Rondell.

"A'ight, God bless each of you."

Rondell stared at him as he made his way down the street.

"Yo, Dee, you alright?" said Mike.

"Yeah, man."

"What's up?" said Tyrone.

"This is the second time in a few weeks that somebody from that church tried to get me to come visit."

He told Mike and Tyrone about seeing the pastor at the grocery store the other day.

"Well, it sounds like God might be trying to speak to you," said Tyrone.

Rondell stared at him. "What you mean?"

"My grandmother is heavy into church, and she always says that you can tell God is trying to talk to you when you keep hearing the same thing over and over again."

Rondell froze. He just realized that what Tyrone said exactly matched what the pastor told him in the parking lot about hearing God speak to you. This was really getting weird.

"What's up?" said Tyrone.

"Nothing," said Rondell, brushing it off. "Let's get to the store."

***

Maria and Rashonda went back a few times to see Shelly, who had taken a leave of absence from school for a couple of weeks, doing her work from home until she felt stable enough to return.

Faleesha was bothered by the fact that Shelly still refused to talk to her. She had been praying about the situation, but she really wished there was a way to communicate to Shelly and let her know that there was no way she could have known that Gesston had been using Shelly to try to get with her.

She sighed and sat back on her couch, reflecting on everything that had occurred within the past few weeks. It seemed like everywhere she turned, there was drama. Every time she tried to bounce back, something new happened.

She hadn't seen or heard from Rondell since he cursed her out. She thought about trying to call or text him, but she didn't know what to say.

She was still hurting from the fact that he had slept with Shalonda. Even though Faleesha had never been in an actual relationship with him, it still hurt to hear that someone she had such strong feelings for had slept with someone else.

And what's worse, Shalonda hadn't thought twice about rubbing it in her face.

What confused her about the situation was that Rondell had always said that he didn't have feelings for Shalonda, and he acted as if he was repulsed by the thought of being with her, but then he goes and sleeps with her, three times in one night!

Faleesha couldn't understand it.

She sat there, lost in her thoughts, glad that she was along and didn't have to talk to anybody when her cell phone rang.

"Hello?" she said, trying not to sound annoyed. It was Maria.

"Hey," Maria said. "Can we talk? Are you alone?"

"Sure, come on up. I'm in my room. And yes, I'm alone, of course."

"Okay, I'm coming now."

"See ya."

Faleesha sat there, puzzled. She wondered what Maria wanted to talk to her about.

About two minutes later, Maria was at the door.

"Hey," said Faleesha, opening the door to let her in. "That was quick."

"Hey, girl." Maria walked in and looked around. "You sure you're alone? Rashonda's not here?"

"No, why?"

Maria looked relieved. "I want to talk to you about something, but I don't want to do it in front of her."

"What's up?" said Faleesha, gesturing toward her couch as she sat down.

"So, first off, I want to say sorry once again for how Shelly won't talk to you."

"Oh, that's not your fault."

"I know, but I feel so bad because she's really blaming you for what Gesston did to her. Me and Rashonda tried to convince her that you had nothing to do with it, but she won't listen. We even tried to remind her that you had feelings for Rondell, but she won't budge."

"Wow," said Faleesha. "Well, hopefully she will see it sooner or later."

"I know. It feels so awkward with just the three of us hanging out without you. And then, when it's just me, you, and Rashonda, it feels weird because Shelly isn't there."

"True."

"And I also wanted to talk to you about the situation that happened with that girl Shalonda."

Faleesha's heart rate quickened. "What about it?"

"I know that everyone has been bothering you about it, and you might feel embarrassed. But I want to tell you, don't be embarrassed, because she didn't even really do much. She hit you once and pulled your hair. She didn't even bruise you, so it's not that serious. I know everyone tried to make it like she put you in a coma or something, but it really wasn't that serious."

"Thanks," said Faleesha, feeling a little weird. Why was Maria saying all this?

"Trust me, I've been jumped before, and it wasn't pretty." She lifted her shirt to show Faleesha some marks on her abdomen. "See that?" she said, pointing to the scars.

"Yeah."

"One hundred sixty-eight stitches."

"Wow!"

"Yeah, girl. I got stabbed. Four girls jumped me at a bus stop in high school. I had a concussion and everything."

"Wow," said Faleesha. "I'm so sorry to hear that."

"And it was all over some guy that I wasn't even dating."

"Wow," Faleesha repeated. "That's crazy."

"I know," said Maria. "So don't feel embarrassed."

"Thank you—really," said Faleesha, meaning it this time. She had no idea Maria had gone through something like that.

"Mmm-hmm. But I had to talk to you about something else." She tucked her hair behind her ear then stared down at her hands.

"What's going on?"

"It's about Tyrone."

"What's going on?"

"Well, like I said, I didn't want to talk about it in front of Rashonda because she has a big mouth."

"Okay," said Faleesha.

"Not like that, but I didn't want her embarrassing me any further because I already feel so bad." Her voice cracked.

"What's wrong?" said Faleesha, grabbing some tissues and handing them to her.

"We did sleep together, more than once." She started bawling. "I just got saved a couple of months ago, and I already messed up big time. God probably won't even forgive me. I'm probably going straight to Hell!"

"He forgives you," said Faleesha, rubbing her back. "Don't worry about that. He forgives you."

"I don't think so. I knew what I was doing was wrong, and I did it anyway. Rashonda told me before it even happened not to go with him, but I liked him. We started hanging out and calling and texting, and then one night, we were in his room watching movies, and we started kissing. Then we did it. I told him it couldn't happen again, but we kept doing it. It's been going on for weeks."

"Maria . . . ."

"I know God won't forgive me because I already said sorry the first time, but then I kept doing it."

"Maria, listen. We all fall into temptation. All of us."

"Do you?" said Maria.

"Yes!" she said. She told Maria what happened between her and Rondell, and how she went to the pastor's wife for counseling. "So you see, we all make mistakes, but God forgives us."

"How come you never told us what happened?"

"I was ashamed," said Faleesha. "I tend to keep things to myself, but now I wish I'd said something at the time, because I didn't know that you were pretty much going through the same thing."

"We should talk more often," said Maria.

"Yeah, and why don't we both start going out with that group that Deborah was talking about—she's the pastor's wife. She said she meets with a group of girls who are all our age."

"I would like that," said Maria. "Because there's a lot of things that I don't understand, and it would be good to be around other Christian girls who go through the same things."

"I agree. So why don't we go to their next meeting?"

"Yes, let's do it!" Maria smiled.

"Great!" said Faleesha, her spirits lifted once again.

Chapter 18

Rondell couldn't stop thinking about all the things that had been happening lately. He remembered the decisions he made at the beginning of the school year because he wanted to change his life. He stopped smoking and drinking, and sleeping with every girl he met.

Then he met Faleesha, and he thought she was the girl he could finally settle down with, but then she played him when things got serious. He understood where she was coming from being a Christian and all, but he didn't see why they couldn't get involved with each other physically, especially since they had already connected on other levels.

It seemed like all of the effort he made to change his life amounted to nothing. He fought Chris, slept with Shalonda, and found comfort in the bottle. It seemed like he couldn't move forward because he was always falling backward.

And now it seemed like everybody was trying to get him to go to church! He had never set foot in a church building before going to Faleesha's church, and now, even though he had only seen her pastor twice, the man seemed to know everything about him. Rondell didn't understand what was going on.

Ever since his parents had gotten him out of foster care, they had tried to get him to come to their church, but he was never interested. He admired Jacob and them because they were cool dudes, even though they were kind of square.

It's just that he could never see himself being "that guy"—a church boy. He had grown up in the streets. How could he ever relate to the church life?

And even if he did try to get into the church thing, would God accept him? He'd done a lot of wrong in his life—selling drugs, fighting, stealing—the list went on and on. Why would God want somebody like him anyway?

These thoughts filled Rondell's mind as he left his last class of the day. He was wiped out after taking three exams in a row, and he just wanted to return to his room, eat, play some video games, and sleep.

He walked across the campus to the Student Center, jogged up the steps, grabbed something to eat so he could take it back to his room, and left the building. He was so out of it that he almost knocked over an older man who was standing on the steps passing out pamphlets that looked like little books.

"Oh, I'm sorry, sir," said Rondell, steadying the man.

"That's okay." He smiled.

Rondell looked at him, wondering why he was on the campus passing out books. He was Caucasian, and looked like he was in his sixties. He had a gentleness about his eyes, and Rondell immediately felt comfortable when he spoke.

"Why don't I give you one of these?" said the man. He handed Rondell one of the little books.

Rondell looked at it and saw that it was a copy of the New Testament. He looked up at the sky then back at the man. It seemed like he really couldn't get away from this God thing.

"Um, I don't want to take all your copies," Rondell said nervously, handing the New Testament back to the man, but he wouldn't take it.

The man smiled again. "Don't worry. I've got plenty more where that came from." He gestured toward a box.

"Have you read all of this?" said Rondell, flipping through the pages.

"Every word," said the man. He gave Rondell a warm smile. "And it didn't take too long to read, either."

"So you read all this," Rondell said in disbelief.

"I've been around a long while, and this book, and the God who inspired it, has helped me get through some of the most difficult times in my life."

"So what's it all about?" said Rondell. He didn't know why he felt so free to ask questions, but there was something about this man that made him feel so comfortable and welcome.

"Well, if I had to sum it up in one word, which is no small feat, if you ask me, I would say that it all boils down to love."

"Love?" Rondell repeated.

"Yup! God's love for you and me and the rest of this world."

"How do you know God loves you?" said Rondell.

"Well, have you ever heard the story of Jesus?" said the man.

Rondell shook his head. "No . . . not really. I mean, I know people think that He is the Son of God, and some people have tried to tell me about Him, but I wasn't really trying to hear it like that." Rondell put his head down.

The man put his hand on Rondell's shoulder. "You're not the only one."

Rondell looked up at him, surprised.

"See, I was a hardcore atheist, then one day, God knocked me right upside the head."

"Huh?" Rondell was confused.

"With life," the man continued. "Let me tell you my story. I don't think I introduced myself. My name is Dan."

"I'm Rondell."

"Good to meet you, Rondell. Here's the thing. I had no respect for anything related to God, church, or religion, but then one day I fell into some hard times. I was drowning in debt. I lost my job, my wife, and was on the verge of losing my children. And the most ironic thing about it all was that they were Christians. Tell me how that happened." He chuckled.

"So anyway," he continued, "like I said, I was down on my luck, and I had nowhere to turn. So I decided to try to pray one time, just to see if it worked. I always heard people talking about God answering prayers, so I decided to see if it actually worked. I didn't really know what to say, so I just said, 'God, if you're real, show yourself to me.' After that, I got up off of my knees, and I went right back to my miserable existence.

"Then, a series of strange circumstances happened. One day, I was sitting at a bar, and a woman came into the bar. She came directly up to me, I kid you not, and said, 'God told me to tell you that He is going to show Himself to you within the next three days.' I said 'What?', but she didn't say anything else. She just left the bar.

"Well, the next day, I wasn't really thinking much of it, but I got a phone call from a job that I had applied to six months prior. They told me that they had conducted over a hundred interviews, and I had been selected as the man for the job. I was blown away because I had only applied to the job on a whim. I figured I would never get it because I didn't really meet all of the qualifications.

"So anyway, the next day, my wife, who I had not spoken to in over a month, randomly called me and said that she and the kids were coming back home, and that God had told her that He was going to help us work out our relationship. This really blew me away because I hadn't spoken to her in over a month, and our last conversation was far from friendly.

"Then the last thing that happened, this thing really touched my heart in the greatest way possible. On the third day, my youngest son, who was about five years old, had his mother drive all the way across the town to give me a card that he had made that day all by himself. The card was simple. It said, 'You are the best daddy in the whole wide world.' When I saw that card, I broke down and cried like a baby, because that was exactly what I needed at that moment in my life, and God knew just what to send and who to send it through.

"That night, I got back down on my knees, and I said, 'God, this is it. I dedicate my life to you.' And I've never been the same since. I've gone through all kinds of trials and errors since then, but God has never left me, and I've found that He always keeps His word." With that, he held one of the New Testaments close to his chest.

Rondell blinked back tears. "That was deep, Dan. Thank you for telling me."

"Oh, no problem," said Dan. "I just hope I didn't bore you with all the details."

"Not at all."

"I've got an idea," said Dan. "How about you try this when you go back to your room. Pray and ask God to speak to you through the Bible, and after you pray, open it and read the first thing you see. Just try it out. I've done it before, and it really helped me get a great start in my relationship with God."

"Okay," said Rondell, nodding his head.

"Alright, well I won't take all of your time, but before you go, I have these really cool bookmarks that I've been giving out along with the Bibles." He reached down into the box, pulled out a bookmark, and handed it to Rondell. "There you go," he said. "That should help you keep your page."

When Rondell looked closely at the bookmark, he was stunned. On the front of it were some scriptures, but on the back were the name of Faleesha's pastor and the address of the church.

"You okay?" said Dan.

"Yeah," said Rondell, nodding. "Thank you for the Bible and for telling me what you went through."

"Anytime," said Dan.

Rondell walked down the rest of the steps, and made his way back to his dorm. When he got to his room, he ate his food then lay back on his bed and closed his eyes, resting. He lay there for a few moments, thinking about his conversation with Dan.

He wondered if what he said would really work. If he literally prayed right now then opened the Bible and read whatever his eyes landed on, would God really speak to him? What if it didn't work? Would that mean he was rejected? Would he get another chance?

Rondell didn't know what to do. The only thing he knew was that he was tired of the way his life was going, and he needed a change. He didn't know if God would answer his prayer like He did for Dan, but he figured it was worth a try.

He grabbed the little New Testament and put it on his bed, and then he knelt down on the floor and clasped his hands like he had seen some of the people in the church do when they prayed during the service. Then he closed his eyes.

"God . . . look, I don't know you, and I don't even know if you're real, or if you're even really hearing me right now. But I want you to speak to me. Please."

With that, he opened his eyes, got up, sat on the bed, and opened the New Testament. His eyes immediately fell on some words in the middle of the page. He read them out loud.

"*All things have been committed to me by my Father. No one knows the Son except the Father, and no one knows the Father except the Son and those to whom the Son chooses to reveal him.*

"*Come to me, all you who are weary and burdened, and I will give you rest. Take my yoke upon you and learn from me, for I am gentle and humble in heart, and you will find rest for your souls. For my yoke is easy and my burden is light.*"

At that moment, Rondell felt as if God was sitting right there next to him on the bed. For the first time in his life, he let his tears flow freely. He usually held them back because he didn't want anyone to think he was soft, but right now, he felt like God had heard him and understood him.

He cried for what felt like a long time.

When he was done, he wiped his eyes and blew his nose. Then he got up and decided to go for a drive.

***

Rondell pulled up in front of his parents' house. He hadn't been there in a couple of weeks, but he felt like he needed to talk to them.

He walked up to the front door and let himself in with his key.

When he got inside, he saw his mother and father sitting at the kitchen table, eating dinner.

"Delly!" His mother said, getting up and rushing over to give him a hug.

"Hey, Ma," he said, smiling.

"Hey, son," said his dad. He reached out to shake Rondell's hand.

"Hey, Pops."

"Is the car still running good?" said his father. Rondell's father had made sure that he always had a good running car ever since he improved his grades.

"Yeah, it's great. I love that Escalade."

"Good, good," said his father, nodding. "I'm glad to hear it."

"So, what brings you here looking all handsome with those long eyelashes?" said his mother. "I bet those girls at the school can't keep their eyes off of you."

"Come on, Ma," he said, blushing.

"There you go. That's my baby's smile."

"So what's up?" said his father.

Rondell stood silent for a moment. "Well . . . I wanted to talk to you . . . talk to both of y'all."

"About what? What's going on?" said his mother, looking concerned.

"Is everything okay, son?" His father looked worried as well.

It was at that moment that Rondell fully understood just how much his parents loved him. All the years and all the pain he had put them through after they got him out of foster care came rushing back to him. They had tried to reach out to him, but he had rebelled and rejected them.

Even though his father had always tried to support him, the two of them had never really opened up to each other like a father and son should do. It was the same with his mother. He was nicer to her over the years, but he still held on to many of his rebellious ways.

Rondell couldn't help it. He broke down and cried again, right there in front of his parents. His mother grabbed him in her arms and held him close. She hugged him like he had never been hugged before.

This was the hug he had longed for as a child, the hug he never received through all the years of pain and abuse he suffered in the system. He cried and held on to her like he never wanted to let her go.

His father joined in the hug, and all three of them stood there with tears streaming down their faces, hugging and holding each other with everything they had.

Rondell's mother spoke first.

"Why don't we go sit on the couch?" she said, gesturing toward the living room. "We were finished eating anyway."

Rondell nodded, and he and his father went over to the couch and sat down. Rondell sat in the middle, and his mother and father sat on either side of him. His mother handed each of them some tissues, and they all wiped their eyes and blew their noses.

"Look at us," said his father, laughing through his tears. "Crying like little babies."

Rondell looked at his mother, then at his father, and then they all burst out laughing. Their tears dried up as they laughed.

When they finally settled down, Rondell's father spoke first.

"So what brought this on? Did something upsetting happen to you recently?"

Rondell told them everything—about God, about the church, about how people kept inviting him; about Dan, and how he had taken his advice and prayed, and how he believed that God had spoken to him through the Bible.

"Thank you, Jesus!" his mother exclaimed when he was done. "Hallelujah!"

"Yes, glory to God!" said his father. "This is what we been waiting on."

"Yeah . . . ." said Rondell, his voice trailing off. Then he spoke again. "I want to apologize to y'all for all that I put you through when y'all got me out of the system. I didn't appreciate anything because I didn't believe you loved me or cared about me. But now I know that you do, and that you did all along."

"It was a hard time for all of us," his mother said in a quiet voice.

"Ain't like you haven't been through nothing as a result of our actions," said his father.

"I know that's right," said his mother. "If I hadn't been on drugs and your father hadn't got locked up, we could have provided a better life for you."

"That's real talk," said his father. "We think about that all the time, how things would have been different if we hadn't made the decisions we made."

Rondell put his hands on their backs and looked from one to the other. "But I'm glad y'all came back for me, and that y'all never let me go, no matter how bad I was to y'all."

"Well, even though it hurt for all of us, I just pray that we can push past this as a family," said his mother.

His father nodded. "I agree."

"Me too," said Rondell.

"So, what are you going to do now?" said his father.

"What you mean?" he said, looking at him.

"From what you're saying, it sounds like God is speaking to you. What are you going to do about it?"

Rondell sat in silence, thinking about this. Finally, he spoke. "I don't know yet. I guess I'll just see how it all plays out."

His father looked like he wanted to say something to him, but he decided against it. "Alright," he said. "Let's just see how it all plays out."

***

Faleesha sat on her couch deep in thought, her TV on mute. She felt like it was partially her fault that Maria had slept with Tyrone. If she had just opened up to her more and shared with her about the temptation she had faced with Rondell, maybe Maria would have felt like somebody was in her corner.

She felt like she had let Maria down, and that hurt. She knew that God was a forgiving God, but she still wished she could turn back time and make better decisions.

Then there was the situation with Shelly, and now Shelly refused to even see or talk to her, even though Shelly was supposed to be coming back to campus within the next couple of days. Faleesha figured that she just needed some space at first, but it didn't seem like things were improving at all.

She had been fired from her internship, attacked by Shalonda, had her name dragged through the mud on social media, and then to top it all off, she found out that Rondell had slept with her worst enemy.

"Lord, what am I doing wrong?" she said to herself as she traveled across campus. She was heading straight for her dorm and her bed. As she passed the Student Center, she heard someone calling out to her.

"Hello, Miss!" She turned and looked in the direction of the voice.

An older gentleman stood near the top of the stairs.

"Are you doing alright?" said the man.

Faleesha didn't usually talk to men she didn't know, but something about this man seemed so kind and welcoming, and it was a public place, so she walked up the stairs to where he stood.

"I want to give you this," he said, and he held out something to her. She immediately recognized it as a New Testament. This made her feel comfortable enough to talk to him.

"Oh, so you're a Christian too. Sometimes it can be a real struggle . . . . " she said, her voice trailing off.

"Well, hopefully this will cheer you up. As you were walking by, God spoke to me and said to tell you that your struggle is not in vain."

"Huh?" said Faleesha, blinking at his words.

"You've been through a lot lately, and God wants you to know that He is still right there with you, and that He's never left. There's a wonderful scripture that I think will really encourage you. Do you want me to mark it for you with a highlighter?"

"Sure," she said, handing back the New Testament he had given her. "Thanks."

He highlighted the verses he wanted her to read, and then he put in a bookmark and handed it to Faleesha.

"Hey, don't I know you from somewhere?" she said. The man looked very familiar.

He smiled. "Yes, I've seen you at church."

"Oh, yes!" she said. "That's it! You're in the senior choir, right?"

"Yep, that's me! Brother Dan!" he said, smiling.

"Well, thank you. I will definitely read this when I get to my room."

Dan nodded, and Faleesha left to go to her dorm. He was already chatting with another student by the time she had descended the steps. *What a great ambassador for the Lord*, she thought with a smile.

When she got to her room, she put all her stuff down, changed her clothes, and went to her sofa to read the highlighted scriptures.

She opened the Bible at the bookmark and saw that he had highlighted Matthew 5:10-12. She read the verses aloud because she wanted to hear the words as well as read them:

"Blessed are those who are persecuted because of righteousness, for theirs is the kingdom of heaven. Blessed are you when people insult you, persecute you, and falsely say all kinds of evil against you because of me. Rejoice and be glad, because great is your reward in heaven, for in the same way they persecuted the prophets who were before you."

When she finished reading, her heart was filled with joy. She hadn't been doing everything wrong!

"Thank you, Lord," she said.

***

Gesston was on his way to the corner store to pick up a couple of groceries. He had heard that Shelly had returned to campus two days ago. He felt horrible for what had happened to her because of his actions. He had hurt her deeply. He struggled to find the right words to say to her to apologize for using her.

He should have listened to Jacob. His friend had told him from the beginning that trying to use one girl to get another was a bad idea, but he didn't listen. He wanted to be cool, and he wanted Faleesha to like him, so he did everything he thought she would find impressive, but as it turned out, she just didn't want him.

Gesston was seriously considering cutting all his losses, giving up this new phase he was going through, and just going back to church. He knew at the bottom of his heart that was where he belonged, but something inside him kept holding him back.

Telling himself he would think about all that later, he parked his car at the curb and hopped out.

"What's up, pussy?" said a voice to his left. Gesston turned and saw Drake standing with a group of his friends. Gesston's entire demeanor changed.

He switched to his "gangsta" attitude.

"Whatchu just call me?" he said, hoping he sounded threatening.

"Ain't no cops around now," said Drake. "Let's get it poppin'."

"What, so you and your boys can jump me? Hell no, nigga. And besides, if I remember correctly, it was you that was flinching when the cops showed up last time, not me. I was ready."

"Yeah, whatever. I see you still talking reckless," said Drake. "But I still ain't seen no hands yet."

"Like I said, I'm not stupid, nigga."

Drake eyed his jewelry. "That's a real nice chain you got there."

"Yeah, that's right. I ball, nigga. That's what I do."

"You better hold on to it real tight," said Drake, "just in case it gets snatched."

"And who's gonna snatch it, huh? You? Try me, bitch. Then you'll see how I really get down."

"You ain't worth it," said Drake, chuckling.

"But I'm saying though. You seeing me right now. You was just saying a minute ago that you wanted the hands. Let's get it, nigga."

"Yo, hit that nigga, Drake," said one of his boys.

"Nah, nah, I'm 'bout to go somewhere." Drake moved toward his car. "But I'll see you around."

"Yeah, nigga, whatever." Gesston gestured, trying his best to look street. "Now who's the pussy?"

Drake and his boys got in his car and drove off.

When Gesston got out of the store, he looked around in every direction to make sure that Drake and his boys hadn't come back for him. Rondell had told him a while back that they were punks who couldn't fight, but they would probably use their guns.

The coast was clear, so Gesston hopped in his car and drove back to campus. He waited at the elevator, which seemed to take forever, and when the doors opened, his jaw dropped in surprise. Shelly walked out of the elevator with Maria and Rashonda and went right past him without a word.

"Shelly!" he said.

"What?" She turned and looked at him, her eyes narrowed.

"I've been wanting to talk to you."

"About what? There's nothing for us to talk about. You played me, and I got over it. So what?" She put her hands on her hips.

"I want to apologize."

"Boy, bye!" she said, waving her hand to dismiss his words. "I don't want to hear your sorry ass apology. You ain't shit, just know that, fuckin asshole."

"Shelly, I was hoping—"

"I don't give a fuck what you hoping for. You wack as shit, and I don't want to ever talk to you again, get it?"

"I understand that, but—"

"So why are you still talking?"

"Because I just want to—"

"Here's what I want you to do," said Shelly, stepping closer to him. "I want you to go on up to your little dorm room and continue being the fake ass, phony ass, hypocritical ass nigga that you've always been with me. I can't believe I actually fell for you. That was the dumbest thing I ever did in my life. But it's over now. We're done, and I have nothing to say to you. Bye."

"Shelly—"

"I said, BYE, BITCH!" With that, she and her two friends headed toward the exit doors.

"I'm sorry," Gesston called after her.

Shelly twirled around. "Oh, I don't know if you're sorry now, but you will be real soon. You gonna get yours. Believe that."

She twirled around and continued walking with her friends. Gesston considered going after them to make her listen to him, but he decided it wasn't worth it. She probably wouldn't listen anyway. His shoulders slumped in defeat as he pressed the button again and waited for the elevator doors to open.

***

Shelly woke up to a knock on her door. She looked at her clock and sucked her teeth. It was 7:30 a.m. She got up and walked to the door, ready to cuss out whoever was knocking this early.

"This better not be Gesston," she muttered. "Who is it?" she called out.

"It's me!" said Rashonda.

Shelly opened the door. "What are you doing at my door at the crack of dawn, girl?" She scrutinized Rashonda's appearance. "And why are you wearing makeup so early in the morning?"

"Please don't hate me," said Rashonda.

"Why would I hate you?" said Shelly, staring at her sideways.

"I need a favor." She clasped her hands.

"What kind of favor?" said Shelly, already not liking where this conversation was going.

"Um . . . so my cousin Craig backed out on me again, and I promised Tyrone I would see him today!"

"Rashonda!"

"Shelly, please! It's—"

Shelly held up her hand to stop her. "Uh-uh," she said. "Not this time. This is about the third or fourth time that you've come knocking at my door early in the morning asking for a ride."

"But Shelly," Rashonda whined. "It's an emergency!"

"An emergency, huh?" Shelly wasn't buying it.

"Yes!"

"What kind of emergency?" Shelly asked in a droll tone.

"It's his birthday, and I HAVE to see him!"

"Today is his birthday?" Shelly didn't believe it.

"Yes, girl, I brought his birth certificate. I got proof, honey." She quickly pulled out Tyrone's birth certificate from her purse and showed it to Shelly.

"You actually brought his birth certificate to convince me? You're unbelievable. Or do you carry it around with you all the time?"

"That's my man, boo," she said. "I got everything."

"You are truly crazy," said Shelly, shaking her head.

"Look, honey, I have to see my man by any means necessary, girl."

"Of course you do," said Shelly, shaking her head.

"So will you take me to see him? Please? Ple-e-e-ease?"

Shelly rolled her eyes. "Yes," she said, sighing in resignation. "Let me get dressed."

***

It seemed to Shelly that she had done this a hundred times: drive to the facility where Tyrone was being held, listen to Rashonda prattling the whole way, go through the interminable waiting process then the annoying security checks, then finally see Tyrone and watch the whole scenario play out of their joyful reunion. It was getting old.

"Hey, baby! Happy birthday!" said Rashonda. She jumped into his arms.

"Hey, girl, you trying to knock me over?" He chuckled as he hugged her tightly. "Hey Shell," he said to Shelly in an offhand greeting, acknowledging her presence.

"Hey," she said. *No thanks for bringing your baby here to see you, huh Tyrone?* She couldn't help it. She was tired of always being the onlooker.

"You been alright?" Tyrone asked Shelly.

"As good as I can be," she said.

Rashonda interrupted.

"Bae, I wanted to bring you a gift, but I couldn't, so I just put some extra in your commissary."

"You didn't have to do that."

"I wanted to. I can't wait 'til you get out of here."

"Me either," he said. "So, did you think about what we discussed?"

"Yeah, I thought about it." Rashonda scrunched her nose and looked at Shelly.

"What?" said Shelly.

"Tyrone keeps asking me to go to Jacob and them's church, but he won't tell me why."

"Church?" said Shelly, wrinkling her nose. "Why you want her to go to church?"

"She'll see," he said. "Will you go with her?"

"Um . . . not me," said Shelly. "I am never stepping foot in no church again."

Rashonda looked shocked. "Why?"

"Too many *hypocrites*," she said, "especially one whose name starts with a G, if you get my meaning."

"I feel you, but that shouldn't stop you from going," said Rashonda. "Plenty of good people in the church. They're not all like him."

"So why don't *you* go?" said Shelly.

Rashonda was silent for once.

"Ooh, checkmate," said Tyrone, watching their interaction with interest.

"Exactly," said Shelly.

"But for real though, Shelly," said Tyrone, "you shouldn't let hypocrites stop you from going to church. Like Shonda said, there's hypocrites everywhere."

"When did you get all religious?" said Shelly.

"Yeah, why you keep asking me to go to church?" said Rashonda.

"Just go, Shonda," he urged gently. "You'll see when you get there."

"I don't know why you're being all mysterious," she said. "I'll think about it."

Just then, an alarm sounded and a voice spoke over the intercom.

"DUE TO AN EMERGENCY SITUATION, ALL GUESTS MUST NOW LEAVE. VISITATION HOURS ARE OVER EFFECTIVE IMMEDIATELY."

"What's going on?" said Rashonda.

"Probably something stupid," said Tyrone. "But anyways, although I hate to see you go so soon, I appreciate you coming out on my birthday."

"Of course!" said Rashonda.

"I love you, girl."

"I love you too."

They hugged and kissed, then Tyrone said goodbye to Shelly. After that, the guards ushered them out.

When they got to the car, Rashonda stared at Shelly.

"What?" said Shelly.

"Why do you think Tyrone keeps trying to get me to go to church?"

"I have no idea," said Shelly.

"Yeah, me neither," said Rashonda.

***

Gesston was up at the corner store again. He was going to pick up a few things he forgot the other day because he was so nervous after his encounter with Drake. He parked at the curb, just like he always did.

When he got out, he heard a voice off to his side.

"Remember me?"

Gesston turned and saw Drake standing there, leaning against a light pole, staring at him, arms folded across his chest, alone this time. This situation didn't feel right. Gesston had never seen Drake alone except for that one time when he had almost hit him with his car.

"Fuck you talkin 'bout, Drake? I ain't got time for memory games, nigga." Gesston tried to sound hard, but he was really just covering up for the fact that he was terrified. His heart was racing. He had no idea what would happen next or how he would handle it.

"How 'bout we shoot the fair ones over in this alley?" Drake gestured toward an alley to his right.

Gesston thought about it, and something told him not to go down that alley, but he ignored it. He was desperate to prove something. "Whatever, nigga," he said. "Let's get this done." He figured that if he fought Drake and beat him up, Drake would leave him alone and stop provoking him every time he saw him.

He followed Drake into the alley. They walked far enough to where they were just barely visible from the street.

"Aight, nigga, we here now, so let's get it poppin'," said Drake. He looked a little awkward, so Gesston played off that.

He cracked his neck to the side. "Whatchu scared, nigga?"

Drake laughed. "Nah, nigga. Ain't nobody scared of you."

"So let's square up then." Gesston squared up against Drake.

Drake squared off as well.

They circled each other for a few minutes, neither one making a move.

Finally, Gesston got tired of playing around. "Hit me, nigga!" he said in frustration.

At those words, Drake swung wildly at Gesston, trying to catch him off guard. He lost his balance when he swung, so Gesston took advantage of the opportunity and slammed him to the ground. He got on top of him, pinned his arms down with his knees, and punched him in the face and chest.

Drake lay there, defenseless. "Y'ALL JUST GOING TO LEAVE ME LIKE THIS?" he shouted between punches, his nose bloody.

In the next moment, Gesston felt himself being lifted and slammed to the ground then kicked and punched from all sides. He tried to fight back, but this time, he was defenseless. They were hitting him so fast that he could barely make out who they were, but he recognized Drake's two friends, and it looked like there was a fourth person that Gesston had never seen before.

He felt himself losing consciousness, and mercifully, they finally stopped hitting him. The new guy snatched Gesston's chain from his neck. He wiped the blood off it and put it in his pocket.

Drake and his friends stood around, catching their breath. Drake looked furious.

"Eyo, Quincy, end this nigga."

The new guy snapped his head toward Drake in shock.

"You said you needed two stacks, right?"

"Yeah," said Quincy.

"Well, you gonna have to earn that shit. Dead this nigga, and you got your two stacks."

"Nah, nah, that's not what we agreed to. You said I get two stacks if I whoop this nigga's ass and snatch this nigga's chain."

"What are you talking about?" said Gesston, weakly. He tried to get up, but he could barely move.

"Your life, bitch," said Drake. "It's over."

"That's not fair!" said Gesston, struggling to get up. One of Drake's friends kicked him in the chest, and he slumped to the ground.

"This the streets, pussy. Life ain't fair."

"That's not what we agreed to," Quincy repeated.

"Yeah, well you had help wit' that beat-down," said Drake. "You gotta do this one on your own. You got the heat, right?"

"Yeah, but that's not—"

"You wanna be down or what? You wanna get money or what, nigga?" said Drake. "Well this is what we do. Drop this nigga, and you get your money. Let this nigga live, and all you got is that chain. Shit probably fake anyway."

Quincy stared at Drake for a moment. He pulled a gun from the back of his jeans. "You said two stacks, right?"

"Yes, nigga. Hurry up!"

"Wait! Please don't kill me, man," Gesston pleaded, his eyes filled with tears. A ripple of fear ran through his body. He was really about to die. Quincy pointed the gun squarely at his face.

"PLEASE! NO!" Gesston screamed.

"Q! EYO, QUINCY!" said a loud male voice from a distance.

Gesston heard a gunshot then footsteps running in his direction.

***

Rondell knew that something wasn't right when he passed Gesston's parked car on his way into the corner store, but he didn't see him in the store when he grabbed his orange juice.

He had decided to take a walk to the store after getting back to the dorm from his parents' house. He had considered driving, but since it wasn't that cold outside, he wanted to get some exercise and fresh air. He was still recovering from staying in his room drinking a couple of weeks ago. He found that once he decided to return to society, he wanted to spend as much time outside as possible.

When he came out of the store, he heard yelling, and something caught his eye. He saw light glinting off of something down the alley, and when he turned to look, he saw Quincy, Drake, and Drake's friends all standing around Gesston, who was lying on the ground, and Quincy had a gun pointed at Gesston's head.

"Oh, shit!" Rondell said. His heart rate increased as adrenaline surged through his body. He suddenly realized that he didn't have his cellphone with him to call 911. He dropped his orange juice and ran back into the store.

"YO, CALL THE COPS!" he screamed at the cashier.

"What?"

"JUST CALL 'EM! TELL THEM TO COME RIGHT NOW!"

He ran out of the store and back toward the alleyway. Quincy still had the gun pointed at Gesston, and he looked like he was about to pull the trigger.

"Q! EYO, QUINCY!" Rondell's voice startled Quincy, and he pulled the trigger out of reflex. "SHIT!" said Rondell, his feet carrying him as fast as they could go.

Quincy just stood there, frozen in place. Gesston was frozen also, but thankfully, the bullet had not hit him, because when Quincy jumped, his aim shifted, and the bullet ricocheted off the wall of one of the buildings in the alley.

"QUINCY! You crazy, nigga? What are you doing?" said Rondell, trying to catch his breath as he arrived in front of them.

"You *missed*, nigga?" said Drake. "What the hell. End that nigga, Q!"

Rondell snapped his head toward Drake, realizing what was going down. "Naw, fuck that shit!" he said, fiercely. "Y'all niggas is not 'bout to have Quincy take the fall for some bullshit." He turned back to Quincy. "Put the gun away, Quincy."

Quincy looked at Rondell. "I can't, Dee."

Rondell heard the desperation in his voice. "Yes you can. Put it away."

"I gotta do this. I gotta eat, man. My daughter gotta eat, man."

"This is not the way, Q!" said Rondell.

"Please don't kill me, man!" Gesston begged from the ground. "Please, I'll do anything!"

"SHUT THE FUCK UP!" said Drake, and to Rondell he added, "AND YOU GET THE FUCK OUT OF HERE BEFORE YOU GET POPPED TOO!"

"AND WHO THE FUCK GONNA POP ME, HUH?" said Rondell, stepping to Drake. "Who gonna pop me, Drake? You? You ain't 'bout this life, nigga! You ain't never dropped nobody. You ain't been nothing but a pussy from jump."

"Yo, Quincy, pop this nigga," Drake said, pointing to Gesston, "and pop this nigga too," he added, pointing to Rondell.

"Oh, so you think you a shot caller now? You ain't no fuckin *boss*, nigga!" Rondell pushed Drake into the wall.

"Dee, stop, man. Please," said Quincy. Rondell could see the fear in his eyes.

"You don't want to do this," Rondell said, wondering why it was taking the police so long to get there.

"I gotta do it."

"Well shoot me, then," said Rondell, stepping in front of Gesston. "I'm a real nigga. You ain't gonna get no credit for shooting no church boy. Shoot me, I'm *from* the streets."

"I'm not gonna shoot you, Dee," said Quincy.

"JUST HURRY UP!" Drake thundered. "SHOOT HIM! WE GOTTA GO!"

"WHY DON'T *YOU* SHOOT SOMEBODY, DRAKE?" Rondell hollered.

Before Drake could retort, everyone froze at the sound of police sirens in the distance.

"OH SHIT! IT'S THE COPS!" said Drake.

Rondell turned to Quincy.

"Run, Q! Go, now! They ain't gonna catch you! Bounce!"

Quincy just stood there, frozen in place.

The sirens were getting closer now.

"QUINCY, GO! GET THE FUCK OUTTA HERE!" Rondell shouted, pushing him backward.

Quincy finally snapped out of it, and he turned and ran, Drake and his boys following him.

Rondell looked down at Gesston. His face was bloody and bruised, and he was crying his eyes out.

"Th-thank you, man," he whimpered.

"No doubt," Rondell said, feeling awkward, and he helped Gesston to his feet.

A black Range Rover whizzed past the alleyway, then three cop cars quickly followed.

Shortly thereafter, they heard a loud crash. "What the fuck?" said Rondell.

"They wasn't even coming for us," said Gesston.

They looked at each other then laughed with relief.

"Ow, it hurts to laugh," Gesston said, wincing in pain.

"You a'ight, man?" said Rondell. "You need a hospital?"

"Nah, I'm good," said Gesston, forcing himself to stand up. "You was right. Them niggas can't fight for shit."

They chuckled again.

"Ey, I'm-a go to the store and get some paper towels or something to clean you up," said Rondell.

"Okay. I'll wait here. I think it's safe now," said Gesston, and he sat against the wall.

Rondell jogged to the store to purchase some first aid equipment, and then he returned to the alleyway to clean the blood off Gesston's face. Most of it was from a bloody nose and lip, and he had a black eye. Other than that, he appeared to be okay.

"You ready to get out of here?" said Rondell.

"Yeah, let's go home."

They walked to Gesston's car, and Rondell retrieved his orange juice from the ground.

"Hey, you wanna drive?" said Gesston, holding out his keys.

"Sure," said Rondell. "You know, it's funny, but I felt like I should walk to the store tonight instead of driving here."

"Good thing," said Gesston. "I don't think I could drive straight the way my head feels right now."

When they got to Gesston's dorm, Rondell parked the car and handed him the keys. "A'ight, man," he said. They got out of the car and gave each other dap.

"Rondell?" said Gesston.

"Wassup?"

"Thank you for saving me, man." He was having a hard time holding back the tears.

Flashbacks of Terry's last moments flooded Rondell's memory. He stood there reliving that day, then he looked up at the sky and back at Gesston.

He smiled.

"No problem, man."

Chapter 19

Rondell stood outside of Faleesha's dorm room too nervous to knock on her door. He had not seen or talked to her since he had cursed her out.

He looked down at his watch and contemplated whether he should bother her. It was getting kind of late, and he'd had a very full day.

She probably doesn't even want to be bothered, he thought. He had been pretty brutal with his words that day. Letting his anger get the best of him was a problem he had struggled with for years.

He thought about it then decided to take the plunge.

He knocked on the door.

He his heart pounded as he heard her soft footsteps approaching from the other side.

"Who is it?" she said.

"Um . . . it's me . . . Rondell." He wondered if she was going to open the door for him. He knew he had really hurt her.

To his great relief, she opened the door.

"Hey," she said, surprised to see him there.

"Hey," he replied.

"What's going on?" she said.

"I wanted to talk to you."

"Okay," she said, opening the door. "Come on in."

She closed the door behind him, and they made their way over to her couch.

"You want something to drink?" she said. "I have orange juice."

He smiled, grateful. "Yes. Thank you."

She blushed, happy that he was pleased that she remembered his favorite drink. She took out a bottle of juice and tossed it to him, then took one out for herself.

"So, what's going on?" she said as she sat down next to him. She turned her body toward him, and he turned toward her.

He decided it was best to get right to it. "Well, I just wanted to start off by saying I'm sorry. I had no right to cuss you out or talk trash about God. I was just going through a lot at that time, and it came across the wrong way. I didn't mean to take it out on you."

She nodded at his apology. "I understand," she said. "I forgive you."

"You sure?" he said, his eyebrows arched in surprise.

"Yeah," she said. "I had a part in it myself. I knew I shouldn't have let things get that far, but I had a hard time controlling myself." Her face reddened, and she looked away.

"Me too," he said. "Faleesha." He grabbed her hand. She turned to face him. "You don't have to be afraid around me."

"I'm just not used to this," she said, tears filling her eyes.

"I definitely understand," he said. "I got introduced to women totally the wrong way." He swallowed a lump in his throat, reliving some of the memories of the sexual abuse he endured from one of his foster mothers.

"I know," she said. "I . . . ." She turned her head as a tear escaped her eyes. She wiped it away.

"What's wrong?"

She looked at him then down at her hands.

"I was going to say that I went through the same thing as a child—if you're referring to what I think you are when you say you were introduced to women the wrong way." She turned her head again, both her face and neck reddening.

"You were molested?" he said, shocked.

She nodded, wiping her tears.

Warmth spread through Rondell's body as he finally understood her. "So that's why you always nervous around me."

She nodded again.

"Hey, we both went through it," he said. "You have nothing to be ashamed of."

"That's why I'm so closed off, and I'm not really assertive toward people," she said. "I feel like I don't know what to do."

"I definitely understand," he said. "I went through the same thing, but mine came out as a form of rage more than anything. I was mad at everybody, including myself."

They were quiet, and then he asked, "Did you ever tell anybody?"

Faleesha's entire body tensed. Her eyes looked frightened.

Realizing what that look meant, he said, "So, nobody knows?" He waited to give her some space.

She shook her head. "I never told because I didn't want to believe it myself."

"I definitely understand that," he said. "You're actually the first person who knows what happened to me outside of Terry, but he passed away, and Mike knows, but only because it happened to him too."

It was Faleesha's turn to be shocked. "Mike?"

Rondell nodded. "By the same foster mother, too." Anger flashed in his eyes. "Me and Terry did our best to protect him, but it didn't work. Fuckin bitch." He looked at Faleesha after he swore. "Sorry. I'm still working on the cussing thing."

"So did Mike ever tell anyone?"

Rondell shook his head. "Not that I know of." He paused then said, "Who did it to you?" He glanced at her then looked down at his hands. He wasn't sure whether he should have asked because she seemed really nervous about it, but he figured it would be best for her to let it out since she had never told anyone.

She looked at the floor before she spoke. "My friend's older brother."

Rondell sat there without saying anything to help her feel comfortable. Finally, he said, "How did it happen?"

She looked at him then back at the floor. "We were at a sleepover. I got up in the middle of the night to use the bathroom. When I got out of the bathroom, he was standing there. He said he wanted me to go back to his room with him."

She paused, trying not to cry.

"I went to his room, but something told me I shouldn't go with him because I didn't know why he wanted me to. That scared me and confused me, but I felt compelled to do what he said because he was so much older than I was. Something about him made me believe that he would hurt me if I didn't do what he said. After he did what he did, I went back to my friend's room. The next day, my mother came to pick me up, and I never went back to my friend's house. I've never told anybody what happened until today."

"Wow," said Rondell. "How old were you?"

"Eight."

"And how old was he?"

"Sixteen."

Rondell said his next words as delicately as he could.

"Faleesha . . . ." he said, covering her hand with his. "You know that none of that was your fault, right?"

She stared at him, her eyes wide and bright as the tears welled in them, and then the pain of the past broke free. He put his arms around her shoulders and let her sob into his chest, getting it all out.

***

Faleesha stood at her bathroom mirror, styling her hair for church. She was reminiscing about the conversation she'd had with Rondell last week. They had talked until three in the morning. They had enjoyed making each other laugh to relieve the tension of their heavy discussion. By the time Rondell finally went to his room, both of them were feeling much better.

Just as Faleesha finished her hair, she heard a knock on her door.

"That must be Maria," she said to herself. She and Maria always rode with Jacob, Ryan, and Jamal to church on Sundays. "Coming!" she said as she hurried to the door.

She opened the door and was surprised to see not only Maria, but Rashonda too!

"What are you doing here?" she said to Rashonda.

"Girl, I'm going to church! I have to see why Tyrone keeps bugging me about it. You should hear him in my ear every week, 'You going tomorrow? You going tomorrow?' I finally decided to go and get this thing over with." She smoothed her skirt nervously.

"You look cute," said Faleesha.

"You do too," said Rashonda, admiring Faleesha's dress.

"Hey! What about me?" said Maria, gesturing toward her outfit.

"Girl, you know you always look good," said Rashonda.

"Thank you," said Maria, with a mock look of satisfaction.

"Y'all are a trip," said Faleesha, stepping into her heels.

"You going to be able to walk in those shoes, Miss Thang?" said Rashonda.

"Of course," said Faleesha. "Then as soon as I get out of the building, they're coming right off!" She threw her favorite pair of flats into her purse.

"I know that's right!" said Maria, holding her purse open. "I got mine too!"

"Y'all the ones who are tripping," said Rashonda. "Heels don't bother me at all."

"That's because you have that crazy arch," said Faleesha. "Hey, is Shelly coming?" she said hopefully.

"Nope." Rashonda shook her head. "I was hoping she would just to get out of her room, but she really doesn't want to go back to church after what happened with Gesston. Girl, you know she cussed him out last week?"

"Really?" said Faleesha.

"Yeah, he tried to apologize when me and Shelly was leaving his dorm after getting Maria, but she shut him *all* the way down."

"Wow. I hope they can resolve their issues one day," said Faleesha, feeling bad for their situation.

"Well, I personally don't blame her. That was real trifling what Gesston did to her. He ruined her life, and he messed up the friendship that you and Shelly had. Plus, he turned her away from God. He going to Hell for that, honey!" She laughed, but then she stopped when she noticed that no one was laughing with her.

"What?" she said.

"That's not funny, Rashonda," said Faleesha.

"We all make mistakes," said Maria.

Rashonda put her hands on her hips. "I know, but that was messed up what he did to her!"

"True, but it's not right to wish Hell on him," said Faleesha.

"Girl, ain't nobody really wishing he went to Hell, but that was just a messed-up situation. That's all I'm saying. But anyway," she said, brushing it off, "are y'all ready to go? I'm trying to get this over with."

***

"Mike, you gotta go with me, man," said Rondell. He was standing outside of Mike's room wearing some dress pants and a collared shirt.

"Dee. Bruh. You *just* woke me up, and you expecting me to go to church with you?" Mike wiped the sleep out of his eyes.

"I feel like I have to go today, and I don't want to go alone," Rondell said.

Mike gave him the side eye with one eyebrow arched as if to say "and that's my problem how?" But he gave in.

"A'ight, man. Hold on."

He let Rondell into his room while he went down the hall to take a quick shower.

"You ready?" Rondell said eagerly when he returned.

"Yeah, man. Chill out," said Mike, spraying some cologne.

They left Mike's room and made their way down the stairs and out to the parking lot to Rondell's Escalade.

"Dang, I should have brought my coat!" said Mike, shivering as he hopped into the passenger seat.

"I'll turn the heat on," said Rondell.

When they got to church, they walked inside and sat down in the last row, just like last time.

"You ain't going to try to leave on me again, are you?" said Mike, staring at Rondell warily.

***

Gesston stood outside the church doors shivering in the cold. The service was about to start, and this was the first time he had been anywhere near the building since the middle of last semester. He knew that he had blown it this time, but he prayed with all of his heart that God would give him another chance. He was full of sorrow for all that he had done and all the disastrous effects his actions had caused.

He shifted his feet, adjusting his sunglasses. He was wearing them to hide the black eye from Drake and his friends.

He contemplated whether he should even go back to church after everything he had done, but he felt like this was his only hope. All he had known his entire life was God, and at one time, he was really on fire for Him. Somehow, he had allowed his desire to fit in and be cool to take that fire away. Now he was standing outside the church building hoping God would take him back.

He took a deep breath and opened the doors.

Gesston was immediately greeted by Sister Shirley, one of the mothers of the church.

"Well, long time no see! Look who we have here!" she said.

"Hey, Sister Shirley," he said, swallowing a lump in his throat.

"Hey, baby," she said, giving him a hug. "Where you been? The young people have been asking about you."

Gesston's heart dropped. He hadn't thought about the fact that people might wonder where he'd been. "I . . . ." he said, but then his voice trailed off. He had no idea what to say.

Sister Shirley rubbed his back. "It's okay, baby. I'm just glad to see you back. Come on in, now." She gently nudged him toward the sanctuary. "You want me to seat you?" she said, looking up at his face.

"Um, no . . . I think I got it."

"Okay," she said, winking at him with a smile. "You know I'm here if you need anything."

"Okay," he said.

She walked away.

Gesston sighed in relief. He had surely thought that she would ask him why he was wearing his sunglasses in the sanctuary, but he was so glad that she didn't.

He looked around, taking in all of the familiar scenery. He found himself choking up as he looked over at the youth section. It hadn't even crossed his mind that he was letting the kids down with his actions. Lots of them looked up to him, and he, Jacob, Ryan, and Jamal were considered role models for the teen boys.

His emotions started to overwhelm him. It was finally setting in—the effects his actions had on him and those around him.

He had spent the past few months searching for something that he already had. He was looking for acceptance, and a chance to be cool and to stand out. He didn't realize that he already had all those things and more. Everything that he had ever needed, he already had in God. He just never realized it before.

His eyes surveyed the church. He was looking to see if he could spot Jacob and them. He wondered if they would ever be his friends again. He was so busy looking around that he didn't notice that someone was standing right in front of him, trying to get his attention.

"Hey, man," he repeated, tapping Gesston on the shoulder. Gesston flinched from the touch. When he saw who it was, he did a double take. It was Quincy, the guy who had almost shot him in the alley last week!

Gesston backed away, full of fear. "Hey, man. I don't want no more trouble."

"Nah, nah, it's not like that," Quincy said, protesting. "I just wanted to apologize."

"Apologize?" Gesston was shocked.

"Yeah—about what happened the other day." Quincy's eyes darted around the congregation to make sure no one was listening.

"We good," said Gesston.

"I'm sorry, man," said Quincy. "I never been the type to pull no gun out on nobody. I usually just carry the heat for protection. But that day I was going through a lot cuz my girl just had my daughter, and we on the verge of getting kicked out of her mom's house. We needed money for food and diapers and shit." After he swore, he covered his mouth in shock. "Yo, I'm so sorry!" he said. "I didn't mean to cuss in church like that."

"I don't think anybody heard you," Gesston said, suppressing a smile. "So did you get everything you needed?"

"Mostly," said Quincy, rubbing the back of his head. "I kind of used the money from pawning your chain to buy it. But I could pay you back though, soon as I get a job."

"Don't worry about that, man. Just take care of your daughter. Matter of fact," he said, reaching into his back pocket for his wallet." He took out fifty dollars and handed it to Quincy. "Here. I know it's not much, but I figure it could do something for you."

Quincy stared at the money and then back at Gesston. He was bewildered.

"You sure?" he said.

"Yeah."

"I just robbed you the other day, and you giving me *money*?" Quincy looked extremely confused.

"It might not make sense to you, but please take it." Gesston paused. "I've done a lot of wrong over the past couple of months, and I figure it's time to start doing right again."

"You sure, man?" said Quincy again.

"Yeah, take it," said Gesston. "Hey, since you're here, I figure you're trying to get your life back on track."

"Oh, no doubt." Quincy finally put the money in his pocket. "Hey, thanks man," he said, shaking Gesston's hand.

"No problem."

***

Mike and Rondell sat in the back row, talking. "I can't believe we in church again, bruh," said Mike. "After that last time, I thought you were never coming back."

Rondell chuckled. "Me neither." He had yet to tell Mike everything that had happened over the past few days.

Mike looked around the church, his eyes roaming the sanctuary.

"Who you looking for?" said Rondell.

"I'm trying to see if Faleesha and them is here. I don't want to stay all the way in the back if I don't have to." He craned his neck and looked in the front rows, then his eyes traveled toward the back of the church.

"Mike," Rondell began, ready to protest about them moving their seats.

"Wait . . . ." said Mike, holding his hand up as something caught his attention. "Is that Quincy? From back in the day?"

Rondell whipped his head around. Sure enough, it was Quincy, and what was even more shocking was that he was talking to Gesston!

"Aw, sh-shoot," said Rondell, almost swearing, as he and Mike got up and made their way over to Gesston and Quincy. He hoped things were not about to pop off here in church.

"Yo, Q, brutha! How you been, man?" said Mike, smiling happily as he and Quincy gave each other dap and a hug.

"I been a'ight," said Quincy, then he looked at Rondell.

"Hey Q." Rondell gave him dap too. He looked back and forth at Quincy and Gesston. "What's up, man? You, uh . . . y'all good?"

"Oh, yeah, we good," said Gesston, realizing why Rondell looked so confused.

"Yeah," said Quincy, "I was just apologizing for what happened the other day. My bad to you too, Dee. My head wasn't on straight, man."

Now Mike looked confused. "What happened between all of y'all?"

"I'll tell you later," said Rondell. "It's a long story."

"So anyway," Rondell said to Quincy, "what you doing in church, man? You looking good too!"

"Thanks, man." Quincy chuckled. "I'm just trying to get my life straight. I didn't tell you yet, but my girl had the baby. I have a daughter now."

"She did?" said Rondell, surprised.

"You got a *kid*?" said Mike.

"Yeah, man!" said Quincy, looking proud. He pulled out his cell phone to show them pictures of him, his girl, and his baby at the hospital.

"That's what's really good, man!" said Mike. "Quincy's a father now."

"I know, huh," said Quincy. "It's a lot of responsibility. That's why I'm trying to get my life on track. I don't want my daughter going through what we went through. It's real in these streets, man." He looked at Gesston.

"I know," said Rondell.

"Hey look, I'm really sorry about what happened the other day," said Quincy, apologizing again. "That night made me face some hard truths about my life. I went online to sign up for that program you told me about, and now I'm starting school on Monday to get my GED."

"Word?" said Rondell, his eyes lighting up with excitement.

"That's what I'm talking about!" said Mike, slapping Quincy on the back.

"That's good, man," said Gesston.

"Thanks," said Quincy. He beamed with happiness at their encouragement and acceptance.

"Yo, you need anything, man?" said Rondell. "You and your girl good with the baby?"

"I mean . . . we a'ight," said Quincy. "Once I get a job, we'll be even better though."

"True," said Rondell, "but babies are expensive." He reached into his pocket for his wallet. He pulled out fifty dollars. "Here. Buy my niece some diapers or something."

Quincy looked taken aback. "You sure?"

"Here's fifty dollars more," said Mike, taking money out of his own pocket and handing it to Quincy.

Quincy was overwhelmed with gratitude. "Y'all really doing all this for *me*?"

"Of course, man. We brothers, yo!" said Mike.

Tears filled Quincy's eyes. "Thank y'all, man. All of you."

"No doubt," said Rondell.

"Dang, if I knew all I had to do was come to church to get some help, I would be here every Sunday!" said Quincy.

"How'd you find out about this place anyway?" said Rondell, curious.

"I don't know, man. I seen this Spanish dude on the street passing out flyers. He was telling his story and everything, and the church address was on the back of the flyer. After everything that went down the other day, I figured I wanted a change. So I came here."

"Was the dude's name Julio?" said Mike, remembering the Hispanic man who had stopped him, Rondell, and Tyrone on the street a few weeks back.

Quincy smiled excitedly. "Yeah! Yeah, that was it!"

"Dang, he must be going *in*!" said Mike, looking at Rondell.

"I know," said Rondell. "Believe it or not, the same dude was talking to us a couple weeks ago."

"Wow." Quincy shook his head in amazement. "It's a small world."

"Well, anyway, how 'bout we go sit back down," said Mike. "They're gonna start church without us, and we don't want to lose our seat."

"A'ight," said Quincy. He and Rondell followed Mike, but then Rondell noticed that Gesston was not following them.

"You good, man?" said Rondell. "You want to sit with us?"

"Nah, nah," said Gesston. "I gotta go to the bathroom real quick, and I might try to find Jacob and them."

"Oh, a'ight."

"Thanks anyway," said Gesston, and they parted ways.

***

When Gesston got to the bathroom, his eyes burned with tears of pain. He felt like a complete fool. All along, he had been trying to be cool, trying to be like Rondell and Mike and them, when the whole time, he never realized that he could have influenced them to come to God.

He was so glad that no one else was in that bathroom. He was full of raw emotion. He sank down to the floor in defeat, wondering how the pieces of his life could ever be put back together.

***

"I am so glad you're here!" said Faleesha to Rashonda as she, Maria, and Rashonda made their way up the front steps of the church. They usually rode with Jacob, Ryan, and Jamal, but today, they rode in Rashonda's cousin's car.

"Girl, I am just here to see what Tyrone was talking about," said Rashonda. She licked her lips in nervous anticipation.

"Well, hopefully you have another reason to come after today," said Faleesha, opening the front door.

As soon as they walked in, the mothers of the church greeted them with warm hugs of welcome. They each hugged the mothers then made their way into the sanctuary. When they got inside, Faleesha's mouth dropped open. Rondell and Mike were there sitting with another guy she didn't know.

Rondell turned and saw her. He smiled, then he motioned to Mike and the other guy, and the three of them got up to meet the girls.

"Hey!" said Faleesha, hugging Rondell and Mike. "You didn't tell me you were coming."

"Surprise," said Rondell, his smile so beautiful that it melted her heart. He introduced the girls to Quincy.

"Where are y'all ladies going to sit?" said Mike.

"Well, we usually sit near the front," said Faleesha. "But if y'all want to stay back here, that's fine."

"Oh, no, we'll move up front with y'all," said Mike before Rondell could open his mouth.

When they all got to the fourth row where there were enough seats for everybody, Rashonda froze. Her mouth dropped open. Everyone followed her eyes. She was looking toward the first row on the other side of the church where a guy had caught her eye and was smiling at her, gesturing for her to come sit with him.

"Who's that?" said Maria.

"That's Tyrone!" said Rashonda, her eyes bright with tears. She blinked them back and smiled at Tyrone, giving him a little wave.

"*That's* your baby's father?" said Faleesha.

"Yes," said Rashonda. "But what is he doing here?"

"Oh, he's been coming here for months," said Faleesha. "He's one of the pastor's mentees at the jail."

"Are you serious?" said Rashonda, looking even more surprised. "He's been coming here for *months*?"

"Yeah, every Sunday."

"I have to go to him," said Rashonda. She made her way over to Tyrone, and they hugged each other and chatted happily. She sat next to him in the front row.

"Aw, that's so sweet!" said Maria.

"I know, right?" said Faleesha, smiling.

"Dang, all *types* of reunions going on up in here!" said Mike.

He, Quincy, and Rondell chuckled.

"Oh my gosh, is that *Gesston?*" said Faleesha, squinting. She looked at the row toward where Jacob, Ryan, and Jamal were standing together talking. A guy that looked just like Gesston had walked up behind Jacob and tapped his shoulder. Faleesha couldn't tell if it was him though, because he had sunglasses on.

Jacob turned around, realized who it was, then gave Gesston a hug. Ryan and Jamal did too.

"Yup, that's him," said Rondell.

"Wow, I am so glad he's back," said Faleesha.

Faleesha was full of joy because almost every person she had tried to talk to about God was actually there with her in church, all at the same time. She was overwhelmed with joy. God had truly kept His Word. Her struggle was not in vain.

The choir sang a few praise and worship songs, then it was time for a special presentation.

"Good morning, everyone!" said Brother Williams, one of the associate pastors.

"Good morning!" said some of the people in the congregation.

"This morning, we have a special presentation for you. As you know, Pastor Bryant and his friend Pastor Jones minister to young men in the prison system each Sunday through the Jail to Jesus program that they founded. They do workshops and seminars as well as job training. In addition to this, they strive to develop a relationship with each of the young men they serve so that when they get out of the jail, they will have someone to count on." He paused as the people of the church clapped.

"Yes, thank you, Jesus," he continued. "Well, today, the young men want to show their appreciation for Pastor Bryant and Pastor Jones by sharing a few words with them." He paused again as more people clapped.

"Praise the Lord. So, without further ado, here is our first mentee, Roderick Adams." Everyone clapped as the young man went up to the microphone. He looked nervous as he spoke, but he thanked the pastor and his friend for watching out for him and listening to him as he shared things with them about his life. He shared how they had both served as great role models through their love and support.

After Roderick spoke, eight other young men came up and gave a small speech of appreciation for the pastors and their dedication.

Finally, it was time for Tyrone to come up to the mic.

"Hello, everybody," he said, speaking too close to the mic and making it squeal. He laughed nervously, and everyone chuckled with him good-naturedly.

"Take your time, baby!" said one of the mothers from the audience.

"Thank you," he said, blushing.

"Well, I have been meeting with Pastor Bryant and Pastor Jones for the past few months, and in that short time, my life has made a tremendous change. They really took me under their wings and showed me how to conduct myself as a man. I grew up without my father in my life, and now I am a father. I always wanted to be the best father I could be for my daughter, but as you can see, I didn't make the best decisions."

He paused, trying not to get choked up. "It's alright, baby!" said the mother from the audience again.

Everyone chuckled along with Tyrone. "Thank you," he said. "That's one of the reasons why I love this church. You guys have shown me so much love and support these past few months, and it didn't matter what I had done. I just want to thank Pastor Bryant and Pastor Jones for not only showing me how to be a better man and a better father, but for introducing me to Jesus Christ and showing me how to be a Christian."

He paused again as the audience clapped.

"Thank you," he said. "But the last thing I want to say is to my beautiful girlfriend, Rashonda." He turned toward Rashonda, his eyes full of love.

She looked up at him from the front row, surprised.

"I just want to thank you for not giving up on me despite my mistakes, for raising our daughter by yourself these past few months because of my mistakes, for taking my phone calls and coming to visit me while I've been in jail, and for loving me through everything. I love you, girl."

"AWWW!" shouted someone in the audience, and everyone clapped again.

When the applause died down, Tyrone said, "Your encouragement means so much, but before I take up all the time, I just want to say one last thing." He took the mic out of the stand and stepped off the platform to stand in front of Rashonda. She looked nervous and excited, not sure what was coming next.

"Rashonda, I love you. We've been together for over six years. We have a family already, but I really want to make things right when I get out of jail." He got down on one knee and pulled a small box out of his pocket. "So I wanted to ask if you would please be my wife."

"Oh!" someone in the audience said, shocked.

Rashonda clapped her hand over her mouth, completely taken aback. She couldn't even speak. She just nodded with tears streaming down her face.

The audience erupted with praise to God and applause as Tyrone slid the ring onto Rashonda's finger, then he stood up and held her hand as she stood so that he could give her a hug and a kiss before he handed the microphone to the associate pastor.

"Aw, come on y'all! Let's give them another hand!" said the associate pastor. Everyone stood and clapped as he wiped tears from his own eyes. "That was truly beautiful," he said. "Thank you to each and every one of the mentees who spoke today, and we wish Tyrone and Rashonda the best in their future marriage. It's time to plan a party, y'all!"

Everyone cheered and applauded again. Tyrone and Rashonda took their seats, sitting close, whispering together, smiling with happiness.

"Alright, alright," said the associate pastor, and everyone quieted down. "The choir is about to come up and sing, and then the service will be in the hands of Pastor Bryant. Everybody, let's give God some praise!"

Everyone clapped and praised God as the choir came up to sing.

After the choir finished, the pastor came up to the pulpit.

"This has truly been a beautiful service thus far," he said.

"AMEN!" someone shouted, and a few others echoed it.

"I just want to thank the mentees once again for all of their kind words. Believe it or not, you guys help me and Pastor Jones just as much as you guys say we help y'all. And I also want to congratulate Tyrone and his wife-to-be Rashonda!"

Everyone cheered and clapped for Tyrone and Rashonda.

"Amen . . . amen," said the pastor, after the applause died down. "Well, I had a word prepared for you all today, but how many people know that sometimes the Holy Spirit has another plan."

"AMEN!" someone shouted.

"Amen," the pastor repeated. "Before I got up here, God spoke into my spirit and told me that there are four people in this sanctuary today that He wants to turn their lives around. He spoke a simple word to me: 'Tell them I said it's time for a change.'"

"AMEN, PASTOR!" someone shouted.

"Amen," said Pastor Bryant. "Now, I have no idea who these four people are, but God told me to tell you that He is ready to change your life right here in this place today. He said that if you will put your trust in Him and come down to the altar, He will turn your life around from this very moment."

Silence swept across the church as everyone wondered who God was speaking to.

Rondell definitely felt like he might be one of the four people the pastor was talking about, but there was no way he was going down to that altar in front of all those people.

"Don't be shy now," said the pastor. "God said He got you!"

At those words, Gesston got up out of his seat and made his way down to the altar. The entire church erupted in praise as he approached the pastor.

"Gesston? Is that you?" said the pastor, looking surprised.

Gesston nodded, and put his head down.

"Glad to see you back, young man," said the pastor, relieved.

Gesston looked up at the pastor then gestured toward the microphone, letting him know he had something to say.

The pastor gave Gesston the microphone.

"Take your time," he said, encouraging him.

Gesston's hands shook as he held the mic. "Hi, church family," he said, shifting his sunglasses.

"Hey, Gesston!" said someone from the audience.

"I bet you are all wondering where I've been and why I'm up here looking all crazy with sunglasses on in the church." He chuckled. Then, with his hands still shaking, he took the sunglasses off.

There were gasps around the room as everyone saw his bruises and black eye.

"The truth is that I've been running from God. For the past few months, I've been searching for something that I thought I wanted, and I didn't realize that I already had it. I hurt the youth, I hurt my friends, and I hurt someone who cared about me very deeply. But most of all, I turned my back on God. I almost lost my life last week, but He spared me."

"Jesus!" someone gasped.

"Amen," he said. "I just hope that God will take me back one day." He handed the mic back to the pastor.

"Gesston, thank you for sharing your story. I want you to know that many of us have been exactly where you are today, and you don't have to wait for God to forgive you. He's already forgiven you, right now, today."

With those words, everyone stood up and clapped as Gesston broke down in silent weeping. Jacob, Jamal, and Ryan went up to the altar and surrounded him, praying for him.

Music began to play softly in the background.

"Heaven is rejoicing!" said the pastor, full of joy. "Praise the Lord! It don't take all day for God to forgive nobody. He is willing to forgive you right now!"

With those words, Rashonda stood up and went to the altar herself, collapsing to the floor and crying out to God. She raised her hands to the ceiling, asking God to forgive her and take her back. The church mothers surrounded her and prayed with her as well.

"Hallelujah! Hallelujah! That's what it's all about! My God IS a God of restoration!" the pastor thundered over the music. "Bless His holy name!"

By this time, everyone in the church was standing up, full of joy over the scene that was unfolding in front of them.

Rondell still felt the tugging in his heart, but even though Rashonda and Gesston had gone to the altar, he just didn't feel like it would work for him. Yes, they had probably done some wrong in their lives, but at least they were in church to begin with. They had started off right and lost their way. *Of course God would forgive somebody He was already associated with,* Rondell reasoned, justifying his hesitation.

"We are praising God for these two right now!" said the pastor. "But God said there are two more. Come on down and receive your deliverance today. My God is able!"

The music continued to play.

Rondell desperately wanted to go down to that altar, but his legs wouldn't move. Suddenly, he felt something moving next to him as Mike crossed over him and passed him on his way to the altar.

The church erupted in praise again, and people cheered as Mike made his way down.

"Hallelujah!" said the pastor. "What's your name, young man?"

Someone handed a microphone to Mike so that he could be heard over the music. "My name is Mike," he said.

"Mike, welcome to the church," said the pastor. "Do you want to share with us why you came to the altar today?"

"I want to be saved," said Mike.

"Praise the Lord!" Everyone began praising and cheering again. The associate pastor came over to Mike and prayed with him.

Rondell could really feel the tugging in his heart now—first Gesston, then Rashonda, and now Mike. He knew he was the fourth person the pastor was talking about, but he couldn't bring himself to go. He looked over at Faleesha. She looked estatic over everything that was happening. When she saw him looking at her, her face showed concern.

"You alright?" she said.

He shrugged his shoulders in response.

"Do you want to go down there?" she said.

"I can't," he said, trembling on the inside.

"I'll go with you," she said, extending her hand.

Rondell shook his head. "I can't. I don't think it's for me."

Just then, the pastor handed a woman the mic.

"Hello, everyone," she said. "I was just sitting there in my seat, and God laid it on my heart to sing this song by Crystal Aiken. The song is called 'Even Me'."

The audience praised and clapped then quieted down in anticipation.

"I don't deserve
The love you've shown

"The blood you shed
Covers my wrong

"Beyond my faults
Oh Lord, you've seen

"And said you'd still use
Use even me . . . ."

At those words, Rondell could not take it anymore. His legs literally started moving by themselves, and before he knew it, he was making his way down the aisle to the altar.

The church erupted in praise once again, but Rondell couldn't hear them. His eyes were focused on the altar. He couldn't hear the lady singing; he couldn't hear the music playing; the only thing he could hear was the pastor's voice as he grabbed another microphone and began to speak, making his way over to the altar with Rondell.

"Young man, God told me to tell you that He is ready to change your life right now, from this very moment, if you will put your trust in Jesus. Is that okay with you?"

Rondell looked up at the pastor and nodded his head. "Yes," he said.

"Hallelujah!" The pastor laid his hands on Rondell's head as he spoke. "Receive ye the Holy Ghost!"

Rondell felt his knees get weak as his mouth began to utter words he had never heard before.

"Hallelujah! Hallelujah!" said the pastor. The entire church was shouting for joy.

All of a sudden, Rondell took off and ran. He ran around the church about five times without catching his breath. He finally stopped in front of the pastor.

"Hallelujah!" said the pastor. "God said that out of the belly there would flow rivers of living water. Praise God for the Holy Ghost!"

Rondell could not explain the joy he felt. He literally felt like God was right there with him, and that He was never going to leave him. He went back to his seat a totally different person on the inside than the person he was when he came in.

**

Rondell and Mike were in his room, talking about the service.

"Yo, that was crazy when you got up and ran around the church, bruh!" said Mike.

"I know!" Rondell was still amazed at how different he felt now.

"I felt it though," said Mike. "I could feel God's presence as you ran around the church."

"Me too," said Rondell. "I didn't notice anything while I was running. But it was the greatest experience I've ever had in my life."

"Me too," Mike agreed. "When I was at the altar, I definitely felt God touch my heart, especially when that other pastor was praying with me."

"Gesston set it *off!*" said Rondell, chuckling.

"I know," said Mike, chuckling with him. "He had me sniffling a little, blinking back tears and whatnot."

"True, true," said Rondell. "With all this crying I been doing lately, everybody gonna think I'm soft."

"Don't let 'em try you though!" said Mike, laughing, and when he calmed down, he said, "So what do we do now?"

"What do you mean?"

"Like . . . we got saved and everything, and I know we supposed to start reading the Bible and going to church and stuff, but is that it? Like, is there anything else we supposed to be doing?" Mike looked concerned.

"Man, I don't know," said Rondell. "I'm trying to connect the dots myself. We could probably ask the pastor when we go to that men's group."

"True, true," said Mike.

"I can't believe all that happened though," said Rondell. "I mean, I knew I was supposed to go to church, but—"

He stopped when he heard a knock on his door.

"Who is it?" he called out.

"It's me!" said Tyrone.

When Mike opened the door, Tyrone walked in, and Chris walked in after him. Rondell's body tensed up when he saw Chris. He hadn't talked to him since the day they fought.

"What's up?" said Chris.

"What's up?" said Rondell, sitting on the edge of his bed. He gestured for them to pull up a few chairs.

"Where y'all been at, man?" said Tyrone, trying to break the ice. "I been blowing up both of y'all phones all morning!"

"Oh, shit!" Mike and Rondell said in unison, then they covered their mouths.

"My bad," said Mike.

"We had our phones off," said Rondell.

"Why?" said Tyrone.

"We was at church," said Mike.

Chris was shocked. "Church?"

"Yeah, we got saved today," said Rondell.

"Y'all did?" said Tyrone, his eyes widening. "*Both* of y'all?"

"Yup!" said Mike.

"Aw, shoot!" said Tyrone, giving them both dap. "Baptized and delivered!" he said jokingly.

"Shut up, Ty," said Rondell, laughing at his joke.

"So how does it feel?" said Tyrone.

"It feels good, man," said Rondell. "Refreshing."

Chris sucked his teeth.

"How about you?" said Tyrone, turning to Mike.

"Oh, I feel great, man," said Mike.

"Here we go," said Chris under his breath, rolling his eyes.

"What are you doing here anyway?" said Rondell, looking at Chris.

"I came to squash this beef we got," he said.

"A'ight. We good," said Rondell.

"Finally!" said Tyrone, letting out a long breath.

"Hey man, but I hope y'all don't start acting all different now that y'all in the church and shit," said Chris.

"Different how?" said Mike.

"You know what I mean. As soon as people get in the church, they start walking around shunning people like they better than everybody, and preaching and shit."

"Chris, everybody in the church is not the same," said Mike.

"All the ones I've seen are like that."

Rondell looked surprised. "Oh, really? Like who?"

Chris sucked his teeth. "Man, like half my family is in the church, and all them niggas act like they got a stick up they ass. And most of them is hypocrites."

"Yeah, you get a lot of that," said Tyrone. "Believe it or not, I actually grew up in the church myself."

"For real?" said Mike.

"Yeah, my grandmother took me all the time. But I never got saved or anything like that because of all the stuff I saw. Mad people was two-faced, talking about each other, out in the club one night then back in church the next day, all of that, man."

"See, that's what I'm talking about," said Chris. "That's why I'm an atheist, because I don't see no point in going somewhere and believing in God when all people do is fake it anyway."

"But that's not everybody, though," Mike persisted.

"Yeah, you say that now cuz you new to it. But wait a couple months. Then you'll see what I'm talking about. See if you still want to be saved then."

Rondell shook his head. "Look, Chris, Mike is right."

Chris just looked at him.

"Everybody ain't the same," said Rondell. "Even among our friends, we got some real Christians. We got Jacob, Ryan, Jamal, and even you was always calling Faleesha a Jesus freak. Ain't no fakeness in them. They all real."

Chris nodded in half-hearted agreement. He still wasn't convinced. "I understand what you saying and all, but I've seen too much. I don't think I'll ever believe in that church shit."

"What about you?" said Mike to Tyrone.

"I mean, I believe there is a God and everything, but I agree with Chris as far as there being a lot of fakes out there. But at the same time, there are fake people everywhere. I'm just not at the point where I'm ready to think about stuff like that right now. I'm focused on graduating, getting a job, then getting the rest of my life together. Maybe after that I'll settle down and start thinking about church and stuff. I think most of the people our age ain't really 'bout that church life anyway."

"Exactly," said Chris. "I mean, look at Gesston."

"Gesston just got back in the church today too," said Rondell.

"For real?" said Tyrone, his mouth dropping open in shock.

"Yeah," said Mike. "It was real, alright."

Chris looked at Rondell. "So you gonna tell me that Gesston is a great example of how to be a Christian?"

Rondell sighed. "Chris, man, I'm not going to argue with you about the church or none of that. I know you don't believe. As far as Gesston goes, yeah, he fell off for a while, but he's back now, and as far as I can see it, that's between him and God."

"So you telling me you don't see anything wrong with that picture?" said Chris.

"I'm not saying that. He has his problems. We all do. I'm just saying that it's none of my business. I've seen Gesston out there trying to be something he wasn't, and now I see him back where he belongs."

"Man, whatever," said Chris, waving off Rondell's words.

"But like I said, I'm not trying to make you believe anything," said Rondell. "All I know is that I believe. God answered my prayers, and I'm going with Him from here on out."

"So you really about to get all into church and stuff?" said Chris, looking disappointed.

"Yeah," said Rondell. "I been looking for a change for a long time, and I finally found it in Jesus."

"Oh, God." Chris rolled his eyes again. "Whatever, man. Look, I respect y'all beliefs and all, but please just don't bring that church shit around me."

***

Gesston looked at Jacob uneasily.

"What's up?" said Jacob.

"Nothing. I'm just a little worried."

"Worried about what?"

"Worried about how people will view me now. I was just out there acting street and being a player, and now I'm standing here with a poster board trying to tell people to come to Jesus."

Gesston and Jacob stood to one side of the steps leading up to the Student Center while Ryan and Jamal stood on the other side. They had started a group called Radical for Christ, an outreach of the Bible study that Jacob, Ryan, and Jamal held in Jacob's dorm room every week. Today, they were each holding a cardboard poster with a short story of what God had done in their lives.

Gesston was originally part of the Bible study, but he had drifted away.

"I understand," said Jacob. "But the way I see it is this. It may be hard at first, but just keep in mind that God has forgiven you, and eventually people will see that you are sincere. Even if some don't, you can't let that stop you."

"True," said Gesston, nodding in agreement.

"And remember, we got your back," said Jacob, patting Gesston on the back.

"Thanks, man."

Just then, Shelly walked by with Maria and Rashonda.

"Oh, God, here we go!" said Shelly in a loud voice. "Here goes the hypocrite!" She smacked Gesston's poster board out of his hands. He bent down and picked it up without saying anything.

"Hi, Shelly," said Jacob.

"Hey," she said to Jacob, but her eyes were still on Gesston.

Finally, when she saw that Gesston wasn't going to look at her, she turned to Jacob. "So, Jacob, one of your crew showed his true colors. When are the rest of y'all going to do that?"

"What do you mean?" Jacob had no idea what she was talking about.

"We already know that one of you is a hypocrite for sure, but when are the rest of y'all going to confess your sins?"

"We're not hypocrites, and neither is Gesston."

Shelly sneered at his last sentence. "Well, Jacob, in case you haven't noticed, your buddy Gesston here has not been acting like a Christian at all. He's been clubbing, he's been drinking, and I'm pretty sure you heard that he was with me in a hotel room on Valentine's Day, and we're definitely not married."

She crossed her arms with an attitude. "So are you still going to tell me he's not a hypocrite?"

"Shelly—"

Gesston cut him off.

"Chill, man." Gesston handed Jacob his poster board. "She's right. I shouldn't be here."

With that, he began to walk away, but Rashonda grabbed his arm. "Wait!" she said.

Gesston looked at her, confused.

"You don't have to leave, Gesston."

Shelly's mouth dropped open in shock. "Shonda, what are you doing? You know what he did to me."

"Yes, I know, honey. What he did to you was wrong, but right is right and wrong is wrong. Like I said to you the other day, he really repented."

"You don't have to leave, Gesston," she said, her eyes brimming with tears.

"I shouldn't be here." He put his head down.

"Hey, look at me." She put her hands on the sides of his face and gently made him look at her.

"Thank you," she said.

"For what?"

"When you gave your testimony in church, that touched my heart. I told myself for years that I could never make it back to God because of all that I had done. But when I saw you get up there and take those sunglasses off, and you shared your story regardless of who was looking, it was at that moment that I finally realized that God is a forgiving God. Thank you for that."

"I helped you?" he said, pointing at his chest. He looked like he couldn't believe what he was hearing.

"Yes, you really did," she said. Then she turned to Jacob. "And I want to thank you too, Jacob."

"Me?" Now he looked surprised.

"Yeah, I don't know if you remember this, but a while back, we were having a conversation at lunch, and you suggested that since me and Tyrone were together for so long and had a child together, we should just get married."

Jacob's his eyes lit up. "Yeah, yeah, I remember that!".

"Well," said Rashonda, "I mentioned marriage to Tyrone the same night that you and I had that conversation, but he didn't say anything, so I figured he didn't want to marry me. But that day in church, I got the surprise of my life. You saw what happened." She held up her left hand to show her ring to Jacob.

"Wow," said Jacob. "Nice rock. I had forgotten all about that conversation. And I had no idea that Tyrone was your daughter's father."

"Well, he is," said Rashonda, her face glowing with happiness. "And now we are getting on the right track."

"When does he get out again?"

"In two months!" she said excitedly.

Jacob smiled. "Wow, that's beautiful. I bet you can't wait, huh?"

"You know I can't!" she said, her eyes twinkling at the thought of Tyrone coming home.

Shelly listened to their conversation with interest, but she felt like it was time to interrupt. "Well, I'm glad Gesston helped you out and everything, but that still doesn't take away from what he did to me."

Everyone looked at her. She was clearly still full of anger at Gesston.

"I don't blame you for being mad at me," said Gesston. "I did you wrong. I used you, and you didn't deserve that. But please don't turn your back on God because of me."

"Oh, you don't have to worry about that!" said Shelly. "I've seen hypocrisy firsthand, so no matter what you try to do to fix it, I'm done with church for good."

"Shelly—" Jacob began, but she held her hand up to stop him.

"Don't try to change my mind. Some things can't just be swept away like they didn't happen."

"That's not what I want you to do—" said Gesston, but Shelly cut him off.

"I don't care *what* you want. I was talking to Jacob. I have nothing to say to you."

"I really am sorry, though."

"And I don't accept your apology. All y'all men are so trifling. We women are willing to do so much for you, but you treat us so wrong in return. Somebody's got to be held accountable."

With that, she walked away.

Gesston called after her, but she kept on walking.

"Well, we gotta go," said Rashonda.

"Okay," said Jacob.

"She'll be alright," Rashonda said to Gesston.

"I hope so."

Maria and Rashonda ran to catch up with Shelly.

***

Faleesha could not believe that finals were just around the corner! In two short weeks, the semester would be over, and it would be time to go back home for the summer. She sat down on her couch, watching TV absentmindedly.

The weather had finally changed. The cold was gone, and the sun had been shining a lot lately. Spring was in full bloom, and soon it would be summer.

Faleesha couldn't stop thanking God for all that He had done in the past month or so. Rondell and Mike had been saved, and Gesston and Rashonda had come back to the church.

Gesston was kind of withdrawn when he first came back because he was unsure of how people would act toward him. At first, he was mostly silent and kept his head down, but after a few cafeteria sessions with Ryan and Jamal telling their silly jokes, he came out of his shell and began to smile again. He was still hesitant at times, but he was making good progress.

Maria and Tyrone had decided to be friends after they talked about their situation. Maria actually met with the pastor's wife along with going out with the group of Christian girls with Faleesha. She decided that the temptation would be too much for her to pursue a relationship with him, so they were better off taking a break. Tyrone seemed okay with it, and he respected her wishes. He tried to get her to come to his room a couple of times after they decided to be friends, but he stopped once he realized that she was serious about her decision.

Shelly was still not talking to Faleesha. She hung out with Rashonda and Maria almost every day, but when Faleesha was with them, Shelly made it a point not to be there. It was driving Faleesha crazy because she really wanted to talk to her so that they could find a way to make peace.

Shelly didn't seem to be interested in being her friend again, however. She ignored all of Faleesha's phone calls and text messages, and she never answered the door when she knocked. Faleesha was still praying about the situation, but it didn't seem like it was going to change anytime soon.

Rondell and Faleesha's friendship had deepened since he'd been saved. He was reading the Bible and gaining a lot of insight. They often talked about scriptures together, along with just hanging out and having fun. Neither of them mentioned anything about being in a relationship, but it was pretty clear that they both had strong feelings for each other. Faleesha felt like she had a deep connection with Rondell because she had shared some things with him that she had never told anybody, and he had done the same with her.

Rashonda was already planning her wedding. She and Tyrone were set to be married in June as soon as he got out of jail. They had participated in premarital counseling sessions each week after the service, but Tyrone couldn't stay for too long because he had to return to the facility by a certain time. Rashonda talked about the wedding almost every day, and she was constantly making lists. She had already visited three bridal dress shops. She hadn't found the perfect one yet, but she was still very excited about it. She said that she wanted Faleesha, Maria, and Shelly to be her bridesmaids, but Faleesha wasn't sure how that was going to work out because Shelly still wasn't talking to her.

Faleesha's thoughts were interrupted when her cell phone rang. She looked at the caller ID, a number she didn't recognize.

"Hello?" she answered, wondering who it could be.

"Yes, may I speak with Faleesha McDaniels?"

"Yes, that's me. May I ask who's calling?" She thought the woman's voice sounded familiar, but she couldn't place it.

"Hi, Faleesha! It's Dr. Spandinelli."

"Dr. Spandinelli?" Faleesha was confused. Why was she calling her?

"Yes, I hope this is not a bad time to call."

"No, no, it's fine."

"So, how is your semester going? Finals starting to kick your butt yet?" Dr. Spandinelli chuckled.

"They're starting to." Faleesha chuckled too.

"Yeah. Well, anyway, I don't want to hold you for too long, but I've been doing a lot of thinking about our conversation regarding your internship."

"Oh?" Faleesha said, shifting in her seat.

"Yes, Faleesha . . . I want to apologize. I think I was too hard on you. Although there were a lot of errors in your work, in retrospect, I realized that all of your work up to that point was excellent, and I see great potential in you for the rest of your undergraduate career here in the department as well as graduate school, if that's the direction you want to go."

"Wow," said Faleesha. "Thank you so—"

"Anyway, I've been doing a lot of thinking, and I want to know if you would be interested in coming back for another internship in the fall semester. I've got another spot opening up, and since you already have experience working on the project, I think you would be the best candidate."

"Wow!" Faleesha said again. "Yes . . . thanks!"

"And did I mention that this position will actually be a *paid* position. Since you already finished your internship hours, you have the credits you need, but since you will be coming back for another semester, I don't see why you can't be paid for your services."

"Whoa, thank you so much!" said Faleesha.

"So, what do you say? Can I count on you?"

"Absolutely!" said Faleesha. "Thank you so much!"

"No, thank *you*!" said Dr. Spandinelli. "Well, listen Faleesha, I've got a meeting in about fifteen minutes, but I really wanted to call you before things got too crazy with finals. I have to go now, but I will definitely be in contact with you over the next week, so please check your emails, or I may talk to you after class one day."

"Sounds good," said Faleesha.

"Great. Well, I will talk to you soon. Have a great evening!"

"You too!" said Faleesha.

They hung up.

"Wow, thank you Lord!" Faleesha said. That was totally unexpected!

Chapter 20

Faleesha was on her way to the Student Center to buy a lunch to bring back to her room so she could eat and take a nap. She was exhausted from all the work her professors expected of her. One of them sprang a twenty-page research paper on them at the last minute, claiming that he had "forgotten to put it on the syllabus."

Since he had it in his mind to assign the paper all semester, he still made it a requirement, despite the protests from the students. Faleesha felt irritated by the situation because she had already planned her time for studying and completing all of her other assignments, and now she somehow had to get this paper done and still have time to study for finals. She loved all of her professors, but some of them could be a trip sometimes.

As she was walking up the steps to the Student Center to buy her lunch, someone called out her name, startling her so much that she almost lost her balance and fell.

She grabbed the railing for support and turned to see who it was.

"Hey girl!" she said, spotting her friend Maria hurrying up the steps behind her. "I definitely almost fell."

"I know," Maria said, chuckling. "I have to admit, it would've been funny!"

"Stop! Hey, you finished your classes for today?"

"Yup! And I only have two finals—thank you Lord!"

"Just two? That's it?"

"Yeah, why?"

"Because, I have finals for all five of my classes, plus end-of-the-semester assignments, plus one of my professors just sprang a twenty-page paper on us at the last minute."

"Wow," said Maria, her eyes widening. "That's why I couldn't be a psychology major. Not at this school." Maria was a communications major.

"Tell me about it," said Faleesha. "But I guess I can't really complain too much, because that's one of the reasons I came to this school in the first place."

"True, true," said Maria. "Well, do you want to come to the cafeteria? Rashonda and Shelly are supposed to be there already."

"I would, but you know Shelly is not talking to me still."

"I know, but she's being childish, honestly. I think you should just come to lunch. Maybe once she sees you, she'll realize that she is being ridiculous."

"I don't know," said Faleesha. "I don't want to cause a scene."

"Well, if she causes a scene, that's her problem. You did nothing to her—absolutely nothing. Seriously!" She sighed. "Please come to the cafeteria. I don't want to walk in there by myself."

"Okay." Faleesha's nervousness increased as they approached the cafeteria. She hoped that Shelly would welcome her.

They entered the cafeteria and immediately saw Rashonda and Shelly sitting at one of the big tables. They went through the line to get their food and made their way over to sit with them.

Faleesha's heart pounded uncontrollably. This was the first time she had seen Shelly since the day she went to the hospital. Their campus was so large that it was easy to take different routes to classes to avoid someone if you wanted to.

Lord, please let this work out, she prayed as she and Maria stopped in front of their table.

Shelly looked up and almost choked on her sandwich. Rashonda patted her back as she drank some water to get her food down.

"Hi, Shelly," said Faleesha.

Shelly nodded in response then looked away.

Faleesha figured that this was at least a start, so she and Maria sat down.

"So ladies," said Maria. "Faleesha says she has five finals. How many finals do you guys have?"

"Girl, I got three!" said Rashonda. "Barely holding it together cuz I'm busy planning the wedding and everything."

"I have four myself," said Shelly, wiping her mouth and looking everywhere but at Faleesha.

"Wow, I really lucked out this semester," said Maria. "I only have two. Thank you, Jesus!"

Shelly rolled her eyes.

"So, Shelly, I'm glad to finally see you," said Faleesha, trying to break the tension between them.

"Yeah," she said, still not looking in Faleesha's direction.

"Oh, come on Shelly!" said Maria. "Don't be like that."

"Be like what?" Shelly snapped. "I don't see why you brought her here in the first place. When I say I don't want to see somebody, I mean that I don't want to see somebody."

"But why don't you want to see me?" said Faleesha. She was really hurt by Shelly's words, but she was trying her best not to let it show.

"It's too much," said Shelly, her eyes filling with tears.

"I'll leave then." Faleesha started to get up, but Maria held her back.

"No," said Maria. "We're all friends here." She looked Shelly straight in the eyes. "Look, I understand that you have been through a lot, but it's not right to do this to Faleesha. She didn't know that Gesston was doing that to you. It's not like she put him up to it."

"It's just too much," Shelly repeated, still not looking in Faleesha's direction.

"Okay, but you have been back at school for two months already! It's really tiring trying to balance hanging out with you and hanging out with Faleesha. I feel like I have two sets of friends, and it's too much!" said Maria.

"I understand, but I need time to heal."

"Yes, but how much time do you need?" said Maria.

"Maria," said Rashonda, cutting into the conversation.

"What?"

"Let her be. That whole incident with Gesston was very hurtful for her. We should let her take her time."

"Oh, I know you ain't talking!" said Shelly, this time getting upset with Rashonda. "You were the one trying to get me to make up with Gesston!"

"I know," said Rashonda. "But—"

"Look, I understand you have your head up in the clouds because you're getting married and everything, but everybody doesn't have a perfect life like y'all. You and Tyrone been together for over six years, and you have a child together. Maria, you and your Tyrone could have been together, but you claiming that you facing all this temptation all of a sudden, and Faleesha, you try your best to act like you don't want Rondell, but everybody knows y'all two might as well be in a relationship. But who do I have? Huh? I have no one. The only guy I was talking to was trifling ass Gesston, and you see how that ended."

"Shelly—" Rashonda started, but Shelly put her hand up to stop it.

"Look, I don't want to hear it. And I didn't even mention the fact that all three of y'all are now in church. How you think that makes me feel, huh? Now who's being excluded?"

"Shelly, you can come to church too," said Maria.

"I already told y'all that I'm not going back to any church. I've seen enough of the church and its people to know that it's not for me. If y'all want to hang around a bunch of fakes and hypocrites, that's on you. But I'm not going there."

"Look Shelly, I don't know what else I can say to you," said Faleesha. "I'm sorry about what happened with Gesston, but I didn't do that to you. I didn't even know it was happening. And I really don't think it's fair for you to hold it against me when I had nothing to do with it."

Shelly sat there in her chair with her arms folded, staring into space. Finally, she spoke.

"You're right. But I just need some time to heal before I can start talking to you and hanging out with you again. Every time I see you, it reminds me of Gesston, and that's just too much for me right now."

Faleesha slumped her shoulders in defeat. "Okay. I understand." She gathered her things to leave.

Maria started getting her things together too.

"Where are you going?" said Shelly to Maria.

"I'm going with Faleesha. I'm not playing this game anymore."

"Maria, nobody's playing games," said Shelly.

Maria ignored her.

"FUCK!" Shelly shouted. "WHY CAN'T YOU JUST FUCKING UNDERSTAND THAT I'M GOING THROUGH SOMETHING!"

Maria stared Shelly right in the eye. "Look, I understand you have a lot going on, but I'm not going to diss one friend just to please another. I'm not doing that anymore."

"Whatever," said Shelly, flipping her hand in the air dismissively. "Bye."

"I'll talk to you later," said Maria.

"Shelly, I'm sorry," Faleesha added.

"Yeah," said Shelly, refusing to make eye contact.

Faleesha and Maria left the cafeteria.

Rashonda reached across the table and put her hand on Shelly's arm. "Shelly, you're going to be alright," she said.

Shelly just glared at her. "Why don't you go with them too?"

"Huh?"

"Why don't you just leave me too, like Faleesha and Maria did?"

"Shelly," said Rashonda. "You basically kicked Faleesha out of the cafeteria, and Maria is just tired of going back and forth."

"So what? So she's just going to stop being my friend now because of Faleesha?"

"No, she's not going to stop being your friend, and neither is Faleesha. She just doesn't want to feel like she has to choose. It's hard on all of us."

"Well, she sure made her choice today."

"That's not fair," said Rashonda.

Just then, Jacob, Jamal, Ryan, and Gesston walked over to their table.

"Hello, ladies, do you mind if we sit down?" said Jacob.

"I mind if Gesston is planning on sitting here too," said Shelly, her face full of attitude.

Rashonda sighed with exasperation. "Shelly, come on. You don't have to talk to him. Just let him sit down. Look, the cafeteria is full."

"You too?" said Shelly, looking like she couldn't believe Rashonda's words.

"What do you mean?"

"You saw what just happened a minute ago, and now you trying to pull this on me?"

"I'm not pulling anything. We're talking about a seat in a cafeteria, Shelly. It's not that big a deal. He can sit all the way at the end of the table if that will make you happy."

"Whatever," said Shelly. "I guess nobody understands me."

"I understand you," said Jacob.

Everyone looked at him.

Shelly was more surprised than anyone. "What are you talking about? And how would you know how I feel?"

"You're speaking out of your brokenness."

"Oh, God," said Shelly, rolling her eyes. "I don't have time for this today." She gathered her things.

"Shelly, you can't just keep on running away from every situation in your life," said Rashonda. "You have to get through this."

"Rashonda! I'm not about to sit here and eat lunch with Gesston!" Shelly spat. "Like, seriously. What the fuck don't y'all get?"

"Let's just talk about it—" said Rashonda.

"THERE'S NOTHING TO FUCKING TALK ABOUT!" Shelly shouted, cutting her off. "NOBODY GETS IT. I DON'T WANT TO DEAL WITH THIS BULLSHIT!" She picked up a chair and slammed it to the floor.

Two campus security guards rushed over to the their table.

"What's going on here?" said one of the guards. The other one picked up the chair and put it back in its place.

"Nothing! I'm leaving." Shelly snatched up her purse and books and stalked to the exit door.

"Shelly!" Rashonda called after her.

Shelly kept on walking.

Rashonda got her things and chased after her. Jacob and the boys were close behind.

When they got outside the cafeteria, they saw Shelly sitting hunched in a corner of the entrance, her arms wrapped around her knees. Tears streamed from her eyes as she rocked back and forth. Her books were strewn all over the steps and the ground where she had thrown them in her rage.

Rashonda sat down next to her, wrapping her arm around Shelly's shoulder. "It's okay," she said. "I'm sorry I upset you."

"Just leave me alone!" she said. "Don't nobody understand me, so it's no point in bothering."

"Shelly, it's going to be alright," said Jacob, crouching down in front of her. She looked at him.

"No, it's not," she said.

"Here," said Jacob, extending his hands toward her. "Give me your hands."

"Why?" said Shelly.

"I want to pray for you."

"I don't want your prayers."

"Here you go," said Ryan. He and Jamal had picked up all of Shelly's books and put them back in her bag. Ryan placed her bag next to her on the steps.

"Thank you," she said.

"Come on," said Jacob gently, his hands still extended.

Shelly just stared at him for a moment, not trusting, not sure of anything, and then she placed her hands in his.

"What is this supposed to do?" she said.

"God can heal your pain," said Jacob.

"How would *you* know?" said Shelly.

"I've had my heart broken too," said Jacob.

"When?" Shelly challenged.

"Don't worry about all that. Let's just pray. Father, in the name of Jesus, we pray for Shelly right now."

As Jacob prayed, Rashonda, Ryan, and Jamal all surrounded him and Shelly, holding hands.

"God, we know that You know her heart, and You know her situation," he continued. "We pray that You intervene on her behalf right now in the name of Jesus. Heal her, Lord Jesus. Restore her, Lord Jesus. Give her her strength back. Heal her like You healed me, Lord. Heal her better than You healed me, Lord. Wrap Your loving arms around her right now in the name of Jesus. God, we know You to be a comforter. Send comfort around this precious woman right now, God. All these things we ask in the name of Jesus. Amen."

By the time Jacob finished praying, Shelly's tears had dried. "Thank you," she said in a small voice.

"No problem," said Jacob. He squeezed her hands and gave her a warm smile. "Like I said, I've had my heart broken too, and God healed me."

"Dang, Jacob!" said a guy named Terrell from Jacob's dorm, who had stopped to listen. They all turned to look at him.

"I ain't know it was like that!" he said. "Can I get on the prayer list?"

Jacob chuckled. "Terrell, you are a fool," he said. "But sure you can, anytime, anytime."

***

Rondell had been doing a lot of thinking lately. He had been reading the Bible regularly, going to the men's meetings, and learning more about the church. It was so different to him. He felt like he had opened the door to a whole new world.

But at certain moments, especially when he was alone in his room, Rondell felt like something was missing from his life. He had heard the pastor talk about finding God's purpose for your life, but the way he made it seem, you were supposed to wait years and go through a bunch of trials before you really knew what God called you to do.

Rondell's problem was that he felt like he already knew what God's purpose was for his life.

He felt a strong urge to tell people from the streets about Jesus. He wanted them to know how much Jesus had changed his life, and He could do the same for them too.

He thought back to the time when he, Tyrone, and Mike were headed to the corner store, and that guy Julio had stopped them and told them his story. He also thought about the time in church when the pastor talked about how he grew up in the foster care system, and God changed him. He even remembered the day he was at the Student Center, and Dan told him how God had worked things out for him.

Rondell felt that he didn't have a whole lot to tell as far as a major transformation, but he still felt a strong desire to tell people what had happened to him. He was just worried that it might be too soon.

Suddenly, he heard a knock on his door, interrupting his thoughts. He got up to open it, thinking it was Mike and the boys.

Instead, to his surprise and delight, it was Faleesha.

"Hey, girl!" he said, opening the door and giving her a hug.

"How are you?" she said, smiling as she walked in.

"Good."

"What are you up to?" she said.

"I was just in here thinking."

"About what?" she said.

Rondell hesitated to tell her. He was afraid he would sound like a fool since he had been saved only a few months. He stood there debating it in his mind, but then he decided just to go ahead and tell her. He trusted Faleesha. He felt like she understood him more than anybody because he had shared some very personal information with her. Maybe she could give him some advice.

"I kind of think God showed me my purpose," he said.

"Really?" she said, her eyes widening.

"Yeah, I think so."

"So, what is it?"

"Well, I don't know all the proper terms and everything, but I feel like He called me to be an evangelist. I think He called me to the streets."

"Wow, Rondell, that's great!" she said, smiling. She was so happy for him. When she noticed that he wasn't smiling too, she was concerned. "What's wrong?"

"You don't think it's too soon after I got saved?" he said. "I don't want to mess everything up."

"Mess it up how?"

"Cuz, like, what if I say something wrong? Like, I been reading the Bible a lot and everything, but I don't know everything. What if somebody asks me something that I don't know?"

"Then just tell them you don't know." She smiled encouragingly. "That will actually endear them to you because it will show them that you're a humble man and not a hypocritical poser."

"I guess so, but I still think maybe it's too soon."

"No, you can always tell people about Jesus," she said. "You can do that from the moment you get saved."

"But how, when I don't know enough?" Rondell's old struggles with self-doubt were creeping back in.

"Did you read the story in the Bible of the woman at the well?" said Faleesha.

Rondell shook his head.

"Well, what happened with her was, she was at the well getting water when Jesus came up and started talking to her. When she found out who He was, it changed her life. At that very moment, she ran back into her town and told everybody to come to Jesus. They all followed her to the well to see what was going on, and Jesus talked to them too. After He was done, they all believed in Him too."

Rondell stood there for a moment, taking in the story. "But that was a chick though. What about a dude?"

"Well, Paul had a similar situation happen with him." Faleesha took a seat on the sofa and Rondell followed her. "You remember Paul, right?"

Rondell nodded. "The one who got knocked off the horse, right?"

"Yes," she said. "But the Bible says that as soon as he got his sight back, he started preaching."

"True, true, but Paul already knew the Bible because he studied it from childhood. I just started studying a couple months ago. I'm barely past Genesis!"

They both laughed at that comment.

"Boy, I don't know what I'm going to do with you," said Faleesha. "But seriously, though, you don't have to know everything in the Bible to tell people about Jesus. Just tell them what He did for you. You can start with that. And if you don't feel comfortable going by yourself, you can go with Julio and them. They go out all the time witnessing. I'm pretty sure Julio could use another guy on his team."

They laughed again. Julio was the only guy on the street team.

"True, true, I can't leave my boy hanging like that." Rondell, Julio, and Mike had had a few conversations after church, and they were starting to develop a friendship.

"See?" Faleesha said, giving his shoulder a gentle nudge. "You can do it." She smiled.

"Thank you," said Rondell, finally at peace. "I'm glad to have you in my life."

"I'm glad to have you in my life too," she said.

"Hey Faleesha," he said softly.

"Yeah?" she said, looking up into his eyes.

"Will you be my girlfriend?"

***

Rondell, Mike, Faleesha, Rashonda, and Maria all piled into Rondell's truck. They were headed to the last church service before summer break.

Rondell and Faleesha sat in the front, and Mike, Rashonda, and Maria sat in the back.

"Y'all comfortable back there?" said Rondell, looking over his shoulder. "A/C cool enough?"

"Of course, man," said Mike. "You know your whip is tight!"

Rondell chuckled. "Pops hooked it up."

"I know," said Mike. "Ask him if he can give me a deal."

"I'll see what I can do," said Rondell.

"Ooh, Rondell! You think your dad can hook Tyrone up with a deal when he gets out?" said Rashonda. "He's got a job waiting on him."

"Rashonda!" said Maria, embarrassed at her friend's boldness.

"What?" said Rashonda, craning her neck to look at her across the back seat. "Girl, he giving out deals! I'm just trying to get while the getting is good."

Faleesha laughed. "Rashonda, you are a trip!"

"Anyways," said Rashonda, "Dee, can you ask him? He's definitely going to need a way back and forth to work."

"I'll definitely ask," said Rondell. "He usually has sales at the end of the month, so if Tyrone comes around that time, he might be able to give him a bigger discount."

"Thank you so much!" said Rashonda.

"Where's he supposed to be working at anyway?" said Rondell as he pulled out of the parking lot.

"He got a job at Archy's." she said. Archy's was a clothing store at the mall.

"Oh, word? I heard they pay pretty decent there."

"Yes, definitely," said Rashonda. "He gets an hourly wage plus commission on his sales. With both of our incomes, we should be straight."

"Well, congratulations to y'all," said Rondell.

"Thank you!" she said.

"When is y'all wedding?" said Mike.

"June fifteenth, honey! Counting down!" She smiled happily and looked at her ring.

"Wait a minute," said Maria.

"What?" said Rashonda.

"I just realized something. How did Tyrone get you a ring if he's in jail?"

Everyone thought about it for a second. It was something that hadn't crossed any of their minds until then.

"Oh, the pastor paid for it," said Rashonda. "He said Tyrone can pay him back when he gets established with his job."

"The *pastor* paid for your ring?" said Maria, her eyes widening.

"Yup! Him and his wife. But it's supposed to be a secret though, so please don't tell anybody, y'all."

"Of course not," said Maria. "Wow, that was really nice of them."

"Definitely," said Rashonda. "We have to get them a really nice card, and one for the church too. The church is paying for our wedding and reception."

"Wha-a-a-at?" said Rondell and Mike at the same time.

"Yes, honey!" said Rashonda. "We are so grateful, because you know we don't really have a lot of money like that. We not having anything real big. Just something really small and nice. Rondell and Mike, you are definitely invited if you want to come, and Tyrone and Chris can come too."

"Oh, no doubt," said Mike.

"Definitely," said Rondell as he pulled into the church parking lot. "Well, here we go!"

They got out of the truck and closed the doors.

"He-e-e-ey!" said Mike as he gave dap to Quincy, who had just arrived on the church bus. Quincy was holding his daughter on his hip. His girlfriend was standing beside him.

"Hey, what's up?" said Rondell as he gave Quincy dap too.

"Nothing man, just maintaining."

"How's school?" said Rondell.

"I graduate next week!" said Quincy, his smile widening.

"Get out of here!" said Rondell.

"Yeah, boy," said Quincy. "It was an accelerated program where they teach you all the courses in just eight weeks. I needed a lot of help, so I stayed after every day for tutoring, but I took the test and passed it my first time. I got my GED, and they holding a graduation ceremony for us on Saturday."

"That's wassup, boy!" said Rondell.

"Congratulations, man," said Mike.

"Thanks." He shifted his baby daughter to his other hip. "Oh, I forgot to introduce y'all." He turned to his girlfriend. "Bae, this is Rondell, but we call him Dee, and this is Mike, Rashonda, Maria, and Faleesha. Did I get everyone right?"

"Yup!" said Faleesha.

"This is Sofia, everybody."

Sofia smiled as she shook everyone's hands.

"Your baby is beautiful!" said Rashonda. "What's her name?"

"Gabriella," said Quincy and Sofia at the same time, and everyone laughed.

"Aw, that's pretty!" said Maria.

"Thank you!" said Sofia.

"Well, how about we get in this building?" said Mike. "It's hot out here!"

They all laughed as they made their way into the service.

***

Faleesha was cleaning out her room. Today was her last day on campus. This had been a heck of a year, but she was so glad she had transferred to this school. She reflected on everything that had happened, and everything that was going on right now.

Jacob, Ryan, Gesston, and Jamal were still going strong with their Radical for Christ group. They had begun witnessing to different people around the campus, and they were planning to do some gospel concerts and other events in the upcoming year. Faleesha was excited because the school had never had any Christian groups up to this point, and it seemed as if Jacob and the boys were starting something big.

She, Maria, and Rashonda had still been hanging out separately from Rashonda, Shelly, and Maria. As Rashonda's wedding date approached, Faleesha was becoming more and more worried because she didn't know how she and Shelly were going to be bridesmaids if they still weren't speaking. She hoped that it would work out soon.

Faleesha and Rondell had been doing well. The whole dating scene was new to Faleesha, but she felt comfortable with Rondell because they related to each other on so many levels, emotionally, spiritually, and as true friends.

Gesston and Shelly still weren't on speaking terms. After the episode in the cafeteria, however, Shelly had stopped cursing Gesston out whenever she saw him. She still wasn't trying to hear his apologies, though, and she still wanted nothing to do with the church.

Rashonda was driving everyone crazy with her wedding plans. She was stressing everyone out with all the little details, such as which color flowers would look best, and how the seating arrangement should go. Thankfully, her mother was wonderfully supportive. She took a load off Rashonda's back by watching her little granddaughter to give her daughter some free time to shop and plan. Tyrone tried to help a little too, but he couldn't do much from the jail. He mostly just offered his encouragement, but that meant the world to Rashonda.

Tyrone and Chris had already left for the summer. They had a big videogame tournament with Rondell and Mike and a bunch of the guys from the dorm as well as those they played basketball with. They were still arguing about who won the most games.

"Well," Faleesha said to herself. "It's almost time to go."

She threw her last bag of trash in the bin at the end of the hall and made her way back to her room. When she was nearly there, she saw the door to the stairwell opening. It was Shelly!

"Hey!" Faleesha said, surprised. "I was just thinking about you."

"I've been thinking about you too," said Shelly. "Maria and Rashonda said you're leaving tonight."

"Yeah," said Faleesha.

"I'm going to miss you, Faleesha." Shelly's voice wavered. Her lips trembled as a tear rolled down her cheek.

"Aw, Shelly!" Faleesha hugged her. "I'm going to miss you too, girl! And maybe Maria and I can come down to visit you and Rashonda after the wedding!"

"I'm so sorry!" said Shelly. "I'm sorry for rejecting you for so long."

"It's okay," said Faleesha. "I understand that you were going through a lot."

"Thank you for understanding."

Maria and Rashonda made their way down the hall toward Faleesha's room. When they saw her hugging Shelly, they said, "Oh my gosh, finally!"

Everyone laughed to ease the tension, and Rashonda hugged Faleesha. "Hey girl!" she said.

"Hey!" said Faleesha. "What are y'all doing here?"

"Girl, you know we had to all hang out before you and Maria go home."

"True, true," said Faleesha.

"I'm definitely going to miss you guys," said Rashonda.

"We will miss you too," said Faleesha. "But we will definitely see you for the wedding."

"Oh, yes, honey!" said Rashonda. "Y'all better be there!"

"Of course we will," said Faleesha. "We wouldn't miss it for the world."

"That's why you my girl!" said Rashonda, slapping five with Faleesha.

"No, that's *my* girl," said a deep male voice.

They all turned and looked down the hall. Rondell and Mike were making their way toward Faleesha's room.

"Okay, I ain't mad atcha!" said Rashonda as Mike hugged Faleesha and the rest of the girls. Rondell hugged the other girls before giving Faleesha a hug and a kiss on the lips.

"Aw, sooky sooky now!" said Rashonda.

"Shonda!" said Shelly.

"What?"

"Let them be!"

They all laughed and went into Faleesha's room where they spent the next couple of hours talking and joking before it was time for Maria and Faleesha to leave. Maria left first because she was catching a ride to her hometown with a couple of girls from her classes.

They all said their goodbyes then Faleesha, Mike, and Rondell carried Faleesha's things down to Rondell's Escalade. He was taking her to the train station.

"You going to be able to carry all of this?" said Rondell.

"I'll manage," she said.

Rondell dropped Mike off at his house first so that he and Faleesha could have some time alone.

When they got to the station, Rondell carried her bags all the way to the train and helped her load them.

After that, he wrapped her in his arms for a long, lingering hug.

"I'm going to miss you, girl."

"I'm going to miss you too."

They lost themselves in a long, sweet kiss, interrupted by the announcement to board.

"Make sure you call me at every stop," said Rondell, holding her hands. He couldn't bear to let go of her.

"I will."

Reluctantly, he released her, and she waved goodbye just before stepping onto the train.

She breathed a prayer in her thoughts as she walked down the aisle to her seat. *Thank you, Lord, for all that You've done in our lives.* It had truly been an amazing year.

As the train left the station, she looked out the window and smiled when she caught one last glimpse of Rondell standing there, seeing her off, making sure she was safely on her way.

She knew one thing. No matter what her future held, he would be in it. She couldn't wait to see what God had in store.

Not ready to let go of Rondell and Faleesha? Well, I wasn't either (lol)! Check out what happens during their senior year in *Even Me, The Sequel*.

Oh, and before you go – please don't forget to leave a review!! ☺

A Note to My Readers

If you enjoyed reading *Even Me*, please sign up for my email newsletter. One of the many benefits of joining the email list is that you get exclusive access to updates, excerpts from future novels, and information about book signing events that may be coming to a city near you! It's easy to join – just sign up at my website at https://www.tanishastewartauthor.com/contact. I love hearing from my readers.

Also, if you enjoyed this novel, please feel free to leave a review on Amazon. Not sure what to write? You can simply comment on your favorite character and your overall perception of the book (no spoilers, please ☺).

If you would like to connect with me on social media, here's where you can find me:

Facebook: *Tanisha Stewart, Author*
Facebook group: *Tanisha Stewart Readers*
Instagram: *tanishastewart_author*
Twitter: *TStewart_Author*

I hope you enjoyed the novel. See you next time!

Tanisha Stewart

Want to see more books by Tanisha Stewart? Just turn the page!

Tanisha Stewart's Books

Even Me Series
Even Me
Even Me, The Sequel
Even Me, Full Circle

When Things Go Series
When Things Go Left
When Things Get Real
When Things Go Right

For My Good Series
For My Good: The Prequel
For My Good: My Baby Daddy Ain't Ish
For My Good: I Waited, He Cheated
For My Good: Torn Between The Two
For My Good: You Broke My Trust
For My Good: Better or Worse
For My Good: Love and Respect

Betrayed Series
Betrayed By My So-Called Friend
Betrayed By My So-Called Friend, Part 2
Betrayed 3: Camaiyah's Redemption
Betrayed Series: Special Edition

Standalones
A Husband, A Boyfriend, & a Side Dude
In Love With My Uber Driver
You Left Me At The Altar
Where. Is. Haseem?! A Romantic-Suspense Comedy
Caught Up With The 'Rona: An Urban Sci-Fi Thriller
#DOLO: An Awkward, Non-Romantic Journey Through Singlehood